Yesterday's Spy

www.penguin.co.uk

Yesterday's Spy

Tom Bradby

BANTAM PRESS

TRANSWORLD PUBLISHERS
Penguin Random House, One Embassy Gardens,
8 Viaduct Gardens, London SW11 7BW
www.penguin.co.uk

Transworld is part of the Penguin Random House group of companies
whose addresses can be found at global.penguinrandomhouse.com

Penguin
Random House
UK

First published in Great Britain in 2022 by Bantam Press
an imprint of Transworld Publishers

A CIP catalogue record for this book
is available from the British Library.

ISBNs 9781787632462 (hb)
9781787630703 (tpb)

Typeset in 11.5/16pt Palatino LT Std by Jouve (UK), Milton Keynes
Printed and bound in Great Britain by Clays Ltd, Elcograf S.p.A.

The authorized representative in the EEA is Penguin Random House Ireland,
Morrison Chambers, 32 Nassau Street, Dublin D02 YH68.

Penguin Random House is committed to a sustainable
future for our business, our readers and our planet. This book
is made from Forest Stewardship Council® certified paper.

To Claudia, Jack, Louisa and Sam

Prologue

Göttingen, Germany, March 1933

IN ANOTHER TIME and place, it would have taken all of Harry's self-control not to laugh at the spectacle in front of him. But this was neither the time nor the place, and he had the growing sense that they ought to have left long ago.

He had found himself captivated, though, by the woman sitting at the table next to them. She had a wide face, full cheeks, a radiant smile and tumbling auburn hair. Her laugh demanded attention and he'd been rewarding it with more than was polite, even if they had yet to be introduced or exchange a word. He told himself that the pimply youth engaging her in earnest conversation must be a brother or cousin, perhaps a friend.

They were in the gloomy basement of a beer hall called the Ratskeller, normally the haunt of students and those leftists still brave enough to show their faces in public. But

1

tonight it was awash with sweaty Nazis, drunk on Pils-ner, their pristine, ridiculous uniforms and the very real prospect – the reality, even – of absolute power. It was a cavernous room, with dark timber panelling, iron light fit-tings that hung low over the bar, and vaulted stone ceilings, which seemed to magnify the Nazis' booming voices into something that resembled rolling thunder. Perhaps it was. The gloom was thick with cigarette smoke, tables draped in stained white cloths packed close together.

Harry, who had been studying under the great math-ematics professors Hermann Weyl and Edmund Landau for his entire term away from Cambridge, was trying to explain to David Wilson, who had missed the first half of the term due to illness, just how much had changed since the Reichstag fire and Hitler's emergency decree, which had been its most direct consequence. The Nazis had real power now and, in his view, intended to use it to extin-guish what remained of Weimar's fragile democracy. Even the Ratskeller's owners had thought it safer to nail up photographs of Adolf Hitler, Rudolf Hess and Hermann Goering, which hung just above Harry's head in the corner.

The Führer was no longer a laughing matter, if he ever had been. And the presence at the long Nazi table of Simon Hughes-Hallett and Ed Haddon, their fellow Cambridge students, only served to underscore that fact. If the cream of the British aristocracy was now paying homage to these dangerous men, the world had a problem. 'We should go,' Harry told Wilson. His friend was not of a martial, or even brave, disposition and he thought it best to get him away before things deteriorated.

The pimply youth at the table next to them appeared to agree. He nodded. 'We should, too,' he told the vibrant woman opposite him.

'I'm enjoying myself,' she shot back. 'I haven't seen anything this funny in years.'

'We shouldn't be laughing.'

'So you say. I don't see why not. They're all fat and sweaty, the ugliest people I've ever seen in my life.'

'Sadly, politics in Germany,' Harry interjected, sensing his chance for an introduction and leaning across the gap between their tables, 'as everywhere else, is not a beauty contest.'

The woman turned to him and gave him the benefit of her mega-watt smile. 'It really should be.'

He offered her his hand. 'Harry Tower.'

She took it, her palm cool to the touch. 'Amanda James.'

The Brownshirts at the table nearest to the wall stood to delight the few student drinkers who had remained with another rendition – their third – of the Horst Wessel Song. Hughes-Hallett rose to his feet beside them. He was a big man, gone early to seed, with a puffy face that made him look like a pumpkin. He was very drunk, too, with a voice that could shatter glass at a hundred paces. 'Isn't he the one who urinated on you from his rooms in the quad?' David Wilson asked.

Harry had forgotten he'd told Wilson that.

'*Die Fahne hoch!*' the men belted out. '*Die Reihen fest geschlossen!*' Raise the flag! Our ranks are closed!

The room fell silent in acquiescence. There were already rumours that Göttingen's world-famous mathematics department was about to be purged of all its Jews, or those married to them, which would likely render it next to useless. The assumption was that every other faculty would soon face similar pressures. Harry had already written to the college authorities back home to outline his concerns, not that it would do him, or them, much good. He was giving serious thought to cutting short his studies here.

'*SA marschiert mit ruhig festem Schritt.*' The SA marches with calm, steady step.

Like hell it does, Harry thought. The SA was the least calm and steady body of men he'd ever had the misfortune to encounter.

'My God,' Amanda said, in horror. 'They are simply appalling.'

As the song ground on towards its inexorable and somewhat telling conclusion – 'Already Hitler's banners fly over all streets. The time of bondage will last but a little while now' – Harry's gaze was drawn to a man who sat alone in the corner. At first, he'd thought him likely to be one of the university's academics, but any reputable professor would surely long since have had the good sense to depart. And this slight, angular fellow just sat there, tugging at his moustache and drinking his single glass of Pilsner with measured care. And watching everyone. Who was he? Harry wondered. And why was he sitting alone, his gaze flicking from Harry to the Nazis and their companions and back again?

He surely wasn't from the Gestapo. It was a facet of life in Hitler's new Germany that you always felt *watched*.

Unable to contain herself, Amanda stood and proceeded to goose-step up and down the room with her finger beneath her nose to imitate Hitler's moustache.

4

Her mockery was so brazen that the uniformed thugs and their companions fell silent. Only Hughes-Hallett's booming voice pierced the hush. 'What the bloody hell do you think you're doing?' He looked at the pimply youth she had been sitting with. 'Can't you control your woman, Carrington? I thought she was supposed to be the daughter of an earl. You'd think she'd have more damned manners.'

The nearest Nazi reached over and tried to grab Amanda's skirt. She pulled away, but he had enough of a hold to force her to slip on the flagstones. She hit the floor hard. Another Nazi, a big sweaty man with dark hair cropped close to his skull, lurched forward, took the hem of Amanda's dress and flipped it over her head to reveal her underwear. There was a roar of laughter.

Amanda screamed. The man stood over her, as if about to contemplate a more serious assault. But Carrington dived at his feet to reassemble Amanda's clothes and beg forgiveness. 'Please,' he said, 'she's very drunk. She meant no harm.'

Yes, she bloody did, Harry thought. And liked her all the more for it.

Carrington hurried Amanda towards the door and, for a moment, it looked as if that might be the end of the matter. But Harry had seen enough of the Nazis to know restraint was not part of their make-up. The men stood and began to follow the couple to the door, hitching their belts and pulling up their sleeves.

Harry caught the eye of the man in the corner. A half-smile tugged at the corners of his lips, as if he was interested to see how this would play out. He was gazing intently at

Harry, his right hand clutching a homburg on the table in front of him. He had his coat on his lap, as if about to leave.

'Stay here,' Harry instructed David Wilson. The last thing he needed was a vicar's progeny as a wingman in a dark alley late at night.

Harry hurried up the steps and emerged into a chill wind, the cobbled alley half lit by a lone street-lamp. He heard voices, then a single, anguished cry. He walked into the gloom and figures gradually took shape. Carrington was at the back, an ineffectual, whimpering bystander. Amanda was somewhere in the midst of the sweaty throng, trying to fight back, grunting and crying in terror.

Harry could not quite discern the men's intention – harassment, humiliation, assault, rape – but if he had learnt one thing in the tumult of his childhood, it was how to handle dangerous odds.

Attack with overwhelming force.

And then run fast.

He hit the men at the back of the group, like a runaway train. They were drunker than he had imagined and scattered like pins in a bowling alley. But the big man who had assaulted her first recovered quickly. He turned, faced Harry. '*Scheisser*,' he grunted. He swung with a giant fist, but Harry was too fast. He ducked easily, then hit the big man such a devastating punch with his right that he careered back into a drainpipe and smashed to the ground.

Harry picked up Amanda, threw her over his shoulder and ran, through the twisting fog, down the winding cobbled street beneath the ethereal glow of the night lamps.

The footsteps behind them faded into rancid curses.

Harry stopped running. He put Amanda down. She had

a hand over her mouth, trying not to laugh, despite the trauma of the assault. 'Whoever you are, you're a bloody maniac,' he said.

She smiled back at him. 'Well, whoever *you* are, you're a good man to know in a tight spot. How did you learn to fight like that?'

'Wait here.'

Harry retraced his steps carefully, wanting to be sure their pursuers had abandoned them to the night. He lurked in the gloom by the entrance to a butcher's shop not far from the scene of their crimes.

The Ratskeller was swallowing the last of the dejected Nazis. Carrington, the pimply youth, had vanished. And only the small, slight man who had been watching him in the bar stood outside still, playing with his moustache.

Who the hell was he?

Perhaps it was Harry's imagination, but he seemed to smile as he raised his hat. Harry turned away from him and headed back, a spring now in his step, to the woman who had just exploded into his life.

1

London, August 1953

AS HE HURRIED along Whitehall, Harry's feet were as damp
as they had been during the Kent winters of his childhood,
but that was no surprise. They'd seen nothing but rain for
weeks. Wimbledon had been a washout, Lord's looked
like an ornamental lake, the trains ran intermittently, if at
all, and the bus he had travelled to work on this morning
might have been surfing over the river.

He ran up Downing Street, banged hard on Britain's
most famous door and stepped briskly into the hall as
soon as it was opened. He shook his umbrella on the
flagstones by the entrance. 'Sorry, bloody weather,' he
grumbled apologetically. The porter returned his smile
and took the umbrella without complaint. 'Harry Tower,
here to see the prime minister.'

'Yes, sir. I believe you know the way.'

Harry hurried down the hall and took the stairs three at a time. He was waved through by the secretary and eased into the study quietly. It was much too small to arrive unnoticed.

Winston Churchill sat slumped in the chair by his desk, smoking one of his infamous cigars and looking every one of his seventy-nine years. Ed Haddon and William Oswald, Harry's colleagues in the Secret Intelligence Service operations department, stood before a map of Tehran on the far side of the desk. 'You recall Harry Tower,' Ed Haddon said. 'We asked him to attend because he had some direct experience in Tehran at the end of the war.' Harry was tempted to ask why they had excluded him from the planning of this operation and all communication with the Americans, but he managed to bite his tongue.

'I'm old, not senile,' Churchill shot back. 'Sit,' he ordered Harry, as if he wished to have company at the level of his steely gaze. 'Go on,' he growled at Haddon.

'Just before midnight, Colonel Nasiri will arrive here to arrest Prime Minister Mossadegh.' Haddon was pointing at the map of central Tehran. 'The PM will no doubt attempt to call out the military to prevent his removal from power, but when he attempts to contact General Riahi, the chief of staff, he will find no one at home.' Haddon tried a smile. It made him look constipated – Churchill had that effect on people. 'Colonel Nasiri and his detachment of the Imperial Guard will already have called there to arrest the general, too,' Haddon continued.

'On whose authority?'

'The Americans have persuaded the Shah to sign a *firman*, an executive order to appoint General Zahedi – a close ally of the royal family – to replace Mr Mossadegh as prime minister. The arrests will be carried out on General Zahedi's orders, after the *firman* has taken effect.'

'Is the order legal?'

Haddon looked at Oswald nervously. Harry had learnt long ago that Winston Churchill would forgive most things, but not being lied to. 'That's a matter of opinion, Prime Minister,' Haddon replied.

'I'd guessed that,' Churchill said, with heavy sarcasm. 'So whose opinion should I rely upon?'

'It's true that, under Iran's constitution,' Haddon went on smoothly, 'the Shah cannot *technically* remove or appoint a prime minister without the consent of the Iranian parliament. But we are confident our colleagues in the CIA – using our contacts, of course – have raised the fear of a Communist takeover to such a fever pitch in Tehran that this move will be widely welcomed, or at least accepted, by the Iranian people.'

'This *coup*, you mean,' Churchill replied. It wasn't offered as a criticism. The prime minister loved nothing more, Harry knew, than his part in the great game of international relations, especially when it was to be carried out in such a nakedly cloak-and-dagger fashion.

'A *transfer of power*, Prime Minister.' Haddon treated him to the more confident trademark grin that had once made him the darling of the SIS typing pool. Harry tried hard to suppress a smile of his own. He knew the prime minister well enough to be certain he would be impervious to Haddon's oleaginous charm.

'Can we deny involvement?' Churchill growled.

'Yes,' Oswald said. 'Operation Ajax is being run on the

ground entirely by the CIA, though, as we said, they're using our former contacts in Tehran and are liaising with our team in Cyprus. So, even in the worst-case scenario that the CIA team is blown, we could still plausibly deny any British involvement.'

'But the Americans remain grateful for our assistance and support,' Haddon said, as if worried he was losing the prime minister's interest. 'They understand they could not be attempting this *transfer of power* without our many contacts on the ground in Tehran and that we would be running the show if Mr Mossadegh had not closed our embassy and expelled all of our people.'

'I don't require a history lesson,' Churchill snapped, 'on this of all subjects. And nor do I need reminding that it was our idea. But how did they get the Shah to sign this *firman*? He has the spine of a jellyfish.'

'I believe the American agent in charge of Operation Ajax is very persuasive, Prime Minister,' Haddon explained. 'He tried at first to enlist the help of Princess Ashraf. As you know, she has an insatiable appetite for men and money so is generally likely to understand the merits of an argument when it is presented correctly.' Haddon spread his arms, as if about to take a bow at what Harry assumed was a kind of joke. 'When even that didn't work,' Haddon swiftly continued, 'the American – the Quiet American, I believe they call him – took to visiting the Shah secretly under cover of night. Certain inducements were offered and accepted, but most persuasive was the sense of unity he was able to convey when it came to the governments in Washington and London. The Shah was told in no uncertain terms that regime change was coming, that you and President Eisenhower were of one mind, and that his choice was therefore to be a part of it, or risk being consigned at a young age to the dustbin of history.'

'The Shah remains in Tehran?'

'We believe he has asked to be allowed to fly to his palace on the Caspian coast on the day of the transfer of power in case our efforts fail and he needs to flee with his family to Baghdad.'

Churchill shook his head slowly. 'That's what I call courage.' He stared gloomily out of the window at the rain still drenching the verdant Downing Street garden. 'It's only a matter of time until we need a new shah. I hope you have some ideas for that.'

They looked at him blankly. 'We could hardly ask for more than a king who does exactly what we want, surely, Prime Minister,' Oswald suggested.

'The world is rarely that simple.' He surveyed them from beneath hooded eyelids. 'So, which one of you is the Iran *expert*?'

Haddon's face flushed. He liked to consider himself an expert in pretty much everything. 'Prime Minister, I am the head of the Near and Far East desks.'

'You know Iran?'

'I made a brief visit in 'forty-four, but—'

'It must be you, then, Tower.' Churchill turned to him. 'Will it work?'

Harry shrugged. He'd had nothing to do with the scheme thus far and had been brought to the meeting, about which Haddon had been extremely nervous, solely because his experience on the ground in Tehran, in 'forty-six, was the most recent in London Centre. All of the staff from SIS's Tehran station, expelled by Mossadegh the year before, were in Cyprus, waiting to jump back in if the coup was successful. And because he knew the prime minister: he had been instrumental during the war in persuading him to switch British support in Yugoslavia from the Chetniks to Tito's Communist partisans. 'It's the Americans' plan,' Harry said.

Churchill rewarded him with the ghost of a smile. They'd always got on. 'I am aware of that. Is it the right one?'

'I wouldn't personally bet my dinner money on the Shah.'

'Why not?'

'He's weak. And vain. And his head is already full of plans to rival the great Achaemenian emperors. It is not healthy to have delusions of grandeur so early in a reign.'

'I thought they were defeated by Alexander at the great battle of Marathon,' Haddon said, looking rather pleased with himself.

Harry turned to him. So did the prime minister, who appeared to share Harry's surprise. Haddon was always at his worst when showing off his imperfect knowledge of a subject, but undermining the achievements of Cyrus and his successors in building the greatest empire the world had ever known at the heart of what was modern Iran took some beating for sheer stupidity.

'Do you know the Shah?' Churchill asked Harry, ignoring Haddon's discomfort.

'No. You have the edge on me there.' Harry was aware that Churchill had met Iran's young king – installed by the

British, of course, after his autocratic father had drifted too close to the Nazis – at the Tehran Conference with Stalin and Roosevelt in 1943.

'But you know Tehran?'

'I visited half a dozen times in 'forty-six.'

'To do what?'

'I went to Tabriz, to assess the situation there after the gendarmes trained by Norman Schwarzkopf had managed to expel the Soviets. We naturally assumed it was only a matter of time before Stalin tried again.'

'The People's Republic of Azerbaijan,' Churchill muttered darkly.

Harry nodded. After Soviet forces had refused to withdraw at the agreed deadline at the end of the war, left-wing Iranian activists had tried to declare a breakaway people's republic in the area around Tabriz close to the border. They had been crushed by the Shah's Gendarmerie, which had been turned into a crack force by the American General Norman Schwarzkopf during the Allied occupation of Iran. But it had been a close-run thing, one of the first stand-offs of the Cold War, though sadly far from the last. 'I spent some time in Tehran,' Harry went on, 'with the army high command and a few of the key ministers. But mostly I was deep in the countryside, with the tribal leaders, trying to prepare some meaningful resistance in the event of a full-scale Russian invasion.'

'That doesn't explain your contempt for the Shah.'

Harry looked at Oswald, then at Haddon. He could tell his scepticism was going down like a cup of cold sick. But what did they expect? He'd got to know the prime minister relatively well during the war and was not in the

15

business of lying to him. 'With the possible exception of Schwarzkopf's Gendarmerie and one or two of the other regiments we trained during the war, the Shah's army is a paper tiger that will fold at the first sign of real Soviet intent. It's still something of a mystery as to why Stalin didn't press matters further in 'forty-six when he had the chance. But despite his death, Moscow won't make the same mistake twice and the current chaos in Iran is the perfect opportunity.'

Harry sensed he had the prime minister's full attention so pressed on. 'Most of Iran is backward, poor and extremely religious. I spent a lot of my time there in the faith schools, talking to the imams. I concluded a combination of resistance in the mosques and by the tribes outside Tehran might at least make an invasion uncomfortable for Moscow in the long-term.'

'What has that got to do with the Shah?'

'He's not especially devout. He has liberal ideas, which may be laudable but will not sit easily with the conservative masses. If we bet the house on him, we'll lose it.'

There was a long silence. 'What do you suggest, then?' Churchill asked caustically.

Harry didn't answer. What he thought was that the British should be bolstering Iran's nascent democracy and accepting that its nationalist leader, Mohammed Mossadegh, had a right to a better deal for the oil being extracted by Anglo-Iranian Oil, but he wasn't going to argue that in this company.

Churchill shook his head impatiently. 'Whether the Shah is the right man to protect our interests in the region in the long-term is a different question. We can deal with him another day – God knows, weak dictators are two a penny. But Mossadegh is a maniac – demented, a lunatic – and we need to defuse this crisis now and get our oil flowing again. The Shah can at least be guaranteed to do that. So my question to you, Tower, this week, here, now, is simple: will the coup work?'

Harry shrugged. 'We have some competent assets on the ground there, to which we have given Washington full access, and the Americans have more money than God. I don't know whether you can buy a country, but they'll be having a damned good go at it. At this stage, there can't be many left in the city they haven't attempted to bribe.'

'You sound like you disapprove of that, too.'

'I'm not sure it's a recipe for stability, even in the short-term.'

'You can buy oil,' Churchill said, 'which is the part that worries me. I've asked the President for reassurance that American companies will not be given special treatment after this coup is successful. It is our damned oil, after all.' Churchill sighed deeply. 'When does this happen?' He was glaring at Haddon.

'We've agreed with Washington that the precise timing will be left to their team on the ground in Tehran. But any day now, sir.'

'Tell me the moment it's done. I'll want to be the first to congratulate the President. What about the Russians? What's the state of play now that Stalin is dead?'

He was looking at Harry. 'The KGB has been preoccupied with endless bouts of score-settling in Moscow since he passed away,' Harry said. 'So I suppose at least this makes it a good moment for us to strike.'

'You think this will wake them up?'

'Possibly. But too late, with any luck.'

The prime minister nodded, then waved them away. He turned to face the window and puffed noisily on his cigar as they filed out.

No one spoke until they had emerged into Downing Street. 'Christ,' Haddon said, 'he puts me on edge.'

It's your relentless ambition that does that, Harry thought. Haddon's raincoat was as snug as his suits – the product of too many long lunches at the Travellers Club and the Garrick. But he'd held off the advances of age in other respects, his thick dark curls – proudly unkempt – still yet to see a trace of grey. Even though Haddon had actually helped smooth Harry's way into the Service – for reasons he had never quite nailed down – he remained the same amoral man who had sung the Horst Wessel Song that night with the Nazis in Göttingen and, back home in Cambridge, sprinkled his working-class scholarship contemporary with exquisitely loaded contempt.

The ravages of age and experience had taken a greater toll on William Oswald – or Oz, as he was widely known – who had cropped his grey hair close to his skull in an attempt to conceal how much he had lost. His nasal hair sprouted prodigiously, adding to the overall effect of a man to avoid on a dark night; his detractors in the Service universally called him 'the weasel'. Oz's background was complex – he was the son of a dispossessed Lithuanian aristocrat with a convert's zeal for his new country – and his psychology still more so. He was a fanatic, as if the world needed any more of them.

Harry had been stuck with both men since the days when the old hot war had turned into a new – if anything, more complicated – cold one. It hadn't been a happy partnership. Too many men they'd sent behind the Iron Curtain had been lost, while Oswald and Haddon managed to combine operational ineptitude, including a tendency to rush almost everything, with world-class blame deflection. They told anyone who would listen that Harry Tower was very much yesterday's spy. They'd been saying as much since the night on Mount Avala that haunted him still, in more ways than one. And he was so disenchanted with the dynamics of the department, he was inclined to agree.

'Have you got your son out of Tehran?' Haddon asked Harry, with what looked like genuine concern. He was sometimes capable of that.

'No.'

'Good God, Harry, why not?'

'You know any young man who listens to his father?'

'I hope he has the sense to keep his head down,' Oz said.

'He is a correspondent for the *Manchester Guardian*,' Harry replied. 'He has no sense at all.'

'God knows what he's doing there,' Oswald said, shaking his head.

He's there because the sudden departure of a grizzled veteran through ill health had offered a young student doing every freelance shift available in London the chance of a lifetime, Harry thought. And one month of emergency cover had been repeatedly extended. But what was the point in correcting someone of William Oswald's myopic perspective?

'Say it's a family emergency,' Haddon pressed. 'Just send him a telegram demanding his return.'

'You may recall his mother's already dead. He has no siblings. And I'm not sure any illness I might claim would qualify as an emergency in his mind.'

They fell into an awkward silence until they parted ways on Whitehall. What else was there to say?

As Harry headed home on the bus, all he could think of was the trip to the airport to drop Sean off to begin his new life in Tehran as a young journalist. He had been unable to penetrate the wall of silence and hostility. So whatever Haddon might have thought, his son's taciturn and dogged refusal to respond to his father's attempts to bridge the chasm between them was no surprise.

The rain was coming down in waves by the time Harry stepped off the bus in Putney, but it was not until he turned into Chelverton Road that he started to become troubled by the regularity of the footsteps behind him.

Not too quick or too slow, a steady pace, so that a pursuer never got closer or fell back.

It was not the way most people walked.

And it left him with a dilemma. If he was being followed and the pursuer knew where he lived, he would clearly reveal that he was aware he was being watched if he chose to overshoot his house.

He had one attempt at being certain. Twenty yards after Harry turned into Charlwood Road, he stopped to retie his shoelaces and glanced back at the exact moment the man ought to have appeared.

But he never did.

Which meant that either the individual following him

was a professional – and a good one at that – or Harry was going mad.

The way things had been this past year, he didn't entirely rule out the latter.

He straightened, brushed the water from his trousers and walked slowly on.

2

London, August 1934

IT HAD BEEN a direct road from those tense days in Göttingen to this humid afternoon on St James's Street, paved with good intentions. At least, that was what Harry liked to tell himself.

He stepped onto the black and white checked floor in the gloomy entrance hall to White's Club and gave his name to a porter, who surveyed him suspiciously. 'Mr Prentice and Mr Haddon are waiting for you in the dining room, sir.' He made the 'sir' sound like an insult. Perhaps it was.

Harry hung up his raincoat and, beyond dark oak doors, walked up a curved staircase to the dining room on the floor above.

Haddon and his superior were tucked into a table by the window, overlooking St James's Street. Haddon rose to meet him, radiating a bonhomie he'd never managed when they were students together at Cambridge. 'Harry, so good of you to come. This is Mr Prentice.'

Prentice was bald, squat and powerfully built. Harry guessed he was in his forties, but he was one of those age-less men who might have been a decade older or younger. Prentice didn't get up or offer his hand. Harry took the seat he was offered and glanced at the menu, heavy with traditional British fare. He ordered lamb.

Prentice leant forward, as if determined to get straight to business. 'Haddon tells me you approached him out of the blue a few months back to ask about a career in the Foreign Service.'

'Yes.'

'Why?'

'I think war with Germany is inevitable. I'd like to do my part to make sure we're prepared.'

Prentice wiped the sweat from his top lip with a clean linen napkin. He was carrying more weight than was good for him. 'You know what *we* do?' Prentice asked.

'I have some idea.'

'Is that why you approached Haddon here?' Ed Haddon looked nervous. Had he in some way vouched for him? And, if so, why?

'Yes.' It hadn't taken him long to work out Prentice was a man who valued truth.

'You were friends at Cambridge?'

'No.'

Prentice nodded. 'That's what he said.' He looked at Harry intently. 'We are not a friends' club.'

Harry doubted that, but didn't say so. 'That may explain

why I'm interested in joining.' He smiled. 'I haven't many friends.'

Prentice grunted. It might have been a laugh. 'We normally reject on principle anyone who shows an interest in joining us. That way, we rule out parvenus, chancers and, above all, socialists.' Harry guessed no answer would provide reassurance, so he didn't offer one. 'Care to guess why I'm contemplating breaking this rule?' Prentice asked.

'War's a tough business?'

'Correct. I can't have the organization entirely staffed by chinless minor aristocrats, like Haddon here.' Haddon flushed. Whatever else he had expected from this lunch, Harry guessed this was not it. 'No offence, Haddon.'

'None taken,' Haddon said, without feeling. In one of the few conversations they'd had at Cambridge – on a walk back to college from the rugby club – Haddon had impressed on Harry his desire to have a 'meaningful career', which was clearly a novelty in the life and history of his family.

'Haddon tells me you were a tough bastard on the rugby pitch and knew how to look after yourself in real life.' Prentice allowed himself a smile. 'I understand you were not averse to putting a Nazi or two in their place.'

Harry offered no response to that, either. Like a lot of men whose backgrounds had demanded it, he didn't like to be known as a tough.

'This is not a formal interview, you understand?' Harry nodded. 'We've vetted you, of course. Spoken to your tutors at Cambridge. I gather you're teaching maths there now?'

'It's a temporary post.'

'You're very bright, they all agree. So we can use a man

with brains and brawn. I'm less confident about Lord Arundel.'

Harry tried to prevent himself bridling. 'In what way?'

'One of your tutors referred to him as a father figure. Does that mean he *is* your father?'

'No.'

'Your mother was his housekeeper?'

Harry hesitated. His background qualified as the subject he most disliked talking about. 'Yes.'

'Your father his chauffeur? But he died when you were fifteen? A veteran of the Boer War?' Harry didn't offer an answer. His father had been a violent drunk whom he'd never mourned.

'By one account, it was your fists that sent him to hospital. They say you came home to find him beating your mother.'

'My father was an alcoholic. He died of blood poisoning.'

Prentice nodded. 'Lord Arundel would not have been the first aristocrat to make provision for an illegitimate child who was secretly his own. Is it not the case that he helped secure you a scholarship to Cambridge?'

'Lord Arundel is a good man.'

'Was he not also your mother's lover?' Harry had been warned the process might be intrusive, but he hadn't expected this. He could see, though, that Prentice was trying to needle him. 'He may have been,' he said eventually. 'I go only by how he treated me.'

'I see,' Prentice responded. 'I've spoken to colleagues who remember Lord Arundel from Eton and Cambridge. They are agreed that he's a poseur, an iconoclast, a rebel, and his socialist ideas are a disgrace to his class. Do you share them?'

'I'm not a socialist, if that's what you're asking.'

'Why not? A man of your background, patronized and excluded at Cambridge by the likes of Haddon here, no doubt. Perhaps, during your time in Göttingen, you concluded only the Communists had the will to stand up to the Nazis. One might argue that, if you're not a socialist, you damned well ought to be.'

'I don't view the world in black and white,' Harry said. It was the first lie he'd told – Amanda said it was his defining fault – but it seemed to be the answer Prentice wanted to hear. Perhaps it merely chimed with his own instincts.

The waiter brought their food. Prentice took some red wine when it was offered, then turned his attention to his lunch. Haddon tried to make small-talk, asking how Amanda was doing with their young baby, Sean. Harry offered sparse, indeterminate answers. He was never going to warm to Ed Haddon and didn't care that it showed.

Prentice finished his meal, drained his glass. He turned to Harry. 'This is what you should know. Not everyone in the Service and across Whitehall shares your view of Nazi Germany, though I certainly do. There are those – Haddon might even be among them – who think Hitler can be accommodated, still others who dream he is positively to be admired. You'll need to accept this if you join us. We don't set the policy, we inform it.'

'I understand that.'

'*Do* you?'

'Yes.'

'And, second, you will always be an outsider. SIS is still a gentlemen's club. I'd like to change this – we need a variety of men in Operations, at least – though not everyone agrees and the current C is only half convinced. I expect you sense what I'm driving at, but I want you to understand it clearly.'

Harry nodded. If nothing else, he thought, he'd written the book on that at Cambridge.

'I'll be in touch,' Prentice said. He didn't move, but it was plain to Harry that lunch was over. He stood, nodded at Haddon and retraced his steps to the muggy air of St James's Street in August.

What, he asked himself, had he begun?

3

London, August 1953

HARRY PUSHED OPEN the front door and stepped into number 27 Charlwood Road, shaking his umbrella as he reversed into the hall, which smelt of fresh polish and Mrs Wilkinson's Player's Navy Cut untipped. Its stillness enveloped him like fog.

The letterbox was empty. He dropped the evening newspaper on the hall table and listened for a moment to the steady drumbeat on the conservatory roof. He brushed the rain off the shoulders of his ancient coat, hung it behind the door, and put his keys on the unevenly polished dresser. He allowed himself a momentary smile at the recollection of Amanda's stoic defence of a cleaner who couldn't clean. 'She's a good woman,' she'd said. 'And she needs the job.' Who was he to disagree?

Harry went through to the living room and stood by the

window. The rain pummelled the pavement and swirled down the corner drain. A couple of weeds still somehow managed to poke their heads above the wall.

But there was no sign of anyone on the street, watching him.

Harry went upstairs to change. He undid his watch, then pulled on a sweater and a dry pair of trousers. He hung his suit in the wardrobe and brushed his fingers lightly along the neat row of Amanda's dresses, prompting a dozen different visions of the woman he had loved. He stepped closer, pressed one of her sleeves to his face and breathed in deeply.

Back on the landing, he paused outside Sean's bedroom, then went in. He stood by the chest of drawers and turned over the watch he had given his son for his eighteenth birthday a year and a half ago, but which Sean had never worn. He stared at the framed caricatures of Sean's friends and teachers that adorned one wall. Sean was a brilliant cartoonist, savage and funny. The teachers had been depicted as animals, his housemaster as a serpent.

Harry sat on the bed. He picked up the picture of Amanda and Sean, as a boy, from the bedside table. His wife smiled at him still, as if reaching through the darkness. Sean had his mother's large doe eyes and a reserved, serious gaze. The photograph had been taken on the day they had taught Sean to ride a bike in a country lane near Amanda's parents' home in Sussex. Sean had set off, crested the hill, ignored Harry's instruction to brake and careered down into a muddy ditch. When Harry had fished him out, Sean had been roaring with joyous

29

laughter as he threw his arms around his father's neck. 'I fell off, Daddy!'

'You crazy fool!' was all the reprimand Harry could muster.

He replaced the photograph carefully.

He glanced outside again. The rain was falling in great billowing waves now, and rattling the panes. Denis Compton grinned from a photograph on the wall, bat held aloft on the day a magnificent century had helped destroy the Australians at the Oval.

Harry went downstairs and tried to read *The Times*, but his mind wandered. He switched on the wireless. The protests against the rule of Prime Minister Mohammed Mossadegh in Tehran dominated the news headlines. The Soviets, the announcer said, were reported to be massing on the border, ready to offer 'assistance' to Mr Mossadegh. The CIA, or its money, was, Harry concluded, doing its job. It never ceased to amaze him how credulous the international media was.

He glanced at his watch, went to the hall and picked up the telephone receiver. He told the operator he had booked a call to Tehran and waited five minutes or more for her to come back to him.

There was no response at the number he had requested, she was sorry to say.

Harry went to check the letterbox, to make sure he had not missed anything. He hadn't. He had written Sean more than two dozen letters since he had left for Tehran and had yet to receive a reply.

He glanced up and down the street, which was still deserted.

He returned to the living room and sat facing the front window as the night crept in, turning over the events of the evening in his mind. Who the hell might have followed him home? And why?

None of the answers he could conjure were palatable.

Harry told himself to move, to do something to while away time, but the distraction that daylight sometimes brought evaporated and he was confronted by the same old demons: anxiety without shape, melancholy without limit, and darkness with no promise of dawn. He reached for the cupboard in the corner. One tumbler led in quick succession to another, until oblivion beckoned. He stumbled eventually upstairs, collapsed onto his bed and stared at the ceiling. He rolled over and stretched an arm across the mattress to the empty space where Amanda had once slept.

He dreamt, as he so often did, about that terrible night last summer.

He had returned home, light of spirit, on a balmy summer's eve. The sitting-room door had been open to the garden, the curtains billowing in the breeze. He had walked down past the immaculately tended flowerbeds that were Amanda's pride and joy and the bench where she sat with her morning coffee.

He had slowed as he saw the severed rope swaying in the wind from the old oak tree and taken the last leaden steps past the rose bush to find his son cradling his dead mother, the knife he had used to cut her down still in his hand.

In this dream, Harry could never move beyond the look in Sean's eyes as he raised them that night: the anger, the rage, the desolation, the naked accusation – this is your doing. *This is all your fault.*

Or the pulverizing sense that his son had been right.

What was left of his life but the possibility of infinite regret?

Harry was dragged awake, soaked with sweat, by the sound of the telephone in the hallway. The clock face glared at him through the empty whisky bottle. Christ, it was nearly three in the morning. The ringing continued, shrill and insistent. He hauled himself up, wiped the sweat from his forehead, and stumbled downstairs, cursing as he went.

He scrabbled for the receiver.

'Mr Tower? Peter Wilson here. Foreign editor of the *Manchester Guardian*. Sorry to disturb you at this hour.'

'Not half as sorry as I am.'

'I'm afraid it's about your son, sir. We're concerned about him. He seems to have disappeared.'

4

HARRY DIDN'T TAKE up the *Guardian*'s invitation to discuss the fact that his son was 'missing'. The last thing he needed the following morning was the assistance of hand-wringing liberals. If he'd developed anything resembling a life philosophy over the past decades, it was of the futility of good intentions alone.

Instead, the first slivers of dawn saw him approaching the grand façade of 54 Broadway, a tall yellow stone building with a prominent mansard roof and a brass plaque at its entrance, which announced that this was the headquarters of the 'Minimax Fire Extinguisher Company', a subterfuge that fooled only people who did not need to be deceived. Its true location as the headquarters of SIS was well known to every KGB agent, and indeed taxi driver, in London.

Harry nodded at Alan, a security guard in workmen's overalls, who looked as if he was about to fix a leaking pipe. Harry signed the book, took off his coat and hat and passed through the security-barrier turnstile to the half-lit corridor beyond.

As he descended the stairs to the basement, he tried to shake off the claustrophobia that enveloped him like fog every time he set foot in the building. It was a gloomy warren of wooden partitions and frosted-glass windows in which he had never felt at home. It had occurred to him more than once that it might have been designed to produce that effect on all its employees.

The corridors were deserted. He'd reliably guessed the office would be empty at this hour since, if nothing else, his colleagues were time-servers to a man. He rounded a corner in the half-darkness and almost bumped into a burly man with a shock of curly dark hair and thick glasses. 'Morning, Tower,' Mike Guildford murmured apologetically, as he stood aside to let his colleague pass.

'In early?' Harry said.

Guildford didn't answer. He looked like the university professor he had once been, his trademark pipe stuck into the corner of his mouth. 'Busy, busy,' he said. He was dressed in a raincoat.

'Something running hot?' Harry asked.

'You might say that,' Guildford said brusquely. He hurried on, and Harry watched him go. Guildford was their defection specialist, the man they usually sent to interrogate any Russian who presented him- or herself at a far-off embassy seeking asylum. It was Guildford's job to work out if they were the real deal or a KGB plant.

Harry was puzzled to see him so early. He'd heard not a whisper of a defector in the offing.

Harry had also correctly predicted Warren Sykes, long-term stalwart of the records section, would be another exception to the staff's general indolence. Sykes sat at his desk, next to another wood and frosted-glass partition, nursing his morning coffee as if it was likely to prove his only sustenance of the day. And perhaps that was right: Sykes was skeletally thin.

'Morning, Mr Tower.' Even though they'd known each other for close to two decades, Sykes considered the use of first names a suspect modern fashion he was damned if he was going to succumb to. He was a veteran of the Great War, stooped now with age and its impact. Harry had no idea how old he might be, but there had long been rumours that retirement beckoned. 'Bloody awful weather,' Sykes offered.

'Terrible,' Harry agreed.

'We'll be lucky if we get any more cricket this summer if it goes on much longer.'

'Lucky indeed. But it must surely turn soon.'

'I wouldn't be so sure, Mr Tower.' Sykes shook his head mournfully. 'You know how our summers can be.'

Since Amanda had always insisted they take their annual break – if the office ever allowed him one – in Nor-folk, Harry had a keen sense of the unpredictability of the British summer, but he didn't want to drag out this conversation any longer than necessary. Sykes nodded, the opening niceties concluded to his satisfaction. 'What can I do you for at this early hour, Mr Tower?'

'I'd just like the file on our Tehran assets, please, Warren.'

Sykes's demeanour, indeed his entire body language, shifted perceptibly. He sucked his teeth, shook his head

35

and leant against the side, as if he needed support. 'I'm very sorry, Mr Tower. Have you not heard?'

'Heard what?'

'I would have thought they'd have the decency to talk to you themselves.' He shook his head again, more vigorously this time. 'Clearance has been revoked for all operational staff. Senior management only until further notice.' Sykes gave him a reassuring smile. 'I should make an exception for *you* of all people, Mr Tower, but rules are rules, I suppose.' He leant closer. 'Word is the Americans have told C he has a Soviet mole. Been in place for years, they claim. They say it's why we've lost so many of those we've sent behind the Iron Curtain. The rot set in that night on Mount Avala, they reckon, and went from bad to worse thereafter. But what would the Americans know, eh? Think they rule the bloody world, these days. But not in my book they don't!' Sykes frowned at him. 'Are you all right, Mr Tower?'

'Of course. Thanks, Warren.'

Sykes smiled. His face brightened. 'It's a load of stuff and nonsense, of course. And I'm sure it won't be long until it's back to business as usual.'

'Indeed.'

'Any reason in particular you needed our Tehran assets?' Sykes winked at him. Harry forced himself to smile back. Warren liked nothing more than to live vicariously through the cloak-and-dagger antics of the senior operational staff. 'Looks like bloody Mossadegh could do with an intervention before the Soviets have him for breakfast!'

'True enough,' Harry said, trying to sound as if he meant it. 'Thanks again, Warren.'

Harry retraced his steps down the gloomy corridor and walked up to his office on the first floor. Oswald and two other senior colleagues were already cloistered in Haddon's palatial suite at the far end of the room. Oswald briefly looked Harry's way, then turned his back to the glass, as if he was frightened he might be able to read his lips.

Harry offered a cheerful good morning to some of the secretarial staff and told himself their half-hearted replies were merely the product of his imagination. He walked into his office, shut the blinds and closed the door.

He went to the window, glanced down at the rain-swept street below, where the morning commuters were now hurrying to work. It took him only a few moments to be certain of the conclusion he had reached climbing the stairs. He picked up the receiver, dialled a number in Fulham he knew by heart. He told the man who answered what he required and cut him off when he offered the usual caveats. 'I'll need them in an hour, Simon.'

Harry walked all the way to Fulham, since it successfully soaked up the time and allowed him to 'dry-clean' his route to be certain he was not being followed. He worked hard, on the Fulham Road in particular, drifting in and out of shops like an inveterate browser and then doubling back on himself.

By the time he reached Parsons Green, he was certain that – today, at least – he had no one on his tail. It ought to have reassured him. It didn't. In fact, it made him wonder more who had been following him the night before.

Simon Ranger was younger than you might have expected in a forger – or counterfeiter, as he preferred to be known. But his was a family business. His father, now dead, had been an antiques and art dealer who dabbled in a little light criminal work, a lucrative business model he had passed on to his son. Harry had bought both father and son immunity from prosecution for more than a decade now, for which neither man had been nearly grateful enough. Harry knew Simon, in particular, hated to be rushed so he had his hand up in acknowledged apology before he had even set foot inside the place. 'I'm sorry, Simon.'

'I'm not going to lie, Mr Tower, you do test me.' Simon was pencil-thin with a moustache to match. He had long hair, with the faintest hint of ginger, and a lisp, which belied a seriousness about his craft that Harry had never ceased to find reassuring. At far-flung borders, with his life sometimes in the balance, much rode on Simon's dedication to deception.

He handed over two passports, one for Harry, a second for his son, Sean. 'I went Irish,' Simon said. 'I know it's been a while, but you know how I like them and, what with the time constraints, I thought—'

'Irish will do just fine, Simon. How much do I owe you?'

'Fifty pounds, sir, if that's acceptable.'

It was steep, but Harry was in no position to argue and Simon knew it. 'I hope your son isn't in any trouble,' he said.

It was a question thinly disguised as an expression of empathy and concern. Harry forced himself to smile. 'None that he couldn't justifiably lay at my door.'

'Isn't that sons the world over, Mr Tower?' Simon shook his head mournfully. 'So many things I would have liked to say to my old dad, but I left it too late.'

'It's always the way.'

'I hope you find what you're looking for.'

Harry returned Simon Ranger's smile once more, but this last comment was so peculiar that, later, he found himself wishing he'd asked what he meant by it. Or, to put it another way, what exactly Ranger had seen in his eyes.

But there was no time for that now. The moment he stepped out into the drizzle, Harry was back on high alert. He returned to the routine that was familiar from thousands of days in dozens of cities all over the world: walk, listen, sweep one's gaze left to right, right to left, never look behind, vary one's pace, go into shops, double back.

Today it confirmed – once again – that he was not being followed. Given that he was probably the most operationally experienced executive officer in SIS, he was inclined to trust his instinct and judgement.

But it left him with the same questions. Who had been following him yesterday? And why?

Harry had one more task to complete. He stopped at a red telephone box just by Sloane Square tube station and called Ed Haddon's secretary. 'Hello, Mr Tower,' she said. 'Mr Haddon is tied up at the moment, but may I pass him a message?'

Haddon was always 'busy'. In fact, Harry had been banking on it. 'Don't worry, Jane. Could you just tell him one of the Albanian exiles from Dassia Bay has contacted me out of the blue with some information on what went wrong with the operation. He's in Paris, so I'll head straight there. I'll be gone a few days.'

'Oh, Mr Tower. That does sound like something he'd like to know about. I'll just—'

'Don't bother him with it, Jane. The less talk about it, the better. You understand. Just explain that I have it in hand and will be back in a few days. It's a chance we can't turn up.'

'If you say so, Mr Tower.'

He did, but was there more than the usual hint of hesitation in her voice?

Or was he still starting at ghosts that existed only in his imagination?

5

Berlin, 1936

'NO, HARRY. ENOUGH.' Amanda turned on him. 'I know Oz is a man of dubious morality and judgement. I understand that the sight of him sucking up to Himmler, Heydrich and the other hideous pantomime dames of this horrible state at Nuremberg was unedifying, disgusting and upsetting. I appreciate that the sheer number of government ministers, civil servants and the assorted rag-bag of misfits and eccentrics from the British aristocracy who paid homage with him was unsettling. But, as you have said many times, that *is* the Board of Trade. The British Empire would do business with the devil if it thought there was money to be made from it . . .

'But, either way, I've heard enough. The sun is shining, our son is content and . . .' she looked up and down the beach by the Wannsee, where Sean was playing '. . . there is not a Nazi uniform in sight. So, imagine they do not exist. Or that you do not work for the British government. Or both.' She pointed at the sun on dappled water. 'This is *joy*, so try to experience it.'

Amanda stripped naked, then walked off the beach and into the water. Sean was playing with his Mercedes-Benz on the sand track Harry had just made for him and was distracted by his mother for only a moment. Harry glanced up and down the beach, but the only other occupants on this autumn day were too far away to pay them any attention.

Harry knelt beside his son. 'How's it going?' Sean waved the car at him. Although he could talk, he rarely bothered to do so. Harry watched his wife's bold, confident strokes as she swam away from them. Halfway out to a pontoon moored offshore she turned onto her back and whooped with pleasure. He was tempted to join her. She'd been on a high for weeks and her mood was infectious. It always was, for good and ill.

Harry dragged his attention back to his son. 'Let's build a proper race circuit,' he said. He got Sean's bucket, poured some water over the sand, then built a wider track and stands. He had no idea why. Sean ploughed through the carefully made structures as he pushed his car round and round the track with abandon, but it didn't stop Harry losing himself in the task. 'Faster!' he yelled at his son. Sean's car sounds grew louder and more extravagant until father and son were lost in laughter.

Harry did not notice Amanda until she plopped down beside him, still naked. 'You see?' she said.

'See what?'

'You know what I mean and don't pretend otherwise.'

She lay on her back and Harry tried to suppress his

desire. He had been away from home too much of late. Perhaps this was her way of reminding him of what he had been missing. 'Easy, Tiger,' she said. 'You're going to have to be patient.'

'Easier said than done.'

'You're a man of immense self-discipline. We all know that.' She propped her head up on a hand, turned on her side and looked at him. 'Tell me something, though. Is it that you think you *personally* must save the world?'

'What do you mean?'

'Oh, I get that these are difficult times,' she said. 'Maybe war is coming, as you keep telling everyone. And God knows I need no convincing that the Nazis have to be confronted. But I don't know anyone who spends so much time inside his head when all this remains within reach outside.' She pointed to Sean, to the sand, the water, the sunlight. 'So why don't you empty your mind, leave the problems of the world to someone else for a while and experience the happiness that is right before your eyes?'

'I do.'

'No, you don't. You're engaged in a permanent dialogue with yourself, which leaves both of us on the outside. As if you're constantly running away from something, or towards it. I can never work out which.' She smiled at him again. There was no rancour in her voice. 'And then, suddenly, you're here. With us. The world recedes. And the love almost makes my heart burst.'

'I see.'

She smiled again. 'I see,' she mocked. 'I see, I see, I see!' She shook her head. 'For God's sake, Harry Tower, get over here and kiss me before Sean and I feed you to the ducks!'

6

Tehran, August 1953

HARRY'S GAZE REMAINED fixed on the parched landscape beneath them. Partly, this was to forestall conversation from the loquacious French divorcee beside him, who was travelling to Tehran to see her sister.

But mostly it was because he was lost in the ghosts of his past. A few hours previously, the flat desert landscape had given way to the rugged hills of the border region around Tabriz, where he had spent the early days of his last visit. He'd been accompanied by a French intelligence officer called Christine Audinette for an intense few weeks he had spent a long time trying to forget. He wondered, and not for the first time, if it had been wise to offer his son an introduction to her.

His mission in 'forty-six had been marked up as a success. Iran had remained in the Western orbit, but for how

44

much longer? He had warned London Centre as soon as he returned that the greatest threat to British interests in Iran was the greed and stupidity of the executives who ran the Anglo-Iranian Oil Company. Despite a tense meeting in their offices in Tehran before he left, they continued to insist that the oil they extracted in vast quantities from the country belonged exclusively to them, and by extension the British Empire, and that the Iranians would never have the right to enjoy anything more than a token income from it.

He could see the Alborz Mountains ahead of him in the distance now and buckled up in anticipation of their descent. So many months away, trying to shape the world. How could he ever blame Amanda for failing to thank him for it? Few others had.

The Viscount's doors opened as soon as the propellers had stopped turning, and Tehran's stifling heat stormed the cabin, like an invading army. The BOAC stewardess wiped a bead of sweat from her upper lip, straightened her hat and gave Harry a weary smile. 'Welcome to Iran, Mr Fletcher,' she said. 'I hope you enjoy your stay.'

Harry forced himself to smile back, put on his sunglasses and stepped out into the blinding midday sun. The sky was clear and the air close, the baking heat only leavened by the faintest hint of a breeze from the mountains, which ringed the airport like the tiers of an amphitheatre.

The first-class passengers were already striding towards the terminal, but Harry found his passage blocked by an official in a peaked cap. 'One moment, sir, if you please.'

He waited as a convoy roared across the shimmering tarmac. It passed directly in front of them and pulled up next to a sleek new Beechcraft plane fifty yards away. Half a dozen men and women in dark suits and fashionable dresses poured out. Piles of luggage were unloaded from the boot of a limousine. Only when the process was complete and the cases safely in the aircraft did the cavalcade's principal occupants emerge. The Shah and his glamorous wife sensed they were being watched, looked up and waved. Harry did not reciprocate.

Flying to their palace on the Caspian to wait out the coup, he assumed. It must be imminent. Courage, indeed, as Churchill had suggested.

'She's very beautiful, isn't she?' the French woman next to him whispered. 'And he's much slighter than in the pictures, don't you think?'

Harry didn't answer. The Shah of Shahs, the Emperor of Iran, gave one last wave – to whom it was not clear – and climbed into the pilot's seat. His wife, in a crisp cream dress and stylish sunglasses, gave her own wave and stepped into the rear cabin. The flunkeys withdrew. Harry and his fellow passengers were forced to wait in the rising heat as the plane taxied slowly away. 'All hail the King,' he muttered quietly to himself.

It was not until it had reached the far end of the runway that the man on the tarmac stood aside to let them pass.

'How exciting,' the woman beside Harry said, trying to fall into step with him. 'Don't you think?'

'Unbearably.' Harry strode on towards the gleaming white terminal, which, like many new buildings in Tehran, was of distinctly utilitarian design. It looked like a Soviet wedding cake, the addition of a curved flight tower at the far end a belated attempt at art-deco sophistication. Just inside the entrance, a portrait of the Shah in stiff military uniform vied with one of Prime Minister Mossadegh reclining on a daybed. The sign beneath said simply: *Welcome to Tehran.*

A fan whirled above the man in crumpled khaki at the immigration desk. He held out his hand for Harry's passport. 'Good morning, sir.'

'Good morning.'

'What is your occupation?'

'Sugar salesman.'

'Are you visiting Tehran for business or pleasure?'

'Neither.' Harry had worked hard on his Irish accent over the years and it was convincing, even if he said so himself.

The man laughed nervously and stamped the document with a flourish. It bore the name James Fletcher. 'Have a good trip!'

Harry walked to the double doors open to the tarmac. He took off his sunglasses for a moment and squinted against the light. He watched the airport staff unload the bags from the back of the aircraft. They were in no hurry. He turned for a moment to scan the terminal behind him. If anyone had followed him from London, he saw no sign of them yet.

Harry hired a new green Buick, with a bright chrome grille beneath its bonnet that made it look like an open-mouthed shark closing in for the kill. He drove along the narrow asphalt road towards central Tehran, a journey that remained one of startling contrasts. A steady flow of British and American automobiles cruised past donkey carts and beaten-up two-tone Bedford buses. Vehicles drove nominally on the right, but this remained optional – certainly for the young boys on bicycles, who hurtled towards the oncoming traffic at speed, forcing it to swerve. Once or twice, Harry almost hit the line of plane trees by the side of Shah Reza Avenue.

He passed the Pahlavi Hospital, where nurses in white skirts and shirts were playing tennis on clay courts, and Tehran University, where he was struck by how the heads of many young women pouring down the steps were uncovered.

Harry was planning to stay at the Ritz, another new white concrete structure with only marginally more archi-tectural charm than the airport terminal, but he decided checking in could wait so he drove on past it and swung right onto Ferdowsi Avenue, named after Iran's most fam-ous poet. As he passed Churchill Street, he thought of the prime minister and allowed himself a smile; the location of the Soviet Union's grand embassy in Tehran had been renamed in honour of Britain's wartime leader.

As he got closer to the bazaar, outside which Sean's office was located, the traffic slowed almost to a standstill. The streets all around him were packed. Men in Western suits wearing slim 'Douglasie' moustaches – after the Hollywood star Douglas Fairbanks – mixed with those in black trousers and white or checked shirts, the uniform of Tehran's middle and lower classes. Young girls in crisp cotton dresses and high heels mingled on the pavements with women veiled from head to toe in black. But only upper-class women, armed with pearls, fashionable sun-glasses and bold block-print dresses, dared to move about bareheaded in the heart of the city. In Harry's previous trips, he'd concluded that the deeply conservative male masses held back from hurling insults only for fear that the woman who strode towards them with such confidence might turn out to be the wife of a senior police officer or general, as indeed she very well might.

Youths lounged in the shade beneath the canvas awnings of row upon row of tiny shops. It was busier than Harry recalled, but there were few signs of the tumult that dominated international news bulletins until he was in sight of the distinctive pepperpot minarets of the Shah Mosque, next to the bazaar.

A crowd blocked the road ahead and shouts drifted in the still, stifling air. It was close to forty degrees in the shade and Harry was already sweating profusely. A group of young men surrounded his Buick and thumped its pristine bonnet. Some carried placards in English demanding Mossadegh's removal, others photographs of the Shah. Many wore braces over their white shirts, some flat caps. Almost all had moustaches and beards.

Harry watched them steadily. '*ShahanShah*,' they chanted. King of Kings. After years in which Tehran's streets had been flooded with demonstrators wanting to show their support of Mossadegh for his attempt to stand up to 'British imperialism', it was notable but not surprising that this was the first group of protesters Harry should encounter. He had no doubt they were thugs from the southern suburbs, bought with CIA money as the groundwork for the coup his organization had helped plan began in earnest.

They crowded his Buick, chewing tobacco and spitting it onto the tarmac. One hammered his window. 'British? British?' Harry did not respond. 'Churchill, America good!' Harry offered them a thumbs-up and they parted to let him through.

He parked between a black Ford Anglia – a car he'd always thought looked like a concertinaed Morris Minor – and a smart new Rover P4, pink with a crisp white bonnet. Clearly, there were plenty of people in Tehran who still had money, despite the British economic boycott.

The entrance to the bazaar was humming. Rows of shoeshine boys shouted for business alongside men selling oranges and lemons, pomegranates, live geese and chickens hanging upside down in their outstretched hands.

Harry had used the bazaar's warren of alleys, densely packed with traders selling everything from coffee to small arms, dozens of times during the war, but it had been many years since he had been forced to check he was not being followed in this kind of heat. Sweat-soaked, he worked his way through a group of narrow lanes full of stores selling spices and copperware. He spoke to traders, doubled back, browsed in a couple of narrow bookshops and made a few small purchases. But anyone who had been watching would have seen a man whose most notable characteristic seemed to be a comfortable insouciance. He was a master of his art.

Satisfied, eventually, that he had arrived in Tehran undetected, Harry made his way to his son's office, which was tucked into a recess three blocks back from the main entrance to the bazaar. A metal sign announced that this was the Tehran office of the *Manchester Guardian*. A heavy wooden door with an enormous wrought-iron knocker gave way to a paved courtyard, in which a fountain fed a wide stone pool and palm fronds curled up towards the open windows of the floor above.

In the office, on the first floor, a middle-aged Iranian

woman with a handsome face rose from her seat and hurried over. 'May I help you?'

'I am Harry Tower, Sean's father.'

The woman looked as if she had been punched in the face. 'Mr Tower?' It was a question, which she buried with an explanation: 'They didn't tell me you were coming. I would have sent someone to meet you at the airport. I am so sorry. I am Nazadeh. What can I . . . May I get you something to eat or drink? Water? Or English tea?'

'Water, thank you. No ice.'

She hurried to a jug in the corner, filled a glass and came back to him. 'I'm so sorry about your son, Mr Tower. He was a good man, such a kind employer.'

'Is.' Harry tried to smile reassuringly. 'Is.'

'Of course. I'm so sorry. Is. Yes. I just meant . . .' She shook her head regretfully. 'We have searched everywhere, alerted everyone. The American Embassy – they have been dealing with British consular affairs since Mr Mossadegh closed the British Embassy and expelled all British diplomats and businessmen – the police. Shahnaz has even spoken to the army. Her father is a general, a personal friend of the Shah—'

'Shahnaz?'

Nazadeh's eyes widened in surprise. 'Miss Salemi. Your son's girlfriend. They have been inseparable for more than six months. She is the cousin of Sean's translator, Ali. I thought your son would have told you about her. They have seemed very much in love. She would have come to meet you at the airport herself if she had known you were coming, Mr Tower. She has worked tirelessly to find your son.'

'When did you last see Sean?' Harry was keen to move

on from the subject of the many things he did not know about his son's life here – or anywhere else.

'He and Ali said they were going to a press conference at Prime Minister Mossadegh's office. That was on the Saturday morning. We have spoken to many members of the press corps, who all agree they never turned up. We have not seen them since.'

'Were they working on something in particular?'

'Not to my knowledge, sir. His last piece was very well received in London, so it is possible he might have been working on a follow-up to that.'

'On the drugs trade?' Harry had read it and considered it unwise and poorly written. He'd yet to develop any regard for his son's journalistic talents.

'Yes, sir.' Nazadeh took a closely typed sheet from a spike by the telex machine in the corner and handed it to him. Harry cast his eye over the article again. In heavy type, the headline read: *The New 'Road to Riches'*.

If you think Iran today is simply about the wealth to be gained from an apparently inexhaustible supply of oil (though not of course by the people of Iran themselves), think again. A senior diplomatic source has told this newspaper of a new, lucrative trade in opium harvested in the wilds of Afghanistan or even in Iran itself. Transported via Turkey and Yugoslavia (where the KGB is said to have a hand in the trade) to the fashionable salons of Paris, it is proving too lucrative for many to easily ignore.

How is it possible that such a trade exists? With powerful connections, comes the answer. It is the new 'road to riches' our source claims, presided over by a gang that involves at least one

senior French diplomat and contacts at the highest level in Teh-
ran's police force . . .

'What kind of reaction was there to this?' Harry asked, though he could guess well enough. He folded the paper and slipped it into his pocket.

'I don't think the organizations named were pleased, Mr Tower,' she said, displaying an unlikely gift for under-statement. 'But your son said no more than that. He didn't seem concerned about it.'

Or most things, Harry thought. Which was part of his problem.

Nazadeh was studying the floor tiles intently. 'Shall I inform the American Embassy and the police that you are here, Mr Tower?'

'No, thank you. Please tell no one that I'm in Tehran.'

Nazadeh did a poor job of hiding her confusion, even consternation. 'Should I call Miss Salemi, sir? She at least would want to know you are here.'

'No. Thank you. I'd just appreciate a few moments to work in peace.'

Nazadeh retreated reluctantly to her space on the far side of the office. There was no mistaking Sean's desk, upon which piles of paper fluttered beneath huge wooden fans. Harry picked up a photograph of his wife and son taken on the sands of a Norfolk beach the year before Amanda's death. Their arms were draped around each other, their warmth and love clearly evident. He dusted the picture carefully and set it down.

Newspaper cuttings filled the wall. A *Time* magazine cover named Mossadegh *Man of the Year* for 1951. Another from *Newsweek* called him *The Fainting Maniac*. There were pictures of the oil refinery at Abadan and of the slums that surrounded it, and an extract from the speech Mossadegh had famously delivered to the UN two years before: 'My countrymen lack the bare necessities of existence. Their standard of living is probably one of the lowest in the world. Our greatest natural asset is oil. This should be the source of work and food for the population of Iran. Its exploitation should properly be our national industry, and the revenue from it should go to improve our conditions of life. As now organized, however, the petroleum industry has contributed practically nothing to the well-being of the people or to the technical progress or industrial development of my country. The evidence for that statement is that after fifty years of exploitation by a foreign company, we still do not have enough Iranian technicians and must call in foreign experts.'

Harry ran his eye along the profusion of thick leather-bound volumes stamped *Anglo-Iranian*. 'Sean talked of writing a book about the company,' Nazadeh explained. 'He believed the crisis could have been avoided if only Anglo-Iranian and the British government in London had shown some sensitivity to the Iranian government's position.'

Harry pulled one off the shelf. It was a set of accounts.

'When Mr Mossadegh nationalized the company and the management fled, a mob broke into the office and scooped up a huge amount of paperwork. Sean has been trying to pull some of it together.'

'Did anyone know he was doing that? Apart from you?'

'I believe he discussed it with Shahnaz and Ali, sir, but I don't know of anyone else.'

Harry picked up a loose sheet from the top of a pile. It was a typed transcript. Sean had written on it: *Extract of an interview with Sean Levy, American oil expert. Levy recalls conversation with ordinary Iranians on Tehran Street.*

LEVY: You realize that if the British technicians leave Abadan you will have to try to run the industry by yourselves?

IRANIANS: Yes.

LEVY: You realize that you will fail to run the industry without the British?

IRANIANS: Yes.

LEVY: So Iranian oil will no longer be produced for the world market?

IRANIANS: Yes.

LEVY: And if Iranian oil is no longer produced, there will be no money in the Iranian treasury?

IRANIANS: Yes.

LEVY: And if you have no money, there will be a financial and economic collapse, which will play into the hands of the Communists?

IRANIANS: Yes.

LEVY: Well, what are you going to do about it?

IRANIANS: Nothing.

Harry seated himself at his son's desk. 'Are you sure you would not like some tea?' Nazadeh asked.

'No. Thank you. Just ...' he smiled '... a little peace and quiet.' Harry put his sunglasses on the shelf and wiped the morning's grime from his face with a handkerchief. He was familiar enough with the unhappy story of

Anglo-Iranian. Without the discovery of an inexhaustible supply of oil in Iran, the British Empire would never have won two world wars. He didn't blame successive Downing Street governments for wanting to control it – though he considered it disastrously short-sighted – or the Iranians for demanding a greater share of the revenue that was rightfully theirs. He had been a lone voice in SIS, advising that they persuade Anglo-Iranian – and the Foreign Office – to be more reasonable.

Harry turned his attention to the chaotic mess. Damned boy, he thought. Never could organize his way out of a paper bag.

He sifted through a few copies of the *Tehran Times*, which sat atop the pile. Nothing was marked or highlighted that he could see, so he threw them into the wastepaper basket. He found a notepad with a couple of pages ripped out and held it up to the light. There was some kind of imprint on the page below, so he put it to one side. He found another handwritten sheet:

Oil:
1950 – \$45 million
1951 – \$23 million
1952 – 0

'Iran's total earnings from oil exports,' Nazadeh explained. For someone who claimed to know little of what his son was working on, she seemed to have a detailed knowledge of every item on his desk. 'He told me he'd got the figures from the foreign ministry and they had fallen to zero last year. Now that Britain has persuaded the world to boycott Iranian oil, and taken to seizing tankers that try to get into the Gulf, there is no one to sell it to.'

Harry picked up a sheaf of paper, still bound together, that appeared to have been ripped from a ledger. It listed names and sums of money.

'Ali found him those,' Nazadeh said.

'What are they?'

'Some of the men Anglo-Iranian was bribing – Members of Parliament, journalists, army officers, police officers, officials from the Shah's court. One of the students who broke into the Anglo-Iranian office gave them to him.'

That would get you into more than enough trouble, Harry thought. He ran through the names, which meant nothing to him. Another sheet listed similar but much larger figures. This time, they corresponded with what appeared to be bank-account numbers.

666074 – $27,000
650193 – $17,000
423837 – $11,000

'What are these?'

Nazadeh shook her head. 'I am sorry, Mr Tower, I have no idea.' But she was staring at the ground again. Harry got up and closed the windows, then the shutters. He took the lamp from Sean's desk, turned it on and placed it on the floor. He switched off all the other lights in the room. He returned to the desk, ripped the top page from the notebook he had set aside earlier and placed it face down. He cleared everything else from around it and raised the lamp to the lip of the desk.

Sean wrote with a heavy, looping hand, like his mother, so it was just possible to pick out the indentation. Harry traced it, then placed the lamp back on the desk. He opened the shutters. Nazadeh was gaping at him. 'Three hundred and twelve Doshtan Street,' he said, putting the paper in front of her. 'Does that mean anything to you?'

'I'm sorry, Mr Tower. I don't understand.'

'This is Sean's notebook. He scribbled an address on the last sheet and tore it off.'

'Doshtan Street . . . Yes, I think it is in the south of the city. A very poor area. Sean did go there. I remember him looking at the map with Ali.'

'When?'

'Shortly before they disappeared.'

Harry leant against the edge of the desk. 'Please tell me what happened. Exactly.'

Nazadeh breathed in sharply. 'Sean . . . Mr Tower . . . came here in the morning that day, as normal. I think it must have been the Thursday. Ali was late, because he had to take his mother to the doctor. They went off into the bazaar to have a cup of coffee. They often did that. I was here, trying to get someone to mend the fans.' She pointed at the roof. A couple were not turning in time with the others. 'They came back and talked on the telephone for a while.' She gestured at Ali's desk on the far side of the room, which was spotlessly tidy. 'Then they came and looked at the map on the wall here. That was when I remember them talking about Doshtan Street.'

'What time did they come back?'

'At about five p.m. I was just tidying up to go. Sean was in a terrible hurry. He ran in and took his jacket from the peg in the corner and shouted that he would see me on Saturday.'

'Would it be normal for Sean to go away for a few days without telling you where he was headed?'

'No, sir. Not at all.' She shook her head. 'I waited for them on Saturday afternoon, after the prime minister's press conference, but they never returned. And then Miss Salemi came in to say he had failed to pick her up at the airport. And that was when we cabled the office in London. We didn't know what else to do.'

Harry slipped his hands into his pockets and looked out of the back window. 'I'd like you to do a couple more things for me if that is possible.'

'Of course, sir. Anything. You have only to ask.'

'Get hold of the telephone company. I'd like a complete record of every call made from this office in the three weeks before Sean's disappearance.'

'I will do my best, sir, but it will take a few days.'

'Then please tell them to be as quick as they can. Have you spoken to the translator's family?'

'Yes.'

'They have no idea where he went?'

'No, sir.'

'Perhaps you could talk to them again, see what else you can find out about what he might have been working on in the week or two before his disappearance. I will see you tomorrow morning.'

Harry got into the lift, pulled the cage noiselessly across and descended to the courtyard below, then walked silently back up the stairs and stood outside the office door he had deliberately left ajar. 'No,' he heard Nazadeh say, into the telephone receiver. 'Just the normal questions.' There was a long silence. 'He didn't seem to, no.' And then another. 'Yes, of course, I will.'

Harry walked carefully down the stairs and out into the blazing sunshine. He had just reached his car by the bazaar when he heard his name being called. He turned to see a striking Iranian woman running towards him. She was tall, with big eyes and lustrous hair that tumbled over slender shoulders. She wore a crisp white fashionably cut dress and moved with the natural grace and ease of an athlete. 'Mr Tower, I am Shahnaz.'

Harry offered his hand. 'I am pleased to meet you, Miss Salemi.'

In the process of running after him, the breeze had blown a brightly patterned scarf off Shahnaz's head. Now, as a group of middle-aged men in workmen's dress – dark trousers, scruffy shirts – walked past, one called out simply, in English, 'Whore.'

Flustered, Shahnaz replaced her headscarf. 'I am sorry,' she said, unsure, perhaps, if she was apologizing for her error, for her country, or both. 'I came to the office and Nazadeh said you had just left. When did you arrive in Tehran?'

'This afternoon.'

'We did not know you were coming.' This sounded like it might have been an accusation, or possibly a question. He didn't offer any explanation. What, he wondered, had Sean told her of his father? He had low expectations and the hesitancy in her demeanour tended to confirm the worst of them. 'Have you been to the American Embassy or the police?' she asked.

'Not yet.' He didn't add that he had no intention of going to either. The last thing he wanted was to alert anyone in officialdom to his presence in Tehran. He had first to work out whether there was any connection between Sean's disappearance and the tail he had spotted before he left London. Like most intelligence officers, Harry did not believe in coincidences.

'We've been getting no help at all,' she said. 'They claim the chaos on the streets has made it impossible for the disappearance of one journalist to be treated as a priority . . .'

Harry waited. Shahnaz avoided his gaze, but he sensed that her hesitancy hid inner turmoil over how far she could trust him. If so, she appeared suddenly to reach a decision. 'I have a cousin in the police,' she said, lowering her voice an octave, 'who has tipped me off that they have found Sean's car south of Tehran.'

7

PERHAPS SHE SENSED his shock because Shahnaz went on, 'I don't think there is any sign of Sean or Ali there, which . . . It is good news, I am sure. Maybe their car broke down or was stolen.' She didn't sound convinced. 'We should go there now. Would you like me to get my car or—'

'I'll drive.' They climbed into Harry's hired Buick. Shahnaz shifted uncomfortably in her seat and tapped her fingers unconsciously against the wooden dashboard. 'I am so sorry, Mr Tower. If I had known you were flying out, I would have come to the airport to meet you.'

'There was no need.'

'I asked the newspaper to give you a message.' They hadn't, but Harry let that pass. He wound down the window. 'It takes a while to get used to the heat,' she said.

Harry allowed the silence to play out. He had long since learnt it was the easiest way to encourage someone to reveal themselves. And her reluctance to trust him suggested she had plenty to elucidate. 'I knew you would come,' she said. 'Sean always said you did not suffer fools gladly.'

Harry did not know quite what she meant, but he felt it was intended as a compliment. He permitted himself a smile. 'That was my good side?'

She tried to smile back at him, still flustered. 'No, of course not. I didn't mean that. I just knew you would come.'

A father willing to search for his son. It hardly made a man a hero, but Harry didn't labour the point. 'When did you last see him?'

'A couple of weeks ago. We drove up to stay with friends whose family have a place on the Caspian coast. I had to fly down to Abadan the next day, so he dropped me at the airport on the way back. We arranged to go out for dinner the night I returned. When he didn't show up, I went to his apartment. He wasn't there.'

'How long ago was that?'

'A week.'

'Is it possible a story suddenly came up?'

'Perhaps. But Sean would never have let a week pass without letting me – or someone in his office – know where he was. And when I got to his apartment, it looked to me as though it had been searched.'

'Why do you say that?'

'Nothing was in its usual place. His clothes appeared to have been rehung in wardrobes in a hurry. That was when I asked Nazadeh to call his editors in London.'

'Who would have wanted to search his apartment?'

She shook her head. 'I don't know.' Harry dropped the

article about the drugs trade onto her lap. She glanced at it and nodded slowly. 'We did talk a lot about this piece. It certainly wouldn't have made him popular at the French Embassy or Police Headquarters. I didn't think it was a good idea to publish it, but I find it hard to believe a single article in a British newspaper would have persuaded someone to kidnap or . . .' She wouldn't, or couldn't, take her fear to its logical conclusion.

'Could he have been working on a follow-up to this?'

'I think he was on to something else. He changed in the few days before I flew to Abadan. He appeared excited, told me he was on to something big, but he wouldn't say what.'

Harry took from his jacket the second piece of paper, with the address on it. 'What happens at three hundred and twelve Doshtan Street?' he asked.

She glanced at it, then up at him. She was frowning. 'I have no idea. Why?'

'That was the last thing he wrote on his notepad.'

'I don't know. I'm sorry. We can go and take a look when we get back.'

'You speak English with no hint of an accent, Miss Salemi.'

'My mother was British.' She smiled. 'Not that you'd guess to look at me.'

'How did your parents meet?'

'She was a ballerina for the Diaghilev. She met my father in Monte Carlo.'

'And what does your father do?' Harry was pretty sure he knew, though he wasn't going to admit it.

'Nothing. He's quite notorious. His default bar-room

story is that he saved Tehran from the Soviets at the end of the war. He was the security minister at the time, but retired when Mr Mossadegh became prime minister. Now he plays cards with the Shah on Mondays and boasts about his friendship with His Imperial Majesty for the rest of the week. Beyond that, I couldn't say. We don't speak.'

As Harry had suspected, it was the General Salemi he had briefly encountered at the end of the war, a man whose booming self-regard bordered on narcissism.

'How did you meet Sean?'

'At a function at the French Embassy.' She smiled for the second time. 'He was hard to miss.' Her cheeks dimpled. 'He's a very handsome man.' Harry found it hard not to smile, too. 'He's rash, though,' she said. 'And that is what worries me.'

And me, Harry thought – but didn't say. She had fear enough for both of them.

It was the end of the working day and the city was still frenetic. Battered old Morris Minors and trucks belching fumes barged impatiently through the donkey carts and buses overloaded with passengers. Groups of young boys threaded through the traffic like shoals of fish, selling cigarettes, or sweets, or the evening newspaper. Labourers toiled on buildings being erected beneath cloaks of bamboo scaffolding. 'Have you been to Tehran before, Mr Tower?' Shahnaz asked eventually.

'Yes.'

'Sean said you were in the sugar business.' He nodded. 'What do you do for it?'

'I manage operations and sales.'

'I see. So what brought you to Tehran?'

'I came to meet our sales team here.'

'How did you like it?'

He smiled at her. 'I've always had a soft spot for Iran.'

'If only the world could say the same. Oil should be our blessing, but it's a curse, just as Mr Mossadegh says.'

The houses were less substantial now and the traffic was blocked not by other automobiles, but by peasant farmers herding flocks of sheep or goats across the fringes of the city. They passed the wireless station, then a military airport, where half a dozen L4 Cub training aircraft were parked just inside the perimeter wire. Harry had learnt to fly in one in his early days in SIS Operations and still had intermittent back pain to remind him of the day he'd crashed it into a field.

After a row of factories spilling bilious smoke into the heavy air, they hugged the railway line for a few miles to the small town of Shahr-e Ray. After that, they were out of Tehran and on an open road.

'Where are we going?' Harry asked.

'The village is called Cheshmeh Shur.'

'What would Sean have been doing there?'

'This is the road to Qom and Isfahan. He is more likely to have been headed to one or the other. But I don't know.'

Harry looked out at dry fields, giant palms and the occasional lone farmer traipsing across the stark horizon. Soon, even the fields receded and they were surrounded by desert scrub and barren hills. It was strangely beautiful, remote and desolate.

As the miles had passed, Shahnaz had sunk into the seat beside him and was enjoying a fitful sleep, her mouth half open. Harry tried to imagine the earnest youth he had said goodbye to a year ago conducting a love affair with this spirited woman. He didn't doubt Amanda would have been impressed.

She awoke with a start and, just a few moments later, said, 'We need to turn left ahead.'

They swung off the road and climbed a hill. A plume of dust twisted through a sky stained deep red by the setting sun. As they crested the rise, they encountered a roadblock mounted by a small group of police. It looked as if it was still in the process of being set up. Harry slowed. One of the policemen strolled towards him as he wound down the window. Behind him, a Caucasian man in a beige suit and white Panama lounged against the police car, smoking.

'I'm afraid you will have to turn back, sir,' the policeman said, in passable English. 'There has been an incident in the village up ahead.'

Shahnaz leant over. 'You have found my boyfriend's car. Sean Tower. He's been missing for almost a week. I am Shahnaz Salemi, daughter of General Salemi.'

The Caucasian man in the Panama straightened, threw away his cigarette and hurried over. 'Mr Tower, I assume?' He took off his hat, bent down towards the window. He was a strange-looking man, with a bulbous nose, thick wavy red hair and a face that looked as if it had been sat on sideways. He was as white as alabaster. 'Julian Grenville. I'm the last remaining British diplomat in Iran, left embedded in the American Embassy, for my sins, to deal with consular matters.' A thin bead of sweat glistened just above his top lip. 'I can take you through, Mr Tower, if you like. Perhaps I could just ride in the back.'

'We'll be fine, thank you.'

'Well, I need to get down there anyway, so if you wouldn't mind . . .'

Harry nodded at him reluctantly.

'When did you arrive in Tehran?' Grenville asked, as soon as they had moved off.

'Today.'

'We weren't expecting you.' It sounded like an accusation. 'Otherwise, I would have come to the airport to meet you. I've been dealing with your son's disappearance ever since Miss Salemi here reported it to the Americans.'

'You never made contact with me,' she said.

'We were just trying to get to the bottom of it.' Grenville smiled at her. It didn't have the desired effect. 'These are chaotic times and, quite frankly, it's very hard to get any sense from Mr Mossadegh's ministries. The scale of their incompetence is staggering.'

They wound their way down towards a small village and glided to a halt beside its well. Harry got out and dusted himself off. The light was fading fast. All around them, chickens and goats roamed freely down a street fringed with single-storey stone-and-wattle houses with straw roofs. There were fewer than two dozen in all, crammed into a narrow gully before a concrete bridge over a stream that wound its way towards a valley floor. A group of children leant against the wall of the nearest house, staring at them in the listless way of the malnourished.

It was hard to imagine a less likely place for a journalist from a British national newspaper to have visited by choice in the middle of a national, indeed an international, crisis.

But as a location to dispose of a reporter asking trouble-some questions, it fitted the bill perfectly. He imagined the price of silence here was cheap, but thought it tactless to say so.

'Please wait here a moment,' Grenville said. 'I believe the car was found abandoned in a lake on the far side of the hill. The police think it must have been stolen.' He walked towards a group of officers at the bottom of the lane.

'The Americans never mentioned a British diplomat,' Shahnaz said.

They wouldn't, Harry thought. He had yet to work out exactly who Grenville was and what he was doing in Teh-ran. 'It's hard to imagine a more remote spot,' he said. 'Can you think of any reason Sean would be here?'

Shahnaz looked down over the village. She shook her head. 'No. I know it a little. I came here about six months ago. We run an intensive programme to get young chil-dren started on reading and writing and to teach them basic hygiene. But Sean wasn't with me and I don't recall ever mentioning it to him.'

'Who is "we"?'

'It's a government initiative. It was started by Mr Mos-sadegh and is supported by some wealthy families in Tehran as well.'

'Including yours?'

'My father finds it a useful way to buy back his conscience.'

'You're a teacher, then?'

'I help where I can.'

Grenville disappeared into one of the houses along the main street. Harry strolled towards the well, where a primitive wooden hoist was being used to extract the water. A couple of women had just filled earthenware bowls and were walking away with them on their heads. He traced his hand along the wall around it. He knelt in the dust.

'What is it?' Shahnaz asked.

'What kind of car did Sean drive?'

'A Dodge.'

'What colour is it?'

'Green. Dark green. Apart from the rusty bits.'

Harry looked up the dirt track. One of the policemen was watching him intently. Grenville emerged from the hut, pushing his Panama down on the rebellious red hair. 'The chief is waiting for us by the car,' he said, as he drew level.

Harry followed him back to the Buick, but Shahnaz stayed where she was. 'I'll walk,' she said.

'Miss Salemi,' Grenville remonstrated, 'it will be dark in twenty minutes. It would be much better—'

'I'm no stranger here. I know my way around. I need to stretch my legs.'

Grenville shook his head. He and Harry climbed back into the Buick and drove up the hill in silence. Grenville could not resist sneaking a glance over his shoulder. Shahnaz had not moved.

Harry looked up at the ridge, now fringed with the last of the dying light. 'Did Sean visit the village?' he asked.

Grenville shifted uneasily in his seat. 'I don't believe so. But we can ask the headman. He's with the police.' They reached the top of the hill and started down towards the main road.

'How long have you been in Tehran, Mr Grenville?'

'Ten months. They settled me in with the Americans as soon as Mossadegh shut the embassy and expelled all our staff.'

'Where were you before?'

'King Charles Street. Due for a three-year stint. My wife wasn't happy to be told she was exchanging Chelsea for Tehran. Not after three years in Romania. All part of the great adventure, I told her. But you know how wives can be, Mr Tower.'

Harry didn't. Amanda had been one of a kind in too many ways to list.

They pulled onto the highway and picked up speed. Grenville leant close to the windscreen in an attempt to spot another track to the left. Once on it, Harry had to proceed slowly, avoiding enormous potholes, until they reached a salt lake. In the heat of summer, it was little more than a moonscape of dried, cratered earth that rose slowly to the craggy ridge that separated the valley from the village beyond. In the fading sunlight, it glowed a rich, deep red.

Sean's old Dodge had been pulled from what remained of the water.

Grenville made the introductions. Harry shook hands with a round-faced police captain and a village elder with flinty, suspicious eyes. Grenville strode towards the car, rattling off questions in Farsi as he went. He turned to Harry. 'A boy from the village found the vehicle here, Mr Tower. It was only half submerged, so they dragged it out. They could find nothing at all inside. He says you're very welcome to look if you wish.'

'How did it get here?' As he waited for Grenville to make the translation, Harry checked around the front of the battered Dodge.

'He doesn't know,' Grenville said.

Harry crouched next to the left wing and ran his hand across it. He found three bullet holes, two in the wheel and a third beneath the window.

He strode back to the Buick, flipped open his briefcase and took a penknife from one of its pockets. He returned to the front wheel arch and knelt in the dust. It was hard to see in the fading light. 'Have they a torch?'

Grenville scurried away and returned a moment later. 'I'm afraid not.'

Harry worked his hand around the side of the tyre, cut through the rubber and fished about inside with his fingers. He pulled out two bullets, slipped one discreetly into his pocket and held up the other to what little remained of the light.

'They were shot at?' Grenville asked, trying to suppress the note of alarm in his voice.

'It would seem so.'

The policeman bent forward and spoke quietly to Grenville. 'The captain will be happy to take the bullet from you, Mr Tower.'

'It's all right, thank you.'

'He wants to submit it for ballistic tests, so they can try to identify the type of weapon that was used.'

'Good idea.' Harry handed it over, relieved they had not seen the one he had slipped into his pocket. He got into the driving seat of the Dodge. There was nothing left inside; no discarded matches or leaves from a notebook. Perhaps they had disappeared or perished in the water. He checked carefully and stepped out again. He faced Grenville. 'Please ask the village elder when he first knew of this.'

'One of his sons came running over the ridge to say that he had found a car in the lake.'

'And that was the first he knew of it?'

'Yes.'

'Had Sean ever previously visited the village?'

Grenville checked. 'No.'

'Is he sure about that?'

'Yes.'

'Not at any time?'

'That's correct.'

'So he had never seen this car before?'

'No.'

Harry scrutinized the man closely. 'Please tell him that I know my son's Dodge was chased into the village, and that it ploughed through the earth wall by the well, which has since been rebuilt.'

Grenville stared at him for a moment, open-mouthed. 'Mr Tower, I understand that you're worried about your son, but I can assure you he did not—'

'The rear section of the wall by the well has been newly repaired. There is green paint on the stone in the garden. The Dodge must have come down the track, out of control, and gone straight through that wall.'

Grenville gaped at Harry for a moment more, then recovered himself and translated. The expression on the man's face didn't alter and neither did his story. 'He says he doesn't know what you're talking about. It happened exactly as he described it.'

73

Harry leant against the Dodge's bonnet. The police captain lit a cigarette. They waited. 'Do you know how long Miss Salemi might be?' Grenville asked.

'No. Tell them to go home.'

'They won't do that. They've been ordered to stay as long as we're here.'

Harry returned to the Buick, replaced his knife in its sheath and took out a packet of cigarettes. He lit one and strolled along the shoreline. The last embers of day had faded into a velvet night. The moon glistened on the still waters of the lake. He sat in the shingle and stared into the darkness. 'Damn you, Sean,' he whispered to himself. 'What the hell have you got into?'

Harry lost himself so thoroughly in his thoughts that he didn't register Shahnaz's presence until she dropped down quietly beside him. Sombre eyes searched his. 'They were chased by army jeeps,' she said. She clutched her knees to her chest. 'I found a woman whose son I taught to read.'

'What did she say?'

'She was incredibly nervous. She said she was in bed, asleep. It was late. She heard the roar of engines, a loud crash. She got out of bed, but her husband told her not to leave the house. Then there were shots.'

'Did she—'

'That is all she would say. After an hour, when her husband had not returned, she opened the door and saw soldiers. There were two jeeps parked at the top of the street, close to the Dodge. I told her she must have been mistaken, that it was more likely to have been police officers, but she was adamant that they were military.'

'Did she see Sean?'

'No, but one of her neighbours told her she'd seen a man being shot as he ran down the alley opposite. The soldiers immediately dragged him away.'

'Was he Iranian or European?'

'She couldn't say.'

'Did you talk to the neighbour yourself?'

'I couldn't. They were all terrified.'

'Then we'll go back and—'

'They don't know any more. We'd be putting them at risk if we went back.'

'Was the man who was shot still alive?'

'They couldn't say.' Shahnaz rocked gently beside him. A tear rolled down her cheek.

'It can't have been him,' he said softly.

'We don't know that.'

'We do. Even in the darkness, she would have been able to tell if it was a European – and if it had been, she would have remarked on it.' Shahnaz stared into the lake as she digested that. After a few moments, she nodded, drawing strength from its logic.

'Is it possible the army was involved in the drugs trade Sean wrote about?' Harry asked.

'No.' She wiped her eyes. 'The police and the military are rivals. One or the other might have been involved in something like that, but not both. Did you find anything here?'

'Two bullets lodged in a tyre. I've slipped one into my pocket. I'll get someone to run a test, back in Tehran. They tried to tell me the Dodge had been driven straight here from the main road.'

'What did you say?'

'I told them I knew the wall at the top of the village had

recently been rebuilt and that there were marks from the car's paintwork in the garden inside it.'

Shahnaz looked towards his feet, buried in the sand. 'You need to watch the scorpions.' She forced a smile.

He didn't move. 'The least of our problems, I imagine.'

'True.' She stared into the darkness, deep in thought. Silence wrapped them, like the night. 'My grandmother used to terrify my brother and me with warnings about scorpions,' she said eventually. 'And *roteil* and *drakoola*. Do you know what they are?'

'I haven't had the pleasure.'

'You'd better hope you don't. A *roteil* is a type of tarantula that is attracted by the scent of blood and bites while falling from ceilings or tree branches.'

'Sounds pleasant.'

'And a *drakoola* is a kind of fire ant that sprays a noxious substance that causes your skin to blister or boil.'

'Iran is a dangerous place.' He smiled at her. 'I think I get the message.'

'Did you go to Kashan when you were here before?'

He shook his head. 'I don't believe so.'

'It was one of the last places to resist the Arab hordes in the seventh century. The Arab commander who was leading the assault grew impatient, so he asked his men to gather up thousands of scorpions to tip over the city's walls. Or so legend has it. My grandmother was very taken with the Zoroastrian faith, and its cosmogony attributes the creation of all of our menacing wildlife to Ahriman, the evil influence of the universe. You know about Zoroastrianism?'

Harry nodded. If nothing else, he liked to think he knew the countries he visited.

'The faith of Cyrus, Xerxes and Darius. It is why we Iranians fight so hard for enlightened leadership. Do you British understand that?'

As if he had been listening, Grenville emerged from the shadows. 'Are you all right, Miss Salemi?'

'Yes, thank you.'

'Do you need a little more time, Mr Tower?'

He stood. 'No. We're ready.'

It was not until they reached the main road back to Tehran that Grenville, in the passenger seat beside Harry, broke the silence. 'I'm sorry, Mr Tower. They were not as helpful as I'd hoped.'

'They were lying through their teeth.'

'Yes ... I suppose ... We shall have to get someone down here to look at that wall. It may be that you were mistaken.'

'I was not.'

'No, well, I'd very much like to think that the police were not involved. It's a professional force and I—'

'It was the army, not the police,' Shahnaz said.

'What makes you say that?' Grenville snapped his head back towards her.

'I spoke to some of the villagers. Two army jeeps chased Sean and Ali into that wall. One of the two was then shot as he tried to escape.'

'Good God. Which one?'

'We don't know.'

'Is he ... all right?'

'They couldn't say.'

'Which hospital would they have been taken to?' Harry asked.

'The Pahlavi Hospital, in Tehran.' Grenville studied his hands.

'Let's go straight there.'

'Of course. I'll get in touch with the hospital's management in the morning.'

'We'll drop in now.'

'Oh . . . yes, if you wish.'

'I'd also like to see the chief of police and the army chief of staff first thing tomorrow,' Harry said. If his original plan had been to move anonymously through the streets of Tehran in search of his son, he understood that that game was up: somehow, they had known he was coming. He wondered if Nazadeh had been talking to Grenville on the phone as he listened from the hallway outside Sean's office.

'It would be ill-advised to trouble the military, Mr Tower. It is almost certainly the case that the kidnappers were simply posing as soldiers.' He looked at Shahnaz for support. 'The army is very powerful here in Iran. Many of the officers are loyal to the Shah and have little respect for the current government. I can't really conceive of circumstances in which they would have behaved like this. It is much more likely to have been bandits posing as soldiers to frighten the villagers into silence.'

'In that case, it's a scandal that I'm sure the chief would want to be made aware of.'

There was a long silence. 'Yes, I suppose so,' Grenville eventually conceded. 'The chief of police will, I'm sure, agree to meet you. I shall arrange it for tomorrow morning. Shall we say midday?'

For the rest of the journey, Harry probed Grenville for any clues as to who he might really be. He asked about his time in Romania, his other foreign postings and his time in London. But he couldn't find any logical flaw in the story Grenville was telling of himself. If he was working for anyone but the British Foreign Office, they'd taught him to cover his tracks well.

Back in central Tehran, the streets were quiet until they turned onto Sepah Avenue by the National Park and were quickly halted by a crowd of protesters. Harry tried to reverse, but was prevented from doing so when another group of young men swung in behind him from Khayyam Street. 'Damn,' he muttered. They surrounded the Buick, thumping its bonnet and pressing their faces to the glass.

'They're opponents of the prime minister,' Grenville explained, as if he thought Harry too stupid to have worked that out. 'They've probably just been protesting at the Parliament building, the Majlis.'

The crowd around them swelled. The men hammered on the doors and roof. 'For Christ's sake!' Grenville shouted. Harry watched him calmly. Grenville looked as if he wanted to get out and run.

'We've had this every bloody day for weeks,' Grenville said, wiping the sweat from his brow and trying not to catch the eye of the men outside his window. 'Lucky it's so hot tonight or we'd have twice the number. Bloody Mossadegh. It seems like most people are just as fed up with him as we are.'

'Most of the demonstrations are still in support of the prime minister,' Shahnaz told Harry, from the rear seat. 'Even now, after the British oil blockade, the years of austerity and hunger, people have not lost faith.'

'I wouldn't believe that, Mr Tower, if I were you. The protests against Mossadegh have been getting bigger, uglier and angrier every day these past weeks. People here are tired of his intransigence. He's an extremely stubborn old man.'

'You don't think he has a point – Iran's oil for Iran's people?' Harry was goading Grenville now. And probably just for the fun of it.

'He may have an argument for a better deal, Mr Tower. Anglo-Iranian conceded that long ago. But he has chosen to pursue his argument with a fanaticism that—'

'The men who protest against the prime minister are unemployed thugs hired by the mafia and the business interests he has so upset, Mr Grenville,' Shahnaz said. 'As you well know—'

'Thugs they may be, Miss Salemi.' He faced Harry. 'But the poor of south Tehran are even more tired of their great leader than we are, Mr Tower. And that is the truth. There are no jobs and nothing to live on. It's as simple as that. Just as we predicted. And all because of the inflexibility of a very stubborn old man.'

'You can hardly say it's Mossadegh who has been stubborn,' Shahnaz said.

'He has bankrupted his country.'

'Or, rather, you did. And all because we had the temerity to demand a fair settlement for our oil.'

'You wouldn't *have* any oil, Miss Salemi, if we had not paid enormous sums to develop its production. As well you know.' He turned towards Harry again. 'Mr Mossadegh's insistence on nationalizing Anglo-Iranian and all its assets was tantamount, Mr Tower, to theft. He's made his bed and now he can damned well lie in it. If his people don't like it, well, frankly, who can blame them?'

Shahnaz was trying not to be goaded. And failing. 'Have you ever been to Kaghazabad, Mr Grenville, the place they called Paper City?'

The diplomat could clearly see he was about to get a diatribe, but he had to concede he had not, although Harry had. It was where the men who worked Britain's oil refineries lived with their families in Iran's deep south. It was an abomination.

'You know,' Shahnaz said, 'in the summer, the shacks the workers live in, made of discarded oil drums, are hotter than a furnace. The sand and the wind whip in from the desert with the air hotter than a blowtorch. And it does nothing to dispel the sulphurous, suffocating stench of burning oil, which sticks in your throat. But even that is not the worst of it. In winter, the land floods and becomes a flat lake, the mud in town knee-deep as people use canoes for transport. The water is a breeding ground for flies like you've never seen—'

'Yes, all right, Miss Salemi,' Grenville interrupted. 'We've all heard—'

'But take a very short trip to the British section of Abadan and you enter another world, of air-conditioned offices, swimming-pools, verdant lawns, gymkhana clubs—'

'If you could spare us the lecture, I'm sure we'd be grateful.'

'And you know the worst of it, Mr Tower?' she said, turning to Harry, with something like light in her eyes. 'Anglo-Iranian swore to reform its ways. In 1933, it promised Reza Shah – of all people – to give labourers better pay and more chance for advancement. It said it would build schools, hospitals, roads, a telephone system—'

Grenville was smiling at Harry. 'Miss Salemi is clearly not familiar with the vicissitudes of running an international conglomerate in the middle of a global depression—'

'In 1947, Anglo-Iranian declared profits of forty million pounds. It gave Iran seven.'

Grenville, apparently accepting defeat, faced the front.

The young men had begun to drift away from them, so that Harry was able slowly to wheel north onto Simetri Street. Grenville was quiet until they were passing the Chinese Embassy at the top of the street, just before the turn-off to the hospital. 'My God, I do hope and pray we don't find anything untoward. But I would have heard if anything had happened to your son, Mr Tower. I'm sure I would.' He nodded, as if to convince himself. 'I'm sure I would.'

8

THE PAHLAVI HOSPITAL was clean, orderly and empty. 'Too expensive for most Iranians,' Shahnaz explained. But it was still hard to find anyone willing or able to speak to them. Grenville eventually located a young doctor who claimed to have been on the night shift for the previous seven days. He said he could not recollect treating any foreigners, save for the child of a Swedish diplomat who had fallen and broken his ankle. He had certainly not seen a young man with a gunshot wound or any injuries likely to have resulted from a car accident.

'Where did you train?' Harry asked him. 'Your English is flawless.' Perhaps it was just his innate suspicion, but he found it surprising that Grenville had managed to produce a doctor who could so conveniently speak for the events of the entire period in which Sean might have been brought there. He imagined Shahnaz had reached a similar conclusion because she had disappeared suddenly.

'St Thomas' Hospital in London. My father is English.'

'An oil executive?'

'Yes. He was. In Abadan and then here in the capital. He is retired now.'

'How long have you been back in Tehran from your studies?'

'A year. My parents are in London, but I intend to stay on. There is a lot of work to do here.'

'Quite,' said Grenville, unnecessarily.

Harry looked from one to the other and back again. 'You know each other?' he asked easily.

'No,' the man said. But he avoided Harry's gaze.

'You don't recall treating a young white man for any injuries at all in the last week?'

He shook his head. 'I am afraid not.'

'Would you mind checking your register? Perhaps he wasn't brought in until after daylight.'

'I have checked, sir.' He pointed at Grenville. 'Your colleague asked me to do so before I came to talk to you.'

'My son, Sean, is a tall lad. Six feet two or so. He has wavy dark hair and a beard.'

'Sir, we don't treat many foreigners here. My colleagues and I would certainly remember him. I have spoken to the nurses and they have no recollection of anyone matching your son's description either. I am sorry.'

'Have you treated anyone else for gunshot wounds?'

The man shook his head. 'Not to my knowledge.'

'Are you sure about that? In the current climate, it hardly seems an unlikely occurrence. A protester, perhaps, shot by an over-eager soldier.'

'Yes, sir. I am sure.'

Shahnaz had returned. She shrugged to indicate that, whoever she had been talking to, she had turned up nothing.

Harry thanked the doctor and they walked out to the front courtyard. 'Are there are other hospitals?' he asked Shahnaz.

'Many – Sina, Varjavad, Karim. I'll get Nazadeh to check in the morning, but they're all small. Anyone would know to bring him here. And even if he had been taken somewhere else, they would simply have transferred him to the Pahlavi.'

Grenville nodded in agreement. 'We'll get along fine from here,' Harry told him. 'Would you like us to drop you somewhere?'

'Ah, no, Mr Tower. I wouldn't trouble you. I can take a taxi home.' He looked as if he was hoping they would insist, but Harry had no desire to extend their acquaintance. 'You're staying at the Ritz, I suppose?' Grenville asked.

Harry was, though he didn't want to give Grenville any more information on his whereabouts or movements than he had to. 'I haven't got to that,' he said.

'It's really the only place in town, these days. I'll call you there in the morning,' Grenville said. 'See what other help I can offer.'

'I'd appreciate that.'

After he'd gone to hail a taxi, Harry and Shahnaz stood in silence, listening to the sound of cicadas in the thick night air. It was still too close for comfort. 'Is he really a diplomat?' she asked.

Harry shrugged. 'Possibly.'

'Did you talk to the Foreign Office before you came out here?'

'No.'

She seemed surprised by this. 'Did you call the American Embassy to tell them you had arrived?'

'No.'

'How did Grenville know who you were?'

'An educated guess, perhaps.' Harry didn't believe it. She didn't look like she did either. 'The doctor and Grenville knew each other,' he said.

'He seemed very on edge,' she said. 'Why?'

'I don't know yet.' Harry checked his watch. It was half past eight. 'Would it be possible to speak to your father?' He was puzzled by the army's walk-on appearance in this riddle.

'Why would you want to do that?'

'You said that he is a general and the former security minister, so, if this was the work of the army, then—'

'We can't speak to my father. He wouldn't help us under any circumstances. And I wouldn't ask him.'

'Then perhaps I could request assistance, father to father—'

'Fatherhood isn't his strong suit. He wouldn't help either of us.'

Harry tapped a cigarette slowly against the side of the packet. It seemed she was making a broader statement than just of her own father, but he let it go. He'd have to contact Salemi on his own.

'What do you want to do now?' she asked. 'The address in Doshtan Street is in a pretty dangerous part of town, so I think we'd be better off going in the morning. I can pick you up at dawn. Where are you staying?'

'The Ritz.'

'It's five minutes from here. But it's probably too late to get anything to eat there.'

'I'd like to go to Sean's apartment.'

She hesitated. 'Of course,' she said. 'I suppose that makes sense. It's not far from here.' They loaded back into the Buick. 'Do you know the way?' she asked. He shook his head. 'It's in a street behind the Atlantic Hotel. You turn off Takht Jamshid, just before you get to the American Embassy.'

Harry swung the Buick back onto a more or less deserted Shah Reza Avenue. It didn't take him long to see why so few cars were about. 'Checkpoint,' Shahnaz explained. 'There's supposed to be a nine o'clock curfew.'

A good-looking young officer swaggered out of the shadows and peered into the rear window. 'What's your name, sir?' He spoke English well, with the faintest trace of an American accent.

'Tower.' Harry was aware there would be a discrepancy with his passport, if asked for it. But he didn't want to alert Shahnaz to the fact that he was travelling under a false name.

'You're from London, England?'

'Yes.'

'Where are you going tonight?' Shahnaz answered in Farsi, but he ignored her. 'And what takes you there?' he asked Harry.

'It's my son's apartment. I'm just visiting.'

'Who is this woman?'

'A friend of my son.'

The officer appraised Shahnaz with a lascivious glare.

He demanded her papers and examined them by torch-light. They heard shouts from a neighbouring street, then a rifle shot. The officer handed back Shahnaz's papers. 'There's trouble tonight. All over the city. Communists are in this area. You might want to visit your son tomorrow.'

A group of students burst round the corner, in fast retreat, some defiantly gesticulating and shouting, others running hard from an army jeep loaded with soldiers. They poured down the empty street, like a flash flood in a dry riverbed. The jeep surged on behind them. Soldiers fired into the air. Some of the young men at the front of the crowd turned again and jeered. One stepped forward to hurl a rock. A single shot rang out and the boy crumpled.

The street was eerily quiet as the displaced dust around his body floated on the still night air.

And then the panic-stricken students bolted past the Buick. Harry noticed how young they were, boys and girls, the women unveiled. The officer stepped back. 'Wait here.' He walked to the prostrate figure, nudged him with his boot, then kicked him when that failed to elicit a response. There was no sign of life. He returned to Harry's window. 'Sir, visit your son tomorrow.'

They edged forward. 'Stop,' Shahnaz said. She got out and ran to the body. She checked his pulse and listened for breathing. There was no sign of either. She began to go through his pockets.

The officer shouted a warning and Harry, who had followed her, reached down to take her arm. 'Come on.'

'He's just a child.'

'So are you. Let's go.'

'The bastards . . . I need to tell his family. I must find out who he is and where he lives.' The officer raised his weapon. Harry lifted a hand to him, yanked Shahnaz to her feet and marched her to the car. 'We can't just leave him here!' she cried. 'Mr Tower, please . . .'

He pushed her roughly into the passenger seat, got in beside her and accelerated away. Harry turned and saw the officer give the corpse another hefty kick. Shahnaz slumped back, her face drawn. Harry turned north on Pahlavi to get away from the trouble but they passed a burning jeep and a bus that had been gutted and turned over in front of the Indonesian Embassy. Shahnaz leant close to the window and peered out. 'I've never seen anything like this up here before. They were just kids, you know. Students. Mossadegh supporters. His house is about two blocks back that way.'

'Communists.'

'Probably members of the Tudeh Party, which is supporting the prime minister. The generals, the British and the Americans would have you believe they're all part of the same conspiracy to tip Mossadegh into the arms of the Soviets.'

'Maybe they're right.'

'They're wrong. The Tudeh Party are socialists and nationalists, not Bolsheviks.'

'But easily confused and conflated, especially by the Russians. As you said, the Soviets have tried before, and your father stopped them.'

'The Soviets aren't the problem here.'

'But naivety might be.'

'I doubt it, but perhaps idealism is one of the casualties of age.' She was looking at him intently, as if to reinforce the fact that it had been an accusation.

'Only if you make the wrong choices.'

'And have you?'

He met her gaze squarely for a moment. He hadn't meant to be this open. Or honest. But there was something about her directness he liked. 'Repeatedly.'

'How?'

There were so many answers he could have given to that question, but he doubted she either wanted or needed to hear them.

'It's just here,' she said. Harry let the Buick glide slowly to a halt beneath a line of jacaranda trees. 'We should get something to eat. This is my favourite restaurant in Tehran.'

Before he could answer, Shahnaz had stepped out of the Buick and was walking towards the building she had pointed out a little further down the street. A string of coloured lights hung along a whitewashed wall and around a red-brick archway with a thick oak door. There was a flea market outside, a laid-back affair in contrast with the hustle and bustle of the central bazaar. An Uzbek sold silks, a Mongolian sheepskin coats and bags, and a wizened old man, with the distinct dress and features of a Turkoman, small, patterned carpets. But Harry could pick out those who hailed from Iran's hard-to-govern provincial tribes, too – a Baluchi, a Bakhtiari – many of whom he had once spent time trying to corral into resisting the Soviets in the event of an invasion. He had generally found them tough, welcoming and fiercely independent of spirit.

Beyond the oak door lay a garden of fig and annab trees, jasmine and honeysuckle, with a tinkling fountain at its heart, and a long bed of damask roses in front of a covered terrace of white and black tiles, lit by hanging lights and flares. 'We had a garden like this at our home in Tehran,' Shahnaz said, smiling at him. 'It reminds me of my mother, especially the scent of the roses.'

A host, in black tie with a starched cotton shirt, stood inside glass doors left wide open on account of the heat. He was sweating profusely. 'Miss Salemi! How nice to see you. Are you not with your friend tonight?'

'No, Amir. This is his father, Harry.'

Amir gave a little nod. 'Mr Harry, a pleasure to meet you. A table for two?' He was looking at Shahnaz.

'Yes, please,' she said.

The restaurant, like the garden, was dimly lit, this time by hundreds of candles, their flickering flames reflected off the floor-to-ceiling mirrors at the back of the room and the tall arched windows at the front. The tables were covered with starched white linen and polished silver, the floor tiles black and white in there, too, scrubbed so clean they might have been installed that morning. 'It's not as expensive as it looks,' Shahnaz said, misreading his thoughts. It was not the Tehran he recalled from the war, that was for sure. No wonder Sean hadn't found time to respond to his letters. One way or another, he could see the place was intoxicating.

There was a group of what looked like intellectuals at the table next to them. One wore a white double-breasted suit with wide lapels, and sported an immaculate Douglasie moustache that the film star himself would have been proud of. His companions, who were engaged in a vigorous debate about a poet Harry had never heard of, were in collarless white shirts and cardigans, with greying beards and hair that tumbled over their shoulders.

On the other side of them a young army officer in a pristine khaki uniform sat with his wife. She wore a dark dress with boldly printed white birds, or possibly butterflies – Harry's eyesight had been deteriorating of late – and a triple row of pearls at her neck. 'This place is popular with some of the ministers from Mr Mossadegh's government, army officers and—'

'I can see.'

'You didn't come when you were here before?'

'I ate in my hotel, which was clearly a mistake.' He didn't think it was a good idea to tell her that he had spent most of the time in the tribal heartlands, far from the sophistication of a place such as this.

The waiter arrived. Harry told Shahnaz to order for both of them, and it took a severe exercise of will to turn down the offer of wine. She ordered them both *dough* instead, a mint-flavoured yoghurt drink. He told himself it would do him good.

'You said the garden reminded you of your mother,' Harry said, when the waiter had gone.

'She died when I was quite young.'

'I'm sorry. Of tuberculosis or . . .? '

'No.' Shahnaz was silent for a length of time that might have felt awkward to another man, but Harry had always been comfortable in silence. 'I overheard my father telling her he would take another wife if she couldn't, or wouldn't, satisfy him. She'd had a very tough time after my brother's death, so . . .' Shahnaz shook her head. 'Perhaps you can see why I don't have any contact with my father and certainly would never ask him for help.'

Harry assumed Shahnaz was telling him her mother

had committed suicide, with all the obvious resonances, but he didn't want to trespass on her sorrow by asking for clarification. He'd learnt that much from Sean, at least. He glanced at the army officer beside them and half turned his back. 'Could the army have been involved in trafficking narcotics?' he whispered.

'Not with the police. The two hate each other. And Sean's source for that story was pretty clear that the police were behind it.'

'Who was his source?'

'He wouldn't say, but I think you can guess. Wasn't it you who gave him the introduction to the French couple?'

The oak door to the garden banged open and three young men in dark trousers and white shirts burst into the restaurant. They were armed with leaflets, and before the waiters could stop them, they were slapping one down on each table. 'Beware, the imperialists are planning a coup!' they shouted in English, repeating it in Farsi.

But the army officer next to them had only glanced at his sheet before he exploded. 'Communists!' he yelled at them. He shoved the young man who had handed him the leaflet into the mirrored wall. It didn't crack, but the lad tumbled to the ground, knocking over an empty table in the corner. 'How dare you?' the officer shrieked in English. 'Get the hell out of here!'

The young men scuttled out, throwing leaflets onto the remaining tables as they went.

Once they had gone, an uneasy silence descended. The young woman who had been dining with the officer looked shell-shocked, as did the group of intellectuals at the next-door table. 'Just kids from the Tudeh Party,'

Shahnaz explained. 'Idealists, like those we saw in the street. You can't blame them for—'

'They're going to get themselves killed.'

'I don't think it's a crime to try to help your country.'

'They'd be better off trying to save it from the Communists.'

Shahnaz gave him a thin smile. 'I sense you're trying to goad me and I can't say I didn't expect it.'

'I wouldn't believe everything Sean says about me.'

'Maybe this is also what you expect, but I feel I should make my case. When the Tudeh first got members elected to Parliament here in 'forty-six, you know what measures they managed to get voted through?'

Harry smiled back at her. He had to concede this precise detail had eluded him.

'Laws to establish a forty-eight-hour week, limit child labour, set a minimum wage and guarantee maternity leave. Revolutionary, right?'

'In Iran, perhaps.'

She gave him a triumphant grin. 'Well, doesn't that tell you everything you need to know?'

Gradually, conversations picked up around them again and the hubbub rose. Their food arrived: baked aubergines in tomato-and-egg sauce laden with garlic, long lamb kebabs and platefuls of highly buttered rice mixed with egg yolk. Only when he started eating did Harry realize how ravenous he was. Nothing had passed his lips since the plane had left Rome very early that morning. 'You look hungry,' she said. She'd barely touched her food. 'I haven't had much of an appetite since Sean disappeared.'

'We'll find him.' But even as he said it, Harry was

gripped by the discomforting sense that he did not entirely believe this bland reassurance.

Shahnaz stared at the table and pushed away her plate. 'I can't think of much else. I just don't know who would have taken him. If the woman in that village was right and it was soldiers, then why?'

'Maybe he was working on something else, as you said earlier.'

'But what?'

As he ploughed his way through a mountain of food, Harry could not help reflecting on the ironic possibility that Sean had been taken for uncovering details of a coup his father's office had helped set in motion. But if so, who would have taken the decision? The trouble was, it didn't explain his tail in London. Not by a long shot.

'What is it?' Shahnaz asked.

'Nothing.'

'You were shaking your head?'

Harry pushed away his plate. 'Come on, let's get over to his apartment.'

He paid and they crossed the street to a lush garden and a set of rickety stairs beneath the extravagant leaves of an enormous palm.

Inside, Harry walked into a room decorated like Aladdin's cave. Rich, dark rugs and cushions covered the floor and a *ghalyan* water pipe hung from a wall alongside Sean's charcoal sketches of mosques and bazaars. Bottles were stacked in a line on one shelf and books on another. There was a photograph album and a picture of Amanda and Sean in a walnut frame. Like the one in the office, it had been taken in Norfolk, at the end of the summer Sean left school. They had spent the afternoon sunbathing and swimming, and the evening eating seafood in a pub overlooking a flat-calm sea.

Harry walked through to the bedroom, which was considerably more spartan but for an embroidered bedspread. He turned to see her standing in the doorway. 'Did they search in here, too?'

'Yes, I think so.'

'Did Sean ever complain he was being followed?'

'No. At least, not to me.'

Harry walked back to the main room and picked up a thin leather book from the coffee-table. A pile of loose photographs spilt onto the floor. One was of Sean with his arm around a young Iranian, leaning against the battered Dodge. 'Ali,' Shahnaz said. 'Sean's translator.'

'What do you know about him?'

'He is my cousin. His father used to be our ambassador to Rome. Sean had been trying to get by on his own Farsi, which was hopeless.'

'Does Ali work for the paper full-time?'

'Not officially. He's still a student. But he's taken to spending most of his time in the office.'

'Why?'

'He loves it. He cares about his country. This is his chance to make a difference.'

Harry took the pile from her and flicked through the photos until he found one of an attractive woman with long dark hair smiling at the camera, in the way only lovers do. 'Her name is Christine,' Shahnaz said, without enthusiasm, while he was trying to hide his own reaction. 'But you know that. I believe you introduced them. She's married to

a French oil executive. They both play in Sean's tennis four.'
She took the photographs back, sifting through them until
she found a picture of the group in front of a court. It
included Christine's husband, Pierre, whom Harry already
knew, and a squat, bald man whom he didn't. 'Who is that?'
he asked, pointing to him.

'Some American, I think. I don't know his name. I've
never met him. He arrived in town three or maybe four
months ago.' She was watching him intently. 'Sean said
you introduced him to the French couple by letter. So how
do you know them?'

'I met them on one of my visits here. I thought it would
help for Sean to have at least one contact when he arrived.'

'How did you come across them?'

'At some embassy function. I played tennis with them a
couple of times.' Harry did not want to get drawn on how
and why he knew the Audinettes.

'They say he is an officer for the French Secret Intelligence Service and that she may be one, too. That his job as
an oil executive is a cover. And so is hers as a photographer
for Agence France Presse.'

'They're pretty convincing in their roles, if that's true. At
least, that was my impression.'

'Sean said he'd heard she'd helped arm and train some
of the tribes to resist a Soviet invasion. He asked her about
it, but she denied it.'

In which case, Sean was dangerously well informed,
Harry thought. No wonder he was in trouble. 'Who told
him that?'

'Ali, I think. His father was in the foreign ministry here
in the final months of the war.'

'Does Sean see a lot of the Audinettes?'

'Too much. I don't like or trust either of them. It's the only subject we don't agree on.'

Harry slipped the picture of the tennis four into his pocket. He didn't need to ask the source of Shahnaz's animosity.

He leafed through the rest of the photographs: unremarkable scenes of Tehran and the surrounding landscape. He opened a nearby cupboard, stared at its contents for a moment, then took out a stack of envelopes and parcels and put them on the table: every single letter he had written since Sean had left London, as far as he could tell, though only a few had been opened. He sifted through them, aware of Shahnaz's fixed gaze. When he glanced up at her, she did not turn away. 'Why didn't he open them?' he asked.

'He wouldn't talk about it. I told him he should at least do you the courtesy of acknowledging he had received them,' she said.

Harry picked up one of the heavier packages and tore it open. He fished out a tape reel and turned it over in his hand. 'What happened to the recorder machine I bought him?'

'It broke.'

'I thought it would make a change from deciphering my handwriting. Perhaps I even hoped he would send some back, so that I could hear his voice again.' Harry crouched by the cupboard, looking for the broken machine. He found only a bottle of whisky. 'Help yourself,' she said.

Harry resisted the temptation. Along with cricket, it was one of the few passions he shared with his son. He moved on to the next cupboard, aware that her eyes were upon him. 'Did you and your wife want more children?' she asked.

'Amanda did. Desperately. But she poured all her love into him.'

'Did you not want siblings for him?'

'I didn't think about it much.'

'He talks about his mother often. And always in the present tense.'

'He's probably not alone in that. Have you any brothers and sisters?' he asked her, keen to change the subject.

'I had only one brother, Cyrus. He died in a riding accident when I was nine, three months before my mother committed suicide.'

'I'm sorry.'

The resonance silenced them once again. 'Everyone is,' Shahnaz said. 'My father won't admit that is what happened, even though he found her. He claimed – and still does – she had malaria.'

Harry wondered how often she and Sean had discussed the shared tragedy of their mothers' deaths. And how they had apportioned the blame. 'Perhaps it helped bind you together,' he said.

'Perhaps.' She didn't need to be told what he was referring to. 'Although I think pain generally makes you an island. But I don't have to tell you that. Would you like coffee?' she asked.

'Please.'

'Turkish?'

'Why not?'

While she was gone, Harry resumed his search of the

cupboards beneath the bookshelf. He found the recorder machine he had bought for his son before he left England, and reels of tape, which looked as if they had been used to record something. Harry took out the machine, placed it on the floor and plugged it in. It gave a low hum but the spindles did not turn.

'It gave up the ghost about a month ago,' Shahnaz said. 'Sean didn't know how to fix it.'

'Sean never knows how to fix anything. He is the most impractical boy I've ever met. Does he own a screwdriver?'

She found one, but it was the wrong size. Harry took the penknife from his briefcase and used the tip of it to unscrew the rear panel. He identified a loose cog and fixed it back into place. Once the panel was on, the motor purred.

The tapes inside each box had been carefully labelled with *Dad* and the date upon which they had been recorded. He rewound the one already loaded on the machine and began to play it.

'Hello, Dad.' Sean cleared his throat, took a sip of something. 'First things first. I'm guessing you're still religiously putting flowers on Mum's grave every weekend. If that's the case, and it's the least you owe her, then would you mind putting some on for me? I'll settle up with you when I get back. And make sure you keep the moss off that headstone – you know how she hated anything to be untidy.'

Shahnaz was staring at him intently. Harry stopped the machine. 'When did he record this?'

'I don't know. He taped a lot of messages for you.'

'Why didn't he send them?'

'He said it was complicated.'

When it was clear she had no explanation beyond that that she could – or would – give, Harry switched it to play again.

'I'm conscious that I usually talk a lot about politics on these tapes, but since it's a subject on which we're unlikely ever to agree, I'll make an effort today to tell you more about my life here in Tehran. You won't be surprised to hear that it's blindingly hot at the moment. There is just no escape from it. It saps your strength and makes it hard to think straight. I'm getting on fine with the paper. Well, as far as I can tell. Every time I file anything, I get a supportive telex by return, but maybe they do that for everyone. I'm sure the cynic in you – or, as you would say, the realist – would agree. The foreign editor seems a decent enough guy. I managed to get a call through to him last week, during which he promised to consider my request for a staff job. He said they'd bring me back to London to talk about it and . . . it will be good to see you if that happens.'

There was a long silence.

'Or perhaps you might come out here to see me. In the meantime, most of the improvement in my output has been down to the new translator I've hired. He's called Ali. He's studying English at Tehran University, but he spends most of his time in the office helping me, for which I pay him bugger-all. He's a great supporter of Mossadegh, who he says is the only Iranian politician genuinely free of the stain of corruption in the last fifty years. He says we should accept that Iran's oil belongs to Iran and stop squabbling over what's already done. He thinks that if Churchill changed his tune, he'd be pleasantly surprised

101

by Mossadegh's response. I don't suppose you'd agree. In fact, I'm sure you wouldn't. But that's how it looks from here.

'I should also tell you about a girl I've met. Her name is Shahnaz. Her father is a general and a politician, close to the Shah. He once saved Iran from the Soviets, or so he likes to claim, so I'm sure you'd find much to admire in him. She is effectively an only child, like me. I haven't mentioned her before, because I wanted to see how things worked out. I think Mum would have approved. She's strong, determined and a hell of a lot of fun.'

Harry stopped the tape again. Shahnaz was staring at the wall, her eyes glistening with tears in the darkness. 'I think it's going to help if we're honest with each other,' he said. Though he naturally intended this to be a one-way street.

'Perhaps.'

'So, let's start with what he told you about me.'

'How will that help?'

'I'd like to know. Did he talk to you about my work?'

'He said you used to work for the Board of Trade but were now the general manager of a sugar company. He said you travelled a lot, that you always had, and weren't around very much when he was growing up.'

Harry had never told his wife or son the true nature of his profession. Before and during the war, it had been forbidden. Afterwards, the office had moved to a new policy of actively encouraging executive officers to tell their immediate family, but Harry had found it somehow easier to continue to live in the shadows, even at home. 'What else?'

'He said he heard his mother accuse you of living a lie.' She turned to face him. 'He thought maybe you had another wife or family.'

'Did he believe that was possible?'

'I don't think so. He talked about you a lot, and I don't think that was his concern.'

'What was?'

'I'll let him tell you.'

'But he isn't here. And it would help to know.'

'He said things that are perhaps easier to talk about with a lover than a father.'

'Such as?'

'He talked about the day your wife died. He blamed you for her death.'

Even though Harry knew this perfectly well – it had been there in Sean's eyes as he'd cradled his dead mother that evening – it was still a punch to the gut. 'Not half as much as I blamed myself,' he said, with more honesty than he'd intended.

'He said your wife told him your own father had beaten you senseless all the way through your early childhood and you consequently refused ever to lay a finger on Sean, either in punishment or affection. It was almost, he said, as if you were scared to show any emotion at all.'

'It's not true to say I never showed him affection. He's rewriting history there.'

'He said he admired you, that you worked hard to rise above your humble origins and won a scholarship to Cambridge. He said you were *very* right-wing – king, queen, country, empire – and there was not a single subject on this planet that he thought you would ever share a view on. He said it broke his mother's heart that you never told her you loved her, and that fact . . . tortured him. What was it that prevented you? It was all, he said, she ever wanted to hear.' They listened to the sound of the cicadas. Harry wiped the sweat from his brow. It was still too warm for comfort. Amanda had known he loved her. He was certain of it. 'Too much honesty too soon?' she asked. 'You said you wanted to know.'

'Perhaps.'

'I'm sorry. My father always says I'm too like my mother – too blunt, too direct.'

Harry picked up the letters and tapes and put them into the box. 'Sometimes,' he said, 'between a father and a son, it is not what you say but what you can't. Or won't. Or don't.'

'Not just between a father and a son.'

Harry thought of his silent trip to the airport to drop off Sean for his flight to Tehran the previous year. It pained him that he still had no idea how to bridge the chasm between them.

The sound of cheering filled the street. Harry moved to the window and looked out. He saw half a dozen army officers and a group of girls in sophisticated Western dress laughing and dancing. 'What's going on?'

Shahnaz joined him by the window. She shook her head. 'I don't know.'

Harry opened the front door and led the way down the steps to the street outside. Two tanks rounded the corner, tracks grinding against the asphalt. They were travelling fast, overloaded with soldiers waving a giant Iranian flag and clutching pictures of the Shah. The officers cheered them on and, for a moment, the vehicles slowed. Palms were slapped, the officers handing bottles of liquor to the soldiers. The tanks stopped. The crowd swelled as residents emerged from their homes and revellers from bars further down the strip. A band from one of the restaurants or clubs began to play an Iranian folk ballad and the men and women danced, stamped and clapped in time to the music. 'What's happening?' Harry asked one of the revellers.

'The Shah!'

'A coup,' yelled another. 'The Shah has taken command. Mossadegh is under arrest!'

More customers spilt onto the street, waving, dancing and cheering. A waiter weaved among them, dispensing the remnants of a bottle of whisky. The soldiers on top of the tank stood and started firing their rifles into the clear night sky. The cheers became a continuous roar. Harry leant closer to Shahnaz. 'Let's get back inside,' he said.

'I need to find out what's going on.'

He took her arm. 'There will be violence, unpredictable, sudden . . .' The tanks started up again and moved off, the soldiers firing once more into the night. Shahnaz shook free of his grip. 'They must be heading for Mossadegh's house,' she said.

She turned away from the throng, towards the distant peaks of the Alborz Mountains, now washed by a crescent moon. She started to run. 'The bastards, they can't get away with it.'

'Shahnaz!'

He had no choice but to chase her. She rounded the corner and ran headlong down the main road until she reached another checkpoint. The traffic was beginning to back up. Some cars honked their horns in celebration and support, but Harry saw plenty of sullen faces as he chased after Shahnaz. She was at the back of a small crowd by the checkpoint when he reached her. 'I think the army has staged a coup in the Shah's name,' she said, breathless. 'They're saying Mossadegh has already been killed.'

The crowd was chanting now. Shahnaz leant closer. 'They are trying to get to his house in a street up to the right here, to see if he is still alive. The students and the Tudeh Party won't take this lying down. It's a constitutional outrage.'

The men and women around Harry certainly looked like students, he thought: young, earnest, angry. None of the women wore headscarves and, on a night when the conservative right was trying to take charge in the country, it was quite the wrong crowd to be a part of. 'We need to get away from here,' he said.

'I told you, I have to find out what has happened. The army has no support for this – just look around you.'

An argument had broken out at the front of the crowd and one of the soldiers fired a volley of rounds over their heads. There were screams as the students dropped to the ground. Harry remained standing – since he could see the volley was fired high into the night sky – but took his chance. He gripped Shahnaz tightly and began to run back the way they had come. She was just starting to resist him when there was another volley of shots. 'Bastards,' she hissed again. But she kept running until they had turned off the main thoroughfare and into the street in which Sean had his apartment. It was now the scene of an impromptu celebration. The crowd was older, wealthier. Officers in uniform mingled with men in dinner jackets and women in long dresses. They were dancing. And many were drunk already. 'I thought you said Mossadegh was popular,' Harry said.

'He is. Even here. I bet half of these people would say they supported him, if you bothered to ask. But the British blockade has made people tense. Something had to happen. They're relieved that it has.'

Once they were back in the Buick, it took them ten minutes just to wind their way through the throng of revellers in Sean's street and a further twenty to navigate through the various checkpoints on the way back to the hotel. They'd seen only small groups of students out on the streets, roaming the city aimlessly.

But the mood changed suddenly as they approached the Ritz on Ferdowsi Avenue. A convoy of army jeeps roared out of a side-street by the Czech Embassy, two abreast, forcing them to pull over. Just behind them, another tank, loaded with soldiers, was surrounded by young men in civilian clothes, carrying banners denouncing Mossadegh and photographs of the Shah. With their thick beards and tattered shirts, they were a far cry from the student protesters by the prime minister's house and they enveloped the Buick in seconds. The men peered in, unsure of what to make of the couple inside. One man banged on the window. 'American? American?'

Harry gave them a thumbs-up. He cranked the window a fraction. '*ShahanShah,*' he shouted.

'*ShahanShah!*' they yelled back, but no one was smiling and, on the other side of the Buick, Shahnaz drew only hostile looks. She had covered her head quickly with a scarf, but it did not appear to mollify them. One man spat on the windscreen, another on the side window.

Others banged the bonnet. They began to rock the car. Harry cranked down the window a fraction more. 'American!' he shouted. 'American!'

The men appeared to hesitate. The tank was pulling away from them. '*ShahanShah*,' Harry said again, offering another thumbs-up. The man closest to him looked older than the rest. He wore a woollen waistcoat over a white collarless shirt. His beard was neatly trimmed. He leant in and spat into Harry's face.

And then he moved off, the crowd with him. Within a few seconds, the sound of the tank tracks and the chanting receded. An eerie silence enveloped them. 'I'm sorry,' Shahnaz said.

Harry took a handkerchief from his pocket and carefully wiped his cheek. 'We got off lightly.'

'It was me they were angry with. They hate women, if truth be told.'

Harry didn't argue with that. He'd seen enough of Iran on previous visits to know that it was many contrasting countries that struggled to co-exist happily. He doubted a coup was likely to improve matters.

When they reached the hotel, they found the lobby heaving with people, most well dressed. It looked to Harry as if some might be trying to take refuge from the chaos and violence outside, and it was several minutes before he could fight his way to the reception desk. He was fortunate: they had only one single room left.

He came back to find Shahnaz by the door. 'Would you like a drink?'

'Yes. Perhaps we can talk about where you want to start in the morning.'

Harry gestured towards the bar. They made their way through the throng, sat at a table beneath a palm tree on the terrace and waited for one of the men dressed in crisp linen to take their order. It was as if the conflict playing out on the streets was happening on a different planet. 'How will everyone react?' he asked her. There was a burst of distant gunfire. The hubbub of conversation on the terrace died down for only a moment before resuming unabated.

'It is hard to say. People are exhausted, so it is possible many may feel relieved for a day or two, but it won't last. Mossadegh is the leader they chose. He is a national hero, just as Gandhi is in India.'

'Power didn't sully Gandhi.'

'True, but even so . . .'

A waiter arrived. Harry ordered orange juice and Shahnaz nodded to indicate she'd have the same. The moon was high above the palm trees, but the air was still warm. The bar was filling with guests. There was only one topic of conversation.

The waiter returned with their drinks. Harry took out a fistful of *rials* and palmed some notes onto the table. They sipped their drinks and listened to the cicadas. 'You should stay here tonight,' he said. 'You can take the bed, and I'll sleep on the floor.'

'I need to get home.'

'But you've seen the men who are out—'

'I'll take a cab from the front of the hotel. I live not far from here and I know how to avoid trouble. I need to find out what's happening and check my flatmate is all right.'

Harry recognized the tone from his attempts to dissuade Sean from various courses of action he considered injurious to his best interests, including abandoning his studies at Cambridge for the precarious existence of a freelance 'stringer' journalist in Tehran. 'Do you want to tell me what you think has really happened to Sean?' he asked.

'I don't know.'

'I thought you agreed that we should be honest with each other.'

'Sean said he thought you were a man with many secrets. So I don't think it's me who is failing to be honest.'

Harry thought about this. The true explanation for his son's disappearance was likely to lie either in Sean's present or his own past. If it was the former, he could spin himself into a role as some kind of saviour, which was a lot more palatable than the alternative.

Shahnaz had been looking uncomfortable ever since she'd walked into the hotel, glancing around nervously. She stood abruptly. 'Let's begin again in the morning.' And before he could stop her, she was heading for the door. Harry watched a couple of male heads swivel sharply as she departed.

It occurred to him she had seemed as nervous as he was.

Someone started to play the piano and quickly the rest of the guests had gathered around and begun a discordant rendition of 'It's A Wonderful World'.

Harry went up to his room. He lit a cigarette, slipped out to the balcony and stared down at the palms that lined the gravel path to the car park. Beneath them, he saw the amber glow of two cigarettes. Perhaps it was his imagination, but he had the sense that the men were watching him.

After a few moments, they stubbed out their cigarettes and retreated into the darkness.

9

London, New Year's Eve, 1938

HARRY FOUND IT hard to believe this was an organization on the brink of the greatest test in its history. Or, if it was, that they had any chance of winning it.

Ed Haddon wore a party hat over thick curls damp with sweat as he danced the conga around Harry's garden between his wife, Lucy, who wore a tight-fitting floral skirt, and William Oswald, who had not wiped an insincere grin from his face all evening. He was drunker than Harry had ever seen him, but still didn't manage a convincing impression of a normal human being.

Harry watched from the bottom of the stairs. He wondered if his reticence would underline an already established reputation for being 'aloof'.

Inviting 'the office' to dinner was his idea of hell. He continued to maintain the fiction with Amanda that he worked for the Board of Trade, but his secrecy about his work was a source of tension, which was why she had pleaded and, in the end, begged to meet his colleagues. He thought she really believed him to be having an affair with someone in the office and he had imagined having them all here would put paid to that notion once and for all. And perhaps it had: she had disappeared to bed long ago with a migraine.

He noticed Sean behind him on the stairs. 'What are they doing?' Sean asked.

'That's a very good question.'

'Why are they dancing like that?'

Harry smiled at his son. 'An even better one.'

They watched for a moment more – perhaps as confused as each other – before Harry hitched his young son to his hip and carried him back upstairs. He laid Sean down, picked up the bear to which he was devoted from the floor, snuggled it under his arm and tugged the curtains tight shut. He sat on the bed and smoothed his son's hair tenderly. Those big eyes gazed at him in the darkness. 'Why do people celebrate New Year?' Sean asked.

'That's another good question.' Harry thought about it for a while. He was in no hurry to return to the party. 'I suppose it's about travelling into the future in hope, not fear.' He shrugged. 'Something like that, anyway.'

'Where's Mummy?'

'She's asleep already.'

'I saw her crying.'

Harry tried to hide his disquiet at this news. 'Perhaps she saw them dancing,' he said, but regretted it. Sean was still much too young for his particular brand of black humour. Harry kissed his boy once more and tucked his bear closer. He walked across the landing and sought Amanda in the darkness of their bedroom. He found her curled up in a ball on the bathroom floor. 'Christ,' he said. 'Are you all right?'

She did not answer. Harry went to the bed, ripped off a blanket and wrapped it around his prostrate wife. He knew better than to move her too precipitously. 'It's okay,' he said quietly.

'Who are they?' she asked.

He knew perfectly well what she meant. 'They're more effective than they look tonight.'

'They're not your people, Harry. They'll never care for you.'

That was not what he expected, or even wanted. The last thing he would ever have wished for was to have them here for an evening in the first place. But he knew better than to explain as much when she was like this. 'Come to bed,' he whispered.

'I feel so alone.'

'I'm here.'

'The fear, the anxiety, the shame . . . it's like a hissing snake in my heart.'

'I'm always here for you.'

'I can't think straight. I try to talk to people, but my mind wanders, my heart goes like a pneumatic drill and my stomach feels like it's falling through my body.'

'Let me get you to bed. We can see a doctor in the morning.'

'No,' she said. 'Please, no more doctors.' Harry gently

scooped her up and carried her to bed. She was as light as a feather.

She did not resist him. They had been dealing with episodes of rampant anxiety and severe – sometimes prolonged – depression since Sean was born, indeed since they had first met. Amanda said she had been wrestling with fear all her life, but that it had increased drastically since Sean's birth. She had been losing weight steadily. He shared her jaundiced view of doctors: so far, they had been of no help whatsoever. 'Is Sean all right?' she asked.

'He's fine – sleeping,' Harry lied. Her fears for her son were alarming enough and he tried to do as little as possible to encourage them. He kissed her tenderly. He hoped the one thing she never doubted was his love for her.

'Do you remember Göttingen, Harry, the night we met?'

'Of course.'

'You were different then.'

'The world was different.'

'I lost you along the way somewhere.'

Harry gripped her hand. 'I'm still here,' he said quietly. 'Always here.'

They both knew it was not true, physically at least. In the last year, he had been anywhere but home. He, Haddon and Oswald had been given responsibility for trying to create 'stay behind' networks in the Balkans and the Middle East in the event that Nazi aggression ever stretched that far. Trying to find suitable people, particularly when time was against them, was not easy and the task had taken him far from home much more often than he would have liked. It hadn't helped that the department

115

had had a very dim view of his conviction that the easiest source of resistance, particularly in the Balkans, was likely to be Communist partisans. 'I'd better go,' he whispered to her. 'But I'll try to throw them out after midnight.'

'I miss you, Harry.'

'I'm here,' he said again. He tried to keep the frustration from his voice. What else could he say?

Harry kissed Amanda, cradled her head. As he closed the door, he told himself again that his wife's illness was a tide that was destined to ebb and flow regardless of the life he had chosen. It was not his fault. Wasn't that what the doctors had told him?

10

Tehran, August 1953

HARRY STOOD IN the darkness just inside his window, the curtains cracked a fraction so that he could see into the car park below. Roughly every half-hour, he had seen the flash of a match and the red glow of two cigarettes being lit in the darkness. Sometimes the two men would emerge from beneath the palm trees to glance up in his direction. Twice already, they had wandered over to check on his Buick, parked the other side of Reception.

They were watching him. He was certain of that now. He just couldn't work out why, or indeed who. A tail in London, now another here. Were those two facts connected? If so, did that mean that colleagues from SIS had followed him out to Tehran?

He thought of his conversation with Warren Sykes in the SIS records section in London. If it was true that his superiors were looking for a KGB spy at the heart of their organization, how much easier it would be to blame the man who had never really fitted in the first place.

Harry doubted they would have anyone in the lobby, but he took the precaution of leaving by the back stairs. Outside, he waited by the pool equipment room, like a hunted animal scenting the wind. It had been an hour or more since he'd heard gunfire in the distance. An uneasy calm seemed to have settled on the city.

He walked around the side of the hotel and out to the road in front, then along the line of vehicles beneath the palms until he found a Packard whose owner had not gone to the trouble of locking it. He hot-wired it swiftly and accelerated gently into the stifling night.

He headed south on Ferdowsi Avenue to avoid the checkpoints. He turned onto Churchill Street and, just past the Soviet Embassy, he drove north again on Hafez. It was the early hours of the morning and central Tehran was a ghost town.

Ten minutes later, he was seated in a wicker chair on the bougainvillaea-clad balcony of a colonial-style white-washed house. Christine Audinette did not spot him until she had the key in her front door. 'I knew you'd come,' she said.

'Then I'm glad I haven't disappointed you.'

'It's been a long time.'

'Don't say you missed me?'

She didn't smile back at him. 'The Americans have been telling anyone who would listen that they're running this coup and there isn't a single SIS officer in all of Iran.'

'I'm here unofficially.'

'Of course you are. That's probably for the best. It looks like the CIA didn't bother to establish tonight if General Riahi or the prime minister would actually be at home when they went to arrest them. So, the coup may be falling apart.'

Harry shrugged. It hadn't been his idea and he didn't care who knew it. 'The Americans are new to the business of meddling in the fate of nations. But they'll learn.'

'I can't wait. Would you like to come in?'

'I thought you'd never ask.'

Harry followed her into the house. The living room was just as he remembered it, cream walls crammed with prints and paintings from Biarritz, Cannes and other seaside towns of her native country. They walked through her study, its shelves still groaning with photographic equipment, and out to the terrace at the rear. Christine fetched a bottle of whisky and two glasses, then came to sit beside him. She had the kind of facial bone structure and slender figure some men lose their minds over and she knew it. God knew he'd come close enough to losing his own. 'You're here to look for your son?'

'Do you know where he is?'

'Honestly, no. But you're not the only SIS officer who is here "unofficially". Some men from London have been asking a lot of questions. About you.'

'Who?'

'British public-school boys.' She shrugged. 'They all look and sound the same.'

'Did they give their names?'

'Not the real ones, I'm sure.'

'How long have they been here?'

'A couple of weeks.'

This was definitely not the news Harry wanted to hear. 'What did you tell them?' he asked.

'That I was just a photographer. When they wouldn't accept that, I said I thought a man who wouldn't even cheat on his wife seemed unlikely to have betrayed his country.' She poured him a glass of whisky and pushed it across the table. 'I told them that, as far as I knew, you spent the months you were in Iran trying to organize the tribes to resist a Soviet invasion, so you didn't seem a likely Russian spy to me.' She shook her head. 'They said your real purpose here was to meet a KGB agent called Oleg Vasilyev in Tabriz. They talked a lot about a place called Mount Avala in Yugoslavia, claimed you sent dozens of royalist soldiers, parachuted in to resist the Communists, to certain death.' She tilted her face to one side, surveying him. 'I told them that if they were hunting a Moscow mole, the working-class scholarship boy from Cambridge must make a tempting target. Scapegoat of the Empire – isn't that the role you were born for, Harry?'

'Whose side are you on?'

She smiled at him. 'Do you have to ask? Besides, no one trusts the French. You know that.' She lit a cigarette and lobbed the packet to him. He followed suit. 'I assume they took Sean to force you out here,' she said. 'Why walk into their trap?'

'Even if that's true, you think I had a choice?'

'As I said, our understanding is that the coup has failed tonight. Once he learnt they were trying to arrest him, General Riahi called out the part of the army still loyal to the constitution to defend the prime minister and tell the

Shah to go to hell. But you know as well as I do that the Americans are bound to try again. Hell, you probably helped them plan it.' He didn't deny it, though the fact he'd been excluded from the actual planning was troubling him more as time went on. 'And if you ask me, the chaos of a city in ferment is the perfect time and place to dispose of a scapegoat. And perhaps his left-wing journalist son, too. So, yes, I think you had a choice.'

She was gazing at him intently. She inhaled deeply and blew the smoke up into the night air. The noise of the cicadas was deafening, the city beyond them now still. 'You think you're going to outwit them, Harry, is that it?'

Perhaps he did, but he wasn't going to admit to that either.

'You always were an arrogant bastard.' She shook her head again. 'Or is it redemption you seek?'

'It might be too late for that.'

'I was sorry to hear about your wife.'

Of all the subjects he didn't want to discuss with Christine, this topped the list.

'Why did you suggest your son got in contact with me when he arrived in Tehran?'

'I was hoping you and Pierre would ensure he didn't get into too much trouble.'

'I was his friend in the first few months of his time here,' she said. 'Did you know that?'

'That's none of my business,' he said, though he was aware he didn't sound entirely convincing.

'He tortured himself that he hadn't been able to do more to help your wife.'

'He's not alone in that.'

'Perhaps it wasn't your fault.'

He rewarded her with a bleak smile. On that, he was inclined to disagree. He feared it was. He was just struggling to admit it. 'How is Pierre?' Christine's marriage was part of the cover she and Pierre shared as long-term agents in the French Foreign Intelligence Service, the DGSE. But if the marriage had ever been real, they had long since agreed to pursue separate emotional interests and attachments.

'What kind of question is that?'

'You formed a tennis four together. You, Pierre, Sean and one other?' Harry had played tennis often with Pierre and Christine in his brief time here. They were accomplished and competitive.

'Sean hits the ball almost as hard as his father,' she said.

Harry found all sports easy, but he didn't return her smile. 'Who was the fourth, the bald guy?' he asked, passing her the picture he had taken from Sean's apartment.

'You mean, you don't know? He's an American, arrived in Tehran a few months ago. He says his name is Brad. He's even more reserved than you.'

Harry had expected this answer, but it still somehow unsettled him. Was it just chance that Sean had found himself playing tennis with a man embedded in Tehran to overthrow the government? 'Did you give Sean the story about the trade in drugs linked to your embassy?'

'No.'

'How about Pierre?'

'Why don't you ask him? We'll both be at a reception at the French Club tomorrow night.'

'Is it possible that's why Sean was taken?'

'This is Tehran. Anything is possible. It was not a very

judicious or sensible piece, which I did try to tell him at the time.'

'Who is the French official behind the trade?'

'The stories that have followed our new ambassador, Monsieur Chevalier, out of Saigon, do not make for pleasant cocktail-party conversation.' She stood. 'It's very late. I have to be up early. Why don't you come to bed?'

'No, thanks.' He didn't move. 'I'll need to borrow your car for a few days, though. I've already acquired a tail.'

'You haven't lost your irresistible Anglo-Saxon charm, you know that?' She went back inside and returned a few moments later with her keys. 'It's good to see you, Harry.'

'And you, too.'

He left without kissing her, found her car and drove back through the city's quiet streets. He parked outside the front of the hotel, away from the watchers beneath the palm trees, extricated a bottle of whisky from the bar and drank himself into sleep upstairs in his room.

Harry sweated through a night of fitful memories and broken dreams. For a time, he was back with his mother on a pebble beach at Hastings on one of the desolate days after his father had returned briefly to promise another new beginning. He could still feel her tears on his cheek. Sean drifted in and out of his dreams, too, not the exuberant and gentle boy of much of his childhood but the quiet, reserved creature who had emerged into manhood and shaken his hand stiffly at the Heathrow departure gate.

But in the minutes or hours before waking, Harry found himself trapped, as he so often did now, in – or by – the memories of his wife. This time, he was back in the evening he'd had to leave for Tehran in 'forty-six. The argument that had ensued had been one of their most bitter, the first time she had explicitly linked her misery with his work. Too late, Harry had realized that Sean was on the landing above them and had overheard it all.

Was Amanda's mental decline, her torment, his fault? He had turned it over and over in his mind and could still find no reassurance, relief or solace. How could he possibly have understood that one life choice would make such heavy work of another?

Harry awoke finally to the muezzin's call to prayer and a strip of morning light beneath the heavy linen curtains. The fan was still attempting to beat the already rising heat into submission. He sat up and tried to dispel the disturbed aftermath of his dreams. Perhaps Shahnaz was right: too many secrets – the worst of which were those he had hidden from himself.

He went to the balcony and looked down into the garden of a neighbouring house where three men lay prostrate in prayer. He tried to assemble his thoughts into some kind of logical order. It was hard in this heat. And the whisky hadn't helped.

Scapegoat of the Empire? Well, on that didn't Christine have a point? Harry had never fitted anywhere. He had always been an outsider. He had sometimes managed to see it as a strength, but now he was less sure.

Was it really possible the past was finally catching up with him? Yes, it was true that many mistakes had been made in Operations over the last five or six years. The debacle on Mount Avala remained its haunting nadir, but too many men had been lost behind the Iron Curtain in a range of botched episodes. And, yes, he could see that the outsider who had never really fitted made a convenient, even compelling, scapegoat. But what disturbed him was that, if this was indeed a trap, how had he not seen it coming?

Down the corridor, a radio turned to maximum volume began to crackle. Harry threw on his clothes and went to locate the source of the noise. He found a group of cleaners huddled around a wireless. 'What's happening?'

'No broadcast!' one said.

The same scene was repeated in the lobby. The desk was deserted, its staff gathered around another wireless in the back office. Harry slipped behind the counter. One of the uniformed porters almost jumped out of his skin. 'I'm sorry, sir. I—'

'No problem.' Harry stayed where he was. 'What's happening?'

'It's difficult to say, sir. Radio Tehran normally begins its morning broadcast at six o'clock . . .' He looked up at the clock. Its minute hand was a shade after the hour. 'But so far . . . nothing. Can I help you, sir?'

'I just wanted to know what was going on.' Perhaps, he thought, the coup was back on. If he'd been in charge of the operation on the ground, his own instinct would have been to strike again quickly.

Harry returned to the lobby and waited. The minutes crawled by, but there was no sign of Shahnaz. He checked outside, where the sun made the buildings glow pink and the heat was rising. The road beyond the hotel was almost deserted. He nodded to the doorman. 'Quiet, this morning.'

'Yes.'

Harry went in search of coffee. Just before seven there was a sudden burst of chatter over the airwaves from the room behind the reception desk. Harry could make out very little, except *Mossadegh.*

'The coup has failed,' the clerk told him. 'Mr Mossadegh is still the prime minister. They say . . .' The man inclined his head closer to the set. 'General Riahi says the plot has been foiled. The coup was led by members of the Imperial Guard. They are . . . Colonel Nasiri . . .' His voice tailed off as he tried to concentrate on the rest of the broadcast.

Shahnaz swept into the lobby, a cloth bag over her shoulder. 'Mr Tower, I'm so sorry—'

'The coup's failed.'

'I know. There are roadblocks and soldiers all over the city. It took me ages to persuade them to let me through. Shall we take my car?'

'No, it's fine. But let's go out the back. Mine's parked this way.'

Once they had gone out past the pool equipment house to find Christine's red Ford Popular, Shahnaz pointed out the obvious: 'It's a different car.'

'I swapped.'

She frowned at him. 'Why?'

'It's a long story.'

Shahnaz got in beside him. 'Where do you want to go? Shall we try that address in Doshtan Street?'

'First I need to go to the bazaar.'

'Why?'

'There is something I have to do.'

'What?'

'It's a personal matter.' She clearly didn't believe him, but Harry was not in a mood to explain why he was about to take a dangerous step back into his own past.

11

THEY ARRIVED AT the teeming square outside the bazaar at the same time as a train of camels, each one heavily loaded. 'The caravan has arrived,' Harry said. Shahnaz didn't return his smile as he navigated carefully around them and parked alongside a gleaming, shark-finned American roadster.

A battered and dusty Bedford bus disgorged a couple of giggling teenage girls in matching cotton polka-dot skirts, a handful of women veiled in the *chador* and a large group of men in business suits.

Harry and Shahnaz made way for a group of youths carrying piles of carpets towards the cavernous entrance to the bazaar. A gaggle of children surrounded Harry. *'Salaam, agha! Salaam, agha!'* He allowed himself a casual glance over his shoulder. He was puzzled that they had left the hotel without anyone on their tail. If they had been prepared to post guards to watch his car last night, why were they not following him this morning? 'Do you know where you're going?' Shahnaz asked.

'Yes.' She followed him through the gate. It was closer, but no cooler in there. Pedestrians had kicked up a curtain of dust. Harry took off his sunglasses and wiped the grit from his face.

The bazaar was like a honeycomb, each tiny store illuminated by a gas lamp or flickering candles. The smell of sweat and tobacco was overpowering, but here and there it was suffused with aromas of spices, roasting nuts, cooking fat, donkey dung, petrol, rotting fruit and offal.

They passed through an alley full of butchers' shops, rancid as an abattoir. They swung into another lane full of stores selling ivory chess sets and elaborately bejewelled plates, bowls and cups. At the end of it, Harry stopped abruptly in front of a neat two-storey building. 'I'll meet you here in half an hour,' he said, pointing to a tiny café opposite.

'I'll come with you.'

'Better I go alone.'

'I love him, you know,' she said, as he departed. He turned back to face her. 'If you think you can't trust me, you're wrong,' she added. 'I'd do anything for him. *Anything*.'

'So would I. Though he might have chosen not to believe it. Just wait here a moment, please. I won't be long.'

Harry weaved his way through a couple more crowded alleys to the street of the money-lenders. He ducked through a narrow doorway into a room filled from floor to ceiling with carpets, watched over by a pair of young men in close-fitting suits. They lounged against the walls drinking tea and smoking a *ghalyan* water pipe. 'Can I help you, sir?' one asked, but Harry ignored him and climbed a narrow staircase to the floor above, where their master lay on huge cushions, like a medieval potentate.

Meshang Rashidian was an athletic man run to fat, with a neat goatee beard and a wide, handsome face. 'Harry Tower,' he said, with an avuncular grin. He pushed himself slowly to his feet and offered his hand. 'How good to see you again. Gentlemen, this is an old friend from London. Mr Tower, this is my brother Said, whom I don't think you met last time you were here, and two colleagues from the bazaar.'

The colleagues stood, shook Harry's hand, muttered polite farewells and left. Said stayed where he was. He was leaner than his brother, with eyes like a stoat's.

'Would you like a drink?' It wasn't really a question. Rashidian conjured a bottle of whisky from under a stool and three glasses from a shelf behind him. He poured a generous measure into each. 'We are always pleased to welcome old friends from London.'

'It's been a while.'

'Mr Tower . . . Harry, if I may,' Said said. 'It is an honour to meet you. I'll wager there is not a man with any knowledge of the Service anywhere in the world who has not heard of you and would not wish immediately to offer any assistance he could. My brother here has spoken of you often.'

Meshang Rashidian smiled in agreement. 'We were not expecting you,' Rashidian went on. 'The message from London was clear: no fingerprints. At least, if there are to be any, American only.'

'I'm not here on official business.'

'I see. Then how can we help you?'

'I'm looking for my son. You may have heard he's missing?'

'Ah, yes, of course.' Rashidian moved to refill his glass. 'You should have no fears on that score, Mr Tower.'

'Where is he?'

'Have you met our delightful chief of police yet?'

'No.'

'Well, no doubt you will. As we like to say here, he is a cock-sucking, motherfucking bastard son of a whore. Your son's article – somewhat ill-advised, it must be said – seems unaccountably to have upset him. Though it was absolutely accurate, of course. He responded by getting some of his friends in one of the criminal gangs that stalk the south of the city to take the boys for an unwanted holiday in the mountains.'

'Where?'

'We don't know yet.'

'Which gang?'

'We're not yet certain of that either. But give us another day or two.'

'Are they all right?'

'I'm sure they will be. We have put out the word that your son is under our protection and the long arm of the British state will reach out and cut off their balls if he comes to any harm. They know that we are *always* as good as our word.'

'Sean was taken by soldiers.'

'No, he wasn't. They were simply dressed as such. It isn't the first time one of the gangs has pulled that trick.'

'Is there any chance they will harm him?'

'They wouldn't dare.'

Harry leant back into the cushions, though he certainly didn't feel inclined to relax.

'May I offer you a pipe?' Rashidian asked.

'No, thanks.'

Rashidian rang a bell and a young boy tripped up the stairs in his haste. He pointed to the corner and the boy prepared a pipe with seasoned dexterity. Harry couldn't help noticing that both men's gaze lingered upon the child. The brothers settled back and took turns in drawing from the pipe.

'Your son is not at all like you,' Rashidian said.

'You've met Sean?'

'Of course. There are few people of consequence in Tehran with whom we are not acquainted.'

'Where?'

'At a reception at the French Embassy.' Rashidian glanced at his brother. 'A good-looking boy. An almost feminine face, like his mother's, one assumes.'

Harry tried to contain his irritation at unctuous mannerisms. 'What did you talk to him about?'

'Revolution! Your boy is no great fan of the British Empire or, indeed, it seems, of anything British.' Rashidian held up the whisky bottle. 'Except perhaps Glenfiddich. A proper Bolshevik! But that's the folly of youth, eh?' He sucked deeply on the pipe, but his small, dark eyes remained fixed on Harry. 'I know you were headed to Yugoslavia after I last saw you. So if you didn't meet him here in Tabriz, you must certainly have run into our friend Oleg Vasilyev there?'

Harry tried to buy himself a moment to think about what they intended by asking this. 'I don't much like to talk about people I've run into.'

'A good policy. But you will have the chance to renew an old acquaintance. Oleg arrived in Tehran two months ago.'

Harry tried to hide his surprise.

'I don't need to explain the reality to *you*, Mr Tower. Iran represents a terrible threat or a great opportunity, depending on where you happen to be standing. Oleg and his KGB colleagues appear a little distracted by the blood-letting in Moscow now that the old monster Stalin is dead. But, despite that . . .' Rashidian glanced at his brother '. . . we sense they still believe they have a chance to bring Iran into their sphere. The support from London and Washington here these last days is not before time. I need hardly tell you the consequences to the West in terms of lost oil, let alone prestige, if Iran were to fall. It would be an unthinkable catastrophe.'

Rashidian was a typical Service major-domo, a local businessman who had used London's backing to create an empire within his own sphere of influence. Harry had met a dozen like him and they were all the same: clever, cunning, unscrupulous, ruthless. He had dropped Vasilyev's name into the conversation for a reason. 'How long have you been in Tehran, Mr Tower?'

'You tell me.'

Rashidian rewarded him with another sly smile. 'You have missed the many weeks and months of protests. The people are angry and desperate. They are losing hope. In the beginning, of course, they cheered their prime minister's populist demagoguery. *It is our oil. Damn those foreigners!* But now they begin to turn on him. Like all revolutionaries, he has not learnt that, in the end, the mob always devours its own. The coup plotters may have failed last night, but I doubt they will be the last. Mossadegh is weak now, his regime teetering.'

'What does this have to do with Vasilyev or my son?'

'With your son? Perhaps nothing.'

If Harry was meant to be picking something up here, he still wasn't getting it. 'Did Sean know Vasilyev?'

'I have no idea.'

'But they met?'

'Not to my knowledge.'

'So why were you telling me about—'

'I merely wanted to remind you, Mr Tower, that you are here at a turning point in our history. Yes, London and Washington have committed finally to act. We applaud that. But Communist students, backed by our friend Mr Vasilyev, come out in support of the prime minister. If we cannot restore the Shah to power in these coming days, then who can say what will become of us?'

'This is not my operation. It is not my war. Not this time. I just want to find my son.'

'Of course. We understand. And find him we will. Have no fear.'

Harry stood. 'I'd be grateful for your assistance on another matter. I need someone who knows his way around weapons. Maybe with a background in ballistics.'

'May I ask why?'

'I'd prefer to keep that to myself for now.'

Rashidian shrugged. 'If you go to the street of the

ironmongers in the bazaar, you will find the man you seek in the last store on the right. His name is Ahmed. Tell him I sent you.'

Harry had reached the stairs when Meshang Rashidian offered his last warning. 'Be careful, Mr Tower. Tehran today is a dangerous place.' He smiled again. 'Anything can happen, even to those most able to fend for themselves.'

12

HARRY RETURNED TO the still, dusty air of the alley outside with a head full of questions, so it took him a few moments longer than normal to sense he was being followed, though it was easy enough to swap positions with the woman behind him. 'Are you looking for me?' he asked, at her shoulder.

Shahnaz whirled around, flustered. 'I— No. I was browsing.' When it was clear he did not believe her, she ushered him to a seat in a nearby café. 'What were you doing with the Rashidians?' she asked.

'Looking for information.'

'How did you know about them?'

'A friend put me in touch.'

'What kind of friend? Every man and his dog knows the Rashidians are the greatest criminals in all Tehran.'

Harry glanced about him. Magazine photographs of Mossadegh and other Iranian politicians were pasted to the wall between ornate mirrors and gilded candelabra. Fresh sawdust had been sprinkled on the floor, and the air was heady with tobacco smoke and the smell of freshly roasted arabica. The customers, all men, were dressed in tatty white shirts with white flat caps or battered Panamas. Most smoked *ghalyan* water pipes with their coffee. A photograph of the Shah had pride of place above the bar, next to a cage full of birds. 'He said Sean's fine.' Harry avoided her question.

'And you believed him?'

'I don't know. Did you ever see Sean with anyone from the Soviet Embassy? At a diplomatic reception, a party, some kind of public event?'

'No. Why?'

Harry didn't answer. What still troubled him was the way Meshang Rashidian had alluded to a relationship between Sean and Oleg Vasilyev. He did not entirely believe Christine's implication that his colleagues had been there a few weeks ago for the sole purpose of fitting him up as a scapegoat. If they were indeed looking for a Soviet mole at the heart of SIS operations in London – and perhaps there was evidence enough that such a search was long overdue – there were more obvious candidates.

But if they *were* going to set him up as a scapegoat, how neat to imply that both father and son had been lured into the clutches of the KGB. Lost near the Soviet border, during an attempt to engineer a Communist takeover of Iran. It was simple. It was the kind of solution he himself might have dreamt up.

'Where is he, then?' Shahnaz asked. 'If they're so confident he's all right.'

'They think the chief of police has got some of his friends in one of the criminal gangs to take them up to the mountains.'

'Where?'

'They're trying to find out.'

'How would that explain the army jeeps?'

'He says they often disguise themselves as soldiers.'

She studied him. 'They say Meshang Rashidian is an agent for the British Secret Service.'

'I wouldn't know about that.'

'How did you get in touch with him?'

'An old friend gave me his name.'

'And was this old friend a member of the—'

'I don't know. And I don't want to know.' He dropped his cigarette into the sawdust and got to his feet. He disappeared back into the street before she could stop him. She trailed half a pace behind, clearly weighed down by questions, until they reached their next destination.

The ironmonger, Ahmed, was a shrivelled old man with a moth-eaten beard and beady eyes. He nodded sagely at the mention of Rashidian's name and led them up to the top floor of his tiny shop. They knocked their heads on the pots, pans, cooking utensils, fire tongs and garden instruments that hung from the low ceilings. There was nothing to suggest an interest in ballistics.

Harry put the bullet he'd cut from the Dodge's tyre on the counter. The man switched on a desk lamp and examined it closely. 'I'd like to know what kind of weapon,' Harry said.

The man picked up a pair of tweezers and held the bullet closer to the light. 'Would you care to tell me why you have not taken this to our police department here in Tehran?'

'No.'

'Mr Rashidian suggested I might be of help?' Harry nodded. 'You may be in luck. My son is a policeman – an honest one, so have no fear. He has just returned from a year's study in America, where he spent some time with their Federal Bureau of Investigation. This is his speciality. I do not know what equipment he has here or what he may be able to do for you, but I will ask him.'

'How long will it take?'

'A few days, perhaps longer.'

'I need an answer today.' The man raised his eyebrows. 'If it is a matter of payment, then I'll gladly . . .'

'I will speak to my son.'

'What time would you like me to return?'

'I cannot promise a result . . .' he looked out of the narrow window '. . . before sunset.' He slipped the bullet into the pocket of his silk jacket.

Harry didn't budge. 'There's one more thing. May I have a word in private?' He raised a hand at Shahnaz to ask her to wait where she stood. She did not look pleased to be excluded.

'Of course.' Ahmed opened a door behind him. Harry had to stoop very low to pass through to a tiny armoury where every kind of weapon was pinned to the walls.

'Christ,' Harry said. 'There's enough here to start a war.'

The old man smiled for the first time. 'Then you had better pick the right side.'

Harry glanced at the machine-guns, pistols, shotguns and grenades. They were all European or Russian models.

He took down a Beretta. It was old, but well oiled. 'How much?'

The man shrugged. 'For a friend of Mr Rashidian . . . Please take it. Just return it to me when you leave.' He took two boxes of ammunition out of a small drawer. 'Enough?'

'Thank you.' Harry slipped the boxes into his jacket pocket. The old man took out a silencer and pushed it across to him. 'What did you wish to speak to me about?'

'Just this. I needed a weapon. Thank you.' Harry picked up the silencer. 'I'll make sure you have them back.'

He clambered down the narrow staircase and out into the bustle of the alley. Shahnaz was waiting for him. 'Wouldn't it be better if we worked together?' she asked. 'If you told me what was going on?'

'Could you find that place in the south of the city?'

'Which one?'

'The address I wrote down from Sean's notepad. Doshtan Street.' Harry glanced at his watch. 'Could you get us there?'

'Probably.'

'I'd like to take a look after I've tried to get some answers out of the chief of police.'

'The car is this way,' she said. They swung left into a quarter where the shops sold fine cloth. The alleys were quieter there and Harry stopped for a moment to retie his shoelace. As he did so, he glanced up at a glass door just long enough to see a man behind them dive into a shop. He straightened and walked on. He cut into another store, pretended to examine some silk and glanced back down the alley. 'What are you doing?' Shahnaz asked.

He stepped into the narrow lane and walked faster.

He'd spotted a second man behind them now, and a pair ahead. He was also starting to lose his bearings. He took Shahnaz's arm. 'Keep moving. How long till we're out of here?'

'You're hurting me.'

'How long if we walk at this pace? Exactly.'

'I don't know. Maybe another minute.'

'Where does it take us?'

'To the side of the bazaar. The car is at the front.' Harry pushed her harder. 'I don't understand – what's going on?'

'Just keep moving.' He could sense the men closing up behind them, but he was careful not to glance over his shoulder. He spotted others now. They burst out of the bazaar. To their right, a crowd was marching towards them, chanting loudly. They carried photographs of the Shah. They were all men. 'Bloody hell,' he muttered.

'Mr Tower . . . Harry, for God's sake . . .'

'Faster.'

The crowd gained on them, chanting more loudly. They stamped their feet. Dust billowed into the close air. 'Where's the car from here?'

'Back the other way. It's . . .'

The crowd was no more than thirty yards away now and the chants were deafening. He swung Shahnaz right into an alley. 'It's a dead end!' she said. But it was too late. The crowd had swarmed into the street behind them.

'Keep walking!' Harry instructed. He took the Beretta from his jacket pocket, ejected the magazine and fumbled for some ammunition. He got a round in, then another. He turned, but too late to raise his weapon. He was punched in the face, then lifted on a tide of seething, sweating men.

140

The Beretta hit the ground. He groped for it, but one of the youths thumped him on the side of his head and he went down again. Hands grappled for his face. Fingers pushed into his eyes and nose and mouth. They dragged him, feet trailing in the dirt. He heard Shahnaz scream and craned his head to see her being carried by another group of men in front of him.

They were swept down towards the end of the cul-de-sac. They smashed Harry's head on a door, then against a wall. He was dragged roughly along a corridor and up some steps into what looked like a deserted schoolroom. As they threw him to the floor, he saw one of their attackers pull a knife, then another. He struggled to his feet. Shahnaz cried out as the men circled her, like animals. She began to plead in Farsi.

Harry took a step back to give himself time and space to assess the threat: two men with knives. Two dozen in the room. The first of the professionals he had caught sight of in the bazaar was by the door, armed with a Colt revolver; the second was on the fringe of the mob that had him cornered.

Shahnaz raked her fingernails down the face of her nearest assailant and was rewarded with a stinging blow to the cheekbone. The man she had bloodied pushed her to the floor and, in the momentary distraction, Harry struck. He punched the first knifeman on the side of the head, twisted around and felled the second with a sharp, open-palmed jab up into his nose, breaking it. The man bent down, squealing.

Harry barged past a startled youth and took three paces to the professional at the back of the group. His prey swivelled towards the approaching threat, but not quickly enough, so the shot from the Colt whistled inches high. Harry kicked the man's legs from under him and smashed the flat of his palm up into the man's nose with a short, vicious jab. The man screamed in agony, but Harry held him as he crumpled, and relieved him of his revolver.

Harry raised the revolver towards the man's accomplice by the door, but fired a split second too late as he ducked away.

The crowd scattered. Harry grabbed the thug trying to rape Shahnaz, yanked him to his feet and shoved him back, the pistol trained on his face. The man lunged for the curved blade on his belt. Harry didn't make the same mistake twice. Blood and fragments of cranium splattered Shahnaz's cheeks. The crowd stampeded for the exit.

And then the room was quiet, except for Shahnaz's sobs. She lay curled up in the corner. Harry moved to the doorway and listened. He stepped out into the corridor, where a well-timed blow caught him on the temple and sent him crashing down. The pistol clattered to the floor, but he managed to kick his assailant's legs from under him as he went down.

Harry was first to his feet, though not by much. His opponent steadied himself and Harry saw the glint of steel in his right hand. Harry advanced. The man retreated, dark eyes glaring. Harry lunged and the tip of the blade sliced the air an inch from his left eye. Harry feinted right, then left, and the man struck again but Harry deflected the blow, gripped his wrist and rammed his knife hand into the wall. The weapon skittered down the steps as they cannoned through the balustrade and tumbled five or six feet to the stone paving below.

His opponent's body cushioned Harry's fall, but he fought on. He landed a punch on Harry's temple and wriggled out from under him. This time he was quicker to rise and caught Harry in the chest with a flying heel. Then he dived for the knife, rolled and came at him a second time. Harry ducked away, caught hold of the swinging forearm and used the momentum of the thrust to turn and twist him to the ground. He felt the man's free elbow snap as it hit the edge of the bottom step. Harry was behind him now, a vice-like grip on his knife hand, his other arm pressed against his adversary's throat.

Harry smelt acid bile on rasping breath as he shifted his left hand to his captive's forehead and angled the blade, little by little, towards his throat. 'Who sent you here?' he growled. 'Who told you to do this?'

He got nothing more than a grunt in return.

Shahnaz appeared in the doorway and watched in horror as Harry pushed the knife closer to their enemy's neck. The man tried to arch his back and buy himself precious extra seconds, but gave up the unequal struggle when Harry pressed his shattered elbow against the stone.

The steel tip pierced his throat.

Harry took in Shahnaz's horrified stare. And plunged the knife in to the hilt.

He held on tight as blood bubbled from the man's lips, then pumped out over his chest and legs. Harry relaxed his hold, shoved the body away and stood. They watched fingers twitch weakly, as if to staunch the flow from the fatal wound. Then Harry turned to Shahnaz. She trembled uncontrollably, too shocked to cry. He picked her up and carried her back to the schoolroom. He skirted the prostrate bodies and the pool of blood from her would-be rapist and sat her on a desk at the back. He removed his jacket and laid it across her shoulders.

He took her face in his bloodstained hands. Her eyes met his, but there was no life in them. 'It's all right . . .' She looked at him blankly. 'They're gone,' he said. 'Just wait here. I'll only be a moment.'

'No . . .' She shook herself from her trance. 'Please . . .'

'Shahnaz—'

'Please don't leave me here.'

'Just wait one minute.'

Harry searched the pockets of the man he'd just killed and found a wad of *rials* but no identification. He picked up the revolver and held it to the light. He moved to the body of the accomplice and repeated the process. He found a second firearm in the corridor: another Colt, of a similar vintage. He dropped both into a discarded satchel with his own Beretta and slung it over his shoulder. He scooped up Shahnaz and carried her outside. Photographs of the Shah fluttered across the deserted street.

By the time he'd eased her into the passenger seat of the Ford Popular, Shahnaz was shaking uncontrollably. He lifted her out again, laid her on the back seat and covered her with his jacket.

At the hotel, staff came running as Harry carried Shahnaz through the lobby. 'Sir, can we—'

'Call the lift.'

The door to his room was already open by the time he reached the fourth floor. One of the bellboys lingered awkwardly on the threshold. 'Sir, is there anything further we can do? Would you like us to call a doctor?'

'No.'

Harry settled Shahnaz on the bed and dispensed with the bellboy. He propped her legs up on some cushions, and pulled the sheet over her. He found a blanket in the cupboard and added it for good measure.

'It'll be all right,' he murmured. 'You need to sleep now.'

He closed the curtains, switched off the light, then picked up the telephone, unwound the cable, carried it into the bathroom and closed the door. Only then did he glance in the mirror. He had blood on his face, neck, arms and chest. He began to wash himself in the basin. When he'd finished, he stared at his reflection. Green eyes gazed steadily back at him. He could hear Amanda's voice: *Is anything in there, Harry? Sometimes the darkness behind your eyes frightens me.*

He picked up the phone and asked to be put through to the American Embassy. It took a few minutes for Grenville to come on the line. 'Good morning, Mr Tower. I trust you've heard about the attempted coup.'

'Yes.'

'Sadly, it appears to have failed. Everything seems to be returning to what passes for normal remarkably quickly, though I doubt that this is the last we'll hear of such things. I've spoken to the chief of police and I'm glad to say he's ready to meet—'

'We need to delay by a couple of hours.'

'Mr Tower, I don't know if that is going to be—'

'Tell him something came up.'

'Er ... I shall do my best, but I'm afraid I can't guarantee—'

'I have faith in you, Grenville. I'll see you there.' Harry terminated the connection and glanced at his watch. He left the bathroom and checked on Shahnaz. She was fast asleep. He slipped out onto the balcony, closing the curtain and the door behind him, then sat and smoked a cigarette. Below him, kids splashed in the pool as the muezzin's call to prayer boomed out from a nearby mosque. This time, it was the women in the neighbouring house who were praying on the back terrace. Harry rested his feet against the balustrade, looked at the Alborz Mountains rising through the haze and tried to banish the idea of going down to the bar.

Harry let Shahnaz sleep for almost the full two hours, but he didn't want to leave without telling her where he was going. He let in a sliver of light and shook her gently awake. She opened her eyes and looked uncertainly into his.

'I've got to meet the chief of police,' he said. 'You'll be safe here, so go back to sleep. If you can tell me where your apartment is, I'll pick up some fresh clothes on the way back.'

'I don't want to stay here on my own.'

'You'll be all right here. I'll tell security. I'll only be an hour or two.' She tried to get up, but he gently prevented her. 'Please . . . you've had a bad shock. You need to rest.'

'I'm fine. I slept.'

'I'll get a doctor. Perhaps you'll listen to him if you won't listen to me.'

'I don't need a doctor. And I'd like to come with you.'

'It will be better if you stay.'

She struggled upright, holding the sheet over her chest. Her eyes bored into him. 'Who are you, Mr Tower?'

146

'What do you mean?'

'I don't think Sean ever believed that you were just a sugar salesman. And if that's your cover story, it just got comprehensively blown in the bazaar.'

The silence stretched between them as he ran through his options. 'I worked for the British Secret Intelligence Service,' he conceded eventually.

'For how long?'

'Many years.'

'Is that what your wife meant when she accused you of living a lie?'

'No.'

'So what did she mean?' He didn't answer. He certainly wasn't going to explain that. 'I know it's none of my business,' she went on, 'but you said we should be honest with each other, so how about you finally explain what you really think is going on?'

He weighed the pros and cons of qualified truth. Increasingly, he was feeling a strange compulsion to unburden himself. 'Our American friends are convinced we have a Soviet mole at our headquarters in London. At this point, it isn't clear to me whether my superiors believe they have one or not. But they certainly need a scapegoat.'

'And they have picked you?'

'It's one potential explanation.'

'They took Sean to lure you out here?'

'Perhaps. But it may be unconnected. I'm not yet sure. It's also possible that Sean found out something here he shouldn't have so they disposed of him and now need to consider doing the same with me. And you.'

'About what?'

Harry shrugged. 'The trade in drugs, the coup we just witnessed. Or something else.'

'If your colleagues in London were looking for a Soviet mole, or someone they could scapegoat as such, why would they pick you?'

Harry was tempted to explain just how much a working-class scholarship boy stood out amid a sea of public-school dandies, but he doubted she would understand. And, besides, he was increasingly convinced there was more to it than that: he had the perfect profile for the role they apparently wanted to assign to him. 'I spent much of the war in Yugoslavia, working closely with Tito and the Russians, which, in the current climate, is enough to mark me out. Then I ran operations in Europe, which meant I had access to a wide variety of secrets. So the failure of every half-cocked scheme can be laid at my door, even if the mistakes were not mine.' He shook his head regretfully. 'I also had a reputation for not suffering fools gladly and there were plenty to choose from, so I made enemies easily. SIS is an essentially clubbable place – Boodle's, White's, the Athenaeum, the Travellers – and I'm not a clubbable man.'

She pushed back the sheet. 'I can't stay here.'

'You must.'

'I'm tougher than you think.' She stood, a little shakily. She watched him intently as he picked up one of the Colt revolvers and slipped it into a leather holdall, which he slung over his shoulder. 'Who were the men who attacked us?' she asked.

'At least two were intelligence professionals,' he said. 'Agents, if you like. Trained in Moscow, Havana, or East Germany.'

'They were Iranians.'

'Born here, perhaps, but trained somewhere else.'

'In the West?'

He still didn't want to concede this possibility. Because if it was so, it implied a degree of preparation and planning that left him in very deep trouble indeed.

'So?'

'We have work to do,' he said. 'That's all I can tell you. But if they have taken my son, they will learn that was a big mistake.'

13

London, May 1945

AMANDA HAD A grip on him and she wasn't letting go.
'Come on, my beloved husband,' she said, 'you can do
this.' She marched him towards a group of women, in
flamboyant floral dresses, who were assembled like a
defending army. 'You remember Marjorie Allen?'

'Yes, of course,' Harry said, with as much sincerity as he
could muster.

'And Jane Corbett?'

'Yes, indeed. Lovely to see you again.'

'It's been a while!' Jane Corbett said. 'The Board of Trade
must have kept you fearfully busy. Thank God it's all
over!'

Harry forced a smile. She grimaced back at him.

'Your wife has been a tower of strength,' Marjorie
added. 'To all of us.' Harry had long since accepted that

neighbours with too much time on their hands assumed you must be doing something secret if you appeared to have a bland civil-service job in wartime. It was just his bad luck that, in his case, it happened to be true.

There were more introductions and handshakes until it felt as though he was being forced to work the street. Harry smiled and took his punishment like a man while Amanda could barely contain her enjoyment. 'Punishment for neglect of neighbours over a prolonged period,' she had told him gleefully, over breakfast, that morning. 'No excuses, no escape, no early release. The war,' she'd said, with a huge grin, 'is over!'

The street was full of bunting, Union flags and tables that groaned with such a feast as rationing permitted. The residents had gone all out for whatever drink they could lay their hands on and Harry didn't blame them. His only regret was that he'd not hit the whisky bottle before emerging.

He eyed the small table outside their own home, where Sean sat, with envy. But Amanda was getting her money's worth. He didn't recognize a single one of their neighbours and he doubted he would even after this episode. He engaged in small-talk as if his life depended on it: the unalloyed joy of this day, collective regret at those who had not lived to see it. And the weather, of course, which had held so far.

Eventually, Amanda was sidetracked and Harry slipped away. He joined Sean, who still sat, long-faced and serious, on his own – as he so often did. 'You all right, my boy?' Harry said easily.

'Is there anyone Mum doesn't know in this street?'

151

'What do you think?'

They looked across at two young brothers who sat at the table directly opposite. 'Do you want to go and say hello to the Corbett boys?'

'I'd rather not.'

Harry knew Amanda would press Sean, since their son's lack of friends was an issue much agonized about. 'We haven't had a chance to chat since you broke up. How was school?'

'You've been away,' Sean said. It might have been an accusation.

'Did you have a good term?'

'It was all right.' The preparatory school he had been sent to at seven was Sean's least favourite subject. It had been Amanda's decision: the traditions of her class had taken precedence over her desire to have him at home. Harry had gone along with it. Perhaps he imagined it would do Sean good to live a life free of ingrained prejudice. 'Were things any better?' he asked, as delicately as he could manage. Amanda had told him that flooring the bullies was quite the wrong advice.

Sean stared at his feet, deep in thought. 'They don't like me,' he said.

Harry searched for a response. He'd told Sean often enough that this was not – that it could not be – because he was not likeable, since the opposite was self-evidently true. Sean was gentle, kind to a fault. Unlike his father, he did not have a bad bone in his body. But this type of reassurance never seemed to help. 'It is one of life's distressing revelations,' Harry said, 'which we all wrestle with sooner or later, that some people are not very nice and most are just sheep. You get a small but wilful group of the former and they can lead a very large flock of the latter. How do you think the Nazis managed to turn a country the size of Germany into a death cult?'

Sean appeared to consider this carefully. If nothing else, Harry thought, his experiences at school would prepare him for life, even if it was not quite in the way they'd intended. Or was he just trying to justify their decision? 'Now I come to think about it,' Harry went on, 'I'm not sure your passage through school has been much different from mine, if not for quite the same reasons.' Even now Harry could recall the sting of the gossip about his mother and 'her fancy lord'.

'How do you make friends, then?'

'You wait,' Harry said, 'and when someone of real quality comes along, you hold on to them like your life depends on it.' They were both looking at Amanda, who was engaged in conversation with Jane Corbett again.

'It's much nicer when she's like this,' Sean said. His gaze had not left his mother. The reflection had been offered without apparent sentiment, but Harry's conscience was pricked all the same. If Sean seemed old and wise beyond his years, it was surely because he had been too often left to cope alone with his mother's mercurial condition. 'I'm sorry,' Harry said.

'For what?'

'Leaving you alone so much.'

'You had to beat the Germans.' Harry watched a smile creep across his son's face as he saw his mother laughing across the street. Their love was so . . . uncomplicated, he thought. So sincere and deep and profound. Not for the first time, Harry wondered if Amanda in some way stood between him and his son. Her love for them both was so passionate and all-encompassing that he and Sean sometimes found it hard to see each other clearly. Or was that just the self-delusion of a bruised conscience?

Amanda caught sight of them and hurried over. 'Uh-oh,' Harry said, winking at his son. 'Here comes trouble.' Sean smiled back.

'Caught!' Amanda admonished. 'Sean, go and say hello to the Corbett boys. They look bored out of their minds. And, Harry, shame on you.' She dragged him to his feet as Sean dutifully followed his mother's instructions. Amanda hooked her arm in her husband's once more. 'This is *such* a great day,' she said. 'Isn't it? Everything's going to be different now.'

It was not a question. And Harry didn't have the heart to tell her that nothing in his life was ever going to be different.

14

Tehran, August 1953

POLICE HEADQUARTERS WAS an uninspiring, dark grey stone building just along from the National Park and opposite the post office. It was in the downtown area dominated by the grander buildings of the foreign ministry, the Bank Melli, the finance ministry and other pillars of Iran's society and government.

Outside, a mechanic worked under the bonnet of a broken-down jeep, and uniformed officers lounged on the wide stone steps, smoking and gossiping. Grenville was waiting for them in a long, dreary corridor, which smelt of the polish that had been heavily applied to its ancient parquet floor.

The office of the chief of police was on the top floor and afforded a handsome view over the rooftops of Tehran. Asadollah Soleimani was a small, rotund individual with a pudgy face and a wide forehead that shone with sweat.

'I am very pleased to meet you, Mr Tower. Do be seated.' He ushered them to a round table by the window. 'Would you like anything to drink?'

They shook their heads, but he rang a bell anyway and asked the servant who popped out from an unseen door for some water. A carafe and four glasses were produced in an instant. Soleimani waited until he withdrew before continuing. 'Mr Tower, I have already spoken at some length to Mr Grenville, and I would like you to know how saddened, indeed horrified, I am at what has befallen your son here in Tehran. I can assure you that we are acting with the utmost urgency.' He retreated behind an enormous mahogany desk. It felt like an audience.

'Where do you think he is?' Harry asked.

'We believe he is being held by one of the criminal gangs that operate in the south of the city. We thought they had removed him to the mountains, but our intelligence tonight suggests he is being held in the city itself.'

'Where?'

'Alas, we do not know.' He looked apologetic but unembarrassed. 'South Tehran is a big place. But we are working on it.'

Taken by criminals, Harry thought. The story they were all sticking to. It meant this was either the truth or that the operation to kidnap Sean had been planned with broad enough support to ensure all interested parties stuck to an agreed line. 'What do they want?'

'I think they *wished* to teach your son a lesson. But I'm afraid your presence here may have complicated matters. It might encourage them to seek a ransom.'

'How do they know I'm here?'

'They are brutal, Mr Tower, but not stupid. Their intelligence is remarkably good. You might say that they are the only growth industry we have in Iran at this time. They will almost certainly have spies in your hotel. In a time of economic . . . discomfort, it is hard . . .' He spread his arms wide. He took a short cigar from a mosaic wooden box on the side of his desk and lit it. He turned the box of matches over and over in his fingers.

He was nervous, Harry thought, and not hiding it well. 'What kind of ransom will they ask for?'

'Until they make contact, we cannot know.'

'How will they contact me?'

'Most probably through us. But it is possible they may seek to do so directly. I hardly need tell you that it would be wise to inform us immediately if that were the case.'

'Are they operating on their own, or is someone else pulling the strings?'

'On their own. But you will no doubt be thinking – on the basis of your son's article – that I am the worst kind of liar and scoundrel. How could I blame you? He wrote of a vile trade in opium, facilitated by an unholy alliance of European diplomats, criminal masterminds – and me. And yet here I am, telling you that these same criminal gangs have mysteriously kidnapped your son, and that I, as yet, know nothing about it.'

Harry did not respond.

'Of course you think that, because if you didn't, you'd be a fool. And I can see you are very far from that.' Soleimani seemed to realize that spinning the matchbox was providing his audience with an insight into his state of mind. He slipped it carefully into his pocket and turned his chair a fraction so he could look out of the window at the Alborz Mountains, visible over the rooftops.

'So my son was . . . mistaken?' Harry pressed.

'No. He was right. There is such a trade, and it is run by the most unpleasant elements in our society, along with the kind of criminal enterprises that really don't bear thinking about. It is carried out with the assistance or connivance of elements within the diplomatic community, whose behaviour brings shame on their country's good name.'

'The French.'

He shrugged. 'We have been investigating these matters for more than a year. If I was in a position to make an arrest – or an allegation – I would have done so.'

'So my son was right about the trade and who lies behind it, but wrong about you?'

'That is correct.'

'A little convenient, wouldn't you say?'

'Yes, but—'

'So how is it able to flourish if it does not have the protection of the police?'

Soleimani faced them again. He leant forward onto the desk. With his fleshy forearms and round head, he looked like a bullfrog. 'The same way any criminal trade flourishes anywhere in the world, Mr Tower. If enough cash is generated, human nature has sadly shown us there appears to be no limit to what one can buy.'

'But your force is incorruptible?'

'I did not say that, and I wouldn't claim it.' His eyes narrowed. He stubbed out the cigar, which he had barely smoked. 'And nor did I say that this trade operated without official protection.' The chief watched Harry for a moment, then Shahnaz and finally Grenville. He got up and moved to a shelf on the far side of the room. He returned with a folder and dropped it onto the desk, which, now Harry came to think of it, was strangely bare. It was as if Soleimani did no real work there at all. 'That's the official report into your son's disappearance. Perhaps Miss Salemi would be good enough to translate.' Harry pushed it across to Shahnaz. She read in silence for several minutes, then looked up. 'Two army jeeps, perhaps a dozen soldiers,' Soleimani added.

'So, it *was* the army who took my son?'

'Initially, yes. We think that a group of rogue officers is working with one of the gangs, and that they handed over your son and his translator.'

'Is it not possible the men were simply dressed as soldiers?'

'It is possible, of course. But my officers were very thorough in their investigations. They are confident these men were serving members of our armed forces.' The chief leant forward. Harry thought of what Shahnaz had told him previously: that the army and the police were notorious rivals. 'Mr Tower, I will help you in any way that I can. It may be that we can prove of use to each other.'

'You say rogue officers. Which ones? Are you seeking to imply that this goes right to the top?'

He shook his head emphatically. 'I know General Riahi, our chief of staff. I don't believe he is the kind of man who would stoop to this. I do not know how familiar you are with what has happened in the city these past twenty-four hours, but the general clearly had no idea a coup was being planned and bravely stepped in to ensure that it was foiled – and that the democratic will of the people continues to prevail.'

'So who are these officers?'

He glanced at Shahnaz. 'Now we are going beyond the realms of my intelligence. From which garrison did the soldiers arrive to kidnap your son? Who supplies the convoys to move the consignments of drugs up towards Tabriz and over the border to Turkey? We don't know. Many in the military are a law unto themselves, as they have demonstrated all too recently.'

'What will they do with my son?'

'I am not certain. Perhaps they are not either.'

Harry thought about the coordinated attack on them that morning. 'Who runs the gang they have handed him over to?'

'There is more than one. They form a loose alliance. There are a number of leaders. It is complicated.'

'But they all pay homage to someone,' Shahnaz said. It was the first time she'd spoken.

The chief turned to her. His demeanour was sympathetic. 'That I can only leave in the realms of speculation, Miss Salemi. If there is a guiding hand, he is adept at preventing us from working out who it is.'

'But you have a theory,' Harry said.

'Yes.'

'Which is?'

'One man controls Tehran, Mr Tower. Not the prime minister. Not the Shah. Not me, or my force.' The chief leant forward to press his point. 'His name is Meshang

160

Rashidian. I'll make no bones about it. Your country created a monster.'

'Steady on,' Grenville said. 'I'm afraid this really is
absurd. I cannot countenance the idea that—'

'Meshang Rashidian has worked for the British Secret
Service for more than twenty years,' the chief countered.
'Throughout that time, there has been nothing he couldn't
or wouldn't fix. Hired muscle? No problem. Bribes to politicians, journalists, judges and military officers? Just keep
the cash coming through. He has used the power and the
influence that come from being Britain's secret factotum to
create an empire that now extends deep into Turkey and
indeed Europe. I returned from Istanbul to discuss the
issue with my colleagues there only last week.'

'You're saying that Rashidian has kidnapped my son?'

'I'm saying that nobody moves without his approval.
Not the military, not even the Imperial Guard.'

'He's not named in the article.'

'But your son was evidently a resourceful man. Who
would have bet against him establishing the true facts
sooner or later?'

'I have to say,' Grenville interjected, 'that I find this theory completely and utterly preposterous, as will every
department of Her Majesty's Government.'

'These are the facts, Mr Grenville, as you most certainly—'

'We know Meshang Rashidian. A respectable businessman. A patriot. No doubt a good friend of common sense.
But he would be most shocked to hear his good name and
reputation being traduced in this fashion.'

'What was my son doing out on that road?' Harry asked.
Soleimani shrugged. 'Had he been to Isfahan?'

'We don't know.'

'Have you traced his movements?'

'We have tried, but if that was indeed his destination, we can find no evidence that he and his colleague passed a night there.'

'Then how did the army know he was going to be on that road? Was the translator working for—'

'Impossible,' Shahnaz said. 'Unthinkable.' Harry looked at her. 'Either they were followed, or someone knew they were coming down the road that night.' They contemplated this in silence.

'Thank you for your assistance.' Harry stood and offered his hand.

The chief took it. 'I'm sure we'll meet again,' he said.

'I have no doubt of it.'

'Mr Tower, one more thing.' Harry turned at the door. 'Even in these lawless times, the discovery of two dead bodies in a schoolhouse in Tehran causes quite a stir. It will be all I can do to keep the matter out of the press. I have made the assumption that the European man seen leaving the area must have been acting in self-defence. But I'm afraid I would not be able to tolerate another such episode.'

'I am sure he must have been,' Harry said. 'Whoever he was. And if I ever meet him, I'll be sure to pass on your message.'

15

GRENVILLE FOLLOWED THEM to the red Ford Popular and looked as if he was about to climb in. 'What was that the chief was saying about bodies in a schoolhouse?'

'I have no idea,' Harry said. 'Thank you for your assistance. I'll call you at the embassy later.'

Shahnaz got into the passenger seat. Grenville didn't budge. 'What are your plans, Mr Tower? If there is anything else I can do—'

'Who's the CIA station chief here in Tehran?'

'The *what*?'

'You heard me.'

'I really don't know if there is anyone of that kind here in Tehran, Mr Tower.'

'Please tell your friends at the American Embassy that we've got to the point where I need to speak to the station chief. They'll know what I mean. I'll be at the hotel this evening. Make sure he comes along, please. I'd also like to talk to General Riahi.'

'I'll do my best, Mr Tower. But I make no promises.' Harry opened the driver's door and got in. 'Where are you going now?' Grenville asked.

'To look for my son.'

Harry yanked the door shut and eased away from the kerb. But he didn't get far. The streets were clogged with traffic. Again a crowd blocked the road by the National Park. Shahnaz's face was ashen. 'It's all right,' he said. He cursed himself for allowing her to accompany him: the signs of deep shock were still all too evident. And, indeed, for not thinking to avoid this section of town. 'You'll need to navigate me to Doshtan Street,' he said.

She nodded. 'I'll show you once we get through here, but you'll have to turn left on Pahlavi and keep going almost all the way to the railway station.'

A couple of youths charged down the line of cars, clutching leaflets. One was posted through Harry's half-open window. He handed it to Shahnaz to translate.

'It's a copy of the *firman* issued by the Shah, deposing Mossadegh and appointing General Zahedi as prime minister.' She sat upright and craned her neck to scrutinize the crowd ahead. 'The Shah's supporters obviously haven't given up.' Many of the protesters were carrying photographs of him and his wife.

Shahnaz seemed to sink into her seat, lost in thought. 'Why would the chief of police make so light of the fact that you killed two Iranians on the streets of Tehran?' she asked.

The same question had been troubling Harry. 'Because

whatever is happening here – whoever took Sean – he's in on it. That's why he looked nervous. And nothing can be allowed to interfere with their endgame.'

'What is it?'

Harry didn't answer. She had been through enough already today and he saw no point in alarming her further. He was concerned enough himself.

'Your death? Mine? Sean's? And you as a scapegoat?'

He certainly didn't want to quantify it like that. He had so long traded in death that his own demise held little fear. But the burden of responsibility for his son and the vibrant young woman beside him was heavier than he could possibly have imagined. As the engine idled, he wiped the sweat from his brow. 'I think I'm going to need to speak to your father.'

'You can't.'

'It doesn't have to involve you.'

'I said you can't and I meant it.'

'I thought you insisted you would do anything for Sean?'

She considered this. 'Not that.'

'Why not?'

'Because he would never help me. And he would never assist you if he thought it would benefit me. And because he is my father. So please . . . leave it.' The traffic was moving now.

Harry braked for a Bedford bus. There was a sleek new green Studebaker two-door sedan behind it, followed by a boxy blue and white Crosley station wagon, then a cart pulled by a donkey. A microcosm of a society, Harry thought, caught in the crosshairs of the past and the future.

He accelerated carefully around the cart and the traffic moved more freely down Pahlavi until they were almost at the station, when it began to clog up again. 'We can go right here,' Shahnaz said.

They turned into much narrower streets where the houses were packed close together and the children playing between them were reluctant to move out of the way. Most of the women were veiled in the *chador*. They passed the hulking iron structures of an oil storage depot, which towered over the primitive brick houses. A nearby tobacco factory belched acrid smoke. Harry tightened the window against the pungent fumes.

'I think it's just down here,' she said.

Harry turned into a wider alley. There were rows of shops on each side, with large canvas awnings. A street market sold fruit, meat and vegetables above an open drain, which ran beneath the tables. Children were playing in it. Shahnaz motioned Harry to stop and took a scarf from beneath her seat to cover her hair. She got out and asked an elderly man the way. She pointed further along the street and continued walking. The houses grew more substantial, with whitewashed walls, brick arches and thick oak doors.

Shahnaz came to a halt in front of the most imposing building in the road, a large white structure with a spacious balcony on the first floor. She put her head through the car window. 'None of the buildings have numbers, but I think this is it.'

Harry climbed out. A group of youths lounging against a wall eyed him with barely disguised hostility. Shahnaz pulled the scarf down tight over her forehead. 'Come on,' she said. 'We need to be careful here.' She hammered on the door. It cracked open and a young boy frowned at her, then stepped back to allow them in. He continued to eye Harry suspiciously.

They walked into an internal courtyard. A woman with lacquered hair and heavy make-up stood behind a counter with a picture of the Shah above it. Ochre walls were half covered with ornate mosaic tiles and, like the flagstone floor, were grimy with age. The house was three storeys tall with an iron balcony on each level. In the centre of the courtyard, men – some in uniform – sat on benches, chatting to younger women, mostly in polka-dot or patterned dresses, who were also heavily made up. Music from a wireless burbled in the corner quietly.

It was pretty obvious what kind of house this was. Harry could see the disgust in Shahnaz's eyes as she surveyed the faces of the waiting men. The older woman behind the counter had come around to face them, sensing some kind of challenge. A wad of *rials* protruded from the top of her dress and she spoke in rapid Farsi that Harry didn't understand.

Shahnaz held her ground and appeared to concede only when she had what she wanted. 'The place we need is the next building along. It's what they call a *koshane* – a kind of wrestling club cum gymnasium.'

As they left, Harry glanced up at a woman looking at them from the balcony above. Unlike the others, she was younger and barely half dressed. She had hollow, listless, lost eyes.

The oak door banged shut behind them as they were more or less shoved back into the street. 'What a horrible place,' Shahnaz whispered, and Harry didn't argue with her.

They moved along to the next building, which was at the end of the row. They knocked and, when there was no answer, stepped inside. In the main hall, about thirty young men were exercising with a wood and brass weight in each hand. Following an instructor, who stood at the front, they swung them up over their shoulders and down again in unison. After a few moments, they dropped to the floor and began to do press-ups. A drummer beat out encouragement, like an ancient slave driver. Shahnaz spoke to a pair who were resting on a bench, then reported back. 'They don't recall any white men coming to visit. And they say whoever's in charge of the gym isn't here.'

Harry sensed movement at the top of a stairwell in the far corner of the hall. A curtain was pulled back to allow a European in a cream suit to emerge. He hurried away through a nearby door.

' 'He's from the French Embassy,' Shahnaz whispered. 'I've seen him at parties.'

Harry moved to follow, but a couple of paces in, the drumbeat grew louder. The gymnasts sprang to their feet and swung the weights in rhythmic loops, effectively blocking his way. Every eye in the place was upon him. He raised his hands in apology. 'Let's get out of here.'

'What?'

He took her arm and marched her towards the door. 'I said let's get out.'

For a brief moment, he thought the men would round on them both, but then they were out on the street and the drumbeat receded as the door was yanked shut behind them.

'What do you think the Frenchman was doing there?' Shahnaz asked.

Harry turned left and left again, and led the way into the shadows. A wall blocked their passage. 'There must be another way in. Here, give me your foot.' He linked his hands and hauled her up so she could catch the top of the wall. She offered to assist him but he took a pace back, grabbed the ridge and they both scrambled into a yard on the other side.

The drumbeat seemed to slow. They drifted through light and shadow before reaching a flight of steps leading up to a wooden door bearing a small brass plate etched with the words 'Global Vision'. Shahnaz was about to climb them when Harry held up his hand. He moved back until he could see through an open window upstairs. Christine Audinette's husband, Pierre, was in conversation with William Oswald, Harry's colleague from London.

'What is it?' Shahnaz whispered. 'You look like someone just walked over your grave.'

Harry didn't answer. He hurried her back to the wall and helped her out. Shahnaz said nothing more until they were back inside the car. 'Who did you see?'

'Pierre Audinette, the Frenchman Sean played tennis with.'

'No, there was someone else.'

He glanced at his watch. 'We need to get back to the bazaar.'

'It was someone you knew. Someone from your past?'

My all-too-bloody-present, Harry thought. Oswald must have been on the plane after – or possibly even before – his own. 'We need to—'

'I'm trying to help you, Mr Tower. I'm not sure you really understand that.'

'I think it's time you called me Harry.'

Her eyes flashed and her silence spoke volumes. Like Amanda, he thought, she wasn't good at hiding her emotions. 'There is a reception at the French Club this evening,' she said. 'Sean and I were invited. Anyone who is anyone in Tehran will be there. Perhaps it would be an idea for us to attend.'

'Perhaps.'

It was growing dark by the time they reached the bazaar. Gas lamps in the tiny stores spilt light into labyrinthine alleyways where young men played dice games or hung around watching girls glide by. Shahnaz drew many admiring looks. The ironmongery was closed. Harry hammered on the door. He stepped back. The windows were boarded up. He looked at the shops around him. All still plied their trade.

A couple of youths watched from the store opposite. 'Please ask them where he is,' Harry said.

She eventually translated for him. 'The old man told them he would be away for two weeks.'

'Where has he gone?'

'They don't know.'

'Where can we find his son?'

'They haven't seen him.'

'Did anyone else visit his store today? The police, perhaps?'

She tried again. 'Not that they saw.'

Harry glanced up and down the street. 'Maybe you'd be

kind enough to tell them that I'm interested in buying a set of fire tongs.'

'I don't think—'

'Just tell them, please.'

She did so, and the bemused young men led him into their store. Harry made a show of looking around. He picked up a couple of ornate metal bowls. 'Fine work,' he said.

'Thank you,' the older one replied. He was slim and slightly effeminate.

'You speak English?' Harry asked him.

'A little.'

'I have just moved to Tehran. My friend is helping me buy some things for my apartment.' He grinned and the youth grinned back. Harry worked his way around the shop. He climbed to the top floor. It was dark up there, and before his guide could light a gas lamp Harry pushed him up against the wall. He placed the muzzle of the Colt under the young man's nose. 'Listen to me, please. I need some information. Nod if you understand.'

He did so.

'I'd like to know who came to the ironmonger's store today. And I want to know where the old man and his son have gone.'

'The police came . . . two officers.'

'What did they want?'

'I don't know.'

'After they'd gone, the old man packed up and left?'

'Yes.'

'Where is he now?'

'I don't know. Aaargh!' The cry died in his throat. 'I don't know. I swear it.'

'Where do we find his son?'

'I will show you. It . . . it is not far.'

He led Harry downstairs, ignored the questions posed by his friend and hurried out into the alley. Harry kept a close eye on him in the event he hadn't got the message, but he didn't seem to relish the idea of a bullet in the back.

The house they were looking for was a couple of blocks back from the western edge of the bazaar. The gleaming shark-fin roadster Harry had spotted in the car park earlier was waiting outside, its engine running. The front door was open and they found a young man in a white shirt and neatly pressed chinos carrying a bag down the stairs. 'You're Ahmed's son,' Harry said, as their guide vanished down the street. 'My name is Harry Tower. I—'

'I know who you are.'

'And this is Shahnaz Salemi.' He nodded at her. 'I spoke to your father this—'

'My father isn't here.'

'He's left town?' Harry glanced in the direction of the fleeing youth.

'Yes.' He looked at Harry, then Shahnaz, dropped his bag and offered his hand. 'My name is Reza. You'd better come in.'

He ushered them through to a sumptuous room decorated in red and gold, and strewn with carpets and cushions. 'I'm afraid I cannot offer you anything. Father sent away the servants before he departed.'

'Where has he gone?'

'We have a place on the Caspian.'

'Did he say why he had gone away?'

'Yes.'

'Members of the police department came calling?'

'Something like that.' He gazed at them for a moment, then waved his hand. 'Please . . . sit.' Once they had done so, he leant forward earnestly. He was a sleek man, with slicked-back hair, a prominent nose and hungry cheeks. 'Let me explain. You are a visitor here, so there is no reason why you should understand that Iran is really two countries. There are men like me, as yet few in number, who have been educated in Britain, or Paris, or the United States. We believe that our nation must modernize and use its vast potential wealth to ensure we join our friends in nations of the first rank in terms of power and civilization and affluence. But there is another Iran that has not changed since the days of Abbas Shah, a country that is corrupt, venal and brutal. Do I lie, Miss Salemi?'

'No,' she said. Harry's knowledge of Iranian history was good enough to understand that many Iranians still revered the Safavid king who had been the first great ruler in the centuries after the Arabs swept into the country, bringing Islam with them. But a man who'd had his eldest son murdered, then two other sons, two brothers and his father blinded, had also become a byword for torture and brutality. In all honesty, Harry thought the current Shah was likely to replicate the worst parts of Abbas Shah's reign, without the epoch-making economic and cultural revival that had gone with it.

'I have a good relationship with the chief of police. I think he is a decent man,' Reza went on. 'I flatter myself that I may be able to assist him in his attempts to modernize the force. But when two members of the department come to my father's door and tell him we would be advised to leave town for several weeks and not to speak to the foreigners again, what do I have to gain by fighting it?'

'Some service to the law.'

'But at what cost?'

'Who sent the men?'

'I don't know. If I did, perhaps we would not be having this conversation.'

'Soleimani?'

'That's highly unlikely.'

'Then who were they working for?' Reza shrugged. 'Did you look at the bullet?'

'My father sent a messenger with it this morning. A department of ballistics was the chief's idea. It was he who dispatched me to America to learn enough in Washington to make sure it was run with the best modern methods and thinking.'

'So you did see it?'

'Of course.'

'And you identified the weapon that fired it?'

'It was not difficult. A revolver of which I have had much recent experience.'

'The Colt?'

'Yes.'

Harry took the revolver out of his pocket and placed it on the table. 'The .45, 1952 issue?'

'Correct.'

'When you were in Washington, I assume you worked with the CIA?'

'Sometimes.'

'I don't understand,' Shahnaz said.

They looked at her. It was Reza who answered. 'The Colt .45 is the revolver most commonly issued to American government departments, like the Federal Bureau of Investigation and the CIA. It is an unusual weapon to find in this part of the world, so its use most likely suggests the involvement of the Americans – or another organization that wanted to give that impression. The KGB, for example, routinely likes to leave a trail that would lead the naive to assume Washington was responsible for an operation.'

'Would you have the bullet?' Harry asked.

Reza hesitated. 'I am afraid not.'

'Could you get it for me?'

'No.'

'Who came to see you this afternoon? Meshang Rashidian?' Reza didn't blink. 'He wasn't alone, was he? There was a man with him? An Englishman, with excessive nasal hair and a narrow face.'

'I'm afraid I must go now. My father will be wondering what has become of me.' Reza moved to the door and held it open for them. Once Harry had gone through it, he said, 'I think you should consider the possibility that your presence here is making your son's predicament worse, Mr Tower.'

'In what way?'

'I think you probably know the answer to that. And, believe me, I'm trying to be helpful.'

16

SHAHNAZ FELL INTO step alongside Harry. 'Who is the colleague you were talking about?' She gripped his arm, forcing him to a halt. 'Please . . . I am very grateful for what you did earlier today. I'd like to think what happened might finally have earned me your trust.'

'I saw someone from my organization. The kind of colleague I'd prefer not to encounter here. He must have come out just before or after me, which again implies a degree of planning and forethought.'

'Who is he?'

Harry turned over Oswald's presence again. He didn't answer until they were almost out of the bazaar. 'After I joined the Service, I was posted to Berlin. I'd studied for a time in a place called Göttingen and spoke the language fluently. The office in the German capital was full of fairly indifferent officers and mostly useless agents. But we did have one source who managed to get close to some of the senior Nazis. He even got the station chief and me invited along to Nuremberg and introduced us to Himmler and Heydrich.

'He liked to pass himself off as a scion of the British upper classes, but he was actually a Lithuanian aristocrat, one Wilhelm Ostrowski, now Oswald – known to every-one in London as Oz – who had fallen on hard times and detested the Russians. He'd fought in the British Army in the Great War, then drifted across to Berlin, where he made a living as a small-time trader and crook. My superiors in London thought the world of him and we had to suffer the revolting spectacle of a steady flow of visitors – from senior officers in the Service, to Whitehall officials, to the many MPs and idle aristocrats who thought there was some-thing to be said for the Nazis – being royally escorted around the Reich's ministries by Oz.

'Once the Second World War broke out, he managed to get across to Switzerland and then back to England, where they decided to take him into the Service. I never trusted him and mostly avoided him, but they parked him in Operations, and after 'forty-five it became difficult to avoid our paths periodically crossing. It did not improve our relationship.'

'So what does it mean that he is here?'

'He is a man without scruple. So it means their pursuit of me – or conceivably of Sean and me – is, for whatever reason, a serious affair.'

'But why not arrest you in London?'

Harry stared at the ground for a moment, contemplating again just how much it was wise, sensible or fair to tell her. He took out the letter he always carried in his pocket and handed it to her. She opened it and started to read. 'This is to inform you that the bearer of this letter is a personal, confidential representative of Prime Minister Winston Churchill. I would be grateful if you would offer him all possible assistance and treat his word as my own.'

'When I returned from Berlin, they didn't have a role for me and I was assigned to some dead-end task, managing a group of cryptographers in a backwater called Bletchley Park. But one of them turned out to be a brilliant mathematician and he, with his team, managed to break the Germans' supposedly unbreakable Enigma codes. It allowed us to read the minds of our enemies throughout the war. Even though it had precious little to do with SIS, we managed to make ourselves the funnel through which this information was fed into Whitehall. The prime minister saw its value very early on and I was instructed to come up personally to brief him. We remained close during the war years. It was his idea to send me to Yugoslavia to make contact with Tito. That was what the letter was for. So, to arrest and interrogate me in London would be politically complicated, to say the least. But . . .' Harry shook his head in confusion. He was still trying to assess the shifting sands of Whitehall's complex politics. '. . . the prime minister's hold on power is more tenuous, his world view steadily going out of fashion.' Harry tucked the letter back into his pocket. 'Perhaps this is not quite the lucky charm it once was.'

He strode on in silence until they reached the door of Sean's office. He ushered her through and pulled it shut behind them. Nazadeh was waiting patiently upstairs. 'Oh, Mr Tower, I was not sure you would come!'

'I'm sorry, Nazadeh.' He glanced at the clock.

'I was getting worried about you.' She turned to pick up a notebook.

Harry sat on the edge of Sean's desk. 'Did you have any success?'

'Can I get you tea? Or something to eat?'

'No, you need to go home. Just tell us what you've found out.'

'The telephone company did not want to cooperate. They said I would need written authorization from the chief of police. I said they could call his office, but he would not like to be put to any inconvenience on this matter. They agreed, but it will still take a number of days, I'm afraid. I pushed them as far as I was able.'

'That's fine, Nazadeh.'

'You asked me to make a note of their movements in the days before they disappeared. I spoke to Ali's mother and tried to fill the gaps from my own memory.'

'Just tell us what you have.'

'I went back as far as Wednesday, the seventh of August. The day his article on the drugs trade was published. Sean had sent it early the morning before and stayed in the office until nightfall. He spoke to the foreign editor on the telephone and they exchanged several long messages via the telex. On the Wednesday, he came in early. I think he was expecting some sort of response from London.'

'And?'

'There was a message from the foreign editor saying how happy they were. He passed on congratulations from the editor. Mr Tower read it to me. He seemed very pleased.'

Harry nodded, willing her to continue.

'I was just making some tea when Ali arrived. They were both as happy as I've seen them. They went off to have a cup of coffee and breakfast, as usual, while I tidied the office.' She breathed in deeply. 'Shortly after he came back, Sean received a telephone call. I answered it.' She glanced at Shahnaz. 'It was from a French woman. I tried not to listen to the call, of course, but . . .'

'It's all right,' Harry said.

'It seemed at first as if she was congratulating him.'

'How did he respond?'

'He said things like, "That's a secret . . ." But he was laughing. Then he grew angry. He took the phone out onto the balcony, but Ali and I could still hear what he was saying. There was an argument.'

'About what?'

'I don't know. I was embarrassed. I tried not to listen. But he kept on repeating, "That's a lie." A few minutes later, the phone rang again. This time it was a French man. Sean also took that call on the balcony. But the tone was still tense. And a few minutes after that, the woman called again. At least, I believe she did. I did not answer the telephone. Sean told her, "You wouldn't do that," and called her a liar again – a number of times.'

'Did the French woman ring here often?' Harry asked.

Nazadeh glanced at Shahnaz again. 'Quite often, yes.'

'Every day?'

'Almost every day, yes.'

'And did the man who called give a name?'

'No.'

'Did you recognize his voice?'

'Yes. He called from time to time, about once a week, I should say. He came in here a few times to see Sean, but he never gave a name.'

'Then what happened?'

'Shortly afterwards, Sean and Ali went off to the bank.'

'Which one?'

'The Bank Melli. It is not far from here.'

'Why did they go there?'

'I don't know. They did not say. They were not there long the first time. But they returned to the bank after lunch and I did not see them again until the evening, as I was preparing to go home. They seemed excited. Mr Tower tried to place a call to the office in London, but it did not come through.'

Harry picked up the note he had seen earlier.

666074 – $27,000
650193 – $17,000
423837 – $11,000

'Did he get this from the bank?'

'I'm very sorry, I did not notice. The fans had broken again and I thought Mr Tower would be upset if I did not fix them before the end of the day. It is so hot at this time of year.'

'So you next saw him the following morning?'

'Yes. I was the first into the office. I had the impression that Mr Tower had started to play tennis again, because his cheeks were red. He asked me to contact London and arrange payment for the article that had been published the day before. I . . .'

'We need to know everything, Nazadeh.'

'Mr Tower was usually out for at least an hour for break-fast, so I went to a doctor across the square to get medicine for my son. He was ill, you see, and . . .' her gaze flicked towards Shahnaz '. . . I was just walking past the entrance to the bazaar when I saw Mr Tower waiting in the shadows. He looked . . . nervous. I was about to call out when a car pulled up. Mr Tower got into the back. Then they drove away.'

'Who was at the wheel?'

'A man.' She shook her head in frustration. 'I'm sorry. It happened so quickly.'

'A white man?'

'Yes.'

'What did he look like?'

'He was wearing sunglasses. He had long hair. Curly dark hair.'

'Had you seen him before?'

'No.'

Shahnaz again was suddenly transfixed by the ground beneath her feet.

'Was anyone else in the car?'

'I don't believe so.'

'How long was he gone for?'

'All day.'

'Are you sure?'

'Yes. Ali came into the office later and asked where he, Mr Tower, was. I said that I did not know. Mr Tower returned a few minutes before I left that evening. That was when I heard them talking about Doshtan Street.'

'Did he say where he'd been?'

'No.'

'So that was Thursday?'

'Yes. On Fridays, obviously I don't work. I was at home. On Saturday I came in early, because a friend of my husband had promised to mend the fans. That was the day Mr Tower and Ali went to the prime minister's press conference.'

Harry moved to the window. 'Have you got any idea at all who the man in that car was, Nazadeh?'

'No, sir.'

'Was it the Frenchman? The one who called here?'

'No.'

'Are you sure?'

'Yes, sir.'

Harry picked up Sean's pad, rooted around in the drawer for a pencil and started to make notes. Both Nazadeh and Shahnaz watched him. He faced the open window and stared out over the uneven rooftops. He looked down into the street, where a group of children was being chased by a pack of noisy dogs. A carpet seller staggered home with his wares.

Harry turned around. 'Nazadeh, please keep on at the telephone company. Call them three or four times a day until they give us what we want.' He held up the sheet he'd taken from Sean's desk. 'We'll deal with the bank.'

He closed the window. 'Now you need to get home.' Harry came to sit behind his son's desk, picked up the silver letter-opener he had given him before his departure and tapped a pile of books, deep in thought. Shahnaz watched him as Nazadeh quietly slipped out. 'If you are still working with the British Secret Intelligence Service,' Shahnaz said, 'why would the presence of one of your colleagues from London so alarm you? Wouldn't you expect to see them here in the middle of a coup they are organizing?'

'The coup was our idea, it's true. But Churchill wanted to be able to deny British involvement convincingly. It's being run by the Americans and we were instructed to make sure no one was in theatre.' Shahnaz looked confused. 'In the country,' he clarified.

'Did they know you were coming out here?' Harry shook his head. 'Does it mean your friends in British intelligence instructed others to kidnap Sean?'

'It might.' Harry didn't want to go further than this. Despite what Christine had said to him the night before, he didn't want paranoia to get the better of him. Perhaps Sean *had* run foul of the gangs of south Tehran and their allies in the city's police force, after all.

'Nice business you're in,' Shahnaz said. She moved wearily to a chair opposite him and sat down with a deep sigh. 'A whole lifetime of it?' She seemed to consider this for a while, then tilted her head to one side. 'You said you met Himmler and Heydrich?'

'Yes.'

'What were they like?'

'Depressingly unremarkable. The crimes they committed were not easily forgotten, but those men were. In my experience, a catastrophic lack of empathy is rarely interesting up close.'

'And what about Churchill?'

'The exact reverse. Complicated. Difficult. Bloody-minded but brilliant. Flawed. Human. Immensely charismatic, even when I didn't agree with him.'

'And Tito?'

'That's enough ancient history for now.'

'What did you do here in Tehran, exactly?'

'I was only in the country for a few months, organizing the tribes to help expel the Soviets in the event they invaded.'

'Did you meet my father?'

She took his silence as consent and appeared to spend a moment calibrating it. 'What did you do after the war? Where did you serve?'

'I moved around. I was tasked with establishing intelligence networks behind the Iron Curtain. Part of my problem now is that it's clear many were compromised from the beginning. We dropped agents behind enemy lines in the Balkans, but later learnt that nearly all of them had been picked up and shot. One of the operations I was involved in, at a place called Mount Avala in Yugoslavia, was the greatest disaster in the history of the Service.'

'Why?'

'We arranged to parachute royalist soldiers in to try to depose Tito. But his partisans knew we were coming.'

'And because you worked with Tito in the war, you were blamed?'

'Officially it was deemed to be intercepted radio traffic or one of the soldiers having been a secret Communist spy, but . . .' He stood. 'Come on.'

'Where are we going?'

'I need to place a call.'

'Can't you use the office line?'

'Somewhere I know no one is listening.'

'Nazadeh has gone home.'

'I mean no one *else* is listening.'

'Oh . . . okay. We can go to the central exchange build-ing. It's probably easier to walk from here.'

Outside, the heat was still relentless and every door was open in search of the faintest hint of a breeze. Families gathered for dinner, cooking, cleaning, arguing. Here and there beneath the awnings, tradesmen could still be seen counting their takings or packing away their wares. Dogs hunted in the alleys for scraps of food or drank from the drains. They walked up Naser Khosrow Street, past the grand and imposing Ministry of Finance building. This area, the central business district of the city, was more or less deserted. It was as if the tumult of the last few days had never happened. 'Who was the man in the car Naza-deh mentioned?' Harry said.

'I was going to ask you.'

'You have no idea?'

'No.'

'Are you sure about that?'

She turned to face him. 'Yes, I am.'

As they walked on, he was struck by two thoughts: that she was lying, and that she was not very good at it.

They reached the telephone exchange, a cavernous and gloomy building with high ceilings and a stone floor. The cubicles for making calls stretched all along one wall. 'Wait here,' she said. 'It's quieter than usual, so it shouldn't take too long. You'll have to give me the number.'

Harry wrote it on a piece of paper and she joined a

queue by the counter. He looked up at a picture of the Shah on the wall, proudly displayed under a sign celebrating the National Iranian Telephone Company.

He sat on one of the benches. A young woman in a cream dress waited in the cubicle closest to him but otherwise the room was full of men in cheap Western suits. They watched him curiously. Shahnaz returned. 'Cubicle ten. But don't hold your breath. It can take up to an hour for the call to come through.'

'I understand.'

'I'll wait here.'

'I'd rather you were outside.'

She frowned, but did not demur. 'If you insist.'

Harry stared at the ceiling and looked at the men in the room watching him. The phone rang after about thirty-five minutes. 'I'm guessing that must be you, Harry.'

'Thanks for taking the call.'

'Where the hell are you?'

'Let's cut the charade, Ed.' There was a long silence. Harry and Haddon went so far back that he had occasionally sensed a hint of meaningful comradeship between them, even if it was filtered through the prism of his superior's ambition. 'I can't speak to you, Harry. You said you were going to Paris, for God's bloody sake. And now they tell me you're in Tehran. You need to get out of there. They've been to Göttingen. That's all I can say. Leave. And leave now.'

'Listen, Ed—'

'No. You listen to me. If you want to know what's happened to your son . . .'

The connection faded for a second. Harry waited until it returned. 'Where is he, Ed?'

'Get out, Harry. That's all I can tell you.'

'What's Oz doing here?'

'You must—'

The connection was severed and Harry listened to the static for a moment before he replaced the receiver.

'Damn,' he said, under his breath.

17

Mount Avala, near Belgrade, November 1945

'LIE STILL, FOR Christ's sake . . .'

Haddon was vibrating with anxiety beside him and, after a night of waiting, it was starting to grate on Harry's nerves.

'How much longer?'

'And be quiet.'

The mist cleared for a moment. Harry wiped the lenses of the binoculars with his shirt cuff and peered through them but could still see nothing. He scratched the beard that had grown so long these past months that the partisans had taken to calling him Rasputin. It occurred to him that even Amanda and Sean would struggle to pick him out of a crowd. Whenever he caught a glimpse of himself in a mirror, he wasn't even sure he recognized himself.

'Something must have happened,' Haddon whispered.

'They'll be here.'

A gust of wind swept the light drizzle hard into their faces, but the movement behind it was unmistakable. Harry raised the binoculars again. 'They're here.'

Haddon tried to get to his feet, but Harry grabbed hold of his belt and yanked him back. 'What the—?'

'Let them find us.'

'How?'

Harry watched as the parachutes spiralled down into the long grass. He waited while the newcomers gathered their lines. Harry let out a low whistle and the men began to jog towards him. '*Zdravo!*' they chorused.

'*Dobrodošli,*' Harry whispered.

'What took you so damned long?' Haddon asked.

Harry was already on his feet. 'Let's go.'

Without looking back, he set off. As he ran, he could hear the soft footfall of the men behind him and the steady drip of rainwater from the pines. Other than that, the forest was eerily quiet in the hours before dawn.

They weaved through the trees and went to ground by the next clearing. The sky was filled with parachutes – perhaps two dozen in all – and a few seconds later the first had floated down into the meadow.

'We're in business,' Haddon said.

One of the royalist soldiers beside him whistled once and waved to indicate that his comrades should join them in the shelter of the trees.

It looked like an orderly procession, as if an invisible thread were quietly drawing all the men into one corner of the meadow, until machine-gun fire shattered the silence.

The young men closest to them were the first to be cut

down. One of the soldiers lying next to Harry cried out and scrambled to his feet. Harry grabbed him, stared into his startled eyes, but the lad shook himself free and charged out into the clearing. The others went with him. They had almost reached their fallen comrades before they were mown down.

Harry pushed himself upright and started to run back in the direction from which they had come. A few moments later, he realized Haddon was not with him. He retraced his steps to find him staring at the slaughter in shock. Harry gripped his fellow agent by the scruff of the neck and yanked him to his feet. He saw the terror in his face. 'Run,' he said, with steely understatement. 'Run for your life.'

Haddon needed no further encouragement. They hurtled back towards the path that had brought them up there two hours previously. As they reached it, Harry turned. 'We must try to warn the others. You take the third landing site, I'll take the last.'

'But they'll be there! We've been betrayed!'

'We have to try.'

Harry pushed him on and, as he watched him being swallowed by the gloom, he was as certain as he could be that Haddon would make no attempt to warn the dozens of royalist soldiers now drifting down towards them.

Harry turned right off the path and moved down towards the clearing on the mountain's western slope. The meadow was just visible through the trees and he stood and watched the first parachute drift into view. He could not hear any sound around him. He scanned the shadows, but saw nothing amiss. He moved forward again, broke a twig and heard an immediate cry. A soldier materialized beside him, his face blacked up. Harry reached for his pistol. Too late: there were others.

He charged at them, bursting through the centre of the group. He swerved to the right, where the ground quickly fell away. He heard another shout – a barked order – but the gunman hesitated long enough for his bullets to do no more than spray the branches above Harry's head.

He didn't look back. He sprinted out of the wood and across the far corner of the clearing, the drizzle on his face, the first hint of sunlight creeping over the horizon ahead of him. As he ran, all he could hear were the fusillades sweeping in across the meadow at his back, a massacre ushering in the dawn of a new era.

18

Tehran, August 1953

'WHAT HAPPENED?' SHAHNAZ asked, when they got back to the Ford Popular outside the bazaar.

'Nothing.'

'That seems unlikely. Can I help?'

'You can drive me to the French Club and stop bombarding me with questions for a couple of minutes.'

She quieted, which gave Harry time to think, but it didn't help much. He wondered if Haddon, far from engaging in a rare act of fellowship, had actually been trying to unsettle him. Why mention Göttingen? What was there to find there?

Of course, they would have guessed he would call, if only to try to assess the lie of the land back home. And he would obviously have chosen Haddon, with whom he went so far back. Who else was there? Being a loner had its drawbacks.

Harry told himself to hold his nerve, as he always had, to trust his judgement and his ability to outwit his foes. In her more critical moments, Amanda had called this his 'defining arrogance', which was the accusation he liked least. Even now – after all that had happened – he didn't like to concede she might have been right.

Shahnaz slowed as they reached the north end of Ferdowsi Avenue. 'Checkpoint,' she muttered.

Vehicles were being filtered through very slowly and it was more than twenty minutes before they reached the head of the queue. A truck ahead carried a group of casual labourers, all of whom were ordered to lie on the ground, where they were closely searched. The truck was loaded again and continued onwards. A young officer ordered them forward. 'Where are you going?'

'The French Club.'

'Passports.'

Harry could make out something burning ahead. 'What's going on?'

'Troublemakers.'

'What kind?'

'They burnt the home of a government minister.' The man waved them through.

They swung slowly onto Shahreza Avenue and drove past the burning house. A group of firemen sprayed water on it from a single hose. They didn't look as if they were trying too hard to put it out. Half a dozen servants ran to and from the swimming-pool with buckets of water through a thick pall of smoke that drifted up and over the treetops. 'Whose house is it?' Harry asked.

'I don't know. They said on the radio earlier that the

Shah was in Rome telling everyone he needed a job because he has a large family to support. He really is a spineless pig. Do your superiors know what a straw man they are backing here?'

'All choices are relative.'

'You'd think standing by democracy was an absolute, but what do I know?'

They lapsed into silence until Shahnaz catapulted the Popular through the entrance to the French Club. Liveried doormen leapt forward to open the doors and spirit it away. She gave a wry smile and gestured towards the gleaming new American and European vehicles that filled the forecourt to underline the contrast.

She led him across the pristine black and white checked floor of the lobby and out onto a terrace glittering with flickering candles. The air was still but for the hubbub of conversation and the tinkle of water in a giant fountain. Most guests were spread around the swimming-pool and the lawn beyond it. A couple of servants tended a bar, while a platoon of them manned the buffet table beneath a striped awning. All were dressed in crisp white uniforms with red braid.

The garden was protected by a high wall, but the price of privacy was the absence of even a hint of breeze. Every face he could see in the candlelight glistened with sweat.

Harry caught sight of Christine immediately. She wore a light blue cotton dress, which Amanda would have described as fitting where it touched. And it touched everywhere.

Shahnaz followed his eyeline. 'Do you want a drink?' she asked, with a smirk.

Harry didn't answer. He lit a cigarette and met the Frenchwoman's cool gaze. He glanced at her husband, deep in conversation with a group of men beneath the awning. One of them was Meshang Rashidian. As Harry approached, they made space for him. '*Bonsoir, Monsieur Tower.*' Pierre Audinette shook his hand. 'Monsieur Rashidian I believe you know.'

Rashidian dipped his head.

The Frenchman gestured at a silver-haired man with film-star looks and an immaculately sculpted Douglasie moustache. 'And you will also remember Adel Salemi, friend of the Shah.'

Salemi smiled easily. He wore a pristine white dinner jacket. 'It is good to see you again, Mr . . . Freeman was it back then? I believe you have had the pleasure of being escorted around Tehran on this visit by my daughter.'

'She is a spirited woman.'

'That's one way of putting it. But which among us can claim to have any control over our children?'

'She has been helping me find my son.'

'Ah, yes. We were all very concerned to hear the news of his disappearance. I am sure he will turn up well – and soon – but if there is anything I can do, please do not hesitate to ask.'

'Where can I find you?'

'These days I am mostly at Latak, our farm. Shahnaz can bring you there.'

'Did you hear, Mr Tower,' Rashidian said, 'that the left-ists have just burnt down a house belonging to a member of the cabinet? Now they are even attacking their own!' He shook his head. 'They do not know what they are doing. It is anarchy, nothing more or less.'

'They wish to create the appearance of chaos to give their Moscow paymasters the excuse to step in, to restore order,' Salemi said. He was looking at Harry. 'Isn't that what you warned me might happen, even after we managed to expel them from Tabriz at the end of the war? You were right. And here we are again, on the edge of the abyss. The Soviets will not give up until they have Iran and our oil within their grasp.'

'We have intelligence tonight that the Russians *are* massing troops on the border,' Audinette added.

Harry doubted that. He wondered if Pierre Audinette believed it.

'It may be that General Salemi here, and those who have the good sense to think like him, are all that now stand between us and catastrophe,' Rashidian said. 'A sentiment, Mr Tower, I'm sure you would share?'

Harry kept his eyes fixed on Salemi's grin. It was hard to avoid the sense that this group somehow deferred to him. And that the conversation – a stilted recital of truths all participants took to be self-evident – was really for the discreet group of diplomats and Tehran notables who surrounded them, half listening while pretending to engage in conversations of their own. Anyone who was anyone knew the power that this group wielded.

'The Russians will enter Tehran to "save" democracy,' Audinette continued. 'They will chastise the British for having stolen Iran's oil and its natural resources and cheated its citizens. They will say they are here to rescue the great national leader Mohammed Mossadegh from the reactionary Shah and his Western patrons. They will say he's Iran's Gandhi, which we all know to be absurd but is a notion easily maintained in the gullible columns of most newspapers. And when the world once more turns its attention elsewhere, and students across the globe have grown bored of rallying in support of this great democratic moment, they will find a leader who is more "in tune" with the wishes of Moscow.'

'Mossadegh is a pawn,' Rashidian said, 'a particularly naive and foolish one at that.'

Shahnaz arrived, carrying a cocktail for Harry. She did not meet her father's eye.

'In the end,' Salemi said, 'in our hour of need, it is about whether one is loyal to one's king and country. And I am sure we all stand united in our dislike of *dis*loyalty.'

'Don't you mean disobedience?' Shahnaz said. 'Isn't that what you really detest? And, in your mind, aren't they the same thing?'

Salemi did not blink. 'My daughter likes to be provocative.'

'Truthful. Some people find that challenging.'

'My daughter is very certain of the world and her place in it, Mr Tower.'

Shahnaz persisted, 'I am just saying that an honest leader trying to do the best for his people deserves our support. I can't really understand what is controversial or provocative about that.'

'There is more than one type of leader,' Salemi said, his voice beginning to sound strained, 'and numerous different ways to do the best for your people.'

'But only one type of elite, the kind that thinks only of its rights and privileges and ways to entrench them.'

'Have we finished with the student lectures?' Salemi said, his urbane mask slipping. 'We have more serious matters to discuss.'

'Like how to get richer? As if any of you need it.'

Salemi looked for a brief moment as if he might explode. Then he bowed his head curtly and departed. The men who had been discreetly listening to the conversation seemed to melt away with him.

'Was it something I said?' she asked.

Rashidian smiled at her. 'I can see why your father finds you such an intoxicating presence, Miss Salemi. Life could never be dull in your company.' He nodded at Harry. 'Mr Tower.'

'I see you have mastered the art of diplomacy,' Harry said.

'And you of sycophancy.'

Harry rewarded her with a wry smile. 'You didn't tell me your father would be here.'

'I told you he is the plaything of shahs and right-wing generals. This is his natural habitat.'

'He has never struck me as anyone's fool.'

'I never said he was.' She sipped her drink. 'But he is undone by ambition. And the rest of them hitch their wagons to his star. Isn't that right, Pierre?'

'He is your father, Miss Salemi,' Audinette said. 'Surely—'

'He wants a doormat for a daughter. I can't be that.'

'Yes,' he said. 'I believe we all see that.'

Shahnaz put down her glass and turned to Harry. 'I'm

afraid this is not *my* natural habitat. I'll wait for you in the car.'

Harry noticed that Adel Salemi's gaze remained fixed on her departure from his new conversation at the far side of the garden. 'I am glad she is not *my* daughter,' Audinette said quietly. 'She really is quite a handful.'

'So is any child worth having.'

Audinette smiled at him. It wasn't wholly convincing. 'It is good to see you again, Harry.'

'And you.' Harry made a point of savouring his cocktail. 'I'm glad to have a moment alone with you. I wanted to ask what you were arguing with my son about on the day after his article on the drugs trade was published.'

Pierre Audinette took a few paces towards the flowerbed, so that they were out of earshot. 'It was not an argument.'

'It sounded like one to the rest of his office.'

'I felt that your son had abused a confidence. He knew of the story about the narcotics trade only because of me. We had been gossiping, I thought idly, after tennis one morning. I did not expect to read about it in his newspaper.'

Harry doubted that. Audinette never gossiped idly. 'He's a journalist, Pierre. Isn't that what they're supposed to do?'

'Even so, he abused a confidence. I was not impressed.'

'What happens in Doshtan Street?'

Audinette gazed into his cocktail. 'I have no idea.'

'My son went to visit a gymnasium there shortly before he disappeared. We saw one of your diplomats leaving it this afternoon. You were there, too.'

The Frenchman glanced across the throng to where Rashidian and Shahnaz's father were now locked in conversation again. 'What is Global Vision?' Harry asked.

'A charity.'

'What does it do?'

'It distributes money to the poor in Tehran's slums. My government is a donor.'

'Then tell me this: what was Sean arguing about with your wife?'

'I have no idea. Who told you they argued about anything?'

Harry weighed his growing irritation carefully. He should have known that here at the epicentre of super-power rivalry, with so much at stake, no one would be straight about anything. 'All right, let's drop the charade, if you don't mind. Sean is still out there and I want him back. He told your wife repeatedly, "That's a lie." What was a lie?' The Frenchman shook his head. He glanced over Harry's shoulder. 'What was a lie, Pierre? Come on, I need your help.'

Audinette put down his glass and beckoned Harry to follow him. They passed a table laden with food, where a half-eaten fish bejewelled with glazed fruits had pride of place, ducked through French windows and down steep stone steps. The basement was cavernous and empty, save for a scattering of rattan sofas. The walls had been newly painted. A dozen records leant against a new gramophone on a dresser. 'We always end with dancing,' Audinette explained. He was a tall man, with a stoop that had become exaggerated since they'd last met.

'I can hardly wait,' Harry said.

Audinette glanced nervously at the stairs. 'I was asked not to tell you about this.'

'About what?'

'It was rumoured that your son's business here was not what it seemed.'

'Meaning?'

'It was suggested . . . that he might have had a relation-ship with the Russians.'

'By whom?'

'I can't tell you more than that.'

'The British? The Americans?'

'On . . . the circuit. That's all I can say. I was told that your son was working with the KGB and might have wanted to make himself scarce while the Russian takeover happens here. I am, of course, aware of what you and your American colleagues are trying to pull off, even if you have chosen not to do us the courtesy of sharing any of your plans. But you heard what was said upstairs. Russian troops *are* massing on the border. They have paid agitators all over the city.' Harry still didn't believe it and he wasn't sure Audinette did either. 'You have witnessed their activ-ities, no doubt. You have seen the house burning tonight. They are trying to give the appearance that this country is ungovernable so they have an excuse to step in.'

'Joe Stalin has only just died,' Harry said. 'We hear the men of Moscow Centre are focusing all their energy on trying to work out who will be held responsible for send-ing so many people to the gulags.'

Audinette shook his head, refusing to be swayed. 'Things have moved on.'

'Who told you my son was working for the Russians?'

'It was a rumour, discussed among colleagues. I was angry that morning at the breach of confidence and it was in that context that I accused him. He became . . . upset . . .'

'What did he say?'

'That it was preposterous. Ludicrous.'

'Did your wife make the same accusation?'

'I told her over breakfast that morning. She didn't believe me.'

'Is it possible she had a brief affair with my son?'

'If so, he was in good company.'

Harry gave him an acid smile. 'I see you have not lost your gallantry.'

'My wife is an independent woman. She goes her own way and I applaud it.'

Harry doubted this, too, but it didn't seem an argument worth having. 'Why was my son "rumoured" to be working for the Russians?'

'It was said that he had been recruited at Cambridge, and dropped out on the orders of his KGB masters.'

'To join a provincial newspaper? There's no end to their cunning.'

'A provincial newspaper that sent him to what they view as a significant theatre of proxy war. Is it not the case that the articles your son chose to write tended to highlight the malign nature of Western influence here – the way in which the British have stolen Iran's oil, the manner in which diplomats have encouraged a vile trade in drugs?'

'That's obviously what he thought.'

'Or what he was encouraged to believe.'

It was Harry's turn to glance up the stairs. 'The Russians aren't interested in kids like my son.'

'Monsieur—'

'You know it, so do I.'

Audinette shook his head. 'Perhaps you have not been in the field enough in recent months. The rules are changing by the day.'

Harry suddenly felt the weight of a lifetime of half-truths, smokescreens and lies. 'Is Shahnaz's father the man I'm really looking for?'

'What do you mean?'

'Someone has provided the Shah with a backbone and liaised with the Americans and the Rashidians here in the bazaar. Salemi is the man I would have chosen if it was my operation.'

'The Shah appointed General Zahedi to be prime minister at the height of the coup—'

'Zahedi is a figurehead, we both know that.'

Audinette shrugged. 'I agree. Salemi is a very dangerous man.'

'The kind to build a lucrative trade in narcotics all the way through to the capitals of Europe?'

Beads of sweat glistened on Audinette's brow in the half-light of the basement. 'I don't know the answer to that.'

'Did you tell Sean it was the police to try to keep your friend and ally Salemi out of it?'

Audinette wiped his forehead. 'I've really done my best to help you, Harry. I urge you to exercise caution in the way you proceed. Whatever you may think, I care about Sean. There is nothing more I can do for you.' The Frenchman turned to go. Harry listened to the squeak of his rubber-soled shoes on the steps. He leant against the dresser and exhaled.

Harry placed his forehead against the cool stone wall, closed his eyes. Fatigue was like a lead weight within him. It had been a long few days, but he knew it was so much more than that. When had he last had a restful night's sleep? He couldn't honestly say.

He felt a hand on his shoulder and spun round. 'Are you all right?' Christine's skin glowed. 'We should talk,' she said. 'Somewhere we cannot be overheard.'

She took his arm and led him deeper into the basement. She retreated into a wine cellar, closed the door.

The skin on her shoulders and neck glistened with a thin sheen of sweat. There was an ethereal quality to her gaze, the product, Harry thought, of some kind of narcotic. For a moment, he thought she might try to kiss him, but that was not what she had in mind at all. 'I heard tonight that Sean and his translator have been killed.'

Harry stared at her. He could feel the colour rising in his cheeks. 'What?'

'I'm sorry, Harry, but I thought it better you heard it from me.'

'Who told you this?'

'A reliable source in the military. He has been working for us for a year, but our contact is infrequent, at his insistence. We met today and that is what he told me. Sean and Ali were shot the day they were taken.'

'That's not possible.' Harry watched the twitch in her left eyelid, a sign of stress he had witnessed before. She gazed at the floor, but he lifted her chin until her eyes were level with his own. 'You think I don't know you're playing me, Christine?'

'I'm trying to give you the chance to save yourself while

you still can,' she said. 'I loved you, Harry. Did you know that? I mean, really loved you.'

He'd suspected it. They'd had a long trip to meet tribal leaders in which her feelings for him had been increasingly obvious. But he had been unable to reciprocate. For all that Amanda's mental instability had often made him howl to a God he did not believe in, he had never stopped loving her. Not for a single second. 'So was sleeping with my son your revenge?' Harry asked.

'Perhaps.'

'Twisted, don't you think?'

'Mixed up. Lesser human beings than Harry Tower can be like that.'

'You think that is how I see myself?'

'I don't know. It's very hard to get close enough to work out who you think you are. I hope Amanda managed it. But, from what your son told me, I rather doubt it.'

'I'd appreciate it if you didn't bring Amanda into this.' She was avoiding his gaze. 'What are you really doing here, Christine?'

'My job.'

Harry shook his head, as if answering his own question. He'd been thinking about what might align the ambitions and interests of men as avaricious and singular as Adel Salemi, Pierre Audinette and Meshang Rashidian. 'Not building a narcotics trade. That's too grubby even for Pierre. But oil? For the French government, perhaps for you personally, for the men gathered here in this garden tonight, that is a business worth any kind of gamble. The men – or women – who control Iran's oil supply here will be wealthy beyond the dreams of avarice.'

She didn't deny it.

'Which brings me to another conclusion that has been creeping up on me,' Harry said. 'That Sean was a better journalist than I imagined. Perhaps he was on to something here and you all decided you had to deal with him. And because you knew I *would* find the truth, you now have to find a way to set me up as well.'

Even as he said it, Harry worried that this was self-delusion. It was so much easier to imagine that what had been set in train here was Sean's doing and not a consequence of his own actions.

'Why does it matter now if he's dead?' She ripped herself free from his grasp, tore open the door and ran down the corridor.

19

SHAHNAZ KEPT HER distance while they waited for the bell-boy to bring the car, and they left the silence unbroken until they joined the queue for the first checkpoint. 'If those are your people,' she said, 'then God help us all.'

'They're not my people and never have been.'

'Then who are?'

At one time, it had been a question Harry wouldn't answer. Now it was one he couldn't. In a lifetime of striving for meaning, that was the sum total of his achievement.

There were more fires burning along Shahreza Avenue and most vehicles were being turned back. A soldier bent to look in through the window and waved them straight through.

Grenville and another man were waiting for them at the hotel. 'Mr Tower,' Grenville said, 'I'd be grateful if we could have a word in private.'

'Of course. Come up to my room.' Harry offered his

hand to Grenville's companion, a squat, bespectacled man in chinos and a sports shirt, with a thick manila envelope under his arm.

'Bill Bryant.' The accent was soft, American.

Grenville halted them before they reached the lift. He glanced around the deserted lobby. The sound of someone singing at the piano drifted across from the bar. 'Mr Tower, I think it would be better if we talked alone.'

'Which is why I suggested my room.'

'I mean, without Miss Salemi.' Harry glanced from Grenville to the American and back again.

'I'm very happy for Shahnaz to be present.'

'Of course. But even so, I . . . we . . . think it would be better to talk alone.'

'She is my son's fiancée,' Harry said. 'There is nothing I wouldn't want her to hear.'

They glanced at Shahnaz in surprise. She didn't bat an eyelid at the lie. Grenville coughed and looked at the American, whose expression remained impassive. 'Very well.'

They rode the lift in silence. Harry could feel the anxiety Grenville was attempting to mask. He let them into his room, opened the balcony doors and drew the curtains half shut. He suggested Grenville and the American take the two available chairs. Shahnaz sat on the bed.

Grenville cleared his throat again. 'Mr Tower, you asked to meet with a representative of the American Secret Service here in Tehran. Mr Bryant is—'

'You work out of Langley or Tehran station?'

'Langley.' Bryant looked grave. 'How much do you know of your son's life here, Mr Tower?'

'I'm learning more by the day.'

'Have you known Miss Salemi long?'

'Sadly not.'

The American glanced at Shahnaz. 'Is it correct to say that your son was at boarding school in England?'

'Is that relevant?'

'I'd be grateful if you could answer my questions, sir, rather than pose your own. I am trying to help.'

'Yes, he was.'

'How much did you know of his life there?'

'Where is this going, Mr Bryant?'

Bryant's eyes glinted. 'Were you familiar with your son's politics?'

'Yes.'

'Did he talk to you about it?'

'Sometimes.'

'Did you meet any of his friends from school . . . male friends?'

'Of course.'

'Did they share his views?'

'Mr Bryant—'

'After school, he spent a year at Cambridge before travelling out here. Is that correct?'

'Yes.'

'I imagine you were not happy at him turning his back on such good . . . prospects.'

'You could say that.'

'Why do you think he took this course of action?'

'My wife . . .' Harry sighed. 'His mother had died. She had been unwell for many years and she killed herself. He wanted to get away, to pursue a dream. His mother put a lot of thoughts like that into his head. But I still don't see what bearing any of this has on—'

'We believe your son had been recruited by the KGB, Mr Tower.'

'What makes you say that?'

Bryant shook his head mournfully. 'I'm sorry to have to do this to you, sir, truly I am. These matters should remain private.' He upended the manila envelope and spilt a pile of grainy photographs across the bed. They depicted two men having sexual intercourse, one white, one dark. The last image was crystal clear: Sean fast asleep in bed alongside Ali.

'The final photograph was shot through the window afterwards,' Bryant said. Harry stared at the image of his son. Sean looked so peaceful, asleep. Harry had a strange yearning to reach out and touch his face.

Bryant tipped out the contents of a second envelope. 'Mr Tower, we don't believe on balance that your son was working for the Soviets when he came out to Tehran.' He spread the new photographs. They were of Ali, getting into and out of a saloon car with the same white man behind the wheel on each occasion. He had long dark curly hair and sunglasses. 'We have been watching Sean's . . . translator for some time. He is a student at the university here, and was recruited by the KGB as a local agitator and agent of influence. He has been a key part of the current operation – Moscow's attempt to take over Tehran by stealth.

'We know that, broadly speaking, your son shared Ali's politics. They held similar views. At some stage, they began a physical relationship, as you can see. We believe this allowed Ali to introduce your son to the idea of working alongside him.'

The American produced a final shot, of Sean getting into the car with Ali and the curly-haired man.

Harry picked it up. Before Bryant could retrieve them, Shahnaz scooped the other photos onto her lap. She began examining each one intently. 'Who do you claim is the boys' controller?' Harry asked.

'His name is Major Ivan Prokopiev. He has been here more or less since the war.'

'Why would the Russians be interested in my son?'

'His articles were generally helpful to their cause: to create the impression in Western liberal circles that Britain and America are a malign presence, intent only on stealing the nation's oil and robbing its citizens of their birthright. The more they can persuade Mossadegh to defy the West, the more he will need to turn to his one "true" friend to keep the country's economy afloat.'

'So perhaps you can now tell me why he has disappeared.'

'We think the Russians are looking for some kind of pretext for military invasion. It is possible that Ali and your son were reassigned to Tabriz, close to the border, and told to go underground.'

'Have you any evidence that they are in Tabriz?'

'No. That's just an educated guess.'

'My son is a little too distinctive to be an underground operative in this country.'

'We assume he's simply helping his friend.' The American leant forward. 'I recognize that this is very difficult for you, Mr Tower.' He gestured at the photographs of Sean meeting Prokopiev. 'Shocking, even. I can only apologize again for that. I'd like to view your son as something of a naive victim in all of this, seduced by a more dangerous and sophisticated companion. When you find him, I suggest that you remove him quickly from this country and from the clutches of the repellent political system that he has decided to serve.' The American looked at him steadily. 'Assuming you are able to do that, I see no reason to pass on the intelligence we possess to our colleagues in London.'

Bryant got to his feet. Grenville followed suit. His pained expression had not altered since they'd sat down. 'But if you gain any intelligence on your son's whereabouts, Mr Tower, I'd be grateful, in return, if you could inform us.'

'So, the idea that he had been kidnapped—'

'That was a police theory,' Grenville said. 'It was all we had to go on. None of us knew when you got here how much progress Mr Bryant had made.'

The American leant forward to scoop up the photographs, but Shahnaz held on to those she had on her lap. 'I'd like to keep these.'

'I'm afraid that's out of the question.'

'But I—'

'Miss Salemi,' Grenville said. 'We have come here in good faith. This is a matter of national security. I would ask that you respect—'

'Give them the pictures,' Harry said quietly. 'But I'd like to keep this one.' He held up the photograph of Sean and Ali getting into the Russian's white saloon car.

'Mr Tower . . .'

'I think I can be counted on to handle this.' He glared at the American. 'And I believe you know that.'

Bryant nodded slowly. 'Yes, sir. I do. Your reputation precedes you.'

'We've agreed to assist each other. I will certainly be true to my word.'

Bryant hesitated a moment more, before picking up the rest of the photographs. 'Very well, sir. Thank you for your time.'

Once they had pulled the door closed behind them, Harry stepped out onto the balcony. He lit a cigarette and sucked the smoke deep into his lungs. The night was warm. The sound of the piano, punctuated by an occasional burst of laughter, floated up to him on a light breeze.

'Please tell me you didn't buy any of that,' Shahnaz said. She came to lean against the rail on the far side of him. A strand of hair brushed across her cheek as she fixed him with an intense gaze.

'Just give me a minute, please.'

'Harry—'

'I said, could you give me a minute?'

'No, I could not.' Her eyes blazed. 'I find it very difficult to understand how you once worked with people like that.'

'They were just doing their job.'

'Oh, really? Did you notice anything odd about those pictures?'

'They were taken with a hidden camera. It's standard procedure.'

'Right. But they weren't *all* taken with a hidden camera, were they? There is only one photograph in which you can definitely say, yes, that is Sean and that is Ali.'

Harry shook his head. 'So what?'

'The last one. The one taken *after* they're supposed to have done whatever they were doing. You're a trained observer, a spy, so you can't have failed to notice the difference between *that* picture and all the others.' She waited. 'Sean's got his socks on! Name me a single man you have ever met – or woman, for that matter – who would put their socks on immediately after making love.'

'I'm a long way past being shocked by what any man – or woman – chooses to do in the privacy of their own bedroom.'

'They don't have any money. Sean is still technically a freelance foreign correspondent. If they ever went out of Tehran, of course they had to share a room, and it's a lot more comfortable sleeping on a bed than on the floor. I can absolutely assure you that Sean and Ali are not . . . Not in any way. If you don't believe me, ask your extremely heterosexual French friend, Christine Audinette.' She took his hand. 'Please, I need you to hear something.'

20

London, January 1946

PRENTICE WAS WAITING for him at his corner table in White's. 'Tower.' He nodded and pointed to the seat opposite. He looked as if he was about to order a firing squad to shoot. But then, they all felt like that after Avala. 'There will be a board of inquiry,' Prentice said. 'There is going to have to be.'

'And so there should,' Harry replied. He'd anticipated it but was still guessing at what kind of reception Prentice was really going to offer him. He'd prepared for the worst.

'What's your take, Tower?' The waiter arrived, clutching a menu. 'I've already ordered lamb for you,' Prentice said, waving him away. 'It's what you always eat.'

'Where do you want me to begin?' Harry asked.

'I don't want a bloody history lecture.'

Harry stared out of the window, thinking of those

parachutes floating down through the darkness. Amanda had asked him why he was so tense as he left home that morning and it was tough never being able to explain. Most women, he thought, would have punished him for it, but this reflection only deepened his already considerable sense of guilt. Wasn't it true to say *she* was paying the price for the life *he* had chosen? Prentice had once told him it was the case with all their wives, and he ought to know: he'd been divorced three times already. 'I can still see their faces,' Harry said. 'Every last one of them.'

'It was a wretched business,' Prentice agreed.

'I suppose one of them must have been a Communist plant. That or an intercepted radio signal. It's all we can think of. We went through every soldier's back story with a fine-tooth comb, but we must have missed something.'

'They were all at the training camp in Bari until departure?' Harry nodded. 'So how the hell did this Communist *plant* manage to communicate the exact time and place of the drop to Belgrade?'

Harry shook his head. 'That's what we can't work out.'

'Could he have sent a message through someone at the camp? One of the ancillary staff? A cook, a cleaner, a chauffeur?'

'They were all carefully vetted. Most are ex-military. Besides, the idea of *two* Communist agents – one a Yugoslav soldier, the other a member of our field staff – working in tandem strikes me as improbable.' Harry knew he was digging his own grave, but what choice did he have?

'Who knew the time and place of the drop?'

'Haddon and I in Belgrade, Oz here in London.'

'And the men themselves? When were they told?'

'The day before they flew. But none of them left the camp in Italy until they were driven to the airfield. So far as we know, no support staff did either.'

'Some kind of hidden transmitter?'

'It's possible . . .' He shrugged regretfully. 'Yes, it's possible. It's as close as we've got to a working theory.'

'Could you or Haddon have been followed out of Belgrade?'

'We don't think so.'

'But that's conceivable, too?'

Harry nodded. With so many men dead, he sure as hell did not want to come across as complacent, still less arrogant. Their food arrived. Prentice accepted a glass of red wine and slugged it down as if it was for medicinal use. Harry didn't blame him. He pushed the lamb around his own plate. He'd lost his appetite of late. He put a silver crucifix on the table. 'The youngest soldier was sixteen. He asked me to give this to his sister just in case. I told him to keep it. Nothing was going to happen except the restoration of the King to his rightful throne in Belgrade. But he insisted.'

Prentice chewed his lamb methodically. He pushed the necklace back across the table. 'I need no instruction on the power of loss, Tower. God knows I've sent far too many blameless young men to their deaths.' He carried on eating, deep in thought. 'We need to talk about Markov,' he said eventually. Harry had expected this, too. He tried not to show any reaction. 'There are some people in the office who want to link Markov and Mount Avala.'

'You mean in the sense that they were both *my* operations?' It didn't take a genius to work out Harry was the primary connection.

'Your explanation for the delay?'

'There was none.'

'That's not the way others see it.'

Haddon, Harry thought, but didn't say. 'It was your decision to assign Mike Guildford?' Prentice asked.

'He was the right man for the job.'

'He was in America.'

'But due to return on that Monday.' Harry was not going to give ground there.

'State your case,' Prentice said. He pushed away his plate, as if disgusted by the food or Harry's answers, or both.

'We needed to handle Markov with the utmost care. I was duty dog and I was damned if we were going to lose a potential defector offering to bring with him details of a spy at the heart of London Centre. That was a prize we could *not* afford to miss. The station chief in Cairo had sent the cable in the diplomatic bag. We knew it was secure. Markov had been warned he was going to have to wait a few days. Back here, only Haddon, Oz and I were aware of the approach. I wanted to brief Mike and send him straight out. He had handled defections before and was indisputably the best-placed man for the job. Haddon hustled to go himself, but I was duty officer and I told him he didn't have the experience we needed. I believed that then and I still do now. It was worth waiting two extra days for Mike. But you're right. It was up to me.'

'And, in the meantime, Markov vanished.'

'He never returned to the embassy in Cairo. I don't know if that's quite the same thing.'

'It seems fairly evident he's in a Siberian gulag, if he was lucky enough to be spared execution.'

Harry shook his head. He couldn't afford to display any sign of lingering guilt or regret. 'The list of questions we don't have answers to in relation to Markov is very long. We don't know who he really was—'

'A senior officer in the GRU.'

'That's what he claimed. We've never been able to verify it independently.' Harry stared out of the window again at the figures scurrying through the rain. London retained the air of singular drabness that had been its defining quality since the early days of the war. 'If you wanted to cause chaos in London Centre, wouldn't you play something exactly like this? Have a previously unheard-of "senior officer" in the GRU appear at a foreign embassy claiming to have a devastating secret – a traitor at the heart of SIS – and then, before anyone qualified can get out to Cairo to cross-examine him, have him disappear into thin air again, leaving the impression that the "traitor" sabotaged this massive and potentially golden intelligence treasure trove?'

'I thought you said you took it seriously.'

'I did. My God, I did. But it meant nothing until we could see the whites of his eyes. And I trusted Mike to know whether he was the real deal.'

Now it was Prentice's turn to gaze out of the window. Harry had little choice but to wait him out. He didn't like the churning sensation in his gut. He knew what was at stake at this table and certainly wasn't misled by the convivial surroundings.

'What do you really think of Haddon?' Prentice asked.

'I've worked with him a long time,' Harry said carefully.

'That wasn't my question and you know it.'

'We've never been close. That's hardly a secret.'

'He's clever,' Prentice said. 'Always has been. That's why I recruited him. Too clever by half, perhaps, but his credentials are second to none. And there are those among my colleagues who will never believe a public-school-educated son of a peer could ever be anything but one of us. But I think he's weak.'

It sounded like a challenge. To Harry. Was he expected to deny it? 'What are you really asking?' he said.

'Do you think Haddon is a traitor?'

Harry hesitated. Was he being encouraged to save himself by denouncing Haddon? 'No,' he said eventually. 'I don't. Vain, self-regarding, weak, yes. But honest. And – probably – decent. A man with no hidden depths, of any kind.'

'You sure about that?'

'Yes.'

Prentice folded his napkin with exaggerated care. 'I agree. In the *end*, I agree. What about Oz?'

'He has depths, many of them very carefully hidden. But I don't doubt his hatred of Communists is genuine.'

'You thought he was too close to the Nazis when you worked together in Germany before the war?'

And I bloody despised him for it, Harry thought. Watching so much of the British establishment and its many hangers-on, like Oswald, kowtowing to the Nazis – even by the mid-thirties, transparently some of the most repellent men ever to walk the face of the earth – had been the defining event of his life. 'That was an observation of fact, not an opinion,' Harry said. 'Oz was one of their fellow travellers. So if we're discussing his morality, or lack of

221

judgement, then, yes, I'm in up to the hilt. But he picked his side. It was never Moscow.'

Prentice stared into the middle distance, lost in thought. The waiter took their plates and offered dessert. Prentice nodded noncommittally and the old man shuffled away again. Like everything else in this place, he hadn't changed since Harry's first visit. 'I can't bring myself to conclude that any one of you is a traitor,' Prentice said finally. 'And I don't want the work of your department to be hindered by a cloud of suspicion. It's too important. The Communists' ambitions are clear enough now so we must accelerate our efforts. However, this is the last such mistake we can tolerate or afford. Is that clear?'

'Of course.' Harry nodded vigorously. 'Of course.'

21

Tehran, August 1953

HARRY WATCHED SHAHNAZ load a reel of tape onto the newly repaired machine in Sean's flat. When she had finished, she turned to him. 'Sean and I talked about you a great deal. It was I who suggested that he voiced his thoughts and feelings for the sake of his own sanity. I can't witness you doubt who and what he is any more.' She switched it on.

'Wait a minute.'

'Why?'

'I don't need to hear this.'

'Yes, you do.'

'I don't.'

'What are you frightened of?'

'I'm not frightened of anything. I'm here to find my son, not to engage in some torturous—'

'We are both looking for your son. But wouldn't it be a good idea if you *actually* found him? Perhaps in more ways than one.' She blew out the candle as the reels began to turn and went to sit in the corner of the room, in the darkness.

'Hello, Dad . . .'

Harry closed his eyes as the pain and the pleasure of hearing his son's voice washed over him.

'You may notice that I've had a drink or two. Well, you know all about that. But I can assure you that, while it might affect the quality of my speech, it has no impact upon the clarity of my thought.

'I know, as I always have, that I'm not the son you hoped for. A dreamer. Worse, a naive idealist. Bullied. A *victim* at that school you insisted on sending me to just so I could join a club that had always excluded you and which no sane man would ever wish to be a part of.'

Harry shifted uncomfortably at the rancour in his son's voice.

'The strange thing is that, right to the end, Mum was your stoutest defender. You were scared of being a father, she said, for fear of the kind of father you might turn out to be. We should understand what you'd lived through, during your childhood, with your father, then during the war, away from home so much, devoted to your work . . .

'I did try to understand. But I couldn't escape the same recurring conclusion: reason or not, just cause or not, where did it all leave us? What use were you to her? Or are you to me?

'I know she forgave you for your absences – mental, physical, emotional. She always said you were the love of

224

her life, and she never wanted to be with anyone else. But in my darkest moments, when I stare into the abyss in the hours before dawn, I believe you broke her heart. She supported you in everything. But when she really needed you, you were not there for her . . .'

There was a long, long silence.

'Shahnaz often asks me what you're like. I say, *Like a ghost*. A man who passes through life without touching the sides. The day you came home to see me cradling my mother's dead body, all I could think to say as I looked at you was, "Who the hell *are* you?"'

Harry stopped the tape. 'I didn't mean to punish you,' Shahnaz said.

'Then what did you intend?'

'I was trying to ignite some warmth and humanity. When I saw you jumping to conclusions about those pictures, I wanted you to understand who he actually was, to have faith in him.'

'That isn't why you brought me here.'

She got up and moved closer. 'I once asked him what his childhood memories of you were and he replied, "Saying goodbye." Perhaps if he had known who you really were, what you really did, what you sacrificed, and why—'

'What difference would it have made?'

'Possibly all the difference in the world. Why did you go away after your wife became ill the last time?'

'Because she had been in hospital before. I thought Sean was at university and she would be safe there until I returned. Her illness, her depression, was overpowering at times. I couldn't reach her, help her—'

'Or was it that she couldn't reach you?' She shook her

head. 'I don't understand. You are a good man. Why did you leave her in that hospital?'

Harry picked up his jacket. He stood. It was not a question he would, or could, answer. Because the truth would haunt him into his own grave. 'I'll see you tomorrow.'

'Stay and tell me.'

'No.'

'Why not? Harry? What else have you got to lose?'

'I had to go.' He walked over to the window and rested his forehead against the glass. The lights of the city seemed distant and blurred. 'I had to go because I'd made a commitment to my life and work a long time ago that I couldn't break. How could I have known the hospital would allow her to discharge herself?'

'If you'd told Sean why it was so important, perhaps he would have understood.'

How could anyone ever comprehend the compromises of the secret life he had chosen? Harry wondered. He no longer understood them himself. Shahnaz pointed at the tape recorder. 'Nobody says the things Sean did on that tape unless they love someone. A great deal. Surely a spy can work that out.'

'What is it you want from me?' Harry asked.

'Sean says that you are a highly intelligent man. So how is it that the one person you can't see clearly is him?'

'Can't I?'

'No! Which is strange, really, because he's so incredibly like you. He likes to keep his true nature hidden, but he has extraordinary integrity. He's much tougher and more tenacious than he seems. He doesn't really care what other people think. He has an unusual purity of spirit.'

'Does that mean you are much more like *your* father than you seem?' It was gratuitous and he knew it. He regretted it as soon as the words left his lips, but he was angry at the way she was forcing him to look at his own reflection.

'You don't know my father,' she said quietly.

'And you don't know me.' Harry picked up his jacket. 'So, if the lecture's over, I've finished for now. I'll see you at dawn tomorrow and we'll start afresh.'

Harry walked out into the balmy night. He could hear a band playing Iranian folk songs in Shahnaz's favourite restaurant as he got into the Ford Popular.

But Sean's words echoed in his head and, as he waited in a queue at the first checkpoint just in front of the Atlantic Hotel, he faced his betrayal of Amanda squarely for perhaps the first time. When he had returned from a trip to Greece to find her once again curled up on their bathroom floor, she had reached for him in abject desperation. It had never been entirely clear what she had sought in these moments – meaning, perhaps, or solace, or some reassurance that their love, their life together, had counted for something. He had struggled to give her what she pleaded for. It had been his decision to take her back to the hospital and there was no hiding the fact that it had been, at least in part, a matter of convenience.

A crisis in Corfu, in Dassia Bay – and in Albania – had been in full swing and he'd told himself his wife's acute mental breakdown could wait, as it had many times before. But the memory of the distress in Sean's face as his mother was taken from the house was unforgettable. He had known it was a mistake, so why could his father not see the situation with equal clarity?

As Harry reached the front of the queue at the check-point, the guards waved him through. But as he accelerated away down an almost empty Takhte Jamshid, he could not shake the recollection of the anger in his son's eyes.

Where was he?

Harry had been intending to head back to the hotel, but he changed his mind and drove on to take a left onto Pah-lavi. He was not certain he would find the gymnasium in Doshtan Street again on his own, so he kept on the main road to the railway station. He lost his way in the narrow streets beyond it and at one stage found himself by the iron gates of the Royal Guards Division, which he had vis-ited in 'forty-six. He doubled back and, orienting from the oil storage depot that loomed ominously over south Teh-ran not far from the station, he eventually found what he was looking for. His instinct was that the gymnasium might well hold the key to Sean's disappearance. And if he had to break in to find out, it was a lot safer to do it with-out Shahnaz.

He parked a short distance away and turned off the engine. The night was clear, the silence punctured by the barking of stray dogs and the distant hum of traffic.

Harry got out and slipped through the darkness to a tall building just short of the entrance, more or less opposite the house in which women were forced to sell themselves. There was no lock on the door and he climbed the staircase to the roof. He took out his binoculars, settled against a wall overlooking the gymnasium and waited. There was a light in the courtyard, but none from the windows above the street. After about half an hour, a gate opened and a jeep roared out. Harry could clearly see William Oswald,

Pierre Audinette and an Iranian in military uniform he did not recognize.

Silence descended again. Only the odd solitary man arriving or leaving the house next door disturbed the quiet of the night.

He waited another hour, then stole back down the side alley and climbed over the wall. He encountered the first sign of life in the courtyard, where a group of guards were playing cards in a security booth. Harry waited patiently, too close to be sure of slipping past unnoticed.

Eventually, one left to take a piss against the wall opposite. Another followed, and the two inside the booth were arguing about the conduct of their game. Harry took his chance and crept silently past them. He waited in the far corner until the guards had returned to the booth and their noisy game resumed.

He climbed the stairs and waited patiently again until a bout of raucous laughter from the booth offered him the cover to break a single pane of glass and force the door of the Global Vision office on the first floor.

Harry waited until his eyes grew accustomed to the dark and took in his surroundings. He lit the candle he had slipped into his pocket at Sean's apartment earlier. The walls were covered with maps and photographs of key locations around the city, from the Shah's palace to the Officers' Club to the home of Prime Minister Mohammed Mossadegh.

There was a filing cabinet and the lock on it took Harry several minutes to pick. When he finally heard the tell-tale clunk, he found it stacked with files. There were more lists, many of telephone numbers: army officers, police officers, journalists – foreign and Iranian – and foreign diplomatic missions. There were files on hundreds of individuals.

The fattest file was one for Global Vision Oil Ltd. It included the articles of incorporation in Tehran and the shareholders. General Adel Salemi headed the list, followed by Pierre Audinette, Meshang Rashidian and his brothers, and the chief of police, Asadollah Soleimani. But there were many more names beneath theirs.

Harry folded the list and slipped it into his pocket.

It didn't take him long to find there was also a file for Sean Tower. He pulled it out and flipped it open to reveal many photographs of Sean on assignment in and around Tehran, some with Ali, others with Shahnaz. There was a shot of Harry walking through Tehran airport.

And finally, tucked at the back, there was a hospital admission sheet, which recorded that Sean had been admitted to Isfahan Hospital with 'injuries from a car accident'.

At the bottom a final entry read *Discharged to Isfahan Morgue.*

22

HARRY PICKED UP Shahnaz, whom he'd woken at Sean's apartment, and they sped in dread silence through empty streets until they were out on a lonely desert road.

The sun rose steadily in the sky, casting unforgiving light across a parched landscape littered with tiny settlements. Harry wound down the window to let the breeze brush his cheeks. His mind never stopped turning, as if determined to dredge every memory and play it through over and over again while there was still time.

Sean and Amanda, Amanda and Sean: it was all he could think of. Both were suddenly, vibrantly, alive in his head.

He recalled Sean's first day at boarding school, aged seven: the tight grip of his hand as he walked between his mother and father and the way he fought hard to hide his tears. He could hear Amanda's furious cry on the morning they had taught him to ride his bike – *Harry!* – and see

Sean's cheery, uncomplaining face as he pulled him from the undergrowth. 'Daddy, Daddy, I didn't brake!'

'Well, you should have done, you clot!'

He recalled Sean's steady, thoughtful gaze on the many, many mornings Harry had left home during the war. 'I hope you're all right, Daddy.' And, as the memories unfurled, the regret – the invisible barrier he could never break, the idealism that suffocated so much warmth and affection – threatened to overwhelm him. In all the years of his own journey, he had never felt so alone.

The Ford rattled on through the building heat. They passed Shamsabad and then the village of Cheshmeh Shur, where Sean's Dodge had been found by the lake. Harry wondered again what his son's car had been doing on that long, lonely road.

Were he and Ali on their way to Isfahan? And, if so, why?

'Have you been to Isfahan before?' Shahnaz asked, as if reading his mind.

'No. Is it as spectacular as they say?'

'More so.' She looked at him. 'You know about Abbas Shah?'

'The king who murdered his eldest son and made Isfahan his capital?'

'It's true he was cruel, like many of the kings who followed him, including the current Shah's father, whose response to religious protesters was to mow them down in their mosques.'

'I didn't have you on the side of the imams.'

'I'm not, at all. If anything, I have some kind of loose Zoroastrian faith, like my grandmother.'

' "Curse this world, curse this time, curse this fate/ That uncivilized Arabs have come to force me to be a Muslim." '

She allowed herself a half-smile and nodded, impressed. 'You know Ferdowsi's work. You are full of surprises. But I guess the point is that everything in my country has always been full of contrasts, even the reign of Abbas Shah. Yes, he was one of the most barbaric rulers in history, but he also built the roads that opened up trade with Europe. He brought in Armenian and Chinese craftsmen, Indian money-lenders, Dutch traders to expand the idea of his grand bazaar. He founded world-leading workshops in silk and ceramics. He was a visionary and his city, Isfahan nesf-e jahan – Isfahan is half the world – is a place every man and woman alive must see.'

In almost any other circumstance but this, Harry thought. But he kept it to himself as they lapsed once more into silence.

It took two and a half hours to reach the holy city of Qom, where the traffic clogged momentarily, but then the houses and factories petered out again and they returned to the lonely desert road, where the many trucks hauling goods north to the capital were interspersed with donkey carts and even the occasional camel.

Shahnaz passed him water in a tin jug as they stopped for a few minutes to stretch their legs and buy something to eat from a roadside stall. Harry smoked a cigarette and stared out into the vast desert. 'How much further?' he asked her.

'Another couple of hours. Shah Abbas moved his capital to Isfahan to protect himself from invasion by the

Ottomans.' She gestured at the arid landscape around her. 'Now you see why.'

The sun passed its peak and began to lose some of the heat that had kept the shirt glued to his back, but the car still felt like a coffin. As they drove on, its sides seemed to press in on him.

'Look after our boy,' Amanda had urged him just before she had been returned to the private hospital – that *asylum*, as she had called it. 'Look after our boy, Harry. That's all I ask.'

He felt a tear come to his eye and he brushed it briskly away.

Shahnaz took over the driving to allow Harry some time to rest. He slept fitfully until she shook him awake. 'You haven't had enough water.' Harry straightened. For a moment, he couldn't recall where he was or why. 'We're almost there,' she said, pushing the tin jug once more into his hand.

He sipped a little. It was warm. She was speeding along a narrow dirt track beside a river. 'Is this it?' Harry asked, as they were halted by a flock of sheep being guided to fresh pasture.

'Yes. The mortuary is on the edge of the city.'

They turned onto a wider asphalt road bordered by tea-houses and shady public gardens. Shahnaz brought the car to a stop in front of a white civic building whose paint was peeling off its façade. 'We're here,' she said.

Neither of them moved.

Harry realized she was waiting for him and forced himself to open the door. After the long night, his legs felt unsteady. He lit a cigarette and a group of young boys watched him smoke it from beneath the shadow of a cypress tree.

Shahnaz drew closer. 'Are you all right, Harry?' He did not answer. She took a pace forward and wrapped her arms around him. He held her tight.

When they released each other, he dusted himself down awkwardly. She tilted back her sunglasses and tried to smile at him as he led the way into the cool interior of the morgue. Shahnaz found the director in a cramped office at the end of a corridor. Whatever explanation she offered in Farsi, the man did not seem convinced and the conversation dragged on. 'Is everything all right?' Harry asked.

'He's saying he needs some paperwork from the public-health director before he can let us see the body. I'm pointing out we have driven a long way to get here and that you have come all the way from England, that we believe your son is the missing foreigner whose body they have—'

'He agrees they have a foreigner's body?'

'Yes. And that they don't know the boy's identity.'

'How old is he?'

She wiped away a tear. 'Sean's age.'

'Does he not want to know who the boy is?' Harry was trying to suppress the feeling of nausea that threatened to choke him.

'He does, but he says he can't do it without the permission of either the chief of police in Isfahan or the public-health director and we must report first to one or other of them.'

Harry stepped in closer, using his height and bulk to good advantage. 'Please, sir,' he said quietly. 'I have come a long way. I need to know if the boy you have here is my son.'

The man looked at him for what seemed like an age, then sighed deeply. 'I understand,' he said. He guided them along a corridor and down to the basement. It was damp here and smelt overwhelmingly of formaldehyde. Dull, ghoulish light leaked from a single lamp. Water dripped from a curved ceiling onto a dark stone floor. Paint peeled in large chunks from the walls. The director spoke to his technician, a spindly man with glasses dressed in a filthy white coat. The man glanced from Harry to Shahnaz and back again. 'They would like to know which of us is to identify the body,' Shahnaz said.

Harry tried to open his mouth to speak.

'I can do it,' Shahnaz said, but he held her arm as she moved forward and nodded to indicate that it was his responsibility. He followed the technician through into another vast room. Paint peeled off the damp walls here, too. The man checked his paperwork, then ushered Harry halfway down the left-hand side. Shahnaz followed him.

'He wants to know if you're ready, Harry,' Shahnaz said. Her voice was unsteady. A fly buzzed around the technician's cheeks and he waved it away.

Harry nodded again. The man opened the nearest of the row of doors and pulled out a trolley. The corpse was covered with a sheet. Harry moved into a position that would allow him a clear view of the face.

The man took hold of the ends of the sheet. He watched Harry nervously as he inched it back to reveal dark hair and pale features.

Shahnaz gasped and her legs crumpled. Harry turned and caught her before she hit the floor. The director shouted for assistance. Harry carried her back towards the technician's desk at the far end of the basement. 'Get her some water,' he yelled at the director.

He eased her into the chair. She was already coming around. The technician arrived with the water and Harry dabbed some across her forehead and forced her to drink the rest. 'I thought it was him,' Shahnaz mumbled. 'It looked like him. He had the same hair and . . . I was sure, I thought . . . Oh, God . . .' She began to cry. 'But it wasn't him, was it? It wasn't him . . .'

Harry leant against the wall and breathed out. He let himself down to the floor. For the first time since Amanda's death, he wept. Tears dripped down his cheeks. Shahnaz came to sit next to him. He wrapped his arm around her and drew her close.

The director and his technician hovered uncertainly nearby. Shahnaz eventually offered them an explanation and they responded with beaming smiles. A rare let-off, perhaps. They discreetly withdrew and left the strange couple to recover.

Harry couldn't speak, or even think. Relief overwhelmed him.

They stayed in the mortuary for another half-hour. They tried to work out who the poor dead Westerner might be. There were few clues. He had been found without a wallet, a passport, a watch or anything else that could have yielded his identity. But the needle marks on his arm gave a hint as to how he had met his end. 'If it is not Sean,' Shahnaz asked, as they left the building, 'then why would his hospital form have said "discharged to Isfahan morgue"?'

Harry did not have an explanation for this, though he

had some ideas, none palatable. If Sean's death was accounted for – a tragic car accident – it allowed his kidnappers to dispose of him wherever and whenever they chose, without fear of reprisal and at their own pace.

By now, Shahnaz was leading Harry down a narrow alley to Isfahan's central square, as expansive and architecturally overwhelming as Moscow's Red Square. 'This is Isfahan,' she told him. 'Like I said, they call it half the world, because it is half of everything you would ever want to see.'

Harry glanced about him. With its green lawns and central pond fed by tinkling fountains, it must have seemed a dramatic oasis, he thought, for those in Shah Abbas's time who had completed the long trek across the arid desert around it on horseback. 'Abbas wanted his new capital to be a visible sign of his drive to centralize the country and draw together all its centres of power,' Shahnaz said, pointing around the square, 'so the Qeysarie Gate on the north side, entrance to the grand bazaar, represents the merchants. The Masjid-i Shah, the Shah Mosque, for the clergy. And, of course, the Ali Qapu Palace on the west side, to represent the power of the Shah himself.' She smiled at him. 'Oh, of course, and the marble pillars at either end, which were polo posts. The Shah liked to be entertained.'

They began to stroll around the maidan. Local craftsmen and small traders had sought shelter from the heat of the afternoon beneath awnings and archways.

They passed the entrance to the bazaar, with its delicate blue mosaics and dozens of cafés packed with men drinking tea and smoking pipes. Shahnaz walked to the fountain at the centre of the square and scooped water onto her face. Harry did the same. He all but immersed his head then shook it like a dog. 'Christ . . .'

'You won't find him here,' Shahnaz said.

'You never know.'

'You don't strike me as a man of faith.'

'Well, I was in there. I was praying to every god in the universe.' Harry lit a cigarette and sucked the smoke deep into his lungs. 'Christ,' he said once more. 'I never want to go through that again for as long as I live.'

'Neither do I.'

'But we won't have to. For the time being, at least. Sean is alive. I'm certain of that now.'

Shahnaz let more water run through her fingers. 'What makes you so sure?'

'Did you notice anything odd about that American last night?'

'Only that I didn't like the look of him.'

'Well, now it's your turn to have missed something. If Ali and Sean were being watched here, if the Americans were on their tail, then how come it was a guy from Langley who came to see us?'

'I don't understand.'

'I asked him "Langley or Tehran station?"'

She shook her head, mystified.

'If our friends in the US Embassy had been trailing Ali and Sean,' he said, 'if they *really* believed them to be KGB stooges, then they must have been doing it for months. So I'd have expected to see a guy from Tehran station. But we got a man from CIA headquarters back in Virginia.'

'I'm afraid I still don't understand.'

'What is he doing here and why would he have been interested in Sean's disappearance?'

'Maybe they flew him over.'

'Maybe, but it sure as hell wasn't because they were worried about some English newspaper reporter flirting with the KGB.'

'Then why was it?'

'I don't know yet,' he said, though he could have made a pretty good guess. If a man from Langley was here, it was because they were interested in Harry, not his son. They'd known he was coming. 'If they have prepared a cover story for his death, but not yet put him in the morgue, it suggests to me that he is still alive.'

Shahnaz stood. 'Come on,' she said. 'Since you're here, you might as well get to see one of the Wonders of the World.'

She steered him across the maidan to the Masjid-i Shah. The interior was cool and quiet, with breathtaking ceilings and intricate blue mosaics. The late-afternoon sun streamed through latticed windows to create pools of dappled light on its smooth stone floors. 'Here,' Shahnaz said. 'Give me your cigarettes.' She took the packet and crouched over a dark stone at the centre of the mosque. 'Are you ready?'

'For what?'

'This is really quite something.' She slapped the packet against the floor and the sound echoed and echoed around the empty space. 'Did you count how many?'

'No.'

'Listen again.' She repeated the trick. An old man had walked into the entrance, but paid them no attention.

'Five,' Harry said.

'No! You can't count!' She did it again. 'See? Seven. Exactly seven, every time.' Her eyes shone. 'Isn't that incredible?'

'I don't know if it's *incredible*, exactly. But it's certainly seven.'

'I wish you'd come in better times,' she said quietly.

'So do I.'

'Sean would have loved to show you all this.'

They gazed up at the dust particles dancing in the fractured light. Harry sat on a stone ledge and looked at her. 'He thought I wanted a son more like me. But that wasn't true.'

'Of course it wasn't. Who on earth would want a son like you?' She gave him back his cigarettes. 'Come on. Let's get going.'

They returned to the car and Shahnaz navigated through a series of back alleys and out onto the road to Tehran. About half an hour into the journey, she turned off the highway and they began to bump down a dusty track. They reached the bottom of a valley, crossed a dry riverbed and started to climb the hill on the other side. 'Where are we going?' Harry asked.

'You said you wanted to see my father.'

'Is this where he lives?'

'It's our farm. Latak. My parents bought it just after I was born. If he's at home, I'll get out at the servants' cottages and let you go in to talk to him.'

The track was rougher still at the crest of the hill and they bumped their way along a ridge. Below was a low-slung, elegant, cream building surrounded by several acres of greenery. The boundary walls sparkled in the setting sun and Harry could see men hard at work tending the gardens. Shahnaz's gaze was fixed upon it. 'My father is not here.'

They reached the floor of the valley and passed a row of simple whitewashed cottages before swinging into the lane that led to the main entrance. The last of the sunlight filtered through the poplar, pomegranate, chinar and acacia trees that stood guard at the furthest edge of the property.

They turned into a neat stone drive and pulled up by the front door. Shahnaz raised a hand to shield her eyes and waved to the gardeners, who responded in kind. She led Harry into a spacious hallway with a highly polished wooden floor and an elaborately painted ceiling. 'Scenes from Ferdowsi's *Shahnameh*. My grandfather's idea.' She smiled. 'You should appreciate them.'

'They're quite something.'

'My grandfather was a fierce Iranian – and Muslim – nationalist. About my only memory of him is sitting on the terrace here while he used to tell my brother and me how the Afghans had so overwhelmed the British in 1842 that not a single soldier escaped, and how the Lezgian chief Shamyl defied the Russians in the Caucasus for thirty years.'

'Bloodcurdling.'

'I think that was the idea.'

Shahnaz turned into the first room on their right, opened the French windows at the far end and folded back the shutters. The fading light glinted on the gold-embossed volumes that were stacked from floor to ceiling all around them. 'My father's study.' She gestured at a painting of a slim and attractive blonde-haired girl. 'My grandmother, Elena. Her mother was the daughter of a grand Russian prince called Major General Dmitri Demidoff, whose family had made their fortune from gold mines in the Urals. She ignited his everlasting rage by eloping with a young British engineer, who carried her away, by a very circuitous route, to live in Tiflis, where my grandmother was born. My grandfather was consul general there, which was how they met and married. Yet even though she herself had eloped, my great-grandmother didn't approve of the match and threw her out of the house. The cycle repeated itself.'

'So you've abandoned the idea of marriage in general?'

'Certainly of doing anything that meets with the approval of my family.'

'And this was your grandfather?'

'Yes. He was a more gentle man when I knew him than he might appear in this portrait. He went on to be the Iranian minister – ambassador, I guess you would say today - in imperial St Petersburg and they lived in this mansion on the left here, which belonged to Prince Bieloselski-Biolozorski. I know all the stories by heart. My grandmother annoyed her husband and the Tsarist authorities by becoming deeply and, in the end, not so secretly involved in liberal and opposition politics, so they had to be moved on some years before the revolution to an equivalent post in Constantinople.'

'A woman after your own heart, then.'

'An outsider, you could say.' Shahnaz led him out onto the terrace, which overlooked an idyllic orchard, its perfectly trimmed lawns and aligned trees inviting the eye to journey between avenues and elaborate flowerbeds.

'I can see why your father chooses to spend his time here,' Harry said.

'He's always said he knew it was home the first time he saw it. So did my mother. We used to go back to Tehran under sufferance, counting the days until we could return.' She pointed towards a cottage in the middle of the far wall. 'We had a Zoroastrian gardener called Bahram, who lived there with his much younger wife. He was a huge man with a grey beard and a passionate love of wild animals that he persuaded my father should have sanctuary here.'

'What kind of wild animals are we talking about?'

'Well, he started with a family of mongooses, which he bought in from Khuzestan. They seemed to co-exist happily enough with the dogs for a while, but eventually came to a sticky end. Then we had a badger, which was quite tame, but had a terrible habit of charging at your legs and biting you. That really annoyed my father, much to my brother's amusement.

'And then Bahram surpassed himself by bringing home a baby bear. My brother and I used to love sitting here, watching her play. She seemed almost human. She used to lie on her back in that pond in the summer and pour water over herself from one of the cans. In winter, she would dance around the garden, throwing up balls of snow and ice and catching them on her nose. As she grew, she became a bit of a liability and Father insisted she was tied to that mulberry tree at night. In the end, Bahram took her away. We never did find out what became of her . . .'

Shahnaz turned and led Harry back into the study and along the corridor to the room next door. She opened the shutters to reveal a formal drawing room with a line of portraits along the walls. 'This is Cyrus, my brother.'

'How did he die?'

'No one really knows. He was out riding with my father. I think he was going too fast, and Cyrus was trying to keep up.'

She pointed to a framed landscape of a mountain stream. 'Cyrus painted that just before he died. He was an artist from an incredibly young age, the kindest and most gentle elder brother you could ever wish for. Exactly the kind my father didn't want.'

Harry moved on to the display in the corner: a stiff military jacket, a sheepskin cap and an enormous cuirassier's sword.

'My father joined the Cossacks as a young man. I don't know how much you know of Iranian history, but the regiment was founded and run by Tsarist officers, who ruled their Iranian soldiers with a rod of iron. It suffered in the immediate aftermath of the revolution when all the Russian officers went home to fight alongside the Whites. But it was built up again as a fully Iranian regiment by the current Shah's father, and he used it to help him seize power.'

'And your father . . .?'

'He decided that the Cossacks still carried too much of a whiff of foreign influence, so he transferred to the Gendarmerie, and then, under the current Shah, to the 1st Pahlavi Guards Cavalry Regiment. He hoped Cyrus would follow in his footsteps, and was always warning him that he was too soft to become the man his destiny demanded. And in public, too.'

Her eyes misted for a moment.

'And then?'

'Then he bullied him relentlessly. Bullied him to death, in fact. At least, that is my interpretation of the horse-riding accident. Why else would Cyrus have been going too fast? He was a talented horseman, but he was always desperate to please our father.'

Her tone was so matter-of-fact that a casual listener might have mistaken it for acquiescence, but Harry knew better. 'Are you thinking about your father?' she asked.

'No,' Harry said. 'I'm thinking about myself. And you?'

'Me?'

'What did your father want for you?'

'He wanted me to care for him, as a traditional Iranian daughter should. To take over the running of the household after the tragic death of his young wife.'

Shahnaz moved another two paces along the wall and Harry followed her gaze. Her mother's refusal to meet the portraitist's eye seemed to heighten the ethereal nature of her beauty. 'I was informed simply that she had passed away, but one of the servants eventually told me the truth, which was that she committed suicide shortly after the death of my brother. My father has never once talked to me about either event.'

Harry was captivated by the tragic beauty of the face above him.

'Now do you understand why I do not wish to ask my father for help?'

He nodded slowly. 'How would he respond if you did?'

'If he were involved in some way, he wouldn't hesitate to lie. He is the type of man who unequivocally puts politics – or, as he would argue, the national interest – before everything. If he is not involved, he would make me feel weak and inconsequential for asking, and do as little as possible to assist us.'

Shahnaz left Harry with the ghosts of the past and their aura of terrible sadness. He sat and watched the sun drop towards the horizon, thinking of his own ghosts: of his mother, of the men who were no more than boys he had sent to die beyond the Iron Curtain, of Amanda. He was struck by the way in which all of these ghosts seemed more real to him – more alive – with each passing day.

Some time later, Shahnaz returned and said her father had gone to Isfahan for dinner, and was not expected back until the early hours. Harry agreed not to wait for him but Shahnaz had instructed the servants to prepare dinner before they departed.

She suggested a swim to wash away the heat. They walked to a pool in the walled garden and she stripped unselfconsciously to her underwear and dived in.

After a while, she got out, dried herself. 'It will clear your head,' she said, throwing him a clean towel.

Harry stripped, dived in. The water was murky. As he swam along the bottom of the pool, he could see her silhouetted against the setting sun.

They retreated to the terrace while they waited for dinner. She raided her father's cellar, returning with a French claret. They settled back into the wicker chairs, watching the parched landscape fade into darkness as the sun turned the horizon a deep, rich red. 'You know,' she said eventually, 'I wouldn't blame you if you were angry that Sean didn't reply to your letters and tapes. I didn't think it reflected well on him and I told him so. If he had hated you, that would have been a different matter. But it was plain that he loved you and thought you a good man.'

'In my experience, few things waste as much time and energy as apportioning blame.'

She lit a cigarette and threw him the packet. 'I suppose that you think I'm a socialist, which means I must be a Communist.'

'An idealist, like my son.'

'You make it sound like a dirty word.'

'Ideals are what men and women sacrifice their humanity for.'

She frowned at him, tilted her head to one side. 'Aren't ideals what give us our humanity?'

Harry shook his head slowly. 'Mankind is beset by two tragedies. The first is that we have enough intelligence to explain how we got here, but not why. So we invent all kinds of attachments to still the internal panic in our minds and give this disordered universe some kind of logical construct . . . religion, political idealism—'

'And the second?'

'The fact that there is no way for men like me to convince kids like you and Sean that you've got it the wrong way round.'

'A cynic, then?'

'A realist.'

'Perhaps if you'd seen children starving for want of food that our oil money could have bought them a hundredfold, you'd be an idealist too.'

There was so much now that Harry wanted to tell her and Sean. The self-imposed vow of silence he had taken all those years ago had never felt more burdensome.

'You love my son,' he said finally. 'That's it. That's all there is.'

'What do you mean?'

'You have all that life has to offer in your hands. When this is over, when we have him back, seize it and don't let anything ever stand in its way.'

'That sounds like a statement of regret.'

'In its own way, it is.'

'Of what?'

'Making the wrong decisions. Of not nurturing the love I was given.'

Shahnaz stared up at the stars in the clear night sky. 'What are we going to do now?' she asked.

'I'm going to do something I should have done as soon as I got here. Ask for help.'

23

London, June 1952

HARRY HAD TRAVELLED home from his last assignment with a head full of questions, chief among them what had happened to the team they'd sent into Albania.

He and Haddon had personally seen the small group of men they had trained for months onto boats in the bay beneath the villa in Corfu. They had watched until they were swallowed by a velvet night. But since then ... silence.

Haddon insisted there was no need to be concerned. This was *not* like Mount Avala. Hadn't they instructed the men often enough to be cautious above all else and to risk making contact only once they felt themselves well established? But Harry feared another storm was coming and that he would be shouldering the blame. He'd kept himself out of Prentice's eyeline since Mount Avala, never leaving himself open to having others land failures at his door.

But it was only himself and Haddon in that villa in Corfu. So who else would there be to blame? He hung his coat from the stand in the corner. 'Sean?'

The house seemed unnaturally quiet. He put his foot on the stairs. 'Sean?' he yelled up.

He tried not to hurry to the drinks tray in the living room, which was a useless piece of discipline he had fallen to imposing on himself. As if it made any difference. Who was he kidding?

The French windows were open, a curtain tugged by the evening breeze. Harry made a stiff gin and tonic and took a gigantic slug.

He stepped outside. The dappled evening sunlight flickered through the leaves on the oak at the bottom of the garden. 'Sean?' he called again.

There was still no answer.

Harry walked past the bench where Amanda always took her morning coffee and was surprised to see her favourite cup unwashed standing on a side table. His wife was supposed to be still in hospital.

He stopped by his vegetable patch. He had been distracted too long: the lettuce was decimated by slugs and the runner beans rotten. He made a mental note to see to the weeds. How was it they grew so fast?

He walked on, feeling the breeze on his face. He'd hurried home from the bus at a furious pace and was aware of the sweat still glistening on his brow.

It was not until he was almost at the bottom of the garden that he saw the rope swinging from the oak tree. His heart quickened and the fear that had stalked him for so many years was suddenly let loose.

He kept walking – slowly, unevenly – until he was the other side of Amanda's favourite rose bush.

Sean sat cross-legged, with his mother's head in his lap. The knife he had used to cut her down was still in his hand.

He looked up. There was rage in his eyes the like of which Harry had never witnessed: a pure, elemental hatred.

'Why?' Sean said eventually. 'Tell me why you had to leave her.'

24

Tehran, August 1953

IT WAS THE middle of the night by the time they drove back into the capital. The streets were almost completely deserted: no police officers, or military roadblocks, or pro-testers. Even the square outside the bazaar was empty. Harry tried to persuade Shahnaz to go home and get some rest, but she wouldn't countenance the idea. In the end, he offered her his bed at the Ritz and he passed out in the chair on the balcony. He awoke with the dawn call to prayer and walked to the square by the bazaar, using the journey to throw off the men who were on his tail as soon as he left the hotel.

He waited in the shade for a few moments as he watched a packed double-decker bus disgorge young male passen-gers, who scuttled off into the bazaar in small groups, like children arriving for school. Harry headed for the taxi rank, in search of a driver who spoke English. When he found one, they set off through streets still waking from a restless night.

The Russian Embassy was a white building with wide steps and grand pillars, shielded by a high stone gateway with the Soviet hammer and sickle at its apex. Harry sent the driver on his way, bought himself a coffee in a café more or less opposite on Churchill Street and positioned himself at a window table. He had to wait about an hour before the staff began to arrive. As soon as the flow of traffic into the building reached a steady trickle, he paid his bill and lingered outside, smoking.

He spotted a suitable quarry fifty yards out and crossed the road to swing in behind him. He took a few quick paces and gripped the man's arm. 'Keep walking and don't say anything.'

The man needed no further encouragement.

'My name is Harry Tower. I want you to get a message to Oleg Vasilyev. Tell him I'll be at the Ritz Hotel at midday today and I need to speak to him. Have you got that?'

'Yes.'

'Harry who?'

'Tower. I will remember.'

Harry peeled off and strode quickly down a cross-street. He did not look back.

Shahnaz was still asleep when he returned, but he had brought coffee to wake her. She smiled, taking in the fact that he was already fully dressed. 'Where are we going?'

'We know the path Sean was following. If we follow it too, sooner or later we'll find him.'

'That's cryptic.'

254

'It's logic.'

The Bank Melli of Iran was situated just a short walk down Ferdowsi Avenue, the grand porticoed entrance guarded by statues of the Achaemenid kings. They passed through to a cavernous interior with a flagstone floor, pot plants and wooden fans. The staff were immaculately dressed and polite, but singularly unhelpful. No, it would not be possible to see the manager, the clerk behind the counter told Shahnaz. He would not be able to find a space in his schedule for some days. Mr Mazandarani was a *very* busy man.

Shahnaz was respectful but persistent. The man's tone grew petulant.

Harry placed his elbows on the counter and leant forward far enough to guarantee the clerk's full attention. He removed a loose strand of cotton from the man's lapel, then said, 'Get him now, please.' He barely moved his lips.

Harry's close proximity and his tone of whispered menace had the desired effect. Without another word, the subordinate withdrew. A few minutes later, he reappeared with an older colleague, whose authority was reinforced by a pinstriped Savile Row suit, a sharply chiselled jaw and an elaborate, neatly trimmed moustache. 'May I help you, Mr . . .?'

'I'd like to have a word in private, please.'

'I'm afraid, sir, that you will have to telephone to make an appointment.'

'We're terribly sorry to bother you,' Shahnaz interjected smoothly. 'Mr Tower has just flown in from London. We are looking for his son, who has disappeared here in Tehran. He is a journalist who works for an English newspaper called the *Manchester Guardian*. Perhaps you remember him?' The two men shook their heads. 'The Ministry of the Interior is aware of our quest. The chief of police is trying to help us.'

'Madam, you have my sympathy. But you will still have to make an appointment.'

'Please, sir. We don't know how much time we have. We do not know exactly where Mr Tower's son is—'

'Madam, I cannot help you.'

'But, sir, these are uncertain times. You don't need me to tell you that. So we are very anxious to locate Mr Tower's son with the utmost speed.'

Harry had stopped listening. A well-dressed young man had just entered the bank. He carried himself with too much confidence to be a customer. As he reached the door at the end of the counter and demanded entry, Harry swept in behind him. With Shahnaz in pursuit, he brushed past the protesting clerk and walked swiftly back towards the manager, now on his side of the counter.

Harry took a firm hold of the man's arm. 'What you're trying to say,' he said, 'is, "I'd be delighted to see you now, sir."' Mazandarani clearly thought better of resisting. 'Which is your office?'

He pointed. Harry released him. 'We have one simple question to ask, and as soon as we have the answer, we'll leave you in peace. Perhaps you'd like to tell your colleagues here that there is nothing to worry about, and they can return to their work.'

The manager brushed himself down in a brisk attempt to reassert his authority. He glanced at his colleagues and spoke crisply to them in Farsi.

'Thank you,' Harry said.

They were led through to a handsomely furnished office. Harry dropped the note from Sean's office onto the gleaming desk. Mazandarani glanced at the figures without showing the slightest glimmer of recognition.

Harry ran his index finger from entry to entry. '666074 – $27,000. 650193 – $17,000. And 423837 – $11,000.'

'I don't understand.'

'My son is a journalist with a British newspaper. He was working on a story when he disappeared. He got these account numbers from your bank. We are not certain how they are relevant, but believe they will help us understand who and what he was investigating. We'd be grateful if you could tell us who they belong to.'

'That is absolutely out of the question!' The man's face twisted with outrage. 'I could not possibly breach the confidentiality of our clients in that manner.'

'Please, sir,' Shahnaz said. 'You may call the office of the chief of police if you wish to be reassured that—'

'But you are not the police! I have not had the police here. I cannot—'

'We are looking for Mr Tower's son, sir. He has been missing for more than a week. We are very worried that—'

'No, no, and no again. I must now ask you to leave. That is a truly preposterous suggestion, madam.'

'But, sir, we cannot leave until we have some progress on this matter. We must find Mr Tower's son.'

Harry stepped forward, lifted the man from his seat by his lapels and smashed him against the wall. The toes of Mazandarani's highly polished shoes scrabbled for purchase on the deep pile carpet.

'Harry!' Shahnaz hissed. 'For God's sake!' He ignored her. 'This isn't going to help!'

Harry gripped the banker's suit more forcefully. He saw the fear in Mazandarani's eyes. 'Do I have your attention now?'

He nodded.

'Someone has taken my son. I would like to be reasonable, but time is running out and my patience is wearing thin. I have to get him back. I need to know who these accounts belong to, where the sums of money came from. So you're going to find that information very quickly, and then you're going to come back and tell me. Is that understood?' The man nodded again. 'Thank you for your assistance.'

Harry let him down more gently than he had picked him up. He reached for the telephone on his desk. 'To save you the trouble later, why don't you call the chief of police now?'

Mazandarani stared at Harry blankly. He straightened his tie and smoothed his hair. As he departed, Harry asked Shahnaz to go with him.

When the door had closed, he went to the window and looked down at Ferdowsi Avenue, where a large crowd of students carrying banners of Prime Minister Mossadegh was making its way north. Police officers watched them idly.

It took them ten minutes to reappear. Shahnaz handed Harry a sheaf of papers. They appeared to list anonymous accounts. 'The last column is where the money came from.'

'Who do they belong to?'

'We have no addresses on file,' the manager said regretfully.

'Why not?'

'These are numbered accounts.' When it was clear Harry did not absorb the significance of this, the manager added, 'A client need only present his passbook, with the number attached, to draw cash.'

'So you have neither a name nor address for these accounts?'

'That's correct, sir.'

'How convenient. Have you ever seen anyone draw money from them?'

'No.'

'The last file was extremely thin,' Shahnaz said. The manager turned towards her.

'Is that a new account?' Harry asked.

Mazandarani shrugged. 'Perhaps.'

'You don't remember the man opening this account?' Harry asked.

'I do not.'

'But this is *not* a numbered account, so you will have an address?'

'Yes.'

'Could you find it for us, please? I'd also like to know when the account was opened, how much was paid into it, from where, by whom and in what currency.'

Mazandarani was about to refuse, but Harry took a step closer to him with an air of menace. The manager raised a hand in defeat and left the room.

Harry moved to the window once more. A small group was burning British and American flags, along with photographs of the Shah.

The manager returned. 'The account was opened six weeks ago. A hundred thousand *rials* was paid in. Cash.' He cleared his throat. 'That is clearly a significant sum, so I spoke to the clerks. They do remember the gentleman. He was a young man.'

'How young?'

'No more than twenty.'

'Iranian?'

'Yes. He brought the money in a briefcase and waited while the paperwork was signed and the account opened. He did give us an address, in Tabriz, but the clerks say they have written to him regarding other documents that need to be signed relating to the account and received no reply.'

'Has he been here since?'

'No.'

'How did these transfers occur?'

'He authorized them on the day he opened the account. We have not heard from him again.'

'The figures given to my son were in dollars.'

The manager shook his head. 'I don't know why that was. The transactions were all completed in our national currency.'

'I'll take this, if I may.' Harry gathered up the paperwork, folded it, and slipped it into his inside pocket. 'And thank you. You have been very helpful. The chief of police will be most appreciative.'

They stepped into the sunlight and stood watching the

stragglers at the back end of the protest. It was big, ten thousand people or more, Harry estimated. The police continued to stand by, tapping their truncheons against their dark blue uniform trousers.

Harry pulled out a handkerchief and wiped the sweat from his face. He watched another small group setting light to a pile of pictures of the Shah. 'The end of an era,' he said, though he didn't really believe it. Had the CIA truly given up so easily? It didn't seem likely. Their belief that they could remake the world in their own image was boundless.

'God, I hope so.'

There was a huge cheer as the photographs of the Shah caught light. 'Who do you think the man from Tabriz was?' Shahnaz asked.

'I don't know, but I don't like the sound of it.'

'Why not?'

'Tabriz is the KGB's stronghold here.' Harry tapped his pocketful of paper. 'I guess these accounts will belong to army officers, and it is therefore possible that the KGB was using the hundred thousand *rial*s to buy influence. Maybe that's the story Sean was chasing.'

'Or perhaps someone was making it look that way to set him up.'

'Exactly.' Harry glanced at his watch. 'We'd better move. I need to be back at the hotel by midday.'

25

'AH, MR TOWER,' the receptionist said, as they approached the front desk at the Ritz, 'we have a caller here for you. Perhaps you'd like to—'

'I'll take it in my room. Ask him to wait.' Harry sprinted up the stairs, Shahnaz in his wake.

The phone was already ringing by the time he reached his room. He took a moment to recover his breath before he picked up the receiver. 'Harry Tower?' The accent was lugubrious and Russian.

'Yes.'

'I have to ask you a question.' Harry let Shahnaz in and waited. 'Mr Tito had a personal assistant in Vukovar over Christmas 1944. What was her name?'

'Elena.'

'And what colour was her hair?'

'Black.'

'There is a café on Sadi Avenue, just off Sepah Square. You must be there at two o'clock sharp. Do not be late.'

The line went dead. Harry replaced the receiver. 'What was that about?' Shahnaz asked.

'An old ally.'

'What kind of ally?'

'The kind that may be able to help us make some sense of this.'

Shahnaz sat on his bed. 'How?'

Harry was about to brush her aside when he caught a glimpse of her acute vulnerability. He sat in the chair opposite and glanced up at the clock. He offered her a cigarette. She accepted. 'One of the places I was posted during the war was Yugoslavia – I think I told you that. We worked with the Chetniks originally, but I didn't trust them. I thought they'd betray their own grandmothers for the price of a bottle of vodka.

'We – well, I – persuaded Churchill back in London to switch our support to the partisans, which brought me into contact with a KGB officer who was on attachment to Tito. His name was Oleg Vasilyev. He was a good man. We fought closely together, helped each other to stay alive.'

'And now he's here in Tehran?'

'Yes.'

'How do you know that?'

'Rashidian told me.'

'As coincidences go, isn't this one a bit convenient?'

Harry grinned. 'You're starting to think like a spy. I'm not sure that's a good sign . . . But no. Not really. He's one of their most experienced operatives, and this is a highly significant theatre. In many ways, it would be more surprising if he wasn't here.'

If the protesters had been headed north to the American Embassy, as Harry guessed, they had evidently swung south again for the parliament building because the roads to it were clogged with traffic and Sepah Square itself packed with milling protesters. Harry parked in a corner of the square and they got out and watched in silence.

Harry guessed the average age in a crowd of ten thousand strong was twenty-five at most. Nor was it just young men. There were many women, too, almost all without their heads covered. The tense disapproval of older men passing was all too evident.

A tall student, wearing a white shirt and braces, with curly hair that tumbled over slender shoulders, was standing on a soapbox and yelling into a loudspeaker. 'Dr Mossadegh has urged citizens to be patient, to withstand the blockade. The British imperialists who have forced this economic crisis on us have now tried to rob us of our freedom. But they will not succeed! We cannot let them!'

'Is this a show of strength?' Harry asked Shahnaz. He had more or less to shout over the noise of the crowd.

'Of support. But the British and Americans won't dare try another coup now.'

'I wouldn't be so sure.' Harry glanced around him once again. Even the most casual observer could hardly fail to notice the seismic difference between the make-up of this crowd and the thugs who had been paid to turn out in support of the Shah. But he very much doubted the CIA would give up so easily. 'Mossadegh, Mossadegh,

Mossadegh!' The cry was taken up around them, hundreds of feet pounding the stones of the square.

Harry glanced at his watch. A minute before two.

The café was on Sadi Avenue, sandwiched between a carpet shop and a vegetable stall. The pavements teemed with people. He leant towards Shahnaz. 'Stay out of sight. I'll join you when I can.'

He spent ten minutes admiring the display of books at the front of a store on the far side of the street. Then he crossed over to sit next to an old man on a low stool smoking a *ghalyan* water pipe, and asked for a coffee.

The tables were shaded, but the heat was impossible to escape. A couple of kids tried to sell Harry cigarettes. Another came and offered him a *ghalyan* of his own before being shooed away by the waiter returning with his order. Harry sipped the dark, sweet liquid and swatted away the flies.

He checked his watch again. It was a moment before he noticed the man at his shoulder. 'You're getting old, my friend,' Vasilyev said. 'And slow.' He took the seat next to Harry, so that they both faced the street. 'I've had a tail for days now,' Vasilyev said. 'It's taken me hours to lose him. It's like a net is closing in.' He took a bottle of vodka and two glasses from a leather bag he carried over his shoulder. 'We hear they hunt a Soviet mole at the heart of SIS.' It was a warning.

'They know we worked together. Here in Tehran. In the mountains with Tito. They'd expect me to seek your help in a time of trouble.'

'Perhaps.'

Harry thought Vasilyev looked older and greyer. And

the eyes that scrutinized him from behind small, round glasses were not as bright as they had once been. 'You really don't look so good yourself,' Harry said.

'You, on the other hand, remain an inspiration to us all.' The Russian handed Harry a glass and raised his own. 'To old friends.'

They drank.

'Is it true your son found her?'

Harry did not answer.

Oleg refilled their glasses. 'Drink,' he ordered.

'To what?'

'Forgiveness, which God knows we both need.'

'How is Tatiana?'

'Fat, old, cantankerous. But in Moscow, thank God.'

Harry enjoyed the sting of the vodka in his throat and belly. He felt more at peace than he had in months. But Vasilyev had always had that effect on him. 'It's good to see you,' Harry said.

'And you.'

'How long have you been in Tehran?'

'A few months.'

'How is the Centre?'

'A madhouse.'

'I assumed things would be better now Uncle Joe is dead.'

'Perhaps they will be, one day. For now, survival is still the name of the game. The word from on high is that someone must be held accountable for the crimes of Comrade Stalin and his merry band of psychopaths. So who will it be?' Vasilyev refilled their glasses and stared sadly into his. 'I tell you frankly, I am afraid to be at home and frightened to be away. Is it better to be far from their gaze, in the hope they may forget about you, or squarely in their eyeline so that you might have a chance to shape your own destiny?' He shook his head. 'There are days when I think it cannot be long before my name is on one of their damned lists. And it is so *tiring*.' He sighed. 'I am sorry for your situation, Harry. First your wife, now your son. The fates are cruel.'

Harry's eyes narrowed. 'The fates, whoever they may be, have very little to do with it.'

Vasilyev nodded. 'Oswald is here. We saw him come through the airport just before you.'

'They arranged for someone to kidnap my son.'

'Yes. We—'

'They took him to force me out here. Even you must be able to see that.' Harry hoped Vasilyev might disagree with him and bolster one or other of the potential explanations he'd been carefully nursing, but the Russian played with his elaborate moustache thoughtfully, just as he always had ever since that night in Göttingen when they had first set eyes upon each other. 'Much easier to dispose of a problem far from home,' Harry said. 'Isn't that what you would do?'

The Russian smiled bleakly. 'Worrying how to dispose of people isn't really our issue.'

'They've tried to kill me once already. If they've been tailing you, they may attempt to get rid of us both together. So let's get down to business. I need your help. Where are they holding Sean?'

'It's hard to say. My guess is his kidnap was organized by his tennis partner, a bald-headed American—'

267

'Brad Vincent. He's from Langley. Some kind of special operations. He's working with an Ivy League type called Bryant.'

'We've been watching both men for weeks. Vincent tells anyone who will listen that he works for a charity called Global Vision. But, if so, he is the first charity official in history with regular and direct access to the Shah.'

'I think Global Vision is some kind of structure aimed at capturing the oil industry after they pull off the coup.'

'*If* they pull it off. That is yet to be determined.'

'They'll try again.'

'Of course. And I wish the minds of the Centre in Moscow were as focused on this as they are on their own survival. But, still, the affair is not yet concluded.'

'They have more money than you could possibly imagine.'

'And we have cunning.'

'You think here, of all places, that is a fair match?' Harry took the bullet from his pocket and put it on the table. 'Sean was taken by soldiers. Maybe from the Imperial Guard.'

Vasilyev nodded again. 'We have tailed both Vincent and Bryant more than once to a compound about ten miles north of the city. It is well protected and carefully hidden from view, so we have not been able to get close enough to see who or what is inside. But the gate is manned by soldiers from the Guard.'

'When Bryant came to see me the other night, he tried to claim Sean was now taking his instructions from Lubyanka Square.'

'How amusing.'

'Not really.' Harry dropped on the table the photograph of Sean with Ivan Prokopiev he had taken from Bryant.

The smile died on Vasilyev's lips as he recognized this was well beyond the rules of the game. 'I am sorry,' the Russian said, with feeling. 'I didn't know of the approach and I have disciplined Ivan since. He claimed to have been informed your son was already practically a Bolshevik. But the approach ended there. What is the man from Langley doing here?'

'I've never met him before.'

'Old, young?'

'Everyone is younger than us. He claimed Sean was down in Tabriz, waiting for the signal.'

'The signal?'

'For your forces to invade in support of a great national freedom-fighter in his battle to escape the imperial yoke.'

Vasilyev smiled. 'A nice story.'

'I've heard wilder ones. But it feels to me as though, whether you intended to or not, you have helped them build the perfect story – father and son, servants of the enemy.'

He knew Vasilyev well enough to be aware he rarely apologized once, never twice. 'If this is, as you say, Harry, the perfect place to deal with yesterday's man, then you should think hard. There is nothing more you can do for your son here.' Harry stared at his boots. He was not prepared to accept this. 'You want to atone for your sins, is that it? You think any of us has the time or grace for that?'

'If I can find the base they're operating out of, how many men can you give me?'

'Half a dozen at best.'

'I'll need more than that. You owe me more than that.'

'I say only this to you, Harry. It is time to run. You *must* accept that.'

'I'll call you when I'm ready.' Harry watched as a car was parked just opposite them. The driver got out and hurried away. 'Oleg . . .' He got to his feet. '*Oleg!*'

The world closed in. Suddenly he was moving, running, his lungs bursting. 'Oleg!' Harry looked back. Vasilyev was too slow . . .

Harry dived for cover behind a parked Morris Minor just as he felt the shockwave of the blast on his back. He hit the ground, dust in his mouth, ears and nose. The sound of the explosion roared in his head and the pain – intense, searing, blinding – ripped through him.

Harry rolled over and gazed up at debris floating in the air above him. He heard screams and shouts, distant and ethereal. He closed his eyes and the pain receded. He felt peaceful and detached. An image of his son floated into his mind, his face creased by an affectionate and mocking smile. 'It'll be all right, Dad. You shouldn't worry so much . . .' Harry fought the seductive pull of the darkness.

He opened his eyes. He saw flames, broken furniture, twisted torsos. Vasilyev's head, detached from his body, in the middle of the road. A man screaming, staring at the stump of what had recently been his leg.

Harry could not move his right arm, but was able to explore his chest and shoulder with his left hand. He forced his fingers up to his neck. He tried to walk them around the back of his head. There was catastrophic pain there, and plenty of blood. 'Harry!' Shahnaz leant over him. 'Christ, what *happened*?'

Her face filled the sky. He thought again how beautiful she was, how lucky his son would be if he were still alive. Harry closed his eyes and tried to marshal some sort of strength. 'Check me . . .'

'Harry? Can you hear me?'

'Check me . . . for bleeding.'

'I'll call an ambulance. Just hang on—'

'No . . . listen . . . to me . . .' She crouched lower. Her hair brushed his face. 'Ignore everything and everyone else. First, check my torso, front and back. Tell me . . . what damage . . .'

Shahnaz peeled open his jacket and examined his chest and stomach, then tried to thrust her trembling hands beneath him. Harry groaned and she stopped. 'Go on,' he growled.

'There's a *lot* of blood.'

'Where from?'

'I can't feel any—'

'My *head* . . .' She knelt beside him and ran her fingertips across his face and behind his ears. Harry recoiled. 'Turn me over . . .' he rasped.

She did as he asked. 'Glass,' she said. 'In the back of your skull . . . I . . . There's a lot of—'

'Get a bandage . . . anything . . . a shirt, my shirt. Rip it. Use it to stop the bleeding. Bind it round the glass, but keep the glass in place. Then get me to a surgeon. Quickly.'

She disappeared for a few seconds. When she returned, Harry did his best to fight off the pain as she bound his wounds, and failed. By the time she had finished, pinpoints of light peppered his blurred vision and all he could hear was the drumbeat of blood pulsing through his head.

She tried to lift and drag him, then other, more vigorous hands joined hers, and her soft perfume was obliterated by the smell of unwashed male bodies. Her voice, gentle but insistent, somehow registered above the cacophony that swirled around him. 'Harry, please hold on. *Please* hold on . . .'

He could sense the movement of a car, her arms around his shoulders. And then the world around him faded into oblivion.

26

HARRY FELT COOL liquid on his forehead, the dab of material against his skin and a palm on his cheek. He opened his eyes.

Shahnaz stepped back, startled. Then she recovered her composure, put the flannel back into the bowl and patted her hands dry against her blouse. 'Where am I?' Harry asked.

'Hospital. They extracted the glass. I'll get the doctor.'

She disappeared from his vision and returned with a plump, middle-aged Westerner. 'Glad to have you back with us, Mr Tower.' He sounded Dutch, or perhaps Danish. Harry tried to sit up. The surgeon raised his hand. 'All in good time. You've been very fortunate. I gather that the Russian gentleman behind you absorbed much of the blast. You probably owe him your life. In fact, all in all, you've escaped rather lightly. We removed an impressively large shard of glass from the back of your head, but as far as we can tell, it's done no neurological damage. We'll need to keep you under close observation, of course.'

'What happened to the Russian?'

The doctor glanced at Shahnaz. 'I'm afraid they had to scrape what was left of him off the pavement.' The image of onlookers skirting Vasilyev's head in the dust swam before his eyes. 'You've suffered a severe shock, Mr Tower. You need at least a week of complete rest. After that, you should be right as rain.'

The doctor disappeared and Harry closed his eyes again. He reached out and touched Shahnaz's arm. 'Thank you.'

'For what?'

'Getting me here. Taking care of me.'

'What did you expect?' He tried to pull himself upright and his head began to throb violently again. 'Lie still,' she said. She sat on the end of his bed. 'I'm sorry about your friend.'

Harry propped himself up on his elbows. 'I assume we are in the Pahlavi Hospital?'

'Yes.'

'At the back, there is the road that goes up to the Officers' Club and the Pahlavi Cavalry Barracks?'

'Jashmi Diyeh, yes.'

'Did you drive the Ford here?'

'No. But I've taken the key from what was left of your pocket. I was going to pick it up now.'

'After nightfall, park at the back there. Headlights off. In the meantime, go to the hotel and bring one of the Colt revolvers from the canvas bag in my room. And a box of ammunition. I'll leave by the window and find you.'

'Harry, you're not in a fit state to go anywhere or do anything. We're fifteen or twenty feet up.'

'We don't have a choice.' Her forehead furrowed. 'Go now,' he said. 'Please.'

'What did the Russian tell you about Sean?'

'I'll explain later. I have to get out of here. Tell the doctor absolutely nothing. Go home. And after dark, make sure you're there.' As he heard her footsteps fade, Harry drifted back to sleep.

His room was shrouded in darkness when he was jolted awake. 'Hello, Harry. Been a while. You don't look so good.'

He waited for his vision to adjust. He could make out Oswald's angular features. Moonlight glinted off his steel-rimmed spectacles and the hair in his nostrils had sprouted still further. Oswald gestured at an Iranian nurse beside him. 'This is Florence Nightingale.'

'Overjoyed to meet you.'

'We're going to need to move you in a minute. Then we'll be able to release your son.'

'Sounds like a happy ending.'

'My favourite kind. Yours, too. Florence works with our new friends in the Imperial Guard, so don't try anything stupid or your son and his beautiful girlfriend certainly won't get to ride off into the sunset together.'

'You'll let them go if I cooperate?'

'Certainly.'

'That *is* the kind of fairy story I like.'

'Just the kind of thing you would dream up.'

Harry reached for the lamp, but the table was pulled away. 'You won't need that,' Oswald said. 'You taught us, remember.'

275

'I seem to remember I also tried to throw in a few lessons on the value of loyalty.'

'You haven't left us a choice, Harry – unfortunately. I need to ask you a lot of questions.'

'You came all the way out here to ask me some questions? What was wrong with the bar at the Travellers or White's?'

'You're not a member of either.'

'Is that where I went wrong?'

'You can't talk your way out of this one, Harry. The game's up, I'm afraid. We have a mole. You know it, I know it. And he's been in place for years.'

'Say the Americans.'

'Says pretty much everyone. I'd think hard before you offer us any more wisecracks. C has the Americans breathing down his neck, it's true. So if you come clean, if you give us what we need to tie things up so that it all makes sense, we'll release your son. We don't make war on twenty-year-old kids, even if they are secret Bolsheviks.'

'Sean doesn't make much of a secret of his views. And the way this is going, I'm inclined to sympathize with him. Why don't you tell me what you're going to want from me?'

'All in good time, my friend.' Oswald shook his narrow head, lips pursed, eyes beady behind his glasses. 'All in good time. Mostly, for now, I need you to accept that this is the end of the line and to offer us your cooperation.'

'Or what? Florence here will stab me with a scalpel?'

Oswald's smile bared his teeth. 'Something like that. I know you will imagine there's some kind of escape here, Harry – we can't change our natures, after all – but I want you to know that you've run out of road.'

'I've been trying to piece it together,' Harry said, playing for time. 'I understand you need a scapegoat and the Americans demand one. I can see how I might fit the bill—'

'A spy, Harry. That is who we are hunting. A Moscow Centre hood who has betrayed his nation's interests for decades and sent countless men to their deaths behind the Iron Curtain – Mount Avala, then Albania. And who knows what in between?'

'Yes, I get it. And it must be so much easier to explain and accept if the man you have your eye on was never "one of us" in the first place.'

'It's too late to play that card.'

'Why? You and your kind have played it all your lives. And in your case it's no more than an invention.' He watched a muscle twitch in Oswald's cheeks. He'd been aiming for a reaction and he'd got one. 'But what I couldn't understand was how you had managed to get such a wide section of Iranian society to sign up to kidnap Sean and use him as bait to lure me out here.'

'Your son made it easy.'

'Yes, he's practically a Russian spy, too, right? And maybe that's enough to bring the Rashidians on side – you only have to click your fingers to have them react, after all – but General Salemi, the chief of police?'

'Patriots.'

'To whom you promised wealth beyond avarice. And I curse myself for being woefully slow to work out what Global Vision is all about.' He could tell he'd surprised his captor, which had also been his intention.

'That's very good, Harry, well done. You always were too clever for your own good.'

'Nobody believes I'm a traitor. And the fact that you haven't arrested me at home is a sure sign that none of you has the guts to tell Winston your theory, because you know he'd laugh in your faces.'

Oswald kept his temper with visible effort. 'I repeat, if you cooperate, we will release your son—'

'You think I'm too stupid to have worked out that you plan to dispose of us all? You're building my cover story still, no doubt – perhaps I'm to die in a final bid to run to the border and into the Soviet Union – but you've already fashioned Sean's: a tragic car accident more than a week ago, discharged from Isfahan Hospital to the morgue.'

'You've brought this on yourself, Harry. But for you, he'd still be alive.' There was a ponderous, regretful tone to Oswald's voice that unnerved Harry.

'He *is* alive.'

'Believe what you want. But one thing is certain: you are coming home with us. One way or another.' He nodded at the nurse, who had been waiting patiently. She took a syringe from her bag. 'Be a good boy, Harry,' Oswald said, 'or you might get hurt.' He always had enjoyed the rough stuff a little too much for comfort.

But few could match Harry's reflexes. As the nurse reached for his arm, he grabbed her hand and used her momentum to help thrust the needle across the bed and right into Oswald's eye. Harry rolled out of the bed and fell on top of him, stabbing the needle into his colleague's face again and again.

Oswald writhed and screamed in agony. Harry turned just in time to duck as the nurse raised an iron chair in an attempt to bring it crashing down upon his head. Harry kicked her feet out from under her so that she tumbled back against the bed and then onto the floor. Harry towered over her. 'Lie down, face down, hands and legs apart,' he ordered. She didn't argue, her broad, ugly face bloody from her fall. Harry put his boot into her back to reinforce his threat, then went to look through the small glass panel in the door at the corridor beyond. It was empty.

He crossed the room to the window overlooking the rear garden, undid the latch and eased it open.

27

OUTSIDE, THE SOUND of the cicadas filled the evening air. Harry eased himself out onto the window ledge, reached across to a cast-iron drainpipe, and wedged a toecap onto the nearest bracket that fastened it to the side of the building. He slid first one hand then the other behind the pipe and, gripping the warm metal, leant back and started to walk down the wall. The last bracket, six feet above the ground, gave way the moment he trusted it with his full weight. He lost his purchase, then his balance, and fell. A low hedge slowed his descent, but his left shoulder, still sore from the bomb blast, took most of the force of his landing. He lay still on the coarse grass, gasping for breath, pain coursing through his body.

Harry glanced up at the window, half expecting whoever Oz might have arrived with to be taking the same route, but – if he had indeed come with back-up – they were nowhere in sight. Harry tested his collarbone, hauled himself groggily to his feet and stumbled towards the line of palms that led to the perimeter. Every five trunks he stopped and listened – and rested – but he seemed to have only the cicadas for company.

There was a shout from the hospital window. Lights suddenly flooded the garden.

He could see no gate, so scrambled over the chain-link fence as best he could, which was neither simple nor silent. Once he was clear of it, Harry kept to the cover of the trees which bordered the road. After a couple of hundred yards he saw the red Ford Popular. He opened the passenger door and climbed in. 'I thought you were never going to come,' she said. She stared at him in horror. 'You're covered with blood.'

As Shahnaz turned the key in the ignition, he put his hand on her arm. 'My gun?'

'Under your seat.'

He reached down for it, checked the Colt's chamber – six rounds – and tucked it under his right thigh. His eyes darted between the windscreen and the side mirror. 'What happened?' she asked.

'I had a visit.'

'From whom?'

'Some old enemies.'

'What did they want?'

'To reminisce about old times.'

'Christ, you're still bleeding.' She took out a handkerchief and dabbed at his neck. 'You should have stayed in bed. They wouldn't have harmed you while you were in hospital, would they?' Harry continued to peer out into the darkness. Then he raised his left hand and placed it on hers.

'What is it?'

'Go on paying a great deal of attention to the back of my head.' He closed his right hand around the pistol grip, keeping it below the level of the dashboard. 'But as soon as I move, duck.'

He breathed deeply through his nose as a figure began to materialize out of the shadows ahead. He heard her do the same. A squat knucklehead from London Operations called Joe Armstrong raised his gun as he stepped out from the trees and pointed it directly at Harry's chest.

'My God, Harry, he's—'

Armstrong's broad, battered face shone in the moonlight. A slighter, more dangerous colleague – a Czech exile called Dvořák – emerged from the shadows to his left.

'*Get out of the car!*' Armstrong shouted.

Shahnaz gripped the steering wheel. 'Perhaps we should do what they—'

'If we do what they say, we'll both be dead in a ditch within the next five minutes.'

'Keep your hands where I can see them.'

'Easy, Armstrong,' Harry shouted. He dropped the Colt onto his lap and raised his hands momentarily. 'I'm coming. I'm not armed.'

'Open the car door, drop your gun in the road or I will shoot first and ask questions later.'

Harry didn't doubt it: both men were the most ruthless killers in SIS's arsenal. But being an assassin was not the same as being a soldier, in uniform or otherwise, and Harry doubted their reflexes were anything like as good as they imagined.

He opened the door, as if about to do as he was asked. And then he rolled hard onto the tarmac.

Armstrong's first two shots shattered the windscreen and punched a hole in the door inches above Harry's head. As Shahnaz screamed, Harry put his first bullet through Dvořák's stomach. The Czech grunted in agony and fell.

Harry felt the shockwave against his ear as Armstrong's third shot ricocheted off the edge of the door.

Harry raised his gun and fired a split second before Armstrong, so that his opponent's final shot whistled past his ear. Armstrong jerked back and crumpled into the dust.

Harry got to his feet. Dvořák clutched his stomach, trying to staunch the blood. Harry grabbed hold of his collar and managed to drag him into the shelter of the trees, where they would be shielded from Shahnaz's gaze. 'Where is my son?'

The Czech gave a low groan, eyes screwed shut against the pain.

'Judging by the look of that wound, Jan, I'd say you have a chance of surviving if I leave you here. But you're not going to make it if I put another big hole in you.'

Dvořák opened his eyes and looked up at Harry. 'He's dead. Our only question has been how and when to bury you beside him.' He grimaced. 'We thought we had you with that bomb. Too sloppy to think we would bug your hotel phone. You're losing your touch, Harry. But you move fast for an old man. Too bad for your KGB friend.'

Harry grabbed him by the neck and pressed the Colt's muzzle against his forehead. 'I mean it, Jan.'

'I don't know where he is.' Blood began to bubble from the corners of Dvořák's mouth. 'Big Boys' Rules, Harry. The New World Order. The Americans are in charge and you don't stand a fucking chance.'

Harry could hear engines somewhere close. He dropped Dvořák and stood up. Armstrong lay sprawled where he had fallen. Two hundred yards down the road a white saloon and a jeep hurtled towards them. Harry opened Shahnaz's door and pushed her across to the passenger seat. He punched out the remainder of the windscreen, slammed the Ford into gear and pulled away, wheels spinning. The white Standard Vanguard saloon and the jeep had split up so one was on each side of the road. Harry had no choice but to drive at them. Behind him lay only the Officers' Club and the cavalry barracks. 'My God, what are you doing?' Shahnaz hissed, clutching her seat.

Harry had his foot flat down. The jeep and the Standard closed up. The gap between them was narrowing rapidly, but Harry rammed the Ford through the centre of it. Shahnaz screamed again and the car shook violently, skidded one way, then the other. But they were through.

Shahnaz glanced over her shoulder. 'They're turning round!'

The Ford was battered but still moving. The wind was howling at them through the fringe of shattered glass.

'Where are you going?' Shahnaz asked.

'We need to avoid checkpoints.'

'Stay on Jashmi!' She pointed dead ahead. 'Just go straight.' She looked over her shoulder again. 'They're catching us!'

The Standard was faster than the jeep and, as it drew level, the Iranian man in the passenger seat wound down his window and began to take aim. Harry put his gun arm through what had once been the windscreen and fired a couple of shots. One must have hit the driver, because the car careered sideways, hit a parked truck, turned over, then rolled again and again, showering sparks across the tarmac.

Harry swerved violently to avoid it. Shahnaz gripped her seat in terror.

They hurtled past the Chinese and Polish embassies, above which the countries' national flags hung limply in the still summer air.

Harry pressed his foot flat down again, grateful for the pace of Christine's new Ford. A bullet from the jeep behind pinged off the metal. 'We can't escape them!' Shahnaz said. 'Harry, for God's sake, it's an army jeep.'

Harry tore past the squat United Nations building and swung into Simetri before careering left into Sepah Avenue. 'We can't outrun them,' she said. 'We have to give ourselves up.'

'They've tried to kill me twice today,' he muttered. 'And this is the last time I'm going to give them that chance.' He handed her the Colt. 'Fill the chambers.'

'What do you mean?'

'From the ammunition box.'

Shahnaz fumbled for bullets and attempted to cram them into the chambers with shaking fingers. 'There!' she said, pushing it back to him. Harry took his foot off the accelerator. 'What are you doing?' she asked.

'You had the right idea. They won't be expecting me to try to give myself up.'

'I don't understand.'

Harry turned round and watched the jeep hurtle towards them.

'What are you doing?' Shahnaz asked again.

'Wait!'

The jeep slowed. Two soldiers stood in the back. There were two more in the front. The longest odds he had faced for many years.

But Harry was the SIS's crack shot and rarely came in second in the annual shooting competition at the range down in Gosport. He calmly opened the door, stepped out, raised the Colt and fired twice at the men in the back, hitting both first time.

Four shots left.

He killed the driver next. But the officer beside him had a revolver with him, too, and he fired a series of shots through the windscreen.

But Harry held his nerve and fired once more. The man slumped back.

The street was still. Traffic had stopped in both directions. A trader pushing a barrel of fruit stared at him.

Harry went to the passenger door of the Ford and helped Shahnaz out. 'My God,' she said, shell-shocked. 'What have you done?'

'It's all right,' he whispered. 'The car is too conspicuous now. We'll go on foot.' He reached in for the rest of the ammunition box and emptied it into his pockets. He shoved the Colt into the waistband of his trousers and folded his shirt over it. 'Let's head for the bazaar,' he said quietly. 'I know somewhere we can hide there while we work out what to do.'

A gathering crowd watched them wordlessly as they walked off. Harry took her arm to keep her moving, glancing over his shoulder to check that they were not being followed. He skirted the National Park and the Ministry of Finance until the distinctive pepperpot minarets of the Shah Mosque indicated they were close to safety. 'What's the time?' Harry asked. He'd lost his watch in the course of the day.

'I don't know,' Shahnaz said. 'Eleven, perhaps midnight.'

But, late as it was, the bazaar was still humming with life. Outside the entrance by the mosque, men sat behind stalls loaded with pomegranates, oranges and lemons, drawing on cigarettes wedged between index finger and flat palm. Donkeys, goats, horses lumbered in and out of the entrance, carrying carpets, copperware, spices. Inside, the cafés were still packed with men in flat caps drinking tea, smoking *ghalyan* water pipes and playing cards or chess, the alleys full of twinkling lights and hushed conversations in darkened doorways. Shahnaz drew many admiring and some hostile looks. Few women were out so late.

Harry swung her into the alley of the butchers, where the stallholders were finally cleaning and shutting for the night, showing little interest in anyone passing as they hurried to finish and get home. The smell of rancid fat caught in the back of his throat and the cobblestones were slick with blood. Two women wrapped in dark *chadors* hurried past them. A couple of men watched them from a doorstep, flicking prayer beads idly in their fingers. 'Where are we going?' Shahnaz asked.

'The street of the money-lenders. There's a safe house I've used before.'

'But won't your colleagues know that—'

'I was the only one who ever knew of it. I made a habit of never telling anyone else the details of my haunts, in Tehran or anywhere else.' Harry stumbled slightly and Shahnaz caught him. He leant against a wall.

'Are you all right?' she asked.

'We need to keep moving,' he said. But his vision was blurred. He straightened. 'We need to keep moving,' he said again.

28

London, August 1952

HARRY HAD ALWAYS believed in travelling light, but Sean's decision to leave for a new life with a single battered leather suitcase that had once belonged to his mother struck Harry as not so much journeying light as empty. Perhaps that was the point, leaving it all behind.

Now, at the moment of departure, Sean had seemed to hesitate and had disappeared into his room. Harry glanced at his watch. 'We'd better get on the road, old boy,' he shouted up. He had never travelled anywhere without turning up in good time, a response to his own father's permanent tardiness.

Harry imagined that running away from the ghost of his dead mother – which he assumed was Sean's driving motivation – was not without its emotional complications. He tried not to hurry him further.

Sean emerged, eyes still glistening from the tears he must have shed in private. Harry took his suitcase and put it into the back of the Austin. For all their arguments these past months, Harry understood. He was half tempted to run away himself.

They drove in silence. This was mostly how they'd existed since Amanda's death, but Harry felt keenly the pressure to puncture it today. He longed to bridge the chasm between them. He just had no idea how. 'Looks like the weather will break,' he said eventually.

'Looks like it,' Sean agreed. He'd grown his hair longer since Christmas and had taken to sporting a beard. Harry had to admit it suited him. 'You see that story about Arthur Wilson in *The Times*?' he asked. 'Ten bloody catches behind wicket. Must be a record.'

'I guess so.'

'You'll miss the cricket.'

'I suppose I will.'

The seconds crawled by. 'Bloody hot in Tehran at this time of year.'

'I imagine so.'

Conversation had never been Harry's strong suit. He tried again. 'If you get the chance, you must head up to the Caspian. If you drive east and wind through the Alborz, you descend into a different world, verdant not arid, and it's as if the landscape has literally exploded into life.'

Sean forced a smile. 'That's unusually poetic for you, Dad.'

Harry tried to grin back. 'You will look up the Audi-nettes? I am sure, if anything goes wrong, that they would—'

'I've said I will and I will.'

'They may be able to help you get started with contacts and so on. You'll obviously need them to—'

'I know what I need to do, Dad. You've told me. Many times.'

Harry tried a different tack. 'You'll miss the Coronation.'

Sean shook his head. 'I'm not much of a monarchist. I leave that to you.'

There was another long silence. Sean had been exaggerated in his civility since Amanda's death. Harry recognized it for the barrier it was intended to be. He'd have preferred almost anything else. It felt like death by a thousand courtesies. 'About your place at Cambridge . . .'

'We've been through this.'

'I'm sure if you – if *we* – wrote, explaining the circumstances, they would agree to keep open your place, just in case you changed your mind.' Sean had been studying English at Harry's old college, Pembroke.

'I'm not going to change my mind,' Sean said.

'Of course. But this assignment is only for a month or two, so—'

'I've said I hope to extend it for as long as possible. And even if they appoint another correspondent above me, I'd hope to stay on to assist him.'

'It's just that—'

'Dad, you know I talked to Mum about this before she died?'

Harry tried to hide his surprise. 'When? I mean, in what way?'

'In the way conversations happen between people who

love each other. I told her that you wanted me to stay at Cambridge to finish my degree, but that I knew I was going to be a journalist, that I'd been doing a lot of free-lance shifts for the *Manchester Guardian* and that I had been told the quickest way to make it as a foreign correspond-ent was to grab any chance going to set yourself up as a stringer somewhere with a running story. She completely understood. So you're never going to change my mind.'

Harry turned his attention back to the road. The traffic was busy – they should have left more time. For so much of his life, silence had been blessed. So why did it now feel like an accusation? 'I'm sorry,' Harry said finally.

'For what?'

'Everything that happened.'

'But for what *exactly*?'

'I should never have sent her back to that hospital.'

'You've said that before. But it was about so much more than that, as you well know.'

Harry hesitated. He understood what Sean wanted, or thought he did. But it was a Rubicon he still could not bring himself to cross. It was not – it could not have been – *all* his fault. If he admitted that his wife's death was his responsibility alone, he was lost. 'No one should have to endure what you have,' Harry said.

Sean turned away and the momentary engagement Harry had sensed evaporated. The chasm widened. 'I don't see the point in going over this again,' Sean said.

'You may be gone a while . . .'

'For an eternity.' Sean didn't look at him or smile. Harry wondered if this was some kind of joke. He tried to chuckle, but Sean didn't notice. Silence descended again, like a dark fog. Outside, the world seemed to respond: it began to rain, first in scattered drops and then in great, thunderous dollops.

'I thought the weather would break,' Harry said. And perhaps it was his imagination, but Sean finally allowed himself the glimmer of a smile.

29

Tehran, August 1953

THE STREET OF the money-lenders was empty, but Harry was dead on his feet by the time they reached the tiny store he sought. Blurred vision had become a pounding migraine and fatigue was consuming him. He looked for the key, which was supposed to be wedged into the ledge above the door.

It wasn't there. Harry leant against the wall. 'What is it?' Shahnaz asked.

They heard the shrill pipe of a police whistle somewhere in the distance. There were shouts from the direction of the entrance to the bazaar. 'They're looking for us,' she said. Harry cast about him for something with which to pick the lock. 'What do you need?' she asked.

'A piece of wire, a hairpin. The key has disappeared.'

'Perhaps the store is being used for something else. You—'

'I bought it in cash.'

'But it was almost ten years ago. How do you know—' She snapped her head round in the direction of another slew of shouts. They were getting closer. 'If they find us . . .' she said. But her voice trailed off again.

She was looking on the ground around her, while fumbling in her pockets. 'Here!' She produced a hairpin and gave it to Harry, who set to work on the padlock. There were more blasts of a police whistle. It sounded like they were only a few alleys away. 'Perhaps we should run,' Shahnaz said.

Harry was trying to concentrate, but the pain in his head was searing and his eyesight had never been poorer. 'I can hear them,' Shahnaz said. 'They're coming . . .'

The padlock clicked open. Harry pulled her hurriedly inside and closed the door silently.

Only just in time. They heard the thunder of passing footsteps, the hubbub of a mob in pursuit.

They waited, holding their breath. Finally, the noise receded. Harry exhaled, closed his eyes and sank to the floor. The store was tiny, filthy, dark, the air thick with the aroma of dust and mould. Shahnaz found a gas lamp and tried to get it alight, to no avail. She knelt in front of him and he opened his eyes as she tried to wipe the crusted blood and dirt from his neck. 'Are you all right?' she asked.

'I'll live.'

She sat back against the wall. It was a bare room, no more than twelve feet across, with damp stone walls, empty shelves, a wooden desk and chair. 'Maybe, in a while, I could go out in search of some water to clean those cuts.'

'I'll be fine.'

'You need to get the dirt out of them or you'll—'

He smiled at her. 'I always hoped for a daughter.'

She seemed to understand it had been meant as a compliment. 'Why did you not have one?'

'Amanda had . . . difficulties. The doctors told us Sean was something of a miracle.'

'I'm sorry.'

'Nothing to be sorry about. The day he was born was the happiest of her life. Of both our lives. An innocent welcomed into a tumultuous world.'

She seemed to think about that. They listened to the distant sounds of the city. The blast of a police whistle was much fainter now. 'What was your wife like?' she asked eventually.

'Simple in her emotional attachments. By which I mean every other woman I had known was complicated in a way she wasn't.'

'I like the sound of that.'

'She could never make up her mind which dress to wear, or what to order off a menu, but was wonderfully decisive about all the important stuff. She was kind. She was loving. She was fun. She had a terrible temper. It was rarely roused, but not to be trifled with. She wasn't shy about hurling half our kitchen at me. She was passionate. She was loyal. Deeply, deeply loyal. Once she'd committed herself to someone or something, it was impossible to convince her otherwise.' He gave a rueful grin. 'She stuck with me, after all.'

'I wish I could have met her.'

'I wish she could have got to know you.' He recalled his

wife's vivid smile and the way it could fade. 'Of course, she had a different side. I could always sense a depressive period coming. It rolled in slowly, like a storm you knew was approaching. And when it hit, it was bewildering in its intensity. For me. For Sean. But most of all for her. She felt like she was drowning and there was nothing any of us could do to help her. It was traumatizing every single time. And then it would pass and we would bury the memory of it and convince ourselves it might never happen again.'

'Why could the doctors not help her?'

'When it comes to diseases of the mind, it seems to me they haven't progressed much beyond the fifteenth century. They tried electric-shock therapy, which horrified me. I insisted they stop that. They medicated her, subjected her to "talking" therapies to within an inch of her life. Finally, I found a small private hospital with a psychiatrist I began to believe in. That was where we sent her the last time. But he turned out to be away on annual leave, she discharged herself and . . .' The pain was still so raw that the words caught in his throat. 'Perhaps if I had been there . . .'

Shahnaz stared at her hands as they listened again to the sounds of the bazaar at night. 'I dream of him so vividly,' she said.

'So do I.'

'What does that mean?'

'It means he's still alive.'

'That is surely just wishful thinking.'

'I don't think so. The paperwork in their file said he had been discharged from the hospital to the morgue. But he was not there. Yet. If he was already dead, why not send him there?'

'I don't understand.'

'They have their cover story. But they won't go through with it all until they've tied up the loose ends.'

'Meaning you?'

'And perhaps you, too.'

She shook her head regretfully. 'I went to Sean's office before I fetched the gun from your room at the hotel. Nazadeh had managed to get the records from the telephone company.'

'What do they tell us?'

'I looked at about the last two months. Called nearly all the numbers. Most were government ministries, voluntary organizations or embassies. He rang the bank quite a few times in the last two weeks. And Pierre and Christine.'

'Did he call anyone in Isfahan?'

'No. That was the first thing I looked for.'

'That's odd.'

'Why?'

'He goes all the way down there without making an appointment? Who was he expecting to see?'

'My father? Perhaps he drove to Latak.'

'Perhaps. Or maybe he suspected someone might be listening at the office and placed the final calls from somewhere else.' Harry took the note of incorporation for Global Vision Oil from his jacket and threw it across to her.

'What is it?' She held it up to the crack of light from the doorway.

'It's a shell company, which looks like it was formed to

try to capitalize on the oil rush that is sure to ensue if the coup eventually succeeds here. I've been wondering how it was that my colleagues seem to have tied so many different people and institutions into cooperation or at least silence over Sean's disappearance – the Rashidians, the chief of police, some sections of the military, at least.'

'My father?'

'My best guess is that he's at the centre of it.'

'Sadly, that wouldn't surprise me. One of his defining characteristics is greed. He's always felt aggrieved that senior military men are excluded from the nation's potential wealth. So what do we do?'

'Our best chance may be to divide and rule. Public exposure would make life difficult for any new regime. But Sean may have been on to this – I'm coming to accept he was a better journalist than I realized – which would make including him in the scheme to do me in even more attractive.' She pushed the piece of paper back towards him and let her head fall against the wall behind her. She looked exhausted and her eyelids were drooping. 'We'd better get some sleep,' he said.

'I'm sorry . . . I feel so tired suddenly.' She lay down and closed her eyes. Harry stood over her, folded his jacket and slipped it gently beneath her head. 'You'll need that,' she said. He squatted in the middle of the floor. 'I won't be able to get to sleep if you watch over me.'

'You look peaceful when you're sleeping.'

'I don't feel very peaceful. I want this to be over.'

Harry lay down beside her and was asleep almost instantly.

*

He was woken the following morning by an agonizingly stiff shoulder, a pounding head and a throat that felt as raw as sandpaper. He rolled onto his feet and tried to stretch. He smoked a cigarette and listened to the tremulous voice of the muezzin summoning the faithful to prayer.

Shahnaz lay absolutely still, breathing evenly, her head tilted to one side.

Harry cracked the door and slipped out into an alley still deserted in the half-light. He drifted towards the entrance to the bazaar as stores were opened for business and wares put on display. '*Salaam alaikum*,' the merchants called.

'*Alaikum salaam*,' he muttered back.

The square by the gate was already overflowing with protesters. Buses were backed up along Sadi Avenue, and wave after wave of placard-bearing men poured out of them. Most looked shabby and unkempt, and milled about aimlessly. They all carried photographs of the Shah and his wife.

Harry started to work his way towards the front of the crowd, looking for some sign of who might be leading the mob. Then he caught sight of Shahnaz, watching him from an archway. He walked over to her. 'What are you doing here?' he asked.

'I woke and couldn't find you. The door was banging so I came out into the street and kept on walking towards the noise.'

'You were watching me.'

'I thought you might be up to something. I didn't want to interfere. Why?'

'Nothing.' Harry held her gaze a moment more, then

turned to face the crowd. He caught sight of a man handing out banknotes as if he was Santa Claus.

'Fifty *rials*,' Shahnaz whispered. 'This must be costing someone a fortune!' A cry rippled through the crowd. And then an increasingly deafening chant. Harry could only make out 'Shah . . . *ShahanShah* . . .'

'King of Kings,' Shahnaz whispered. They were swept along. As each group left the square, a placard adorned with the Shah's face was thrust into outstretched hands. Drums began to roll. 'Let's get to the front,' she said.

'Stay here,' Harry instructed.

'I want to see who they are and where they're going.'

'Remember what happened the other day.'

'This is different,' she insisted.

'It is. You're the only woman in the entire crowd.'

She took his hand. 'Come on.'

They turned onto Sadi Avenue and made their way through to the front of the procession. At least two hundred enormous men with huge, muscular torsos waved barbells above their heads or juggled heavy pins over their shoulders to the rhythm of a drummer. Almost all the men were naked but for loincloths and extravagant moustaches. 'The Zurkhaneh giants,' Shahnaz said.

'Where do they fit in?'

'Weightlifters who use an ancient Iranian exercise routine to build up their torsos. They train in places like that gymnasium we went to the other day and they mostly come under the control of the gangs that operate in south Tehran.' A group of slimmer men emerged from behind the Zurkhaneh and began to whirl like dervishes. The drumbeat quickened.

Protesters wheeled away from the crowd and charged towards a white three-storey building. A guard standing by the gate was knocked to the ground and set upon. Others rushed past him and smashed in the front door. Harry was about to follow them when Shahnaz grabbed his arm. 'Don't,' she said. 'It's a pro-Mossadegh paper. They'll tear the place to bits.'

Within seconds, chairs and desks were being hurled out of upstairs windows, typewriters and anything else of value looted. Then smoke began to billow from the upper floors. A photographer was down on one knee on the small lawn in front of the building. It was a moment or two before Harry recognized Christine Audinette. She retreated to his side, as if she had been aware of his presence all along. 'It's really happening, this time,' she said. She let her camera drop for a moment. 'You have to hand it to the Americans. They know how to do things in style.'

Harry looked at the swelling crowd. 'It must be costing them a king's ransom.'

'But it's nothing compared to the fortune they'll make here when it's done.' She looked at him. 'Isn't that the truth?' Harry shrugged, though it was self-evidently the case. 'Have you found him?' she asked.

'Not yet.'

Christine leant closer. 'Run, Harry. Down to Tabriz. While you still can.' And then she was gone again, swallowed by the crowd.

'Let's get out of here,' Harry said, as he rejoined Shahnaz. 'I've seen enough.'

'No. Something is happening. I need to see what they are going to try to do,' she insisted.

'You don't.'

'*I do.*' She charged ahead.

He had to run to keep up. 'If we get into trouble in this kind of mob,' he yelled, 'I shan't be able to—'

Shahnaz ignored him and kept on walking. The front section of the march had reached Sepah Square, where it wheeled into a crowd already several thousand strong. 'Long live the Shah!' they cried in ecstasy. '*Long live the Shah!*'

A soldier on top of a tank fired his rifle into the air, then jumped down to join them.

Harry hoisted himself onto the railings and watched a group of men move through the throng, whispering into every available ear and pressing a ten-, twenty- or fifty-*rial* note into every palm. Others hurried along behind them, distributing leaflets as they went. Harry reached out for one and passed it to Shahnaz.

'The *firman* again,' she yelled. 'The Shah's executive order to appoint Zahedi his prime minister. They're still trying to make it happen.'

Harry gave it a closer look. 'Let's follow them.'

'Why?'

Harry didn't bother to reply. The pamphleteers had reached Sepah Avenue. By the time he got to the far side of the square, they were climbing, empty-handed, into a waiting car. It turned and pulled away.

'We need a taxi.'

They found one at the corner. Harry pushed Shahnaz in and jumped in beside her. 'Tell him to follow that white Packard.' He pointed through the windscreen. The driver nodded and set off in pursuit.

'Where are we going?' Shahnaz asked.

'Take a look at the *firman* again.'

'What about it?'

'It's not printed, is it? But copied. And the machines to do it are huge, cumbersome and expensive. They are also very rare. We have one in the office in London, the Americans in Washington. But I'll wager there hasn't been one in all of Iran until now.' He took back the copy. 'And if it has been installed recently, it can only have been for this purpose.'

Harry leant forward in his seat, pointing and encouraging the driver to keep pushing through the waves of protesters still filling the streets. Eventually they left the crowds behind them and the driver began to navigate his way through the morning traffic.

Harry stayed at the driver's shoulder until they reached the northern tip of the city, where the Alborz Mountains rose through the morning haze. Harry flicked sweat from his forehead and wound down the window for some air.

They left the tarmac and hit a dirt track. Dust flew up from the tyres as they bounced along it. Harry touched the driver's shoulder. 'Take it easy . . .'

Shahnaz translated and he took his foot off the accelerator. But he was beginning to look nervous. He started gesticulating, and talking to Shahnaz in animated Farsi.

Harry kept his eyes on the car they were following as it turned into a compound surrounded by a high fence topped with huge rolls of barbed wire. Half a dozen Iranian Army guards in steel helmets manned the gate, and another with a dog patrolled the perimeter wire. 'Stop here,' Harry said. The driver didn't need to be told twice.

Harry's eyes didn't leave the compound as he pulled out the Colt and filled its magazine. He tucked the revolver into his pocket and put on his sunglasses. 'Stay here,' he said. 'And make sure the driver does too. We might have to leave in a hurry.'

Harry left the dirt track almost immediately for the scrub-covered hillside. He worked his way through the rocks to the far side of the compound, then climbed above it to an outcrop that afforded him cover and a clear view of the bungalow at the centre of the property. Two guards prowled along this section of the perimeter fence.

The young men they had followed from Sepah Square emerged from the front of the bungalow with more armfuls of the *firman* leaflets and loaded them into the boot of the car. They made a couple of trips before driving back past Shahnaz and the waiting taxi. As the sun rose to its zenith, the guards retreated into the shade and kicked their heels. Nothing else stirred. Harry could feel the temperature rising.

He crouched as a bald-headed white man in chinos and a sports shirt stepped out onto the terrace – the American from Sean's tennis four. He was gesturing to someone who took a couple of minutes longer to leave the shadow of the overhanging canopy. Pierre Audinette fought a losing battle to cool himself with his Panama before both moved back into the house.

Harry was preparing himself for another long wait when the Frenchman hurried out of the front door and into a car that had been waiting by the gate. His companion emerged from the bungalow a few moments later with a jerry-can and started dousing the exterior with what must have been petrol. He dropped a lit match, watched the blaze take hold, then sped off after the Frenchman.

As soon as both vehicles had left the compound, the guards loaded up into a jeep and a truck. They drove out of the gate, stopped to lock it, then roared away down the hill.

Harry waited until he was sure they had gone, then ran round to the front gate, which was the only section that did not have barbed wire above it. He climbed over it, ran to the bungalow and kicked in the back door. He covered his nose and mouth with his handkerchief and ran through the accelerating fire. In the first room, he saw caricatures scrawled into the wall with a stone or rock.

Of the Shah, of Mossadegh. But they were in a circle and at its centre was a face with the unmistakable features of Shahnaz's father, General Adel Salemi.

'Sean!' he bellowed.

Harry tore through the house. There was no sign of his son, but in the room at the far end of the corridor, he found himself in a makeshift office. Before departing, someone had pulled everything from the walls and emptied the drawers of a desk into a pile at its centre, which had also been doused in petrol and set alight. All that was left was a blackboard covered with names and numbers and a column headed 'timeline'. In it, the coup was laid out, with the final entry ringed: *Zahedi, Officers' Club.*

The intensifying fire and gathering smoke forced Harry to retreat. He returned to the gate and to the waiting taxi. It was clear it had taken all Shahnaz's powers of persuasion to get the driver to stay. He looked terrified at what he might have been talked into. 'Sean was here,' Harry told Shahnaz, as he climbed in, flooded with relief.

'Where?'

'There were some of his caricatures on the wall. A series of figures surrounding a man at the centre: your father.'

Shahnaz digested this. 'Where is Sean now?'

'He's alive. That's what matters.'

She pointed at the taxi driver. 'Where do you want to go?'

'The Officers' Club. That's where the coup is about to reach its conclusion.'

30

EVENTS HAD MOVED rapidly in the hour since they'd left the city. Many of the streets were now thronged with traffic and crowds carrying pictures of the Shah. They passed a building on fire and then, five hundred yards later, a second.

'Damn,' Shahnaz muttered, beneath her breath.

'What was that?'

'It's *Bakhtar-e-Emruz*, a pro-Mossadegh newspaper owned by Foreign Minister Fatemi.' She craned her neck. 'It looks like they're trying to take over the city.'

She turned to see a column of tanks grinding towards them. Soldiers stood proud of their hatches, waving pictures of the Shah. The crowds cheered. A burst of gunfire split the air and the taxi driver, now petrified, ground to a halt. Harry told him to keep driving, but progress was slow.

Another burst of gunfire, and the crowd around the car

split and spilt past to allow Harry to see that a battle was raging in front of a tall white stone building. A machine-gunner at the rear of a jeep raked the walls with bullets. A couple of men in civilian clothes were firing back from the upstairs windows and a handful of pedestrians caught in the crossfire lay sprawled in the road. A group of protesters, who were trying to shelter behind a line of cars, thumped the taxi in fury.

'Keep going,' Harry shouted.

The traffic moved a little more easily again, but not for long. All the main squares in central Tehran were choked with demonstrators waving banners supporting the Shah. Soldiers and some policemen seemed to have joined them. More tanks and jeeps appeared, loaded with joyful opponents of the prime minister.

Once or twice, they passed lorries that appeared to be full of captured Mossadegh loyalists, and soldiers who had attempted to rally to his cause. Passing cars honked their approval at the captors. They had to pull up and park short of the Officers' Club. The crowd that surrounded it was more relaxed and welcoming than any Harry had yet encountered in Tehran, and they passed through it with ease, until soldiers in crisp khaki uniforms barred their way at the gate.

None of Shahnaz's arguments had any effect, and men clustered around them thrust copies of the *firman* at Harry. 'Zahedi, Zahedi!' they shouted excitedly, pointing at the low white building on the far side of the courtyard.

Harry moved closer to Shahnaz. 'What's happening?' he asked.

'General Zahedi has just arrived. They say they're

discussing the new cabinet and the arrangements that need to be put in place for the Shah's return from Rome. He has categorically instructed them not to allow in any visitors whose names are not on their list.'

A cheer from inside the building rolled across the courtyard and was taken up by the crowd. 'What are they cheering about?' Harry asked.

'I have no idea. And neither do they.'

Harry took an envelope out of his pocket, unfolded the letter from Winston Churchill he always carried with him and handed it to Shahnaz. 'Give them this, explain what it is and make sure that one of them takes it directly to General Zahedi, or his closest aide.'

Shahnaz glanced at Churchill's signature and turned to the young officer in charge. He read it, shrugged and disappeared across the courtyard. He came back ten minutes later, opened the gate and clicked his heels. 'It is a pleasure to meet you, Mr . . .'

'Harris,' Harry said.

'Please come with me.' The man led them across the courtyard, past a group of young army officers, who lounged against an ancient cannon. They were smoking and laughing, obviously in high spirits. 'This is a very great day for the people of Iran, Mr Harris.'

'I understand that.'

'We always had every confidence that our countrymen would rise up, and that their loyalty to the Shah was not in doubt. It was only a matter of time. We could not go on as we were.'

'Well, your faith has certainly been rewarded.' They slipped through the huge doorway into a blessedly cool corridor. The hall was packed with men, who were listening to an officer address them from the stairwell above.

'Zahedi,' Shahnaz murmured.

The general was surrounded by his supporters and cronies and spoke with fluency and passion.

'He is telling them that this is one of the most important moments in the entire history of Iran,' she whispered. 'And that the people will never forgive them if they do not rise to the challenge. He has not yet spoken to His Imperial Majesty in Rome, but he understands the news of the dictator Mossadegh's removal has been conveyed to him and that he is delighted. He apparently never doubted the loyalty of his people, or that events would come right at the end of the day. He – the general – intends to place a call to His Majesty within the hour, and to make arrangements for what he expects to be a triumphant return to his beloved country.'

Zahedi ploughed on. Harry cast an eye across the faces of the crowd around him. Most of the officers wore expressions of ecstasy, but his attention was drawn to the corner beneath the stairwell. Adel Salemi was regarding Zahedi with more than a hint of triumph. Next to him stood the bald-headed man from Sean's tennis four and Pierre Audinette.

'Now, enough,' Shahnaz relayed. 'There is an enormous job to do to get this country back on its feet, to restore the economy and prosperity, to give people work and hope, and to beat back the influence of the leftists, the Communists and the Russians before it is too late. He says he will not rest until their beloved monarch presides over a country at peace with itself.'

The roar around them as Zahedi concluded his peroration and departed for the floor above seemed about to take off the roof. The officer who had escorted them from the gate waited a moment until the crowd had begun to disperse, then nodded towards the stairwell. 'Please follow me, Mr Harris.'

Salemi, Audinette and the American were watching Harry now, though Shahnaz appeared not to be aware of her father's presence. Harry nodded acknowledgement to Pierre and Salemi, who gestured curtly in response.

'It is so good to have an inspirational leader at last,' the officer said. He was a good-looking man with a friendly manner and a guileless face. 'Like your Mr Churchill.'

'Indeed.'

'I'm sure General Zahedi will tell you that we are very grateful for Mr Churchill's unstinting support.' The officer delivered them to the landing. 'Please wait here. General Zahedi's aide will come to find you in a few moments. He knows you are waiting.' They shook hands again. 'It was a pleasure to meet you both.' He departed with a more than moderately appreciative appraisal of Shahnaz. 'And thank you again for your assistance to our country in its hour of need.'

Harry glanced around them. They were at the heart of a crowd that seemed pumped up on adrenalin and excitement. Their exchanges were animated and forceful. 'Some of his cabinet, I suppose,' Shahnaz said.

'Do you recognize them?'

'One or two, all the most devoted of the Shah's loyalists. I'm surprised my father is not here.'

Before Harry could answer, the double doors opened

and an expectant hush descended. Another young officer – a much taller man, with a regal bearing all of his own – sought out Harry and Shahnaz and invited them to enter, to the astonishment of the waiting grandees.

They were ushered into the club's library, deep armchairs surrounded by low tables and high bookshelves stacked with ancient leather tomes. The general was alone, save for his aide. Close up, Harry was struck by his stature. He had thin grey hair and a gaunt face, but bounded towards them with the energy of a man half his age. 'It is a great honour to meet you, sir. Mr Churchill's timing is impeccable, if I may say so.'

'This is my daughter-in-law, Shahnaz Salemi,' Harry said.

The general took her hand cautiously. 'I know your father well, Miss Salemi. And your beauty by reputation, of course.' He turned back to Harry. 'Your son is a very lucky man.'

He sat them down and offered tea or something stronger, which they both declined. The aide took a seat close to the door. 'This is a very important moment in the history of my country,' Zahedi said. 'Without the events of the past few days, that mad old fool would have had us under the Soviet yoke in a matter of weeks. A proud nation would have lost its independence and been reduced to the status of mere vassal.

'We are happy to have fought for our freedom, and many of us would have done so until the last man. But we could not have carried off such a victory without the support of our friends, and I would like you to convey to your prime minister that I, personally, am deeply grateful. We know who our allies are, and we will not forget it.'

'I'm pleased to hear that, and I have no doubt the prime minister will be too. As you say, yours is a nation with a strong history of independence, standing at the crossroads of the world.' Harry sensed Zahedi expected a speech. 'Were we to have lost Iran to Soviet influence, who knows what other threats we who live for freedom might have faced in the coming years? Her Majesty's Government – and the prime minister in particular – want you to know that it is our intention to provide you with every assistance in the future. We have been – and the prime minister hopes will remain – close friends and allies.'

Zahedi nodded and, now the formalities had been concluded, took a silver cigarette case from his uniform pocket and offered it to both of them. Harry accepted and they lit up. He was still trying to assess whether the general was involved in the kidnap of Sean. He struck Harry as the kind of man who liked to maintain an elevated view of himself and who perhaps preferred to skate above knowledge of the grubby realities and compromises of his grab for power.

'We couldn't have done it without you,' Zahedi said. 'But then, you know that. His Imperial Majesty is a man of many talents, but I think we can both agree he would not have been brought to the point of signing the *firman* without Mr Vincent's confidential visits to the palace, and the assurance that he spoke directly for President Eisenhower and Prime Minister Churchill.' Zahedi sucked deeply on his cigarette, never taking his eyes from his guest. 'I assume you are well acquainted with Mr Vincent?'

Harry shook his head. Vincent was the bald-headed man he had seen downstairs, the CIA agent who had run the coup. The so-called Quiet American. 'I was sent here to stand back, to *observe* events as they unfolded,' Harry said, 'and advise Downing Street on any action that might be necessary if things had not gone to plan. You will be aware that Mr Churchill does not like to be associated with failure.' Zahedi glanced doubtfully at his aide. It was clear they were confused by Harry's presence and perhaps uncertain of his credentials. But who in their right mind would think Winston Churchill incapable of undermining his own operation, if circumstances demanded? 'But the happier part of my mission was to make contact to offer congratulations and support in the event of the outcome we were all hoping for.'

Zahedi nodded slowly. 'Is there a leader in the world more capable than your Mr Churchill? I somehow doubt it. It is an honour to receive his seal of approval.' He tugged at the seams of his immaculately pressed khaki trousers, then leant forward and stubbed out his cigarette. 'Well, Mr . . .'

'Harris.'

'Harris, yes. I do not wish to appear impolite, but we have a country to recover, and some of the prospective members of my cabinet await.' He stood. 'It was a great pleasure to meet you. Please convey my thanks directly to Mr Churchill. I have not seen him since the conference here at the end of the war and he would not, of course, recall me, but—'

'He certainly does.'

'How flattering. Our meeting was a fleeting affair. If there is anything else I can—'

'Now you mention it, General, there is one other thing

that is concerning us, which we would be grateful for your assistance with.'

Zahedi lowered himself to the edge of his seat, as if to indicate that Harry's request should not be too time-consuming. 'Please . . .'

'An English journalist is missing. He disappeared about ten days ago. You perhaps haven't had the misfortune of dealing with our colleagues in the British press, but they are quite aggressive when it comes to protecting their own, and we predict a great deal of trouble if he is not found imminently. Perhaps you are already aware of the matter.'

Zahedi's face clouded and he glanced at his aide. 'This is something Mr Churchill himself is concerned about?'

'Yes.'

There was a long silence. Zahedi sighed. 'Mr Harris, you look like a military man . . . A man of action.'

Harry did not answer.

'You must understand that for the last few days we have found ourselves essentially at war – the battle for the soul and the sanity of a nation. You will also be aware that things happen at such times, which would have been unthinkable in calmer days.'

'Are you telling me he is dead?'

Zahedi glanced at his colleague once more. 'No, I am not. I have no knowledge of his fate.'

'But you knew he was missing?'

'It was mentioned to me. In passing. You asked if I was aware of the case – I am. I know that matters of this kind have been dealt with by our American friends since the decision to expel your representatives, and I believe it was they who raised the matter with my staff. But I gather we have been unable to provide much assistance. I would simply advise you to caution your prime minister that it may not be a story with a happy ending.'

Harry glanced at Shahnaz. 'The prime minister will be most disappointed to hear that.'

'Disappointed? About the disappearance of a journalist?' Zahedi chuckled. 'Are there not more where he came from?' The smile evaporated almost as soon as it had appeared. 'Of course, I understand that the disappearance of any young man is no laughing matter. And no doubt his family are distraught. But I am sure the prime minister needs no lessons from me in the vicissitudes of conflict.'

'Sir, I have reason to believe that some of your supporters are not being entirely straightforward with you on this matter.'

Zahedi glowered at him. But he didn't ask him to leave.

'I think they are trying to use an event that has official backing from the prime minister at home in London – this *transfer of power* – to provide cover to achieve something that most certainly does not.'

'Is this an issue I *need* to know about?'

Spoken like a true politician, Harry thought. 'The prime minister believes so. It is important this new era of Anglo-Iranian relations begins on a sure footing, with complete transparency on either side.'

Zahedi clearly wanted to ask his aide's advice, but he also did not wish to lose face in front of his guest. Harry wondered what the general had been told. 'It was our understanding that the young man in question was a KGB spy,' Zahedi said. 'And that his father was also a KGB asset that mole hunters in London had been searching for across more than two decades.'

'We are hunting a KGB agent in London,' Harry said, holding Zahedi's gaze. 'That much is true. But the prime minister is anxious that we find the right one. He is not interested in scapegoating outsiders for an easy life.'

Harry could see the doubt in Zahedi's gaze now. Could they really be sure that Harry was not the personal representative of the prime minister he claimed to be? After all, that was exactly what he had been during his time here in the war. Meshang Rashidian, Salemi and others would have been aware of it. Perhaps this fact had filtered through to Zahedi.

Zahedi stood abruptly and offered his hand, as if that was the only answer his confused mind could come up with. This time it was clear that their audience was over. 'I will look into the matter. It has been a pleasure to meet you.'

As they were escorted out, Harry could see no sign of Pierre Audinette, Adel Salemi or any of the other conspirators in the hall below.

31

THE CENTRAL TELEPHONE exchange was more or less deserted. Whatever else the city's inhabitants were doing in these tumultuous times, they weren't making long-distance calls. Harry listened as Shahnaz worked her way politely through the management tiers until someone who might actually be able to assist stood behind the grille.

The general manager was small and rotund and wanted to oblige, but couldn't help being wary. If it had been busier, it might have been more difficult to persuade him, but since they were more or less the only customers in the cavernous room, Shahnaz was able to convince him that the normal rules did not apply.

It took an age to find the right documentation. Harry listened to Shahnaz politely making conversation and gently encouraging the bespectacled clerk assigned to help them. He searched the columns for Sean's and Ali's names and methodically copied down each entry on a sheet of paper. They soon had a list, which Shahnaz stared at for almost as long as the clerk had taken to compile it.

'What?'

'We have our answer,' she said.

'And . . .'

'He made ten calls from here. Seven were to England, to this number.'

'Our home,' Harry said quietly.

'The other three were all made on the day before he disappeared.' She handed it over. 'To Isfahan.'

'Whose is it?'

'It is the number for Latak, my father's farm.'

'Could he have thought you were there?'

'No. Until I took you the other day, I hadn't been back for months. Sean knew that.'

His eyes bored into her. She lowered her head and sighed. *'Inshallah.'*

There was a roar from outside. A cavalcade of jeeps and tanks rolled past, plastered with photographs of the Shah and festooned with Iranian flags. The soldiers cheered and waved.

Shahnaz asked the clerk to place a call to the farm and Harry waited while she spoke to the housekeeper. 'He telephoned an hour ago to say he is on his way home,' she said. They emerged into the fading daylight. 'I just have to place one more call,' she added, preparing to turn back.

'Don't.' Harry continued to observe her intently. The pieces of the jigsaw puzzle were assembling themselves in his mind.

'What do you mean?'

'We don't need any help. Not any more. Either of us.'

Shahnaz looked confused, even a little frightened. 'I just have to call my flatmate,' she said. 'I will join you in the car.'

'You don't need to call anyone else.'

'Yes, I do.' She tore herself away from his gaze and ran back inside.

Twenty minutes later, when they started to roll through the outskirts of Tehran, having recovered Harry's hired car from the hotel – and established that it did not appear to be being watched – the sun was dropping below the horizon. Shortly after, they were plunged into a close, dark night. The car rattled and hummed as the wind tugged at Shahnaz's hair. She didn't seem to want to meet his eye.

Harry found himself turning over the meeting with Zahedi in his mind. Neither Salemi, Pierre Audinette nor the American had been visible as they left. But why? Where had they gone?

He glanced in the rear-view mirror. He had been fairly sure they had avoided a tail as they left Tehran, but now he had his suspicions about the headlights in the far distance. The vehicle they belonged to never came closer or dropped back.

'What was Tito like?' Shahnaz said eventually.

'Tito?' He had the impression she was trying to distract him.

'Churchill's letter. You said you were flown out to Yugoslavia. I was wondering what he was like. You didn't answer the other day when I asked.'

'Why?'

'What do you mean, why?'

'How could you possibly give a damn about Tito?'

'A lot of people in my generation think he's an interesting role model, a socialist leader with a human face.'

'A Communist, you mean.'

'You can define it however you like.'

'There is nothing human about Josip Broz. He's just as ruthless as the rest of them.'

'It was your idea to switch support to him from the Chetniks?'

'Yes. I told you that.'

'It's just that it doesn't seem like an obvious move for the British government to make.'

'The Chetniks had more or less stopped fighting. They were a bigger group originally because they were led by a former Royal Yugoslav Army officer who brought a lot of his troops with him. But the Germans took terrible reprisals on the civilian population, which Mihajlovic and his men could not stomach. Some of them gave up and others collaborated with the Germans. They were of no use to us.'

'But Tito didn't mind the civilian casualties?'

'He thought it was a price that had to be paid.'

'And did you agree?'

Harry was silent for a long time. 'I didn't know then, and I don't really know now, to be honest. In war – any kind of war – there are always casualties. How do you set one off against another?'

'Did you like him?'

'That wasn't really the point.'

'But you knew him. On a human level, did you like him?'

'Respected, perhaps. He was direct. Decisive. Honourable,

within the limits we knew we had to accept. He was quite shy, but had a good sense of humour. He was pragmatic, independent-minded and inclined to consider every question on its merits. And he had a slightly mystical romanticism about his country. He was prone to the line of argument, advanced at a pertinent moment, that this course of action, or that one, did not befit an ancient, honourable and civilized nation.'

'It sounds as though you did like him.'

'He believed in something and was prepared to die for it.' Harry was aware that in answering her he was framing an argument for himself. He hoped she wouldn't notice.

'The Nazis believed in something, so it is surely *what* you believe in that counts.'

'Perhaps.'

'What do you mean, perhaps? You should give me a proper answer,' she said quietly, 'because I think you want to.'

'Is that so?'

'Yes. And I'd say it has been ever since you came out here.'

'All right. Well, I told you before, as a race we spend a lot of time dealing with the meaning of life, which is to say rationalizing death. Or, to put it another way, we all devote a lot of energy to trying to convince ourselves we shuffle through this mortal coil with some purpose. We are thus uniquely susceptible to crowd psychology. We all want to be caught up in the big idea that will give life meaning. Our opiate could be religion, or it could be political ideology.'

'You can't compare the two.'

'Can't you?'

'No. One is about defending the established order. It's about hierarchy and obedience. The other should be about the pursuit of equality.'

'Or the pursuit of power.'

'Are you telling me you no longer believe in equality?'

'I haven't stopped thinking it's a noble idea.'

'What went wrong?'

'I was misled.'

'Then you allowed yourself to be.'

'No. That's not true.'

She shook her head, exasperated. 'You can't have completely backed away from the need to confront injustice on the scale that we have here.'

'I grew up in Berlin in the thirties. I saw the Nazis up close – manipulative thugs preying on humanity's basest instincts. Envy. Jealousy. The desire to feel superior to others. And as I watched the British ruling class troop out to kowtow to these monsters, there was a moment when I thought that only the Communists could stop them. And it was true, factually speaking. Without Russia, there would have been no victory. But look at the price we're paying.'

'So you *were* almost a Communist?' Harry didn't answer. 'That's a long way from the right-wing cynic of Sean's imagining.'

'The trouble is, as I said before, that age teaches you ideology is the enemy of humanity. And thus, in the end, of equality too.'

Shahnaz sighed. 'After so much loss, after so much

grief – my brother, my mother, the alienation from my father – I have to have a purpose. And right here, right now, it makes sense to me.'

'So you're telling me that, after all, love isn't enough?'

'Right now, I honestly don't know.'

'I thought I had purpose. Amanda said it blinded me. I understand that now. I devoted myself to a cause at the expense of the people who needed me most, for fear of the vulnerability love brings with it. I have seen many, many deaths. I have been responsible for more than a few. And yet, until her death, I felt nothing.'

Harry glanced over his shoulder into the darkness, as he had periodically since they'd left Tehran. He caught her eye as he turned back. 'It's different now,' he said. 'I cannot have Sean taken from me. I . . . cannot.'

'How did you first meet your Russian friend?' she asked.

'Oleg? He was attached to Tito's group when I arrived.'

'What was he like?'

'He was everything you would expect in a senior KGB officer.'

'Ruthless?'

'When he had to be. Shrewd. Lugubrious. Darkly humorous, but never to the point of publicly questioning the system he served. He was one of the architects of Tito's rise to power after the war. I was organizing the coup that might have prevented it.'

'What happened?'

'It was over before it began. We were betrayed, and a great many young men lost their lives at a place called Mount Avala, ambushed as they parachuted in.'

'Betrayed by whom?'

'Someone who must have made the mistake of thinking that the end justified the means.'

'But you blame yourself, nonetheless.'

His knuckles whitened as he gripped the wheel.

Harry drove on, keeping a weather eye on the head-lamps that glinted periodically in the rear-view mirror, then disappeared again. 'What do you and Sean talk about?' he asked.

She smiled at him. 'Fishing?'

'Only for insight. When a boy grows into a man, he pulls away from his father and remains a mystery to him ever afterwards.'

'I don't think he's a mystery to you. At least, he shouldn't be. We talked about everything, of course – politics, family, friends. And dreams.'

'And what are they?'

'I guess, for me, security. For my country, for myself. I'd like to be with people who actually care who I really am.'

'And Sean?'

'To secure himself a front-row seat at the great events of our era. But as a commentator, not an activist.'

'In my generation, no such distinction was possible.'

'I feel the same. But Sean would argue that we're simply taking different routes to the same destination.'

'And how do you feel about that?'

'I admire his willingness to fight other people's battles.'

'Even if, tomorrow, they might not be your own?'

'Perhaps there will be enough here for him. Perhaps we can travel elsewhere together. I love him. That's all I can say now.'

They settled back into a companionable silence. She rested her head against the passenger window and appeared to fall asleep. In the darkness, Harry was left alone once more.

He reached a small settlement and pulled up alongside a solitary petrol pump. Shahnaz stretched awkwardly. 'How long have I been asleep?'

'Long enough to keep me awake with your snoring.'

'Very funny.'

'I'll be back in a moment.'

An old man shuffled towards them to fill the tank. Harry indicated that he wished to go to the WC and was directed down a side alley. The ammonia-laden stench of urine caught in the back of his throat as he bypassed the latrine and kept walking, occasionally glancing over his shoulder at the dim lights of the petrol station as he looped back along the side of the road. Most of the local inhabitants kept goats or donkeys in their gardens, and dogs barked their alarm as he strode past. He stopped far enough from the last house to be swallowed by the desert shadows, crouched on his haunches, and waited.

As their pursuer's headlamps pierced the darkness, he retreated further, to the cover of the nearest palm tree. The vehicle slowed a couple of hundred yards before the settlement and pulled quietly onto the edge of the road, engine running.

He took out the Colt and circled behind it. Crouching low, he moved swiftly and silently towards the boot, swung round to the rear passenger door and slipped in behind the driver. He put the muzzle of the weapon against the back of the man's neck before he had time to turn. 'Don't move.'

He didn't.

'Name and rank?'

No answer.

'I'm an old friend of Oleg Vasilyev. We fought together. But if you move, I'll kill you. If you pretend you don't speak English, I'll kill you. If you don't tell me the truth, I'll kill you. Is that understood?'

'Perfectly.'

'So what is your name and rank?'

'Prokopiev. Ivan. Major.'

'Was it you who tried to recruit my son into the KGB?'

'Yes.'

'Did you succeed?'

'No.'

'Do you have any idea where he is?'

'No.'

'And what about the young woman in front of us?'

'A fellow traveller, not an agent. She said she thought she would have news of who was behind the coup.'

'When you get back to Tehran, I want you to send a cable to Yuri from Harry Tower. Tell him that we don't make war on the young, the naive and the foolish. Do you understand?'

'Yes.'

'Now drive up to the girl's car at the petrol station. When you get there, wind down the window and call her name. Do not give any indication of my presence, or it will be the last thing you do.'

They rolled up alongside the pump. He didn't have to call her name before she lunged towards him. 'For God's sake, Ivan,' she hissed. 'What the hell . . .?'

328

Her voice trailed off as Harry emerged from the rear of the car. He tapped his Colt against the driver's door. 'Go. Don't come back.'

The tyres spun, found traction, and Prokopiev, Ivan, accelerated away.

'Harry . . .' He turned. 'You were right. I'm a terrible liar. But I'm with the Tudeh Party, not the KGB.'

'Is there a difference?'

'This is my country. I'm trying to do something to help.'

'You think the Russians want to *help* you?'

'At least they're not trying to buy my country to rape it of its natural resources and source of all wealth.'

Harry bought himself some time by tucking the Colt into his waistband, then looking up at the stars. He breathed in the warm night air. Finally, he said, 'Do you want me to tell you what it's like to serve a country like the Soviet Union, or have you got that message by now?'

'Our only chance here is to play off the superpowers against each other. Surely you can see that.'

He pointed towards the rear lights of Ivan Prokopiev's car, disappearing into the night. 'I understand only that it is the first step along the road to perdition. And once you take it, there is no going back. What you once saw with pinpoint clarity melts into a thousand shades of grey. And, most searing of all, the commitment and the dishonesty it demands become a barrier to every kind of human warmth you might reach for. It's the truth you can never tell, and it eats away at you until there is absolutely nothing left to give.'

She looked at him, unclear of his meaning. 'All the British have ever done is steal from our country while the poor starve before their very eyes. Am I supposed to ignore the cries of starving children?'

'You have my son. You love him. I hear that in your every breath. Don't let any kind of politics stand in its way. Ever. That's all I ask.'

32

SHAHNAZ WAS SILENT as they made their way down the track that led to Latak. Harry pulled onto the drive and switched off the engine.

She steeled herself, then got out and strode to the porch, Harry behind her. She knocked loudly and the door was opened by an elderly gentleman with a shock-white beard.

'Good evening, Hamid.'

'Good evening, Mistress.'

'Is my father . . .?'

'The general is indeed in residence. I will tell him you are here.'

They were ushered inside. Harry watched her tug at her dress in agitation. He reached down gently and gripped her forearm. 'It's all right.'

'Good evening, Shahnaz.'

Adel Salemi materialized in the hallway. It struck Harry

that he, too, looked nervous. 'I am pleased to see you tonight,' Salemi said. He was gazing at his daughter.

'I'm sorry to arrive so late, and without warning.' Shahnaz seemed subdued suddenly, as if paralysed by the occasion.

'This is your home. You are welcome at any time. Good evening, Mr Tower. Please . . . do join me.' He led them into his study, which was filled with the heavy aroma of Havana cigar smoke. He had evidently been reading by the light of a single desk lamp, a solitary existence that struck Harry as a more exotic mirror of his own in Charlwood Road. 'Can I offer you something to drink, Mr Tower?'

'No, thank you.'

'Shahnaz, tea?'

'No, thank you. We have something to ask you.' The years appeared to have fallen away from her. She was a child once again in her father's study, her voice and manner subservient and apologetic.

'I would be happy to help. Have you found your son, Mr Tower?'

'Almost.'

'How almost?'

'We have established that his road led to your door.'

'Some time ago, yes.'

'The night he disappeared.'

'I'm sorry, I didn't know that.'

'He came to talk about the coup,' Shahnaz said. 'And your part in the planned aftermath, through Global Vision Oil.'

Salemi tried to hide his surprise. 'He came to ask me about matters of which I knew little. That much is true.'

'How did it come to this, Father?'

'What do you mean?'

'I am a child of great privilege in a country of immense poverty.' She gestured at the room around her. 'And yet, far from being grateful, I may in fact leave this house tonight and never see it or you again.'

'That would break my heart.'

'Mine was shattered long ago.'

Salemi sighed. He was a far cry from the arrogant narcissist of Harry's previous acquaintance. 'That was never my wish. Indeed, I would have given anything to protect you.'

'Like you protected Cyrus?'

Salemi stared at his hands.

'Like you protected my mother?'

'I don't know how or why we have hurt each other so much.'

'Yes, you do. It is because of the pressure you placed on all of us to be the people you wanted us to be, rather than who we actually were.'

Salemi slowly shook his head. 'No ... no, it was not that.'

'It was. Once, I thought you did not know it. I see now that you do.'

'I have always tried to do what I thought best, for you, for them, for our country.'

'And now you sit here, alone.'

Salemi closed his eyes. 'Yes. Alone.'

'I love him, this boy, as you once called him. Do you know that? Perhaps it is not the love you wanted or sought for me, but it is a fact nonetheless, just as you once said it was for you the night you first saw Mama on that stage in Monte Carlo. I know he came here. I know he was kidnapped on the way back to Tehran, and that you know who took him.'

'You are mistaken.'

'No, I am not.'

'I . . . do not know.'

'Don't lie to me, Father. Please at least do me that service, after all we have been through.'

'I . . . cannot . . . help you, Shahnaz.'

'Cannot, or will not?'

'It is not in my gift.'

'I am your *daughter*. Please allow us the chance tonight to take a couple of steps back from the abyss.'

To the ticking of the mantelpiece clock, Harry watched another man wrestle with his soul.

'Father, I must warn you that if you do not tell me where Sean is tonight, I *will* leave this house now and never, ever speak to you again.'

Salemi shook his head, slowly, mournfully.

'You must make your choice,' she said.

'You cannot force me to choose between my child and my country,' he said quietly.

'Sean is no threat to this country so that is not a choice you can claim to be making.'

'These are matters beyond your understanding.'

'Why? Because I am a woman? Because I am your daughter? Or just because you think I am stupid?'

Salemi got up and went to the window. He stared out into the darkness. 'If I were to tell you what I know, it would lead to all of our deaths.'

'If anything happens to Sean, I will have nothing to live for.' Shahnaz turned to Harry. 'Come. We're wasting time. He has made his choice.'

She had reached the door before he broke. 'He's in the fort at Alamut.'

'He's alive?'

'I believe so, yes. But now that our plan has come to fruition, I don't know for how much longer. General Zahedi . . .'

'We have to go there.'

'The camp in the old fort is heavily guarded.'

'We have to try.' She looked at her father once more. 'When we leave, will you tell anyone?'

He did not answer.

'Because you must know that if you say anything at all, if you warn them in any way, you will be condemning your own daughter to death.'

33

'YOU CANNOT BE sure of that,' Shahnaz said, as they reached the main road.

'I can. Only a monster would imperil the life of his daughter, and despite everything, your father is not a monster.'

'Sometimes I think it would have been easier if he had been.'

'That is never easier.'

She turned to face him. 'Do you know about the fort at Alamut, Eagle's Nest?'

Harry shook his head. 'I'm aware of it, but no more than that.'

'Have you heard of Hassan Sabbah?'

'The Ismaili leader?'

'Yes. According to legend, the castle was given its name by a ninth-century king of Daylam, who watched an eagle take flight and land on a high rocky outcrop, which seemed to him an ideal and impregnable location for a fortress – hence Eagle's Nest. But when Sabbah was being persecuted by the Sunni leader Sultan Malek Shah here in the eleventh century, he retreated to Alamut and created an army of *fidais*, followers who would spend years infiltrating the households of key members of the regime and winning their trust before suddenly murdering them. They would make no attempt to flee, resigning themselves to their gruesome fate and bolstering a reputation for blind fanaticism. That's why they call Sabbah the father of terrorism.'

'But the fort is a ruin?'

'Yes, they must have created a makeshift camp. It is remote, so perhaps that is why they chose it. There is only one entrance, up steep stone steps.'

'How far is it from here?'

'A long, long way. We'd have to go back to Tehran, then begin the journey west past Karaj and through the Alborz to Qazvin.'

'Then we had better get moving.'

The journey was as long and arduous as Shahnaz had predicted. They took it in turns driving through the night to reach Tehran, their headlights illuminating only the occasional donkey cart or truck. They moved quickly through the empty streets of the capital, and dawn saw them in the western Alborz Mountains, where the jagged blue-grey rocks of the peaks were in sharp contrast to the deep green of the forests and lush plains.

The road was winding, with precipitous drops. Shahnaz was visibly exhausted so Harry had to do most of the driving. He felt little better himself, fatigue tugging at his eyelids.

All conversation had petered out. They had to stop repeatedly and Harry did not want to admit to his exhausted, frightened companion that he also felt close to the end of his endurance. But as the sun climbed high into the sky, Shahnaz said, 'We're nearly there.'

When they crested the next rise, the craggy, crumbling grey sandstone towers of Alamut towered over a valley vibrant with fields of wheat and orchards of fruit trees. They passed through the village of Gazor Khan, a picturesque collection of mud huts, and then along a stretch of road flanked for almost a mile by cherry and pomegranate orchards. Finally, all that was left was the approach to the fort: a short road, then wide stone steps leading up to walls that might have been hammered into craggy brown rocks.

Harry parked, waited. He got out. There was a crisp, cool wind. Shahnaz came to stand next to him. There was no sign of life in the fort above them and no way of approaching it without being seen. 'You think your father has betrayed us?' Harry asked.

Shahnaz paused for a long time before answering. 'If so, what should we do?'

Harry glanced around him. If he had not been so tired, perhaps he'd have thought about this more clearly on the journey, but if Sean was held anywhere near here, it was certainly not at the fort. 'It's a trap,' he said. 'Let's go.'

He hurried back to the car, got in and spun it around in the road.

'Where are we going?' she asked. 'Perhaps he is here.'

'He's not in that bloody fort. And I should have known as much.'

As they approached Gazor Khan, the road was blocked by two army jeeps. Soldiers stood on the verge beside them, Kalashnikovs raised. Harry slowed, looked in his rear-view mirror to watch two jeeps swing onto the road behind him. 'Damn,' he said.

'What shall we do?'

'I can't fight my way out of this. We're about to see Sean again. And our fate will be his.'

Shahnaz put her face into her hands and began to cry. 'It's all right,' Harry whispered. 'It isn't over. Not yet.' But he was aware as he said it that he was not even convincing himself.

The soldiers in front of them advanced on foot, guns raised. They looked nervous, but although they hand-cuffed and blindfolded Harry and Shahnaz, they treated neither of them roughly. They were loaded into the back of a jeep and driven for what felt like two hours or more. 'Qazvin,' Harry whispered to Shahnaz.

'Be quiet,' one of the soldiers shouted. But the noise of traffic suggested to Harry that he was correct to think they had been taken back to the provincial capital.

The jeeps stopped and they were manhandled through what felt like a warren of corridors. When he was unmasked, Harry found himself in a small room with whitewashed walls and a stone floor. Ed Haddon sat opposite him. Shahnaz was nowhere to be seen.

Haddon leant across the desk between them to undo his cuffs. Harry didn't take that as a good sign. 'Where are they?' he asked.

'They're safe. All of them: your son, his charming girlfriend. Even his translator. And they will be fine as long as
you cooperate.' Haddon took a thick file out of his briefcase and placed it carefully on the desk. 'Oz did a thorough
job before you killed him. He was a good man, Harry.'

'I think we both know that is not true.'

Haddon ran his hand through his wavy dark hair. He was
wearing a white shirt, jeans and desert boots. He was con-
centrating hard, his washed-out blue eyes seeking some
truth. 'Oz suspected you a long time ago. He almost convinced Prentice of your guilt. I wouldn't – *couldn't* – believe
it.' Haddon leant forward suddenly. 'Why, Harry? Those
men we trained together. You met their wives, their children. And you sent them behind the Iron Curtain to an
execution you'd already arranged. From Mount Avala to
Albania . . .'

The room was as silent as death.

'I wouldn't accept it until I had the evidence before me.'
He gestured at the thick file. 'But you have to tell me why,
Harry. I need an answer.' There was desperation in his
eyes that Harry had not expected. 'A higher cause, a
greater purpose. I have to know why you sent those men
to their deaths.'

There were shouts from somewhere else in the compound, then screams. A shot was fired. 'Communists,'
Haddon explained, when it was clear Harry was going to
offer him nothing else.

'You're executing people already?'

'The new regime is rounding up anyone guilty of sedi-
tion. I wouldn't expect you to support that, given
everything we now know.'

There was another long silence. It disturbed Harry that Haddon was making no effort to follow any known interrogation technique. It was the kind of approach you would only take if you already knew the conclusion.

'There is a section of opinion in London,' Haddon continued, 'in Whitehall, I should say, rather than in the office where your perfidy is better understood, that finds it hard to believe you are the Moscow spy we have been looking for.'

'The prime minister, you mean.'

'Indeed, although the brutal way in which you murdered poor Oz may finally give him food for thought. I think he just doesn't fundamentally understand how any man with your service record could have served such a disgusting regime for so long. Why on earth would he do it? he asks. I have always answered that it must have begun in Berlin. That is the only explanation that makes any kind of sense.'

Harry leant forward, so that their faces were only a few feet apart. 'Tell me something, Ed. Was it Sean you really needed to get rid of? Did he find out too much? About the coup? About the carve-up of the country's oil you've all been planning? And was painting me as a scapegoat for your problems back home a bonus? Or was it the other way round?'

'I'm sure it would assuage your conscience to think that Sean was the architect of his own predicament. And, of course, I'm not blind to the benefits of killing two birds with one stone. Your son was a better journalist than any of us anticipated and appears to have uncovered things that might be harmful to our interests. But in the end I wouldn't want you to kid yourself that this was his fault, Harry. This is all about you.'

Haddon flipped open the file. 'When we first opened the investigation, I said my hunch was that it had begun back in Germany with those damned Nazis. I often think of the night when Amanda almost caused a riot in the *Bierkeller*. But there are those who say that wasn't enough, that it must have been Maurice who persuaded you.'

'Lord Arundel convinced me of the value of friendship and intellectual rigour.'

'I have no doubt he did, when he wasn't trying to get his hands on your mother. But we've done a little digging. In fact, more than a little. We thought Arundel was an eccentric. But we now believe he was a Communist, too.'

'Well, if he was, he kept it a secret from me.'

'You didn't know?'

'I *doubt* he was. But *if* he was, then no, I wasn't aware of it. We barely talked about politics.'

'I find that hard to believe.' Haddon turned the page, switching tack dramatically. 'Let's talk about Markov. I'd like to wind back the tape. Markov presents himself at the embassy in Cairo and announces his wish to defect. He says he has sure knowledge of a traitor at the heart of the SIS and he will bring that with him in return for certain guarantees. He is nervous of discovery and believes time is of the essence. The night manager at Cairo station puts a confidential briefing on the approach into the overnight bag and it reaches your desk on a Friday evening. You were weekend duty man. Was it your decision alone to assign Mike Guildford? You never consulted Prentice or any of our superiors?'

'You know it was.'

'But you knew he was on the west coast of America and couldn't be in Cairo until the middle of the following week at the earliest.'

'Mike had handled defectors before. Everyone agreed he was the right man for the job.'

'Not everyone. You didn't think to consult *anyone* upstairs?'

'Do we have to go through with this charade?'

'We do, yes.'

'If I'd consulted some genius upstairs on every operational decision, nothing would ever have got done, as you well know. I also believed, as I've already said, that the widespread dissemination of information was becoming a problem for the organization as a whole. It was the reason too many of our operations were failing. You wanted to go to Cairo, but you were not the right man for the job. And the fact that you were so damned persistent about it, then and since, makes you the likely suspect – if there is one – not me.

'Markov was in a hurry,' Harry went on, 'but he must have spent years considering his move and he wasn't going to run away in a matter of days. The briefing had been correctly and swiftly sent in the overnight bag, with knowledge of the approach restricted to the ambassador only. We had time and we needed the right man to handle the operation and make sure Markov was not a double.'

'So how did Moscow find out?'

'We don't know that they did. All we know is that we never heard from Markov again.'

Haddon pushed a sheaf of papers across the desk. 'Take a look.'

Harry started to read.

'There was a huge increase in radio traffic between London and Moscow on the Friday night. An hour later, there was a similar increase between Moscow and Cairo. What were you up to? Sharing holiday memories?'

Harry flicked through the pages, then handed back the file. 'There could have been a hundred reasons for an increase in radio traffic from the Soviet Embassy in London.'

'Could there? Involving Cairo? Really?' Haddon shook his head. 'I don't think so. The only sensible explanation is that the news of Markov's desire to defect was betrayed from London. As you say, information was tightly restricted and we believe it can only realistically have been passed to the Russians by you.'

'That's not evidence, Ed, and you know it.'

Haddon pushed another sheaf of papers across the table. 'Let's move on to the most shameful episode of all. The betrayal of those young men on Mount Avala as they tried to stop Tito seizing power. Forty-seven dead royalist soldiers, twenty-three captured. The operation you once described as having the most terrible outcome of any in the modern history of the Service. We've been back through this, Harry, in very great detail. We have spoken to almost every survivor, and all those involved. And you know what we found, in the end? The exact same thing: an increase in traffic between Belgrade and Moscow on the night before the operation. Only you and I were in Belgrade that night.'

'So does that make you the spy the Americans are looking for, Ed?'

Haddon didn't return his mirthless smile. 'When I went back over these files, I realized how much we had missed. I finally thought to ask for the detail on the increased traffic from the Americans. But why had no one ever asked them that question before? Why had *you* not asked it? You were handling the wash-up. The answer was obvious: because you were too busy with the cover-up.'

There was another long silence. 'I helped you train some of those men, Harry. You might as well have killed them with your own bare hands.' Haddon leant back in his seat. 'Aren't you going to say something, you fucking bastard?'

'Like what?'

'You can't kid yourself it was just collateral damage. They were young men with their lives ahead of them, lambs to the slaughter.' Haddon leant forward again, as if he was about to jump out of his chair and punch Harry. 'Are you going to look me in the eye and tell me they were the price that had to be paid for your ideals? For Comrade Joe? For his gulags? Not even a man as cold and lifeless as you could possibly believe that.'

Harry didn't respond. What answer was there to give?

The door opened and Christine Audinette walked in. She took a seat next to Haddon. Harry offered her a bleak smile. 'I should have known.' He turned back to Haddon. 'At least we'll both agree you can never trust the French.'

'Christine has given us a signed affidavit to say she saw you on more than one occasion with Oleg Vasilyev during the war. Here and in Tabriz.'

'You seem to have forgotten we were on the same side then.'

'I don't think a court is ever going to believe that we were on the same side as a man like Oleg Vasilyev.'

'Oh, I *love* the fiction that this is going to end up in a British court.'

'You do understand this is the end of the road, right, Harry?'

'Is it?'

Haddon took a book from his briefcase and pushed it across the table. 'You want to tell me what this is?'

Harry knew right away. 'Those Germans and their obsession with records,' Haddon said, as he flicked through the opening pages. 'Of course, the original was destroyed by "someone", but how very efficient of them to have completed two copies. The Nazis were nothing if not pedantic. So . . . Göttingen. That bed-and-breakfast in Marienstrasse. I remember it. Here *you* are . . . Harry Tower.' Haddon pointed at Harry's signature. 'And here, a few pages later, guess what? Max Wisler. Well-known alias at the time for the man we later came to know as Oleg Vasilyev, deputy to the head of the KGB's Foreign Directorate, Yuri Menkov.'

Harry stared at Vasilyev's scrawl.

'A coincidence, you may say. But look here . . .' Haddon turned the pages. 'Three months later, just before you depart for Cambridge, who should be back staying at the Schwarzer Adler guesthouse but Wisler again.' Haddon stared at him. 'It was you who always said we should never believe in coincidence in intelligence work – right, Harry? Since we found this, we've gone further. We've mapped your movements over the years with what we know – or have been able to find out – of Oleg Vasilyev's.

And guess what we found?' He smiled. 'Indeed. There can be no doubt as to who is our Soviet mole.'

'You want a confession?' Harry didn't bother to keep the sarcasm from his voice.

'I want an *explanation*.' Haddon stood. 'All right, Harry. Have it your own way. You always bloody did.'

He walked out, leaving Christine and Harry alone. 'You going to tell me how sorry you are?' he asked.

'No.'

'Was that why you tried to seduce me?'

'No.'

'And Sean?'

'Perhaps.' She stood. 'You always were an arrogant bastard, so it is no surprise to learn you thought you could outwit us all.'

'It's always good to know,' he said, 'that you were right not to trust someone.'

'Coming from you, that really takes some bloody nerve.'

She followed Haddon out. Neither had closed the door. After a few moments, Harry stood and walked through it, as he imagined he was expected to do. He found Sean sitting in front of a desk and a bank of recording machines.

Sean slowly removed the headphones through which he had been listening to the conversation in the next room. His curly hair was a shaggy mop and he had a thick, dark beard. But his gaze remained just as sombre, as unblinking, even as hostile as on the day Harry had last witnessed it. 'Do you think Mum knew?'

'That I worked for the Secret Intelligence Service or that I was really a spy for Moscow?'

'Either. Both.'

Harry shrugged. 'Neither, but, on some level, both. She knew I had a job in government. She understood my journey from youthful idealist to servant of the Empire. She just didn't know why.'

'And what is the answer?'

'It began in a far-off time and place. In Göttingen, that much is true. The world was different then.' Harry met his son's level gaze. 'It's what they demanded of me. I don't know what other explanation I can give you.'

'She once said to me it was not how often you went away but where you were when you came home. I guess this explains why you were never really there.'

'Not that it will make any difference, but it was a prior loyalty not a higher one.'

'But if it began in Göttingen, that can't be true.'

'It began before then,' Harry said, but he didn't know what more he could add. How could you explain a resentment that became something close to a religion, dissipated to a cause and ended as a matter of everlasting regret?

Sean stared at his hands for a long time. 'You're right. It doesn't make a difference.' He raised his head, fixed Harry with the same penetrating gaze. 'Do you regret it?'

'I gave up my humanity for it. And I long ago passed the point where any kind of redemption was conceivable. So I'm not sure regret quite captures it. We learn too late in life that the real traps are those we make for ourselves.'

'But that is the great flaw in our species, isn't it? When a human being is selfish, it's rarely he – or she – who pays the price.'

'I wouldn't be so sure of that.'

Harry took a seat opposite his son. The longing to reach

out and embrace him was unbearable. 'She would want me to forgive you,' Sean said quietly. 'But I don't think I can.'

'It's much too late for forgiveness.'

'What will happen to us?'

'I don't know.'

'I fear that isn't true,' Sean said. 'I think you owe me the benefit of your experience.'

Perhaps that was fair enough but, even so, Harry couldn't bear to tell his son the truth.

Three Iranian soldiers armed with AK47s stepped into the room. 'Come with us,' one said.

34

THEY WERE RUSHED down a series of dark corridors until a huge, heavy door was kicked open and they emerged, blinking, into the bright sunlight of a courtyard. Thirty or forty men and women were lying face down on the ground, arms stretched in front of them, wrists cuffed, legs wide apart. More soldiers surrounded Harry and Sean as an officer swaggered towards them. 'Good morning. My name is Captain Khan. I am in charge here.'

He led them to the far side of the courtyard. Shahnaz was lying close to the wall and Sean fell to his knees to try to embrace her. Khan stepped forward and kicked Sean so hard in the back that he stumbled and fell face first into the dust. 'Time for that later,' Khan said. Harry briefly thought of lunging for him, but he felt the barrels of half a dozen AK47s sizing him up and stayed where he was.

Khan pushed them all close to the ground, making sure they were at least two metres apart. Harry was next to a young Iranian he recognized from the photographs in Sean's apartment. His face was badly bruised and his nose looked broken. 'Ali, meet my father. Harry, this is the man who kept me out of trouble until your friends came calling.'

If there was a hint of bitterness in his son's voice, Harry couldn't blame him. 'What are they going to do with us?' Sean asked.

He got his answer a few moments later when a large truck lumbered into the courtyard. It had canvas sides and a roof that rested on thick wooden slats bolted to iron struts. Khan bellowed at the men and women lying prostrate before him and the soldiers forced twenty or so – including Harry, Sean, Shahnaz and Ali – to their feet and herded them towards the truck. Now that they were no longer just figures in the dust, Harry searched the faces of the men and women around him. They were all young and very frightened.

Harry was one of the last to reach the back of the truck and Khan rewarded him with a savage kick to his legs. Harry went down on his knees, then took Sean's outstretched hand and clambered into the rear. There were no seats so they were forced to sit or kneel or lean against the sides, packed in closely together.

The back was slammed shut and the truck moved off. Harry pressed his face to the thin canvas side. He could just make out a gate as they went through it, then the desert beyond. 'Are we in Qazvin?' he asked. 'On the outskirts, right?'

Sean's translator, Ali, was closest to Harry. He nodded.

'This is the road back to Tehran?' Harry asked.

Ali pressed his face to the side. 'I think so,' he said.

Harry peered out at the scrubland beyond the canvas. 'What are we going to do?' Sean asked him.

Harry had no answer.

'Where are they taking us?'

To somewhere they can shoot us and dispose of our bodies in a shallow pit, Harry thought. God knew it had been done often enough before. 'Anyone have any idea where we're headed?' he asked loudly.

One of the men, whose nose was broken and mouth swollen, turned to him. 'There were reports of them shooting students and burying them just outside Qazvin. We came down here to investigate.'

'How far is it?'

'Fifteen minutes' drive, maybe twenty.'

They were silent as they absorbed the brutal reality that their lives were about to be dramatically cut short. 'What are we going to do, Dad?' Sean asked.

Harry still did not offer an answer. This, his final failure, was too overwhelming to allow for clear thought. Amanda would never forgive him.

Never.

Sean shuffled round so that he was facing his father. 'Dad?' Harry looked at his son. 'This is your world, right? Come on. How do we get out of it?'

'Sean—'

'No, come on. Think. You're a man of action. If that's been your life, then get us out of here.'

'We're in a truck. There is no way out of it. There are heavily armed soldiers in the front. When we get to our destination, no doubt in the middle of nowhere, they'll jump out first, fan out, create a field of fire that if any of us—'

'Then we need to get the hell out of here before we arrive.' Sean gripped Harry's shirt with both hands. 'Come on, Dad. You think Mum would want you to give up?'

There was desperation in Sean's voice, but determination too. And perhaps it was that, or the mention of Amanda, that snatched Harry from the despair that was threatening to envelop him.

He looked about him. The back of the truck was solid metal, as was the floor. The metal girders on the sides were spaced at short intervals, so it would be a struggle to wriggle between them, even if you could punch out the thick wooden slats.

But it was a different story on the roof of the truck. Here the gaps between the girders were big enough – in theory – for a human to get through. If you could somehow remove the slats, which were like prison bars. Harry stood, balancing himself against the side, and looked up. 'What is it?' Sean asked.

'Put me on your shoulders, you and Ali.'

They did as he asked, clinging to the side of the truck. Harry was nothing if not heavy.

He climbed off his son's shoulders.

'What are you going to do, Dad?'

'Have you got a coin?'

They checked their pockets, without luck. But all the men and women in the truck had worked out that something was going on and one offered a shiny coin.

'All right,' Harry said. 'I'm going to need more than the two of you.' Ali nodded and explained to their fellow captives. He picked the two burliest and they all discreetly shuffled around each other until they stood together.

Harry got back onto Sean's shoulders and the other three men crammed closely around him, following Harry's instructions. They clung to the slats at the side to bolster Sean, who was struggling under Harry's weight.

Harry could only just reach the slats at the top and it took interminable stretch, patience and effort to turn even one screw. After ten minutes, he had made barely any headway and had to get back down to rest.

He tried again, but still had only a single screw about halfway out.

Sean took charge. They agreed a shift system, replacing each other every couple of minutes. Before long, both screws at one end of a single slat were out. Each plank had three sets of double screws, at each end and in the middle. And Harry calculated he needed at least three, possibly four slats out to get someone through. He prayed the man beside them had been wrong in how far outside Qazvin their final destination lay.

It took them another ten minutes. Wherever their intended destination, time at least had been on their side.

When Harry said, 'All right, enough,' the relief on every face was clear. He had the disconcerting sense that, over the course of the journey, unreasonable hope was being invested in him.

He steeled himself. One man against an unknown number of heavily armed soldiers in the front cab of a truck. He didn't fancy his chances. But perhaps Sean was right: if he had a remaining purpose, this must be it.

Sean was kneeling before him again, those brown eyes searching his. 'Can you do it, Dad?'

'I don't know.'

'How will you—'

'It's my job. You're right. There's nothing you can do to help me and you'll make it worse if you try. Just wait here.'

Harry stood. He was tempted to cross himself, for reasons unclear to him. He assembled Sean, Ali and the burliest men around him. He felt the squeeze of Shahnaz's hand and saw the hope in his son's eyes. It brought him a measure of the peace he had long sought. 'All right,' he said. 'Let's do it.'

Harry climbed onto Sean's shoulders. The truck hit a bump in the road and he almost flew off, but managed to hold on. 'Do it,' Sean gasped.

Harry punched the slats whose screws he had removed out of the way. It took every ounce of strength to force himself through the gap and then, miraculously, he was on top of the truck, the wind in his hair, as it roared along the main road. The driver of a car coming the other way honked his horn in astonishment and Harry realized he had to move fast. He dragged himself forward on his belly and was just getting to his knees when the driver below sensed something amiss and rammed his foot on the brakes.

In desperation, Harry lunged for the metal hook used to keep the canvas in place.

As the truck shuddered to a halt, he was thrown forward, slamming into the windscreen and cracking it, then bouncing against the driver's door and smashing the huge wing mirror.

Every muscle in his body screamed in agony, but he could see the shock and horror in the soldiers' eyes. He scrambled for purchase on the front of the truck.

He got his knees onto the bonnet, stood and tumbled to the ground.

As a soldier opened the door to climb out, Harry pushed himself to his feet and charged with his shoulder. The door caught the soldier's head and he slumped to the road. Harry grabbed his Kalashnikov, raised it and fired at the first man to come round the corner from the other side of the cab.

Harry waited. He had to assume the remaining soldiers would come from both directions at once.

Silently, he rolled under the truck. He saw pairs of legs, working around the sides, as he'd imagined. He aimed, fired once. A soldier screamed. The last two were too slow to realize what had happened. Harry shot them in the legs as well.

When he emerged, the men were on the ground, clutching their wounds. Harry disarmed them and opened the rear of the truck. The captives staggered out into the sunlight.

Shahnaz put her arms around Harry and hugged him. Sean leant his tousled head against his father's shoulder and, briefly, the tableau afforded Harry a moment of contentment that, in any other circumstances, he might have relished.

Up ahead, two cars had stopped, their occupants watching but keeping their distance. Another was slowly coming to a halt behind them. They were in the middle of nowhere, surrounded by scrubland punctuated by craggy grey rocks and the occasional wych elm or sycamore.

The young men and women in the truck were milling around, still dazed. Harry went to look at the soldiers. The one he had shot through the heart was obviously dead, another still unconscious. Harry dragged him to the side of the road and put him onto his side, so that his tongue would not get trapped in his throat.

He checked the others' leg wounds. Shahnaz was trying to bind them, using a shirt that had been offered by one of her fellow captives. 'Tell them they'll be fine if they stay here and wait for help,' Harry said.

'What are we going to do?' Sean asked, looking at the dazed faces around them. None seemed quite to believe their escape and Harry didn't blame them. It was far from complete.

'They'll stand a better chance if they're away from us,' Harry said. 'Tell them to get into any passing car that will take them.'

'What about us?'

'We'll take the truck.'

Sean looked as if he was about to argue but thought better of it. He explained what Harry had suggested to the others and one by one they came to offer their thanks, then fanned out along the road to wave down and climb into the few passing cars.

Sean and Shahnaz tried to persuade Ali to stay with them, but he was adamant he could not and would not leave his country. After a brief but emotional farewell, he joined the other freed prisoners and climbed into a passing flatbed truck.

When they had all gone and Shahnaz had done her best to make the soldiers comfortable, they climbed into the cab of the truck. Harry smashed out the shattered windscreen, started the engine, shifted it into gear and accelerated away, leaving the wounded soldiers on the side of the road. 'How long until someone comes after us?' Shahnaz asked.

'A few hours at best.'

'Perhaps we could go to one of the neutral embassies in Tehran,' Sean said. 'I met the head of the Swedish mission a few times.'

Harry glanced at his son. 'After what just happened, and the story you'd have to tell, a bunch of peace-loving Swedes won't stop them making sure we never leave Iran.'

'I guess we could head for Tabriz,' Shahnaz said.

'We'd never reach there. Not in this thing, anyway.'

'So what, then, Dad? At least if we try for Tabriz, we'd have a chance of getting across the border. We can tell the Soviets our story and, whatever they decide to do with it, at least we'd be alive.'

'They'll have every soldier in Iran searching for us by nightfall. Two white men and a young woman . . . we'd not get far.'

Sean's attempt at a level gaze and the fear he was trying to hide reminded Harry achingly of his son's reaction to Amanda's illness, her descent into the final slough of despair.

'What are we going to do?' Sean asked again.

Harry was trying hard to think straight. He was looking at Shahnaz. 'The first time we drove south to find Sean's car at that village on the road to Isfahan, we passed a military airfield. I saw a couple of L4 Cubs just inside the perimeter wire.'

'L4 Cubs?'

'Training aircraft. I learnt to fly in one before the war. They're simple to steal, simple to start and simple to fly. They only have two seats, but you two can squeeze into the back.'

'I didn't know you could fly a plane.'

Harry looked at his son and Shahnaz, and was touched

by the faith in their eyes. 'There's an air base at Van in Turkey. I was there a few years ago and I know it. I can keep
the L4 low and hug the valleys to avoid radar detection up
to the border. The Iranian air force doesn't have any jets, so
we might make it.'

They didn't look convinced. Harry couldn't blame them.

'It's not a perfect plan, but it's the only one I have. Otherwise I don't think we'll have any chance of getting out of
the country.'

'They'll have roadblocks in the city and certainly near a
military airport,' Shahnaz said. She thought about it. 'We'd
have to work around Tehran and maybe hike the final ten
miles or so through Wasfanard and across the railway line.
It would probably be safer.'

Harry nodded. 'All right.'

Sean was stroking Shahnaz's hair gently and, within a
few minutes, she was asleep in his arms. 'What are our
chances of making it?' Sean asked eventually.

'They'll be trying very hard to make sure we don't.'

Sean indicated his sleeping girlfriend. 'Would she stand
a better chance if we hid her and went on alone?'

'Not if Captain Khan and his band of psychopaths inside
that camp have anything to do with it. But I don't think
she'd let that happen anyway and, from what I've seen,
you'd break her heart if you left her behind.'

Harry looked at his son, whose hair was being blown in
every direction by the wind whipping through his non-
existent window. 'You look like the neighbours' Old
English Sheepdog.'

'Marmaduke.' Sean's smile lit his face. He dipped his
head and kissed Shahnaz lightly.

'She's quite something,' Harry said, glancing at her. 'Can't think what you've done to deserve her.'

'I'm sorry, Dad . . .'

'What on earth for?'

'Not writing, for a start. Being so angry with you.' He paused. 'Did Shahnaz tell you? I used to listen to the tapes you recorded over and over again. Just to hear your voice.'

'I'm the one who should be saying sorry,' Harry said. 'For not being the father, or the husband, I could have – and should have – been.'

'I've had some time to think,' Sean said.

'That sounds dangerous.'

'After the last few weeks, perhaps I understand more than you realize about what you've done, the choices you made. I don't agree with them.' Sean appeared lost in thought. 'I don't, but—'

'You've no idea of the lies I've told.'

Sean gave him a wry, lopsided grin. 'That's the sugar industry for you, eh?'

'And I don't think you should seek to excuse me.' Harry kept his eyes fixed on the road ahead. 'I told myself that my rage was triggered by principles, by idealism. But maybe it was plain old-fashioned resentment – the chip on my shoulder that even Uncle Maurice couldn't remove.' For a moment, Harry closed his free hand over Sean's. 'I cannot tell you how good it is to see you, my son.'

Sean smiled at him. 'I hope you can remember how to fly a plane, or we really are screwed.'

'We've come this far. We'll make it, I promise you.'

35

THE L4 CUBS didn't look like they'd make it to the end of the runway, let alone Turkey. They each boasted a single propeller, and a wing that appeared to have been stuck on top of the cockpit as an afterthought.

'Are you sure about this?' Sean asked, crouched beside his father in the shadow of a makeshift hut at the edge of the airfield furthest from the terminal.

'Do you have a better idea?' Harry glanced up at the clear, star-filled sky. 'At least someone up there seems to be watching over us.'

'About time,' Sean said. 'Will there be maps in the aircraft?'

Harry shook his head. 'I doubt it. I'll have to fly by sight.'

'What about fuel?'

'If you leave an air pocket in these things for any length of time, you end up with a serious condensation problem.

Only complete idiots leave them without full tanks.' Harry stood. 'Come on.'

He climbed onto the wing strut of the nearest aircraft, flipped up the top half of the door and folded down the bottom. He leant across the front seat and tapped the sight glass on the fuel tanks. Satisfied that the ground crew hadn't cut any corners, he flipped the two magneto switches and opened the throttle a quarter of an inch. He stepped down and unhooked the tarpaulin draped over the engine cowling. As he dragged it off and threw it towards the hut, Sean climbed into the rear seat. Harry helped Shahnaz scramble on top of him.

Harry loaded two Kalashnikovs he had brought from the truck and shoved a pistol into his jacket pocket. Then he moved to the nose of the aircraft, picked up the rope linking the wheel blocks, glanced across the tarmac to the terminal, and turned the propeller. Once. Twice. The third time, it caught.

He darted back to the cockpit and climbed in. He released the blocks, then steered the Cub onto the runway and ducked his head closer to the windscreen. Everything was still. 'This isn't going to be easy. We're a bit heavier than they're designed for,' he said. 'So hold on.'

He slammed open the throttle and the plane lurched forwards. As they picked up speed, Harry wrestled the waggling tail with the rudder-pedals. A jeep appeared behind them, gaining ground, its headlamps flashing. The airframe strained and groaned. On and on they went, still without the momentum or speed to get into the air.

The jeep closed in. 'Come *on*,' Harry hissed. He pulled the stick back, the tail lifted, the wheels bounced, once, twice, and, finally, they climbed into the cloudless night. Harry glanced back and watched the jeep skid to a halt as it came to the edge of the airfield. Sean reached out and gripped his shoulder.

Harry squeezed his son's hand. 'You'll need to direct me,' he shouted. 'I'm aiming to fly over the Alborz with the Caspian to our right until we see the lights of Tabriz. Then I've got to find the northern tip of Lake Urmia so that we can locate the lights of Salmas, the last town before we cross into Turkey.'

'I'll try.' Shahnaz leant forward so that her mouth was next to his ear. 'Head north-west over Tehran until we see the waters of the Caspian.'

She peered out into the darkness, then thrust herself far enough forward to see through the windscreen.

The twinkling lights of the capital soon disappeared beneath them and he had to fly on by the light of the moon. As they saw the still, calm waters of the Caspian, they banked left and flew on, keeping the sea to their right, the jagged peaks of the Alborz below them dramatic in the half-light. 'Will they put aircraft up to chase us?' Shahnaz asked.

'Yes.' Harry tried to think of something that would reassure her. 'But, as I said, they don't have jets, so they have a lot of sky to cover with limited speed. But I imagine they will be patrolling the border areas. It will get more dangerous the closer we get.'

Harry kept low. The effort of flying by sight required intense concentration. Shahnaz stayed close to him until they located Tabriz. Her first effort to get them up to Lake Varmia and then Salmas by locating the road from Tabriz

failed and they had to turn back towards the city and
start again.

This time she was confident they were heading in the
right direction. They flew across soaring mountain tops,
then sought the protection of the valleys. 'We're very close
now,' she said. 'I think this must be Salmas, the last town
before the border.'

They passed over another sprinkling of lights and
climbed towards a particularly jagged peak. As they crested
it, there was a sudden flash and a bullet pinged off the propeller blade. A split second later, a fighter roared past.

'*Damn*. A Hurricane.'

Harry rammed the stick forward and threw the Cub
into a dive. He kept on pushing down, but he knew they
couldn't escape the second run. The next fusillade slammed
into the engine. Oil squirted across the windscreen. There
was a thunderous clanking and the Cub started to shake
uncontrollably. Within seconds, the cabin was filling with
smoke and the noise of the aircraft's death rattle.

Harry thrust his face against the windscreen, wrenched
the stick forward and tried to line up the nose with the rib-
bon of road that snaked across the valley floor. As they lost
power and altitude, he pulled the stick back and fought to
hold off, but he could barely see anything and they hit the
ground with crushing force. The Cub bounced twice on
the tarmac and turned over, spinning out into the sand
until it came to a shuddering halt.

Choking on the smoke, Harry fished the revolver from
his pocket, gripped its barrel and smashed the side window with the handle. He wriggled free and pulled Shahnaz
out behind him. She reached back inside to free Sean. Harry

retrieved the Kalashnikovs and scanned the shadows for cover.

'*Down*,' Harry yelled, as the Hurricane made another swooping, strafing approach and flew past thirty feet above their heads.

They waited for it to return but, save for the hiss of the Cub's devastated engine, the valley was silent.

Harry led them back to the road. 'How far do you think we are from the border?'

'I've never been further than Salmas,' Shahnaz said, 'but I think we must be close. Turkey has to be the other side of that mountain.'

'Then we're going to have to walk.' Harry looped both Kalashnikov straps over his right shoulder.

They set off uphill, but it was soon obvious that Sean was too weakened by his time in captivity and the exertions in the truck to make much progress on his own. Shahnaz and Harry placed themselves on either side of him and draped his arms across their shoulders.

'I'm sorry,' he whispered. They hushed him into silence.

As they staggered on, they heard the sound of engines rising from the valley floor. They turned their heads to see three jeeps advancing swiftly towards them.

Harry let go of Sean and unslung both Kalashnikovs. 'You keep walking.'

'Not on our own.'

'I'll catch you up.'

'No, Dad.'

'Go.'

'Give me a rifle.' Sean gripped his father's arm. 'I'll help you.'

'You're moving much more slowly than I am,' Harry said. 'If I can hold them off long enough for you to get a decent way up that mountain, we might make it.'

Shahnaz gently prised open Sean's hand and Harry passed her one of the Kalashnikovs. 'In case of emergencies,' he said. 'Make sure he doesn't get any bright ideas.'

He gripped the butt of the other and sprinted towards an outcrop where the rock had been blasted to make way for the road. He took cover, then glanced back to make sure they had slipped away into the darkness. He couldn't see a thing. They were moving faster than he'd imagined.

Harry checked there was a round in the chamber, slid the safety catch onto semi-automatic, focused on the bend in the road fifty yards away, and waited.

The jeeps began to slow as they approached the bend. His opening salvo ignited the petrol tank of the lead vehicle. It veered off the tarmac and turned over, providing him with enough of a fireworks display to pick off the driver of the second and throw the soldiers now clambering from the third into sharp relief.

It took them long enough to realize that they were silhouetted against the flames for Harry to take another three down, but then someone – perhaps an officer – ordered the remaining troops to spread out before they continued to advance.

Some found cover and began to return fire.

Harry loosed off a burst from the left side of his outcrop, another from the right, then slipped away. He crawled at first, then ran, keeping his head down and his body low to the ground. The enemy lay low, too, and he made distance. Then a stream of tracer arced out into the gloom, and a couple of 7.62 rounds whistled just over his head. Two hundred yards later he sensed two figures struggling up the hill ahead of him. Harry ducked under Sean's right arm and pulled it across his chest with his left, leaving himself some freedom of movement with the Kalashnikov.

'You made it,' Sean whispered.

'We've got to move faster.'

Harry forced the pace. It wasn't easy. Sean was becoming a dead weight.

'Go on without me,' the boy said. 'Take Shahnaz.'

'Don't be so bloody stupid,' Harry hissed.

A volley of shots kicked up the dust around their feet. Harry unhooked Sean's arm and fired back at the figures now zigzagging from cover to cover behind them. They were getting closer.

'Come on . . .' Harry picked up Sean's arm again, presenting a stationary target as he did so. A bullet tore into his back and exited through his shoulder.

'Dad . . .' Sean rasped.

Harry took three more paces before he fell. He lay on the ground, staring up at them. Shahnaz bent and tried to free his jacket so that she could assess the damage, as he had taught her back in Tehran. Sean knelt beside him.

Harry looked at their anxious faces and the bright stars above them. He reached for the Kalashnikov, which had fallen with him. 'Go,' he whispered.

'No,' Sean said.

'Listen to me. I can hold them off long enough to give you a chance. If we all go, we'll all die.' Harry took hold of his son's wrist. 'Please, my boy. I owe you this.'

'You don't owe me anything.'

367

Harry looked into his son's solemn face and watched the tears run down his cheeks. 'I owe you your freedom.'

Sean kissed his forehead. For one last time, Harry drank in the sight, the sound and the feel of him, then gently pushed him away.

Shahnaz touched her soft cheek to his. 'Thank you,' she whispered.

'Look after him.'

They hesitated a moment, then crawled away into the darkness.

Harry half stood, switched the Kalashnikov to fully automatic and fired a two-second burst from the hip. He dropped down again, clenched his jaw against the pain in his chest and crawled to a ledge. He waited a moment. As the shadows danced below him, he brought the assault rifle clumsily up to his shoulder, immediately regretted it, held the pistol grip away from his body and sprayed his next burst for longer, across a wider arc. He had no idea whether he'd found his target, but he didn't really care any more. He just wanted their pursuers to stay where they were for as long as possible.

Silence followed, then shouts. If they hadn't already, he knew it wouldn't be long before the soldiers realized he was on his own, and had dug in.

They started to move towards him again. The flames from the burning jeep were still backlighting the soldiers who were too single-minded to bother trying to outflank him. He caught sight of two more and cut them down.

Harry no longer knew how many rounds he had left in his magazine. He gazed up at the night sky. Tried to close his mind to the pain. Tried to block out the ghostly presence of the boys whose fate he had sealed as they had run the gauntlet behind the Iron Curtain or on the slopes of Mount Avala. Rivulets of sweat ran down his face, but he suddenly felt terribly cold.

He glanced back up the mountain. There was no sign of Sean and Shahnaz in the darkness.

He needed to move. Thought he saw a ridge a hundred yards to his right. Squeezed the trigger of the Kalashnikov one more time, vaguely aware that he was now only stitching holes in the sky.

Then he heard a click.

The dead man's click.

His instructor had bollocked him good and proper for failing to keep track of his Sten gun's rate of fire. Where was that? On the range at Shrivenham. 'Now what, Mr fucking Tower? You, sir, are in *deep* shit. Oldest mistake in the book . . .'

He dropped the Kalashnikov and felt for the Browning. He disentangled it somehow from the lining of his jacket. Flicked off the safety. Propelled a round into the chamber with the top-slide. Some things you never forget.

Hauled himself up and stumbled towards the ridge.

Took three steps.

Three more.

Then a searing pain ripped apart his dorsal muscle and right lung. He fought for breath, already knowing he would never get enough. He managed to raise his sleeve to wipe the dark liquid frothing from his mouth.

Two more steps, and the ground rushed up to meet him. He used his one good elbow to lever himself onto his back, and lay there, listening to the rattle in his chest. *I'm drowning here*, he thought. *Drowning in a fucking desert . . .*

With a last, superhuman effort, he forced himself to sit upright.

Back against a rock.

Heard footsteps.

'Sean . . . my boy . . .'

He had no idea whether he had said the words out loud. But he was absolutely certain the approaching figure was not his son.

He raised the Browning and fired. His arm dropped and his head sank to his chest. All he could glimpse now was his life melting into the night.

He heard voices. Harsh. Manic. Excited.

He raised the pistol again, but could not persuade his arm to lift more than six inches off the ground. Or his finger to hook itself round the trigger.

Harry hung his head and allowed the darkness to flood in.

And as the last of his strength drained away, he imagined what he could not see: his boy running and running and running.

To freedom.

He closed his eyes and smiled.

Afterword

THE COUP AGAINST Mossadegh turned out to be one of the defining events of the early Cold War. It gave the Shah absolute power, which the American and British governments appeared willing to tolerate as long as he remained a staunch ally in the fight against Communism. It is fair to say that he remained a reliable friend to the West, but ever greater levels of domestic repression led to the Islamic Revolution of 1979, and everything that we have seen since – perhaps one of the most compelling examples of the law of unintended consequences in the history of the modern world.

Arguably of more significance was how the actions of 1953 formed part of the Central Intelligence Agency playbook that was to be used time and again in the following decades. The CIA officer who organized the coup against Mossadegh, Kermit Roosevelt, was so pleased with his work that he later wrote a book about it entitled *Countercoup*.

One can see the direct influence of these events in the removal of Diem in Saigon in 1963 (not that he was democratically elected), and of Allende (who definitely was) in Chile a decade later. And they were not alone.

The CIA intervened with impunity all over the world, and many of its actions were inspired by and even modelled on Kermit Roosevelt's early work in Tehran. Was it all justified in terms of the desperate battle to defeat the Communist threat? Or was it one of the darkest periods in American history, which undermined that nation's right to be considered the guardian of the Free World?

The debate still rages.

Acknowledgements

My primary thanks, as always, to my brilliant wife, Claudia, my partner in life and in my writing. I'd also like to thank my agent and my editor, Mark Lucas and Bill Scott-Kerr, both of whom have been with me on this journey for a quarter of a century or so now, along with Eloisa Clegg and the rest of the fantastic team at Transworld.

TOM BRADBY is a novelist, screenwriter and journalist. He has written nine previous novels, including top-ten bestselling *Secret Service* and its two sequels, *Double Agent* and *Triple Cross*. *The Master of Rain* was shortlisted for the Crime Writers Association Steel Dagger for Thriller of the Year, and both *The White Russian* and *The God of Chaos* for the CWA Historical Crime Novel of the Year. He adapted his first novel, *Shadow Dancer*, into a film, the script for which was nominated for Screenplay of the Year in the Evening Standard Film Awards.

As a broadcaster, he is best known as the current anchor of ITV's *News at Ten*. In his first year in the job he was named Network Presenter of the Year by the Royal Television Society. He has been with ITN for thirty years and was successively Ireland Correspondent, Political Correspondent, Asia Correspondent (during which time he was shot and seriously injured while covering a riot in Jakarta), Royal Correspondent, UK Editor and Political Editor – a job he held for a decade – before being made the anchor of *News at Ten* in 2015.